Rare Blend

MICHELLE NAOMI MOSLEY

Rare Blend

A RED MOUNTAIN NOVEL

Publisher: Mariposa Books, LLC

Cover designer: Lia Ramirez

Editor: Editing by Andrea

Spanish editor: LC Editing

Proofreaders: Kari LeAnn and Lauren Rossi

 Formatted with Vellum

To my mom, who filled my childhood with romantic comedies and soap operas, igniting my love for romance and inspiring me to write this book. I'm a storyteller because of you. I miss you endlessly and love you always.

"There's no such thing as being lost in a vineyard. You're always in the right place."

— FRANCIS DUFLOT, *A GOOD YEAR*

Author's Note

Dear Reader,

One of the main characters in Rare Blend is a biracial, Mexican-American woman. As a biracial, Mexican-American woman myself, and the daughter of an immigrant, my experiences are weaved into this story. Please remember there are many different subcultures within the Mexican-American/Latinx communities and not all experiences are alike. It is my hope that I have done justice in portraying a realistic representation of a multifaceted young woman, who also happens to be Latina. Often times, in media, Latinx characters are pigeonholed into stereotypical archetypes. My goal was to step outside of that box and create a character who feels like the women I know and love in real life.

For my Spanish speakers, the Spanish in this book is informal Mexican Spanish. However, there is a phrase Marisa says to Ethan that is more of a direct translation rather than what would be spoken between two native speakers. Because Ethan is not a native speaker, this phrasing is intentional.

This book is intended for adult audiences and contains sexually explicit content as well as emotional themes that may be sensitive for some readers. To avoid spoilers, I've listed content warnings at the back of the book.

You can also find them at www.authormichel lenaomimosley.com/

I hope you enjoy Marisa and Ethan's journey.

Happy reading. ¡Salud! (*Cheers!*)

Michelle

Spanish 101

Dialogue spoken in Spanish is directly translated on the page, however there are some terms and phrases littered throughout that are not defined or translated. For your convenience, I have listed them below.

- **Amigo** - Friend
- **Bruja** - Witch
- **Caldo de pollo** - Chicken soup
- **Champurrado** - A warm chocolate and cinnamon beverage made with corn flour
- **Dios te bendiga** - God bless you/common way to express goodbye or good wishes
- **Hola** - Hello
- **Jefe** - Boss
- **Mija/Mijita** - Term of endearment, meaning my daughter/my little daughter
- **Nada** - Nothing
- **Novia** - Girlfriend
- **Pan dulce** - Sweet pastry, similar to a donut

- **Para español, oprima el dos** - For Spanish, press two
- **Pinche pendejo** - Fucking asshole
- **Sí Dios quiere** - God willing
- **Tamale** - A corn-based dough steamed in a corn husk and filled with meat
- **Telenovela** - A Latin American television serial drama or soap opera, often referred to as a "novela" for short

Playlist

Motion Sickness - Phoebe Bridgers
I Did Something Bad - Taylor Swift
no tears left to cry - Ariana Grande
Autumn Town Leaves - Iron & Wine
I Fall Apart - Post Malone
Dreams - The Cranberries
Breathe - Faith Hill
Under My Skin - Nate Smith
Let It Happen - Gracie Abrams
Cherry Wine - Hozier
Your Heart Or Mine - Jon Pardi
Everything Has Changed (Taylor's Version) - Taylor Swift
I Found - Amber Run
girl who drank wine - Ella Langley
Iris - Justin Miguel
Wreckage - Nate Smith
Rare - Selena Gomez
Butterflies - Kacey Musgraves
Don't Know Why - Nora Jones
NIGHTS LIKE THIS - The Kid LAROI

Cherry - Lana Del Rey
Maybe We Do - Zach Seabaugh
Love Me Like You Mean It - Kelsea Ballerini
Dress - Taylor Swift
Before You - Boone Benson
I Guess I'm in Love - Kole Larsen
Wildflowers & Wine - Marcus King
Radio - Lana Del Rey
Stargazing - Myles Smith
Catching Butterflies - Eddie Flint
Linger - Royal Otis
Never Be the Same - Camila Cabello
We Fell in Love in October - girl in red
Everything We Need - Wilfred

About This Book

Marisa Castilla's life is in need of a rewrite. Her ex-boyfriend/boss just fired her, the guest room she's occupying is about to be taken over by a newborn, and she's drowning in student loan debt. Swallowing her pride, she reaches out to her estranged father and makes the temporary move to Red Mountain, leaving behind her beloved city and corporate ambitions. Transitioning to being a lowly reporter for her father's small town newspaper is a culture shock, and constantly bumping into Ethan Ledger, her less-than-friendly neighbor, who also happens to own the vineyard cottage she's staying in, doesn't make things easier.

Ethan Ledger recently assumed the role of CEO of his family's wine empire. An anxious over-thinker, he wears a grumpy facade like armor. Still adjusting to running the family business, he can't afford any distractions, especially not the beautiful one next door. He only has two rules for his new neighbor/tenant: no visitors and no expectations of friendship. But when Marisa breaks through his tough exterior, friendship soon blooms into late-night texts and telenovela marathons.

Feelings develop and lines blur, and Ethan is prepared to break every rule he's ever had for Marisa. However, an enticing offer for her dream job back in the city clashes with Ethan's roots in Red Mountain.

Sparks fly and wine flows between the most unlikely pairing, but sometimes the rarest blends are the most satisfying.

CHAPTER 1

Marisa

GIANT BALD SPOT. HUGE.

There better be a damn good reason why the *other woman* is gracing me with her presence this early in the workday.

"Brandon wants to see you in his office at ten o'clock," Quinn says, standing at the threshold of my cubicle with her arms crossed and nose scrunched as if she smells something unpleasant.

Curious eyes flick our way. I'm sure they're all wondering if this will be the Jerry Springer moment everyone has been waiting for. While I could definitely take her, I would prefer to hang onto the small shred of self-respect I've managed to maintain.

Despite her obvious distaste and overall attitude, she's beautiful. The kind of beauty that stops you in your tracks—head-turning gorgeous. It's no wonder Brandon cheated on me with her. He is a man, after all.

Forcing a smile onto my face, I may or may not be imagining scenarios that could land me my own episode of *Snapped*; the thought widens my smile. "Okay, I'll be there."

1

She whips back around with a huff, her blonde hair swaying and heels clacking against the tile floor. She hates that I'm nice to her. I honestly think she would prefer it if I were mean; maybe it would alleviate some of the guilt she undoubtedly feels.

"Now I know he did not have the audacity to send his side piece to come get you for a meeting," Zoe, my cubicle neighbor, says, watching me dumbfounded.

"She's his admin, who else is he going to send?"

She snorts. "An email, like a normal person. That man is trash. Straight, hot garbage, rotten trash. He did you a favor revealing his true colors before trapping you with a ring."

I nod silently, because she's absolutely right. Things are bad, but they could have been so much worse.

"What do you think he wants to meet with you about?"

I shrug. "Who knows. You never know with him."

I can actually think of a few reasons he would want to meet with me. There have been rumors of a layoff coming for weeks now. And my direct manager is conveniently on short-term disability until he's recovered from knee surgery, leaving no one in my corner if things go south.

Zoe's lips purse, but I disregard her implication. I have thirty minutes to let my mind wander down the *what if* rabbit hole, and I'd rather stay blissfully ignorant for as long as possible.

To pass the time, I get caught up on emails and listen to Zoe as she updates me on her latest dating app match. I used to enjoy her dating stories when I was perfectly happy, in what I thought was a very secure relationship. Being on the other side, though, newly single and fast approaching my thirties, the stories sound a lot less rom-com and a lot more psychological thriller. At some point, I'm going to have to get back out there and try to land myself a fish in what is likely swampy, shallow water. Just thinking about it makes my stomach roll.

I'm a relationship girl through and through, but I'm nowhere near ready to start dating again. Brandon, on the other hand, is such a relationship guy that he started an entirely new relationship while still being in one with me. Pig.

When the clock reads 9:55, I rise from my chair, every muscle feeling more tightly wound than a twisted corkscrew. My breathing turns ragged as I walk the short gauntlet to Brandon's corner office. Ignoring the watchful eyes and questioning looks of my coworkers, I keep my gaze fixed ahead. Murmurs and mumbles burn my ears and heat my neck as I pass each desk.

Shoulders back, neutral expression, steady, deliberate steps. More importantly, never let them see you sweat. I repeat the mantra over and over in my head, hoping if I think it enough, I'll embody it. Of all the times to try out this manifesting bullshit.

Quinn is noticeably absent from her desk outside Brandon's office. I can't decide if that's a good thing or a bad thing. Feeling petty, I walk up to it and deliberately knock over the glittery, pink cup of pens. Surprisingly, it does slightly brighten my mood, only for it to darken the moment I cross through the doorway.

Ignoring the blob of a man seated at the desk, I choose to be greeted by the view of the Seattle skyline instead. It's an unusually clear fall day, and the Olympic Mountains stand out against the light-blue sky, their crisp edges defined by snow-capped peaks.

Seconds after I walk in, Aaron from human resources is at my heels, apparently joining us. HR is never a good sign—in fact it's just the opposite. The door closes behind him with an ominous thud. My throat tightens as I swallow down the lump threatening to rise, and my heart beats heavy in my chest.

"Thank you for coming, Marisa," Brandon says.

3

Hearing him say my name stirs a storm of emotions within me. The painful clenching of my heart and the fiery anger I feel toward him collide with the utter sadness sitting deep within me. Even worse is his professional tone—no warmth, no familiarity, all business. We've managed to keep our interactions to a minimum since the breakup. In truth, I've made it my sole mission to avoid him at all costs. A lot of good it did me.

I take the chair opposite his desk. The very chair I used to sit in when we would eat our lunch together that once felt comforting and sturdy. Now, it feels shaky, rocking unevenly beneath me as I sink into it. It creaks with a loud echo as it depresses under my body weight.

Mustering all of my willpower, I try my best to avoid looking directly at Brandon, but I fail. My mind may loathe him, but my stomach still dips when I see his classically handsome face, his broad shoulders, that dimple in his chin, his slightly crooked nose that adds a subtle edge to his pretty face. I'm intimately familiar with him, yet now we exist as strangers, despite knowing everything about each other.

Brandon is wearing the tie I got him for his birthday last year, the one that brings out the blue in his eyes. I threw the majority of his clothes in the lake across from our condo, so it must be one of the survivors. Not my finest moment, but it was incredibly satisfying. I had to unleash my rage somehow. Especially after literally catching him in the act, pounding into Quinn in a way he never had with me. If I close my eyes, I can still hear the relentless slapping of their skin; my stomach churns at the memory.

What better way to take out some aggression than to destroy all of his fancy clothes? He's always been so vain and obsessed with looking the part. He wouldn't be so obsessed with it had he actually earned his position. But when your daddy owns the company, why work your way up when you can be handed everything instead?

Brandon's eyes won't meet mine; they wander about the room but never land directly on me. I am definitely about to lose my job. The rumors of layoffs, talks of budget cuts, Brandon's recent erratic behavior—he yelled at Diane, our sweet office coordinator, because she brought in homemade cookies for everyone. He called her a distraction. Then there was the company-wide email about not backfilling positions and learning to manage larger work loads with less employees. The puzzle pieces are forming a picture, and it isn't pretty.

Brandon clears his throat. "Well, let's go ahead and get started."

His hands clasp together over the imposing mahogany desk. The tension in the room is so thick it feels hard to breathe.

"As you know, it's been a difficult year. The tech industry as a whole has seen a downturn, and it's resulted in us having to make some difficult decisions..."

He drones on for a while longer, speaking his corporate talk to me as if I don't know how rehearsed this script is.

"Get to the point. I think we all know where this conversation is going," I snipe.

Sighing deeply, he finally looks me in the eyes. I'm not prepared for how physically painful it is to have those piercing eyes I used to adore look at me with such indifference.

"Unfortunately, we're going to have to let you go."

I knew it.

I knew it was coming. All signs pointed to this conclusion. But hearing it—having it spoken into existence—nothing could have prepared me. Would I be sitting in this seat if we were still together? Would someone else be getting this speech? Of course, it makes sense to get rid of me, the ex-girlfriend who's a constant reminder of his indiscretions.

When we started dating, Brandon made sure we filled out the appropriate paperwork with the company. He didn't want to hide us—me. He was proud to call me his girlfriend, and while we didn't advertise it, everyone was very aware we were together. He could have easily kept us a secret since it wasn't the best look for our jobs, but his insistence at being out in the open made me feel special. How pathetic is that? The bar is so low, it's in hell.

When news spread that we had broken up because he cheated on me with Quinn, sides were taken, lines were drawn. Team Marisa significantly outnumbered Team Brandon. He can't have that—I'm the thorn in his side that keeps poking deeper the longer I stay here.

"Is this because of what happened between us?"

He pinches the bridge of his nose with his thumb and index finger—his telltale sign of annoyance. "I knew you would make this personal," he hisses under his breath.

Aaron leans forward. "Miss Castilla, I assure you this is all on the up and up. You are simply the first in a significant layoff that will be occurring throughout the day. In fact, it was Brandon's suggestion that you be the first, because he understands how delicate the situation between you two is."

My focus remains on Brandon. "How generous of you. Really thank you. I forgot how sweet you could be. And sending Quinn, of all people, to come get me. You're disgusting."

"Risy, please don't make this harder than it needs to be."

Oh God, that nickname. I could gag. How hard is it to say Marisa?

"Don't call me that. You don't get to call me that."

"Fine. *Marisa*. Can you be professional about this?"

I stand from my seat. "You've got some nerve thinking you can fire me to make your life easier."

He rises, leaning across the desk, his face too close. I always forget how intimidating his height is until it's up against my short stature.

"You're being laid off, not fired. And I'm sorry to inform you that the world does not revolve around you and your feelings. This has nothing to do with us. I don't think about you, and I sure as shit don't care about you anymore. This is business. Nothing more."

My head jolts back like I've been slapped. His words sting to the point I can feel the swell of a wave threatening to wash over me. *I will not cry. I will not cry.*

Aaron stands and puts his hand on Brandon's shoulder, steering him back. "Okay, folks, it's getting a little heated in here. Let's keep it civil."

Brandon shakes out his shoulders and straightens his already straight tie. His hand glides over his perfectly coifed hair, ensuring not a single piece is out of place. "There's no sense in arguing about this. You're being let go, and that's that."

My eyes fill with tears, and I blink rapidly in an attempt to hold them back before they fall out of me like an uncontrollable stream. They're from anger, not sadness, but I start to well up all the same.

Brandon's jaw tightens, a hint of guilt surfacing on his face before he quickly masks it with apathy once again. He never could handle my crying.

"If you leave now, you can still walk out of here with your dignity," he whispers, as if what he's saying is supposed to bring me some sort of comfort.

My dignity? *My* fucking dignity? He's the one who should be worried about his dignity. Cheating asshole.

"Fine," I say, my voice a touch too high and wobbly as I try to remain collected. I walk to the door, ready to face the shame of my coworkers' awkward glances. Through all the emotional fury burning inside of me, something finally snaps, pouring kerosene over my growing fire. Enough with being the bigger person; it's clearly gotten me nowhere.

I yank open the door, and a ripple of heads jerk their attention back to their monitors. A slow, satisfied smile eases across my face as I wipe the moisture from my eyes.

I lean against the open door. "You know, there's something I've been meaning to tell you." I speak louder than would be considered conversational, throwing my voice so it reaches the far corners of the office suite.

Brandon freezes, his eyes widening. I see it happen in slow motion, the realization that he has no idea what I'm going to say but whatever it is, I intend to humiliate him.

"Marisa," he drags out my name, unease dripping over each syllable.

Aaron has made himself scarce, clinging to the windows to distance himself from the situation. Such a weak little man.

"I lied."

Brandon says nothing. I'm not even sure he's breathing.

"That time you asked me about your hair," I continue. "I lied. It's thinning horribly. Especially in the back. Giant bald spot. Huge."

The office is completely silent, save for the low hum of office equipment.

His hand instinctively rubs at the back of his head, and his face turns red hot.

With that, I march to my desk to grab my bag. My gaze lands on Zoe, whose mouth is covered as she holds back a laugh. Nobody says a word, nobody so much as moves, as I leave the office suite without looking back.

I could've gone much lower and made a comment about what's lacking under the belt or criticized his abilities in bed, but I knew he'd be able to talk himself out of those claims. His ego would refute it. But his hairline—particularly that bald spot—there's no denying that.

Aaron's voice calls out to me as I make my way to the elevators. "Wait, we need to conduct your exit interview."

There is an incredible amount of adrenaline pumping through my veins as I step inside the elevator. "Sounds like a personal problem, Aaron."

The elevator doors shut before he can close the distance between us. Normally, I would feel terrible, ever the people-pleaser. But right now, I'm all out of fucks to give.

CHAPTER 2

Marisa

PARA ESPAÑOL, OPRIMA EL DOS

"I'm going to kill him," my best friend Hillary says while folding a onesie on her cute, little belly, using it like a tabletop. "I'm serious. He should be very afraid of me."

It's hard not to laugh at her when she gets riled up like this, even if it is to come to my defense. When she came home from work and saw that I was home already, she instantly went into detective mode, asking me a million questions. I quickly filled her in, and she's been in a state of rage ever since.

Hillary is standing in the middle of the living room, surrounded by heaps of baby clothes—it's as if OshKosh B'Gosh threw up everywhere. Ever since she found out she's having a girl, she's been obsessed with buying everything in pink.

"Calm down. We don't want to induce early labor because your blood pressure spiked."

She takes a squatting stance and then eases her way down to sit on the couch. Hillary, whose petite frame is struggling to carry the weight of a growing baby, often looks like she's about to tip over.

"How are you not more upset? I'm shaking." She shoves her arm in my face to show me.

I internally roll my eyes. "When was the last time you ate? You're probably shaking because you're hungry."

"Archie is bringing home takeout. And stop trying to change the subject. You need to get a lawyer. There's no way what he did is legal."

I curl myself into one of the several throw blankets adorning the couch. "Legal or not, I'm still out of a job."

"Well, you've been applying all over the place. Any hits?"

Ever since Brandon and I broke up, I've been on the hunt for a new job. Obviously, I didn't want to keep working there, but it's not like I had the luxury to quit. Unlike some people, I don't have a trust fund to fall back on.

"I've applied everywhere that's hiring technical writers and haven't gotten one call. It's a lost cause."

She gives me one of her new motherly stares. "Don't give up. Something will come along. And you know you're welcome to stay here as long as you need to. We love having you."

I highly doubt the newlyweds with a honeymoon baby arriving in less than five months want me crashing in the nursery forever. The daybed in there is supposed to be for Archie's mom, who's planning to fly in from London after the baby is born.

"We'll make it work with Joanna," she says, reading my train of thought. "I could probably convince Archie to move his workout equipment to the garage and we can make that room yours."

I know she's trying to be positive and helpful, but staying here—no matter how temporary—makes me feel guilty enough. Nothing I can say will change her wanting to fix my current disaster of a life, so there's no use arguing with her.

She's stubborn like that. I need to figure things out, and I need to do it soon.

Hillary has been my rock throughout this whole ordeal. In some ways, despite being a few months younger than me, she's been the mother figure I've needed as of late. My own mom has been busy living her best life. And I'm happy for her, if not slightly—and only slightly— resentful. You go through your childhood and teen years assuming you'll grow up one day and not need your parents anymore, only to find you need them even more as an adult. I can't fault her. She had me young, and I'm sure her current adventure is a way of reclaiming some of that lost youth. I can support it and still be annoyed by it. At least that's what I tell myself so I don't feel completely selfish.

The front door opens, and Archie bursts through with his arms wrapped around two large, brown paper bags over-flowing with styrofoam containers. I scramble off the couch and grab one of the bags before it slips out of his hold.

"Thanks," he groans while we set both bags down on the kitchen counter.

"Oooo, what did you get?" Hillary is already tearing into the bags like a wild animal.

Archie and I share an amused look.

"Thai food from that place you like on Roy," he says.

"Have I told you how much I love you? Because I freaking love you," Hillary says between bites.

He laughs, shaking his head. "Thank you, love. I'm quite fond of you as well." He kisses her forehead and removes his suit jacket, tossing it onto one of the accent chairs Hillary doesn't allow anyone to sit on.

"You're home early," he says to me.

"She got fired," Hillary says, around a mouthful of spring roll. "By dick face."

"Laid off," I mumble. As if that's somehow better.

"You're joking." His voice rises to a squeaky pitch, making

him sound even more British. "What an idiot. He's asking for a lawsuit."

Hillary pinches her chopsticks, pointing them at Archie. "That's what I said."

"I never did like him," Archie claims.

I call total bullshit. Brandon and Archie had standing pickleball dates twice a month, all of last spring and summer. Archie introduced Brandon to the world of football—aka soccer, and Brandon would often invite Archie out to Mariner's games after work. They were buddies, but Archie is Hillary's, and by default mine, so their friendship came to a close when our relationship imploded. It's nice of him to pretend, though.

It's one of those things that feels like a punch to the gut if I dwell on it too much. Brandon and I were two halves of a whole. Our lives were so intertwined that his friends became my friends, and vice versa. Brandon's side of our friend group has been crickets since the breakup. Not even a polite *I'm here for you,* text. Nada. And to think, I considered Ashleigh and Kiera, the wives of his two best friends, actual friends. They were on the bridesmaid list, which is kind of a big deal. Clearly, I won't be having any bridesmaids any time soon, seeing as the guy I thought was going to propose to me had other plans, like fucking his secretary. Decades from now, I'll still be bitter that Brandon turned our entire relationship into the biggest cliché ever.

I busy myself by making a plate even though my appetite is nonexistent and give Hillary a look that says I no longer want to talk about it. One perk of being best friends for most of our lives is that we can speak without saying anything. She gives me a nod before returning to her food.

Forcing myself to eat, I listen to the happy couple chat about their days. He subconsciously rubs her stomach while she reminds him of the CPR class they're scheduled to take later in the week. It's all so easy, so natural. The envy seeps in, rotting my already wounded heart. It sucks feeling like this, like Hillary has surpassed me in some way. Logically, I understand it's not a competition. But the jaded, broken part of me feels like I'm entering a race and everyone is already at the finish line. What if Brandon was it and there is no next guy? What if no one else ever comes along and I'm the perpetual single friend? I'll be alone at weddings, pity invited to couples' trips, and slowly faded out because I'm depressing to be around. I think women have more than proven their ability to lead full lives without a man at their side, but society doesn't really care about that. Our world was designed for couples, and now I'm like a square peg trying to fit inside a round hole. I don't know where I fit anymore, and it's terrifying.

Suddenly, the last thing I feel like doing is being around all the love wafting off them. It's like putting salt on scabbed over cuts in various states of healing, that reopen at the most inconvenient times.

I quickly clean up after myself and silently make my way upstairs. I think I've made a clean exit, but Hillary's voice calls to me from downstairs.

"You're only allowed to sulk today and then tomorrow, it's back to being a badass bitch."

"Okay," I shout back, trying to sound positive and not at all defeated, like I feel.

Once I'm inside the nursery with the door closed and locked, the weight of recent events crashes down on me. I don't want to be angry anymore. It's such a useless emotion that does nothing but drain me. Today took so much out of me, I'm not even sure there's anything left. I'm just incredibly sad now. Sad that my life is in this messed-up state. Sad that nothing has gone according to plan. Sad that the future I so perfectly mapped out no longer exists. In the span of a month, a bulldozer plowed through my life, wrecking everything I thought was stable. My career, my hopes, my dreams, my plans —all gone. Moisture pools in my eyes, effectively breaking the dam. Tears slide down my cheeks like a flood. I'm so taken aback by their sudden onslaught that I pat my face to make sure I'm not imagining them, but sure enough, my palm is covered in wet, streaky mascara. Still crying, I crawl into bed and hug myself. I've never felt so broken in my entire life, but Hillary is right. Today I can sulk, tomorrow is a new day.

The morning light hits me like a freight train. There's a headache sitting behind my eyes from crying myself to sleep, pulsing at an annoyingly rapid pace. I may as well be hungover with how achy every limb feels.

Sliding out of bed, my body snaps and pops, evidence of how tensely I slept, likely balled up in the fetal position. Glancing at the clock, I see it's well past my normal wake up time. Not that it matters because nothing matters when you have nowhere to be and nothing to do. I flop back onto the bed with a groan, cocooning myself under the heavy down comforter. I'll just stay in here all day. It's much safer than stepping out of this room and facing my new reality.

At some point, I must've drifted back to sleep, because I wake up to my phone buzzing against the nightstand, practically shaking it. It's a 1-800 number. Normally I wouldn't answer, yet for whatever reason, my thumb hits the accept button.

"Hello?"

"Hello." It's some kind of automated message. Maybe the universe is gifting me a fake vacation.

"This is EDU Financial Services. Reminding Marisa Castilla that the first payment to the student loan ending in

6547 is due on October twenty-fifth. To speak to a financial representative, press one. Para español, oprima el dos. For more options, visit our website at www.edufinancialservices.com. Goodbye."

My body jolts upright so fast I feel a little dizzy. *Shit, shit, shit.* With shaky fingers I log-in to my account, my heart beating erratically as the page loads. I have been deferring my student loans, and I was supposed to start finally paying them last year. In a moment of stupidity, I ended up consolidating them into one giant loan with a third party for future Marisa to worry about. Money was tight, and I wanted to buy myself another year of not having to pay. Which would all be fine and good if I wasn't currently broke and jobless.

They say your life flashes before your eyes right before you die. Well, what happens when it feels like you're dying? Because I'm pretty sure that's what's happening when I see how much my payment will be. My eyes blink several times. That number can't be right. How is it possible I owe $2,500? Not total, that's the monthly payment amount. I don't even want to look at the total, because it's a hell of a lot more than I took out. Stupid interest. Aren't there laws on this now? I could've sworn this was all over the news.

That payment would be hard to make even if I still had my job, now it seems impossible. An overwhelming sensation knots my stomach, gripping so tightly I can't think straight. My first instinct is to call my mom. She's nothing if not a problem solver. As the first on my favorites list, I select her name and wait for the call to connect, but nothing happens; no ringing, nothing. She must not have any service. It's sometimes difficult to get in touch with her when she's out at sea. The cruise lines always have Wi-Fi, but she's not the most tech savvy.

"Fuck!" I scream. There's no one home, so at least I can have my meltdown in peace.

I go to the next name on my list, Hillary. It used to be Brandon, but he got deleted and Hillary got promoted.

She answers on the second ring. "You just woke up, didn't you?"

"Yes, but that's not why I'm calling."

She must note the panic in my voice, because I hear rustling and the sound of a door closing. "What's going on?"

I relay the disaster that is my student loans.

"Shit," she says. "That's a house payment. Well, not here, but somewhere, that's a house payment."

"What am I going to do? I have enough for the first payment, but that was money I was saving for a down payment on an apartment, and now I can't even do that because I don't have a job."

"Don't panic. You're a month away from the due date. You didn't tell your mom, did you?"

"Well no, not yet. Only because I couldn't get through. Why? Do you think I shouldn't tell her?"

She used to think my mom was one of the cool moms, but her opinion has changed as we've gotten older. I don't really know when things started to shift, but it's become a point of contention between us.

Hillary lets out a long breath. "It's just that she can be really judgy and ends up making you feel worse than you already do. Maybe don't tell her, or at least wait until you've come up with a solution."

"She's my mom, Hill."

She's quiet for a moment. "You know, you could—"

"No!" I cut her off. I know what she's going to say. And I can't.

"He would help you, you know he would."

I don't want to go down that road. "I should go. I'm going to try to apply for unemployment."

She sighs. "Okay, but think about it. I'm serious."

17

We say our goodbyes, and somehow I feel even more panicked after our phone call.

I spend the next hour trying to navigate the unemployment website. I'm convinced they make it difficult on purpose because they don't want people to actually figure it out. When I have everything completed and filled out, I click submit and it loads and loads and loads. After several minutes pass, I get hit with a red error message: *Insufficient Information*. Great. That's just great. I slam my laptop closed and head for the bathroom. I need a scalding hot shower, hot enough to match my frustration, or I'm going to lose my mind.

The guest bathroom may not be the luxurious spa-like one I left behind at Brandon's, but it's been recently remodeled with high-end finishes and a rain shower head that beats down on me, alleviating some of my tension.

Mid-shampoo, Hillary's words come back to me. *He would help you, you know he would.*

Long after I've finished scrubbing every inch of my body, to the point that my olive skin is now a raw, pink shade, I stand under the searing water and almost succeed in temporarily melting away the little voice telling me to give up and call him.

The voice festers in my head as I towel dry my hair and lather my body in a thick layer of lotion. Why did she have to bring him up? Now it's all my mind seems to want to think about.

By midday, my resolve is hanging by a thread. I've had ample time to envision every possible outcome, and none of them seem promising. I have no place to live, I don't have a job, unemployment is screwing me, my car payment is due next week, and then there's that lovely student loan lying in wait for me in the shadows. And the cherry on top, my mom is MIA in a time when I desperately need her.

It seems I may be out of options. Except for one.

Before I can talk myself out of it, I reach for my phone. With trembling hands, I dial the number from memory. My breath hitches in my throat and doesn't release until the line picks up.

"Hello?" he sounds hesitant, as if he isn't sure I meant to call him.

"Hi, Dad."

CHAPTER 3

Marisa

BRAWNY PAPER TOWEL GUY

A ccording to the GPS, I'll be in Red Mountain in about ten minutes. It's music to my ears after driving for nearly four hours, clutching the wheel a little too tightly for most of the drive due to nervous jitters.

Most people don't realize there's more to Washington than evergreen trees and rainfall. While I do love the *Twilight* aesthetic, there are several different landscapes across the state. After crossing the Cascades and heading east, cheatgrass and tumbleweeds gradually replace the tree line. It's like a dry desert on the eastern side of the mountains. Not nearly as pretty, in my opinion, as the western side of the state, but there is something kind of calming about the desert view. Must be all the beige.

I can't believe I'm really doing this. I keep thinking I'm going to wake up at any moment and this will all have been a nightmare. Unfortunately, it's been five days and that still hasn't happened. When I caved and finally called my dad, I didn't expect him to be quite so welcoming. I was thinking something more along the lines of a small loan to keep me afloat, but I should've remembered Robert Stephan doesn't do anything I've ever expected him to. Why start now? He was insistent that I come stay with him while I figure things out, and for the life of me, I couldn't find one excuse good enough not to.

Our relationship hasn't been the greatest, and apart from birthday and holiday texts, we haven't spoken in almost two years. It's been even longer than that since we've seen each other. I try not to think about it too much, because I grew up a daddy's girl, and somewhere between my parents' divorce and emerging into adulthood, our relationship fell apart.

A little over four years ago, my dad had, what I refer to as, his midlife crisis. He retired early from his cushy job at Rainer Publishing and bought a crumbling newspaper in Red Mountain. Things were already strained between us for several reasons, but his decision to move over two hundred miles away really hammered the nail into the coffin. I know he's married because I received an invitation to the wedding, but I've never met his wife. I never intended to either. I guess that's out the window now.

Unease twists and swirls in my stomach when the *Welcome to Red Mountain* sign comes into view. I can't believe my life has come to this. At twenty-eight years old, I'm unemployed and running to my daddy with my tail between my legs—teenage me would be so disappointed.

Rolling hills of vineyards flank either side of the road as I approach the downtown area, further confirming I'm no longer in Seattle. My clammy hands grip the steering wheel while I take in the main stretch of town. The street is quaint, lined with various brick storefronts and old-fashioned lamp-posts. Rustic artisan shops display handcrafted goods in their windows, and flower boxes overflowing with colorful mums hang from the buildings. At the heart of Main Street stands a

21

picturesque archway with a festive banner stretching across it announcing *Winetober*. Considering it's Monday and Red Mountain is a small town, it's fairly busy. Lots of people mill about, strolling in and out of tasting rooms and restaurants.

"In half a mile, turn left onto Bordeaux Lane," the GPS tells me.

I thought the town appeared charming when I looked it up online, but seeing it up close, it's like a picture-perfect Hollywood set. I have yet to see any big box stores or commercial businesses. No Starbucks, no McDonald's, and sadly, no Target. Red Mountain may as well be another country, with everything appearing homegrown, mom and pop, and local. Even the sidewalks are cobblestone, like something you would see in Europe. From what I gathered during my internet deep dive, the town was a ramshackle of dilapidated buildings and farmland before the wine industry took off. Today, it's considered the Napa of the Pacific Northwest.

"In two-hundred feet, turn left onto Bordeaux Lane."

My heart rate increases. There's a nagging feeling telling me to turn around and go right back, that I don't need to do this. I ignore it, because the truth is, this is my last option. Whether I like it or not.

I take the left and drive down the narrow road, downtown disappearing in my rearview mirror. The further I drive, the rougher it gets. This can't be right. There's nothing but vineyards surrounding me. Not a house in sight.

"The destination is on your right," the GPS claims.

I look to the right and then to the left, but see nothing indicating a house is nearby.

As I continue coasting further, the GPS announces, "You have arrived."

Again, my eyes take in the expansive vineyards and desert terrain, looking for any sign of a house. Nothing.

I pull over to the side of the road, my car half on the shoulder, half on a mixture of loose dirt and sand. Off the shoulder, the road is walled in on both sides by large vineyards that seem to go on forever, taking up acres of land.

Re-reading my dad's text, I confirm his street is Bordeaux Lane, and according to the app, I'm at the location. This is ridiculous. Only in a small town would the GPS send me on a wild goose chase. I can navigate Seattle rush hour traffic with my eyes closed, but send me to the middle of nowhere and I'm lost in what looks like the setting of *The Hills Have Eyes*. I give up on the accuracy of my phone's directional abilities and call my dad. Of course he doesn't answer. Well fine, I will figure it out myself. His house can't be that hard to find in a town this small.

I put the car in drive, but when I try to pull back onto the road, instead of going forward, my car does the opposite and starts rolling backward. In a panic, I slam my foot down, flooring the gas. My little car practically screams as it tries to fight gravity, a cacophony of tires screeching and my engine revving roars loudly, yet the downward journey continues. I stomp my foot down on the brake and yank up on my e-brake, even though it hasn't worked in years, but I'm too late. I can't fight the momentum. Bracing myself for an impact to jolt me, I hunch my shoulders and squeeze my eyes shut. Blood rushes to my head, and my entire body tenses. This is it, this is how I die.

And then, like someone hit pause, everything stills, save for the small little thump that brings my uncontrollable car to a stop. With the car finally at a standstill, my body slumps, relief uncoiling my tensed nerves. As I come down from the panic of a potential accident, the blood pounding in my ears starts to ease. I put the car back in park, something I probably should've attempted when my car refused to stop, and a sudden bubble of laughter jumps out of me. The laughter seems to have opened a door that won't close, and now I'm full on laughing. It's a deranged kind of cackling, but it's the first time I've laughed in days. The hilarity of the past month, the reality of where I am, and the fact that I'm lost both mentally and physically—it all hits me at once, harder than I'm prepared for. Thank goodness I'm alone, because this is by far the ugliest I've ever looked, bursting with a witch-like cackle, frothing at the mouth. I'm beside myself, spiraling into oblivion.

I'm not sure how long my spiral goes on for, but eventually, I'm spent. I pant and wipe the tears from my eyes. The episode seems to be behind me, and my sanity returns.

I make a few attempts to get up to the road, but each time I'm met with the same result; my car simply cannot handle the terrain.

As I start trying to figure out how I'm going to get myself out of this, a flash of black catches my attention, and I see a truck barreling down the traffic-free road. It comes to an abrupt stop near where I was originally pulled over, and a man jumps out. My first thought is he's a Good Samaritan here to help me. There's also a chance he's a serial killer coming to murder me, but he doesn't seem like the murdering type. I don't think murderers look like the Brawny Paper Towel guy. The thought makes me want to laugh again, but I tamper it down. I truly am losing my ever-loving mind.

The man walks toward me with fast, determined steps. I start to unbuckle, but he's fully ignoring me. His eyes don't so much as acknowledge me. Instead, he bypasses my car completely and practically sprints out of sight.

What the hell?

I get out, not really sure what my intent is, but my car is stuck and I need help. On shaky legs, I round the corner and that's when I see it.

That little thump I felt was my car bumper colliding with one of the many rows in the vineyard. I managed to take out a pretty big chunk.

Shit.

On a positive note, my bumper looks unmarred.

The man stands and stares at the damage. His fists clench at his sides, and his mouth draws into a thin, narrow line. I take back what I said earlier. He looks absolutely murderous.

"Is this your doing?" the man demands.

I practically jump at the deep timbre of his voice. Something about his smooth, authoritative tone awakens a little flutter in my stomach. I'm definitely losing it.

"I'm so, so sorry. It was an accident," I squeak. "I pulled over, because my GPS led me astray, and then the sand swooped my car, sending it flying away. I've been meaning to get my brakes looked at, but I'm so bad at car stuff. This wasn't intentional, I swear."

My rambling seems to irritate him even more.

He pulls out a radio, dismissing me. "Go for David."

"David here. Over." A man's static voice comes through.

"Yeah, David, this is Ethan. Can you come out to quadrant sixteen? There's been some damage"—his eyes cut to me — "due to an *accident*. Over."

"Ten-four."

"Do you have insurance?"

It takes me a moment to realize he's speaking to me and not the radio. "Yes?"

He nods and looks me up and down, seeming to realize for the first time that I'm an actual person and not some giant inconvenience. His gaze lands on every one of my flaws: my messy bun with greasy roots, my bare face in the middle of a period breakout, and my outfit, consisting of a threadbare crewneck sweatshirt and worn leggings. I'm dressed for comfort, not style, and I don't appreciate the judgment.

His features tighten, the scrutiny so obvious I feel naked under his stare. "Well? Are you going to get it?"

Heat creeps up my neck and fans out across my cheeks. This guy is such an asshole. Whatever remained of the drunken-like hysteria I was experiencing mere moments ago dissipates, and I'm stone-cold sober.

I stomp around to the passenger side, making a show of my irritation, and dig through the glove box until I find my insurance card. It's so unlike me to act this way, to not be overly polite, even if he is being rude. Apparently, a long car drive and a shit streak of bad luck have dimmed my usual sunny disposition.

I thrust the card out to him roughly. *That'll show him.*

Standing this close to him, I realize I'm at a disadvantage. Not only is he angry with me, he's also a very large man. Taller than me—which isn't saying much—at least six foot three, maybe even more. He's lean but solid looking. His well-defined biceps bulge beneath his flannel. His rich, brown beard, while full, is neatly trimmed and groomed. Despite his darkened, fuming eyes, the mossy green swimming in a mosaic of browns adds an unexpected softness. He's handsome, unfortunately—all the assholes are. I take notice of it purely for the purpose of describing him to authorities, if he is, in fact, a crazed killer.

As more of a suit girl—Hillary calls my type "tech bro"—it seems I've neglected to appreciate what a pair of well-fitting Wranglers can do for a man. Strong, thick legs fill out his snug jeans, and as he turns to pull out his cell phone, I definitely don't look at his butt. Nope, not at all.

He takes a few pictures of the card with his phone and then hands it back to me, the tips of his calloused fingers brushing against my skin. The sensation sends a shiver down my spine. Not sure where that came from. Clearly, I'm exhausted. Flutters and shivers within minutes of each other, truly flu-like symptoms.

"Why do you need my insurance?" I ask, unable to help the attitude pouring out of me. I resist the feminine urge to place both my hands on my waist and pop a hip.

His face scrunches as he looks at me like I'm an idiot. "Your negligent driving destroyed my property. We're in the middle of harvest, and there's no telling how much this will set us back or eat at potential profits."

Is he serious right now? Yes, I took out a few grape plants, but it's nothing in comparison to what remains.

"So you're going after my insurance? Does this mean I get your insurance information too? Only seems fair, don't you think?"

His jaw works side to side. Wordlessly, he pulls out a pen and small notepad from his Carhartt vest and begins scribbling on one of the sheets. He tears it off and hands it to me. "That's my name and number."

I look down and see that his name is Ethan, just like he said into the radio, and the number looks legitimate, but it's not as if I can confirm it at this very moment. He's conveniently left off his last name, which is suspicious. And it's not the insurance information I asked for, but something tells me this is the most I'll get out of him.

"I'd rather not be contacted," he continues. "If there's any damage to your vehicle, which by the looks of it, there isn't, who knows what you'll be charged at the overpriced city shop you'll no doubt take it to."

I scoff. The audacity of this guy. "What makes you think I'd take it to some crappy city shop?"

His eyes drag over me again, slowly, deliberately. "Wild guess."

What's that supposed to mean?

Without another word, he turns and stalks back to his truck.

"Hey," I yell.

He turns excruciatingly slow, his eyebrows raised.

"Little help here." I lift my arms in frustration.

He walks back to me, his hands shoved in his pockets. "What now?"

"I'm kind of stuck."

He looks between me and the car. "What's the issue?"

"I can't get out." I wave my hands from my car, up to the shoulder of the road to demonstrate. "I can't get up the slopey part."

The corner of his mouth ticks upward, almost forming a quarter of a smile. Almost. He's amused at my expense, yet some *I can fix him* part of me wants nothing more than to draw a genuine smile from his lips. Obviously, I need therapy.

"It's called a drainage ditch." He says it like I'm supposed to know what the heck that means.

He looks at my car again and then back to the road. "Crank your wheel all the way to the left and drive along that dirt pathway. Eventually, the grade will even out and you can pull back onto the main road. If that doesn't work, call a tow company. Impractical German cars don't do well in this desert sand." This time he does smile, pleased with his dig at my girly vehicle.

I roll my eyes. *Dick.*

"Is that all?" He's back to being irritated.

I flash him my fakest smile. "Yes, sir."

His eyes widen, exasperation flickering in those hazel irises, and a sense of triumph fills me.

"Word of advice, stick to downtown," he says, his voice low and condescending. "Tourists have no business driving on these back roads. Go on your little wine tour and then go back to where you came from."

My mouth drops open. I'm completely stunned by his obvious contempt for me. Not to mention his completely inaccurate assumptions.

With a curt nod, he hops back in his truck and drives away without a second glance.

Annoyingly, his directions work perfectly, and I'm quickly back on the road. When I finally get back to Main Street, my dad returns my call.

CHAPTER 4

Ethan

THE SECOND CHOICE

Fifteen pairs of eyes stare at me like I'm the world's biggest idiot.

"Meeting's over. You guys are dismissed," I repeat. Did they not fucking hear me the first time?

Alex, the foreman, clears his throat. "We usually do some stretches before returning to work."

"Stretches?" What the hell is he talking about?

"Yeah." His eyes dart around to the rest of the field crew nervously. "Your dad would lead us in some stretches. He said it helps with injuries."

Oh, nice. Yet another thing my dad failed to mention. We're five weeks into harvest, and this is the first I'm hearing about this. Granted, I'm also not a regular at these field meetings, but I'm trying to make more of an effort. Trying being the key word.

I nod at Alex. "Alright, how about you lead it?"

I make my way off to the side and let Alex take front and center. Fat fucking chance am I going to bend and squat and do whatever yoga-type shit my dad implemented, especially in front of this many people.

As I suspected, the stretching is a combination of your standard arm and leg stretches, sprinkled with some hippie-looking shit I'm assuming is yoga poses. A few years ago, my parents vacationed in Bali and my dad's been into the stuff ever since. He's probably the most flexible man in his sixties I know, so I'll give him that.

Following the completion of their stretches, the crew disperses and I head back to the office.

Tawny, my admin—who's also my cousin—greets me with a cheery smile. "Sooo," she drags. "How did it go?"

"Fine."

Her head cocks, and she looks at me like I'm a small child. "Use your words, Ethan. Grunts and single word sentences aren't going to cut it."

I really wish I could fire her purely for being annoying.

She remains standing in the middle of my office with her arms crossed, apparently waiting for me to elaborate.

"I don't think they like me very much," I admit.

She snorts. "Of course they don't."

My face contorts, and she tosses her head back and laughs. *Fired!*

"I fail to see what's so goddamn funny."

She flops down on the leather chair. "You show up here, don't so much as go around and introduce yourself to anyone, and suddenly you're their boss. No shit, they don't like you."

"I didn't ask for this," I grit.

"Believe me, I know," she says, scowling. "We all know, yet here you are. Better suck it up and get used to it."

I feel a headache coming on. It seems to be a daily occurrence for me. The consequences of trying to fill my dad's impossible shoes. In early summer, just as preparations for harvest began, my dad made an announcement that shocked the entire family—he was going to retire. We all knew he would retire one day, but we weren't prepared for him to do so without even warning the family. We all assumed Gavin, the oldest of us siblings, would fulfill his legacy and run the family business, but he turned it down. He said his daughter Lily came first and that he couldn't be both a good dad and run this place successfully. That's how I, the second choice, ended up CEO and operations manager of Ledger Estate Winery and Vineyards.

I rub the bridge of my nose, trying to release some of the pressure. I was already being pulled in multiple directions the second I showed up this morning, and then the trail cameras caught a car plowing down the Syrahs, so I had to go deal with that, making me late to the afternoon field crew meeting and adding one more reason for the crew to not like me.

"What do I have on my calendar for the rest of the day?"

She pulls out her tablet and starts scrolling. "Surprisingly, that's all for today." Standing, she straightens her blouse. "If you're hungry, Shane dropped off some lunch for you. It's in the fridge."

She starts to walk away but then spins on her heels to face me. "I wasn't going to say anything, but I fear I can no longer hold it in."

My shoulders tense. Something tells me I'm not going to like what she has to say. "What is it?"

Crossing her arms, she inches closer. "You are not your dad. You're your own person, and you don't have to do everything just as he did it. Do things your way, make the job work for you and how you want to operate. No one is expecting you to suddenly become the gregarious Jack Ledger after a lifetime of being prickly, Ethan."

"Is that little speech supposed to make me feel better? Because if so, maybe you should've practiced it a few times in the mirror beforehand."

She tosses back her head, her eyes rolling to the ceiling in frustration before returning to meet mine. "Don't be difficult with me, because I guarantee you will not find a better admin willing to put up with your mood swings. Just because we're family doesn't mean you have permission to treat me like I'm expendable."

I have a nasty habit of lashing out at those around me when I feel any sense of pressure. It's why I never wanted to be in charge to begin with. I was content with remaining in the background, quietly handling the financial end of the business. There are so many unspoken expectations put on me now, none of which I'll ever live up to. I'm not charming like my dad, or friendly like Gavin, or funny like Shane. I don't have an ounce of Ledger charm in my genetic makeup. What it all boils down to is I'll never be enough, and it's a tough pill to swallow.

I release a sigh. "You're right. I'm sorry."

"Just remember, I'm on your side. I want you to succeed, and success can look however you dictate. Be yourself, but maybe slightly friendlier," she says with a small smile.

With that, she walks out, and I'm left alone with my nearly debilitating imposter syndrome and the four corners of my dad's former office closing in on me.

I didn't realize how hungry I was until I sat down to eat the fancy-ass sandwich Shane made for me. Surprisingly, it still tastes fresh despite sitting in the fridge for hours, well past lunchtime. Perks of having a chef for a brother, I suppose.

I've been up and going since well before the sun came up, and I feel it. My neck aches, my eyes are dry and heavy, and overall I'm completely worn out.

On the edge of drifting off at my desk, I'm shocked back to life by the loud shriek of my radio.

"Go for Ethan," David's voice blares.

I give my head a shake and rapidly blink until the blur goes away. "This is Ethan. Over."

"We have repaired the damage at quadrant sixteen. Good as new. Over."

"Thanks for the update. Ten-Four."

My mind flashes to the woman from earlier. It wasn't funny at the time, but now, thinking back on it, it's pretty fucking funny. I've never seen so much fire spit out of a five-foot-nothing little thing. I'm used to pissing people off, but very few give it right back. It wasn't until she was digging for her insurance card, bent over with her ass in the air, that some of my anger started to dissolve. Those leggings of hers left little to the imagination. I quickly averted my eyes, because it felt wrong to check her out while also being on the verge of yelling at her. In truth, she barely caused any damage, but I had to scare her straight. These damn tourists need to learn to stay off back roads with their ill-equipped vehicles. Maybe I could have been slightly less of a dick, but after a week of one thing after another going wrong, I'd had it. Not that it matters. I doubt I'll be seeing her again.

For the next hour, I fight the desire to fall asleep and force myself to answer a few emails from distributors and forward a few others to my management team, delegating as much as I can, so I don't fuck up anything.

A *tap, tap, tap* has my eyes looking up to see my sister, Elyse, filling the door frame.

I can tell by the look on her face that she's not here for a friendly visit.

"Did you get one of these?" She slaps a white envelope on my desk.

I look down at it and then back up at her, slowly nodding my head. "Yeah, I got one."

"Can you believe that bitch?!" she practically yells, the anger radiating off of her like waves from a scorching sun.

"Elle," I chastise.

She throws up her hands. "Don't start defending her now. As a girl's girl, I can confidently say we do not claim her."

The headache that was slowly fading comes back with a force.

"Sometimes I don't know what half the shit that comes out of your mouth even means."

Ignoring my comment, she continues her rampage. "I mean, not only did she cheat on you with your best friend, now she's going to marry him!? *Bitch*. And to invite us, the gall."

"I know the story. I was there, remember? And I don't care. They can do whatever they want."

She groans. "Why aren't you matching my energy on this? Be mad, throw something, punch a wall."

I laugh, because what else can I do? I saw the envelope yesterday when I checked the mail and immediately knew what it was. Not many envelopes show up stark white, trimmed in gold, and addressed in swirly calligraphy. I would've preferred not to be invited, and I'm still working on figuring out their angle. They both know there's no way in hell I'm going to that wedding.

"I'm done with all of it," I say. "I don't give a shit anymore."

She rolls her eyes. "God, you're so sensible. It's disgusting."

Elyse is dramatic, to say the least.

I was angry for a really long time, but all that anger did was make me feel worse. I upended my life because of what happened between Laura and me, thinking if I moved away from it all, I could pretend it never happened. But as it turns out, you can't run away from your problems. They follow you, no matter how hard you try to escape them. When I accepted this new role in the family business, I made a choice to let it go. Does it suck? Yeah, it's humiliating. But I can't let it dictate my life anymore. I've got other things to worry about now, none of which include my ex and former best friend.

"Do you have a reason for being here, or are you just throwing a tantrum over a wedding invitation?"

Elyse's eyes narrow, and her lips draw together. "You should've stayed in Woodinville. You're already annoying me." She hands me the folder that was tucked under her arm. "I need your signature of approval for a corporate holiday retreat we're hosting in December."

Elyse is the event coordinator for the winery, which mostly hosts weddings, and she's pretty damn good at it. My little sister, the ball-buster who could easily make a grown man cry and rarely dates because she doesn't put up with shit. Yet somehow, she manages to work successfully with loving couples and plan romantic weddings. It's as if she can switch into a completely different person.

"Since when do we host corporate retreats?"

She shrugs. "Since some ritzy company is willing to pay us a fuck ton to do it."

I glance over the contract. I trust Elyse. I don't ever feel the need to scrutinize her decisions; she's the most meticulous person I know. I flip to the last page, sign it, and hand it back to her.

"Happy doing business with you," she chirps on her way out. "I leave tomorrow for a wedding expo in Vegas. I'll see you on Sunday."

"Have a safe trip," I tell her.

Sundays are reserved for the weekly Ledger Family Dinner, one of the few times I allow myself to double up on my anti-anxiety meds. Five siblings, two meddling parents, and my six-year-old niece. Individually, they're fine; all together, they're pure chaos.

CHAPTER 5

Marisa

THE MESSENGER, THE SPY

I guess I should've turned right instead of left, because once I'm back on the road, I quickly find my dad's house. He stayed on the line with me until I pulled into the driveway of a pretty, white farmhouse.

I put the car in park and jump out, but then pause, unsure if I should greet him with a hug or not. Fortunately, he makes the decision for me and pulls me into a familiar, bear-like hug. My body gently sags in his embrace, a combination of exhaustion and a rush of emotions from not having seen him in so long. He still smells the same, and I breathe him in as memories flood my mind. Images of the doting dad he was in my childhood eventually distort to the uncompromising, demanding dad he became in my teen years. I was never good enough, could never quite measure up to the impossible standards he held for me. It only got worse when I went to college. The last time we were in the same room, he told me I was a disappointment. That was the last real conversation we had. Until now.

Too quickly, he releases me, keeping his hands on my shoulders and inspecting me.

"You look so much like your mom," he says, his eyes tracking me, laced with something I can't quite identify.

There's no *so good to see you*, or *I missed you*, or *I'm so glad you're here*. No, none of that.

A quiet sigh slips through my lips. "Thanks." I'm not sure if it's a compliment or not.

He nods, turning toward the house. "Come on in."

The inside of the house is beautifully decorated with a purposeful mixture of fabrics and finishes that complement the space, making it both modern and classically farmhouse without being kitschy. Jennifer's doing, I'm sure, because my dad couldn't identify a throw pillow if his life depended on it.

The house is eerily quiet, too still for anyone else to be home. I know for a fact that along with Jennifer and my dad, there are two teenagers—Jennifer's kids—who live here, too.

Seeming to read the question in my eyes, he says, "Sadie is at her barista job and Caleb is at football practice. Jenn will be home from work in about an hour."

We get settled in the open concept living room, and he offers me a glass of water, which I down in less than a minute. I avoided drinking much of anything for the drive because I hate stopping at random places to pee, so I'm sure I'm pretty dehydrated.

An awkward silence hangs in the air between us. Instead of trying to fill the gap with my rambling, I take in the surrounding space. Sunlight streams through sheer curtains, casting a glow on the rustic hardwood floors. Large wooden beams draw attention to the vaulted ceilings, making the room appear much larger. It's a dream house, vastly different from the 1970s ranch-style home I grew up in. It's strange to think of my dad living here, acting as some sort of father figure to two kids who aren't his. Is he as hard on them as he was on me? Does he hold them to the same expectations?

Though it's been some time since I've seen him and our

interaction has been brief, it's evident that he's different. Calmer maybe? Less tightly wound? I can't quite put my finger on it, but something in him has clearly changed.

He clears his throat and blows out a long exhale. "Jenn and I did some talking...and we think it would be best if you didn't stay here."

My stomach plummets, the water I chugged churning like a whirlpool. He couldn't have told me this over the phone before I packed up my whole life?

My face must give away every emotion, because he quickly shakes his head.

"I'm sorry, that came out wrong. What I'm trying to say is we've arranged with Jack Ledger, a friend of ours, for you to stay in one of the rental cottages at his winery. Give you a little privacy, allow you to have your own space. I figured you would prefer that."

Both relief and disappointment weave through me. While I appreciate having my own space, it's clear that my dad doesn't want me intruding into his new life. Why bother adding me to the mix and tarnishing his shiny house and new family? He can pretend it's for my sake, but this is equally about him having no idea what to do with me. He never has.

"Should we go see it? Get you settled in?"

I arrived maybe ten minutes ago, and he's already trying to push me out the door.

I assumed I would be meeting Jennifer and the kids today. I guess I assumed wrong. I plaster on a fake smile. "Sure, let's do it."

The cottages are a block away, bordering a vineyard. Ten identical homes with sage-green clapboard siding are scattered across the land, partially concealed by the tree-lined street. My dad parks along the sidewalk, and I pull in right behind him. Together, we walk toward the cottages, a knot of wariness tightening in my stomach with each step.

As we approach, I take in the steep gabbled roofs topped with rustic shingles and the weathered wooden shutters framing each window. A meandering gravel path winds from the entrance of the vineyard, connecting each cottage. We pause in front of the one marked with the number seven, and my dad jingles the keys in his hands with his brows raised in excitement. He unlocks the door, and it swings open with a soft creak.

The inside is a little outdated, but it's clean and appears to have everything I'll need. There's a small kitchen and dining room off the side with a table and two chairs. The living room is simple, with a small couch, two accent chairs, and a TV. Off the living room is a bedroom with a decent-sized closet and the bathroom is your basic three-piece bath. The wall paint is faded and covered with awkward strips of wallpaper, and the cabinets are a yellowish maple, but the space is perfectly livable. All in all, I can't complain.

"The only thing missing is a laundry setup, but you're welcome to do your laundry any time over at our house."

I nod, looking around.

I'm not sure how long I'll be in Red Mountain, it all depends on my luck in getting a job. It could be a couple of weeks or months. Not having a definite end date is a little terrifying. How long can I go with my life on pause?

"What do you think?"

I give him a faint smile. "Love it. Thank you for making the arrangements. How much will this cost?"

He shakes his head. "Free of charge. They're not active rentals anymore."

"So, there isn't anyone else staying in the other cottages?"

His forehead knits, and he shakes his head. "Not that I'm aware of."

I'm not sure how I feel about staying somewhere without paying for it. And while the idea of having my own place to stay is nice, it's kind of creepy to think I'm the only one out here, surrounded by empty little houses.

"I take it you have plenty to unload from your car?" he asks. "If you're anything like your mother, I expect you packed a year's worth of stuff."

My eyes dart to him. My defenses tend to rise when either of my parents brings up the other. I tense, waiting for a negative comment that never comes. Instead, he continues on as if it's normal to mention her in passing and not add on a snarky quip.

He's not wrong about my overpacking, though. It takes us an hour to unload my car. Once we've gotten everything inside, it feels like the small cottage is going to bust. With my funds lacking, renting a storage unit was out of the question. It was either pack everything or get rid of stuff, and by the looks of it, I didn't get rid of one thing.

He gives me a rundown of things to expect while I'm staying. Most of it goes in one ear and out the other, except the part when he mentions everything in town, besides a convenience store or two, shuts down at 9:00 p.m., and if I need anything past that hour, I'll have to drive the thirty minutes it takes to get to Badger Canyon, the next town over. In Seattle, there's always something open at any given hour. It's going to take some time to adjust to living within the confines of small town life and without the amenities I'm used to.

"About your student loans," my dad starts.

I wince just thinking about them.

"While you're here, I would like to take over the payments."

I'm already shaking my head before he can finish the

42

sentence. "No way. You're already doing more than enough. I don't need to burden you with more."

"Marisa," he says in that patronizing tone I'm all too familiar with. "The purpose of you staying here is to get back on your feet. And that's not going to come easy if you're paying an exorbitant amount on that loan. I already have a meeting set with my financial guy to see about your options, and at the very least, try to find a way to lower the interest rate."

His offer is nice—it's more than nice—yet I feel like a child being scolded. He may have relaxed in this new life of his, but he's still an expert at making me feel foolish.

Rather than answer him, for fear of my voice cracking, I simply nod as shame floods my skin with heat.

Thankfully, he doesn't press me on the matter and changes the subject, inviting me to breakfast tomorrow morning. It's an in-service day, meaning the kids won't have school, so I'll be meeting everyone at once. At that, he leaves, claiming I should take the rest of the day to get settled in. The stillness that emerges in his absence stirs my growing regret for making this move, however temporary it is.

With nothing but time on my hands, I shoot a text to Hillary, letting her know I made it safely and promising to call later. While my phone is still in my hands, I decide to call my mom, even though I haven't been able to get through to her. I'm hoping she's at least gotten the half-dozen voicemails I left her.

It rings for the first time since I've been trying to reach her, and a seed of hope starts to sprout that maybe this time, we'll actually get to talk.

"Hi, mijita," she greets, casually.

My neck stiffens. She sounds so nonchalant. In fact, I'm pretty sure I hear laughter in her voice.

"Mom! Where have you been? I've been calling you for days."

I sound like a whiny child but I can't help it. I really needed her and she was nowhere to be found.

"I dropped my phone in the pool and it took a while to get a new one set up. What's the big deal? Did someone die?"

Yes, because only death warrants a reason to answer your daughter's phone calls.

"No, no one died. But I lost my job and my student loan payments restarted, so I'm staying with dad." It's the cliff notes version of events, but I don't have the patience or desire to rehash every detail to her. Especially when it's apparent she hasn't checked one voicemail I left her.

She's silent for a stretch. No doubt stunned. "You're telling me that *pinche pendejo* fired you?"

I groan. "Yes. No. I don't know. I guess, technically, I was laid off."

"Mija, what did I tell you?" And there it is. I was waiting for the *I told you so*. "I told you getting involved with him was a mistake. When are you going to learn to stop letting a man be the center of your life? Look what happened, he cheated on you, because that's what men do, they cheat. Even when they seem like they're not the type, they are. He got rid of you the moment someone shinier caught his eye. I bet he has the new girlfriend sitting at your desk and doing your job."

I hadn't thought of Quinn in all of this. My mom is probably right, I was completely replaced in every single way. Still, her words make my chest burn with humiliation. She *did* warn me about Brandon, several times, and I ignored her. It's hard to see the flaws in someone when you're caught up in the excitement of new love, blinded by affection and hope. Not to mention I was incredibly vulnerable. My mom was already on her self-discovery journey, and things with my dad were rocky. I needed someone who made me feel valued and loved, and Brandon seemed to fit that role.

"Can we stop talking about Brandon? I get it, okay. Let's talk about literally anything else."

I don't want to fight with her, but the resentment I work so hard to keep at bay starts to simmer. I need to shift the conversation before I let it boil over.

"Fine," she sighs, and the tension in my shoulders dissolves. "I'm assuming you're in Red Mountain now?" Even through the phone, I can detect her disgust. My mom loathes small towns. When she's not traveling around the world singing on cruise ships—which it feels like all she does these days—she's in Seattle, enjoying all the perks that come with living in a metropolitan area.

"Just got here."

"How is he?" Her tone is light and uninterested, but I see right through it.

"Who?"

She breathes a frustrated sigh. "Your dad."

The worst part about having divorced parents is this— being the go-between, the messenger, the spy. As bad as it sounds, it was easier when my dad and I weren't talking as often, because then my mom would ease off me a bit.

"He's Dad. You know how he is." It's better for everyone if I don't divulge too much. The less she knows the better.

"Hmmm. So, have you met her yet?"

I don't need to ask who "her" is. "No, not yet. I'm sure I will soon."

"How long are you planning to stay there? Not long, I hope."

"I haven't gotten that far yet. At least a couple weeks, maybe a month. The town is cute, though."

"Marisa," she says like a warning, her accent adding emphasis to my name.

I switch the phone to speaker and start unpacking my toiletries, needing a reprieve from our conversation. "What?"

"Don't get distracted and end up stuck there."

"Obviously, this is temporary. I'm allowed to like the town."

"You need to stay focused. The last thing you need is to end up meeting some local boy and giving up your future and independence for a simple little life in a simple little town."

My head flops back, and I close my eyes, willing myself to not snap.

"You're young, you need to be out there, traveling and having fun. Because believe me, this time in your life will fly by, and one day you'll wake up and realize your best years are behind you. I don't want that for you."

She's notorious for these tangents. I don't think I'll be getting distracted by any "local boys," as she put it. If they're anything like the asshole I dealt with earlier, I'm going to be just fine. I may not have the greatest taste in men, but I can confidently say it's definitely not rude and entitled dicks who dress like they should be on the cover of a lumberjack magazine.

"You're really going hard on the *distracting men* lecture today, aren't you?"

"All I'm saying is we don't need a Brandon repeat.," she continues, paying no mind to my snarky comment. "Stop letting men hold you back. They can't be trusted. You can have a little fun, sure, but keep it at that. Attachments lead to heartbreak."

It's nothing I haven't heard before. My mom has been lecturing some version of that since I was old enough to think boys were cute. To say she was disappointed when I called her after Brandon cheated would be an understatement. She was livid. Not at Brandon, but at me, for not being smart enough to predict he would do what he did. I should've been more prepared, had more money put aside, I should've never gotten involved with a coworker, let alone one of my superiors. The list goes on and on. It's my own fault for telling her in the first place. If I hadn't been so emotional, I would've lied and said we decided to part ways. Make it sound amicable and mature. Silly me for thinking she would comfort me instead of lecture me.

I've long since come to terms with the fact that my mom will never fully accept any of my romantic relationships. No man is good enough simply because he's a man.

"Okay, okay. I hear you." This conversation has grown exhausting. "Listen, I have a lot of unpacking to do. Can we talk another time? I'll call you later on this week after I've settled in."

She hums her agreement and, in the background, I hear laughter and her name being called. "Alright. Sí Dios quiere. I'll be near the Bahamas. Check time zones."

"I will. Love you."

"Love you," she happily sings like she didn't just lay into me. "Dios te bendiga," she adds, never one to end a phone call without tacking on a blessing.

The call with my mom depleted any remaining energy I had. Abandoning the suitcases and boxes begging to be unpacked, I crawl into bed. I'm usually only the napping type when I'm sick, but as soon as my head hits the pillow, not even the bright sun can prevent me from drifting off.

CHAPTER 6

Ethan

KILL ME, DO IT FAST

Tawny taps on the door frame of my office. "Hey, why don't you go home? Get some rest. You look like shit."

"Jesus, tell me the truth why don't you."

"You don't pay me enough to lie."

It's only six, and there's still so much to take care of; the pile is never-ending. But I'm gassed, and if Tawny is telling me to go home, who am I to argue?

I've only been back in Red Mountain for about a month and a half, and due to the short notice, my options for accommodations were limited, forcing me to freeload in one of the winery rental cottages until I find a more permanent solution. There's a foundation poured on the plot of land my parents parceled off to me, but the walls never went up. The thought of dredging up that mess overwhelms me. That was my old life, my old plans.

I park my truck on a dirt pathway and make the short trek to the cottages. As they come into view, I get an odd feeling that someone has been here. It's like the sense you get as a kid when you know a sibling has been in your room, even though

48

nothing looks disturbed. But when I look around, nothing seems suspicious, so I chalk it up to my lack of sleep.

Goose greets me at the door, his tail wagging with excitement. My little sister, Ariana, came by to check on him earlier and let him out for a potty break. I feel bad that he's been alone for most of the day. I would love to bring him with me to work, but with it being peak season, it would be too chaotic to have a giant German Shepherd, who thinks he's a puppy, running around the place.

"Hey, buddy." I crouch down and scratch the spot behind his ears.

He groans and pushes his head further into my hand, trying to get a deeper scratch.

"Where's your leash?"

His ears perk up. Damn dog is too smart for his own good. A leash means a walk, and he lives for our walks. Goose runs off and then quickly returns with his leash between his teeth.

"Alright, bud, let's go." I snap the leash in place to his collar and let him drag me out the door. It's dog walking 101 to not let your dog drag you during a walk, but this guy has had me wrapped around his fingers since day one and I let him get away with just about anything.

Goose happily trots along, kicking up sand and gravel with each bounce of his step, and pausing a few times to pee. There's less than an hour of daylight left before the sun disappears behind the ridge. For now, though, it casts an array of oranges and pinks across the river valley, bathing everything in a glow you can only experience this time of the year. Despite the days getting shorter and the unpredictable temperature highs and lows, nothing beats Red Mountain in the fall. Even a few years away couldn't make me forget that.

As we walk, I take in the rows of vines stretched out before me. Their leaves are fading from green to gold, a sign that fall is in full effect. The crisp air is tinged with the earthy scent of soil and ripe grapes, a nostalgic smell that always reminds me of my childhood and the chaos surrounding harvest.

Goose starts tugging on his leash, snapping me back to the present, trying to get out of my hold. I could probably walk him out here without a leash since there isn't anyone around, but he's a little shit and would find trouble, just like he's trying to do now when he spots a jackrabbit a couple hundred yards away.

I give the leash a tug. "Goose, inside. Now."

Like a good boy, he obliges, while glancing longingly at the jackrabbit he doesn't get to attack today, and we go back inside.

After eating dinner, which consisted of a random concoction of leftovers my mom snuck inside my fridge, I take care of a few more work tasks I didn't get to when I was at the office. By 7:30, the sleep I've been fighting off finally starts to win. How fucking sad is that? This schedule is making me feel a hell of a lot older than thirty-two. Only a few more weeks of harvest remain, and then I'll be on a more manageable schedule.

Goose joins me in bed, taking up the entire right side, like a human would, body sprawled out, with his head on a pillow. I attempted to train him to not get on the furniture, because German Shepherds are notorious shedders, but I gave up fighting it. It's his space, too. In fact, he's home more than I am, so the way I see it, he should get to enjoy the furniture along with me. And, if in some alternate universe or very, very distant future, I actually allow another woman into our lives, she's going to have to be okay with that. If I'm ever made to choose between Goose or some chick, it's Goose every damn time.

My eyes glaze over, the narrator on the History Channel and Goose's whir of snoring lulling me to sleep.

It feels like I just closed my eyes when I'm jolted awake by my dog's low growl. My eyes adjust to the pitch-black room, and I prop myself up on my elbows. There was still a faint glow of light when I fell asleep, but now it's completely dark. Tapping my phone, I see it's almost midnight. Goose growls again, more aggressively, and my hackles raise. He hears something, something foreign and wrong, because in all the years I've had him, he's never woken me up like this.

Using the glow of my phone to discreetly light my way around the bedroom, I throw on a pair of sweatpants and slip into my boots, making sure to grab a hoodie. Despite how warm it was today, once the sun is down, the temperature drastically drops. Before heading out the door, I grab my pistol, just in case. There's always an uptick in cougar sightings this time of the year, and I'm not about to find myself facing a snarling cat without some protection.

Goose walks quietly beside me, aware that we are now on a mission that requires a little stealth. It's probably nothing, but I'd rather check it out than sit and wonder. Tourist season is in full swing, and you never know what kind of crazies are going to roll into town. I hope to hell this is nothing but a lone coyote or wandering deer.

The moon is almost full in the night sky, but heavy clouds dull its brightness and block most of the light. Luckily, I know the landscape like the back of my hand. I'm not dumb enough to use a flashlight and draw the attention of whatever—or whoever—is out here. We make it just past the front steps when Goose pauses, lifting his nose, sniffing the air. His ears pin back as he takes his attack stance, dropping his back legs so he can spring off of them. I grab hold of his collar to stop him before he goes on the attack. If someone is out there, they're dealing with me first.

We move forward together, one step at a time, slowly, crouched low, my hand still gripping the collar. I think I see movement near the trees, but I can't be too certain. I don't want whatever it is to see me coming and try to hide, or do worse. Goose whines, seeing it, too, and yanks himself out of my hold to jet off after our unwanted visitor like a bat out of hell.

Before I can change my mind, I race after him, watching as my hundred-pound dog tackles a small figure to the ground.

"What"—a feminine choking gasp—"the"—a shriek that could cut glass it's so high—"fuck!" Strangled sounds push out of the person Goose flattened as he stands over them, barking profusely in their face.

I run up, shoving him out of the way, and replace him so that I'm standing over the intruder instead. His barking comes to a halt as he sits and waits for a command. At least some of his training stuck.

I look down at the tackle victim and shine the light from my phone in their face.

Recognition surfaces.

It's the woman from earlier. The one who crashed into my vineyard.

Fuck.

She's sprawled out on the ground, gasping for air, and there's an assortment of...garbage around her.

Her eyes widen to the point I can see the whites all the way around her brown irises. Then, like a fish flopping on land, she throws her body into the fetal position.

"Do it fast," she croaks. "If you're going to kill me, do it fast!"

I step aside so I'm no longer standing over her. "I'm not going to kill you."

She stays frozen for a few beats, holding the fetal position like she thinks I'm going to strike her. Apparently, my staying still is enough reassurance that I'm not going to hurt her, because she slowly starts to uncurl, keeping her eyes trained on me.

"Well then, will you at least help me up?" she yells, her voice raspy.

I grab hold of her reaching hand and pull her to stand. She clutches her chest, huffing as she bends over, hands resting on her thighs.

"What the hell are you doing wandering around here in the middle of the night? Are you following me?" I ask, much louder than I intended.

Rather than answer me, she puts up a hand, gesturing with her pointer finger that she needs a minute.

"Shit. Fuck. Are you hurt?" My eyes inspect her for any possible injuries, but it's hard to get a good look with her hunched over the way she is and the lack of decent light.

She shakes her head no, but her head is still hanging off her shoulders as she continues to try to catch her breath.

Minutes pass as she slowly starts to breathe a little better. I wait, staring at her and unsure of what to do.

"My dinner," she whines, and it comes out wheezy.

Dinner? I look down to see what I initially thought was garbage is actually a variety of gas station food. Two taquitos, a burrito, some nachos, a hotdog, and a large pop, spilled and soaking into the ground. How was she carrying all of this? It's ruined now, unless she enjoys the taste of sand. Goose doesn't seem to mind, though, as he helps himself to the hot dog.

Fucking hell.

I'm startled by what I think is a cry escaping her. My gaze flies to her face, ready to see tears rolling down her cheeks—she did just get the shit tackled out of her—but instead of crying, she's laughing. It's not a cute, girly laugh either—more

53

like a honking bird mixed with a cackling hyena. She throws her head back, unrestrained, her eyes sparkling as they pick up light from the few stars shining above. Her laugh is so unexpectedly genuine I can't stop my lips from lifting into a smile. Our eyes meet, and we both deflate, laughing together at the sheer ridiculousness of what just happened.

My shoulders shake, my fist covers my mouth, and a wheezing laugh crawls up my throat. It feels good to laugh a real laugh. And for the dumbest fucking reason, my greedy dog and his addiction to hot dogs. The tension I've been carrying in my back begins to unravel, loosening like a tightly wound spring finally releasing its grip. The stress, the pressure, and the anxiety are carried away with each breath. I look to the cackling woman, astounded that such a hideous sound can be attached to someone very far from hideous, and it makes me laugh harder.

After a while, her awful laughter fades into a phlegmy cough, and I'm jarred back into reality, the slap-happy feeling dissolving as quickly as it appeared. Reality sets in, and I'm reminded she could very well be some unhinged criminal.

"I'm not following you," she clarifies, her breathing still irregular.

I cross my arms and raise my shoulders with a firmer stance. "Then what are you doing out here? This is private property."

The atmosphere between us takes a dive. Her eyes narrow, looking up at me with an icy, penetrating stare. The speed at which her eyes shifted from wide and bright to cold and detached is startling.

"I'm staying there." She points to the cottage to the left of mine.

"That's not possible."

She rolls her eyes and places her hands on her hips. If I

wasn't so weary of her, I'd find her display of determination slightly comical given her short height.

"What part of 'I'm staying there' do you not understand?"

"See that name right there?" I tell her, pointing to the arched, wrought iron sign at the end of the pathway that says Ledger on it. "That's my name, Ledger. Ethan Ledger."

Her eyes cut back to mine, unimpressed. Bored even. "Is that supposed to mean something to me?"

"My land. My winery. My cottages."

A sharp laugh escapes her lips. She's laughing at me, and the tips of my ears singe. I don't know who this woman thinks she is, but she's dangerously close to getting tossed on her ass by the cops I'm seconds away from calling.

"All I heard was *my, my, my*." She laughs again, and it grates my ears like a goddamn crow cawing in the dead of night. "Lighten up, crabby pants. My dad set this up for me with some guy named Jack. Take it up with him."

I should've known my dad had something to do with this. Just another thing he couldn't be bothered to tell me about. I whip out my phone, not giving a single fuck what time it is. I should've been informed of this. While I wait for the call to connect, Goose trots up to our intruder and starts rubbing his head on her legs. *Guard dog, my ass.* I expect her to shoo him away, but instead she pets him mindlessly, giving him gentle little scratches along his head. He soaks in the attention, tail wagging.

Traitor.

The phone rings three times before my dad picks up.

"Hello?" His voice is gravelly, and a pang of guilt hits me. I could've waited until the morning. It's not as if she's an actual threat. But then I remember he's been a lot less helpful in this transition than I thought he would be, leaving me to figure things out blindly, and some of the guilt dissipates.

"Did you book someone to stay in the cottage next to mine?"

"Sure did," he says, sounding more awake.

There's no way she heard my dad through the phone, but the satisfied smile she's shooting my way says otherwise.

"And you didn't think to tell me?" I ask through gritted teeth.

He yawns, an exaggerated, long yawn. "Slipped my mind."

"You should've told me. Goose attacked her because he thought she was sneaking around."

He groans, cursing under his breath. "It was an honest mistake. Is she hurt?"

My eyes rake over her, and I let myself indulge slightly with her focus off me and firmly on my dog. She's attractive, there's no doubt about it. But I have an aversion to women who are too attractive for their own good. They blind you with their beauty, making it difficult to see what's been right in front of you the entire time. I don't know why she's here, and I don't know for how long, but I don't like it one bit.

"She's fine."

He breathes a sigh of relief. "Good. That's good. She's Robert's daughter, so be nice to her, will you?"

I'd never guess the two were related. Robert, a pale, average looking white guy, who doesn't look nearly old enough to have an adult daughter, looks nothing like the olive-skinned, brown-eyed woman before me. She clearly takes after her mother.

"Marisa I think is her name. She drove down from Seattle today," he adds.

I tip up my chin at her to get her attention. "You got a name?"

She cocks her head at me, annoyance dripping off of her. "Marisa," she says, in a dry, dead voice.

"Son, what did I just say about being nice?" my dad chastises.

"I'll work on it," I tell him and then hang up the phone.

Marisa's back is to me, and she's squatting in front of Goose. "And what's your name, handsome?"

Thank God it's dark and she's facing away from me, effectively hiding the smile I almost let slip. I've never heard a baby voice quite like that one. Sugary sweet, yet husky.

"His name is Goose."

Ignoring me she extends her hand out to him. "Shake," she commands, and he puts his paw out to her. "I'm Marisa. That grumpy man gave you such a terrible name, didn't he? Naming you after a bird."

Something south of my belt twitches at hearing her baby-talk voice. Christ. Now I feel like a pervert. One more reason I don't need her around.

"He's not named after a bird. It's from the movie *Top Gun*." Not sure why I feel the need to elaborate.

She stands, dusting off some of the sand still stuck to her. "Never seen it."

Who the hell hasn't seen *Top Gun*?

I remain silent, the awkwardness growing with each passing second.

Her smile is devious as she walks closer to me, invading my bubble of space. She cranes her neck up at me, all doe eyed and smug. "Satisfied?"

"Mildly," I retort, slightly distracted by the vanilla smell coming off her.

"Well, now that we have all that sorted out, I'm going to go back inside and try to find something to eat."

She walks to the cottage. Her hand glides along the railing as she takes the front steps up to the door. Before going in, she pauses and looks over her shoulder at me. "I will be expecting an apology from you for ruining my dinner and for being a total ass about this."

"I wouldn't hold my breath," I mumble.

Her lips purse, eyebrows raising. "What was that?"

"Nothing." I shrug. I doubt she heard me, but she knows it was something smart ass.

"Maybe tomorrow, after you've had some much needed beauty rest, we can try this again."

"Try what again?"

"Meeting." Without giving me a moment to respond, she's inside, the door slamming loudly in her wake.

Goose looks at me with disappointment.

"Yeah, yeah," I whisper to him as I gather the gas station food still lying all over the place. "I'm an asshole, I know."

CHAPTER 7

Marisa

A TOOTHPICK INTO A LOG CABIN

I *can do this. I'm calm. This isn't weird at all.*
Preparing myself, I stand in the backyard, feet stuck
to the grass, as I creepily look through the sliding glass
door at the scene in front of me. Two teenagers, who I assume
are Sadie and Caleb, are seated at a dining table while my dad
and Jennifer are working together in the kitchen. It radiates
staged perfection as rays of light filter through the windows,
providing a golden backdrop to the image. Perfect weather,
perfect family, and then there's me. My feet remain planted for
several more seconds, battling my fight-or-flight instincts.
Taking a few deep breaths, I gear up to enter this new world. A
world where my dad is married to a woman I've never met and
I have two step-siblings. It's much easier to pretend none of
this exists when it's not right in front of my eyes.

Here goes nothing.

"Good morning. Come join us." My dad is standing in
front of an electric griddle, pancakes laid out in perfect, even
circles. He's wearing an apron that says *Kiss the Chef.*

A woman—Jennifer—stands at the sink with her back to
me. She turns at the sound of my dad's booming voice and

wipes her hands on an apron that matches his, except hers says *I Kissed the Chef*. Her arms open as she approaches me.

"Marisa," she says, enveloping me in a hug. It's a real hug too, tight and warm. She pulls me in so close I can feel the bones in her chest press against my cheek. My hands remain at my sides, clutched down by her arms. She releases me, keeping her hands on both of my shoulders and admiring me. "My goodness, you're beautiful. It's so good to finally meet you."

"G-g—good to meet you, too, Jennifer."

Her hand waves off my formalness. "Please, call me Jenn."

Smiling at me brightly, she practically exudes warmth. She has the kind of smile that immediately puts others at ease, her eyes crinkling at the corners, cheeks lifting beneath deep smile lines. Even her blonde hair, with hints of gray, glows like the sun is shining down on it. I was prepared to hate her. Mentally, I was going to catalog all of her flaws and use them to build an evil stepmom narrative. Unfortunately, she's nice and it seems sincere. I can't help but feel as if I'm betraying my mom by having one positive thought about her.

"Sadie. Caleb. Come meet Marisa. Your phones will survive if you set them down for a few moments." She gives me a look that tells me this is a daily annoyance for her.

"Hi," Sadie says shyly. She looks like a young Jennifer with her long, honey-blonde hair, a youthful round face, and the most piercing, cornflower blue eyes. She looks nervous, and I'm reminded of myself at her age—painfully shy, nose always buried in a book. I give her a half wave, and she smiles back.

"Sup," Caleb says, sounding every bit the teenage boy he is. He looks similar to Sadie, but his features are sharper and his hair is chestnut brown. His cheeks and jaw are covered in patchy, uneven hair, an attempt at growing a beard that forces me to bite back a smile. It's comforting to know there are some things, like teenage boys, that remain utterly predictable.

"How do you like your eggs?" Jenn asks.

I walk around to the kitchen island, using it as a barrier between us. "Over easy, but I'm not picky, whatever is easiest."

"We are a runny yolk household." She gives me a wink. "Oh, and if you're a coffee drinker, help yourself."

After making myself a cup of coffee, I take the far seat at the table, wincing from the giant bruise on my ass, a reminder of last night's debacle. I clasp my hands in my lap, unsure of what to do with myself. Sadie and Caleb are focused on their phones, randomly kicking each other under the table. I'm guessing it's some form of sibling communication, but as an only child, I can only assume.

My dad and Jenn work in the kitchen like a well-oiled machine, sensing and anticipating the other's movements before they even happen. It's a rehearsed dance they seem to perform often, and I'm hit with a pang of jealousy. I never got the two parents in the kitchen happily working together as a team. My parent's relationship was rocky for as far back as I can remember. If they weren't fighting, they were silent. Seeing this version of my dad is so foreign to me, he may as well be a stranger. In many ways, he is a stranger. I've never met *this* man.

The breakfast spread is akin to something from a TV show—impeccably prepared and ready for the main characters to take a single bite of toast as they race out the door. All of Jenn's dishes are a matching crisp white porcelain. So unlike my mom's array of colorful dishes, acquired over years of thrifting.

Dishes are passed around the table, family style, while Jenn walks around, serving each person their preferred egg order. Is this real? Do people actually live this way?

Finally, she takes her seat next to my dad. "Is there anything you need for the cottage? Kitchen supplies, towels, household basics?" she asks, spreading a layer of butter on her toast.

"Not that I can think of. The cottage seems fully stocked with things like that, and I also brought a ton of stuff."

Jenn looks to my dad. "Did you show her around the property?"

He shakes his head. "I figured she was tired."

"We definitely should, or have one of the Ledgers do it." Focusing her attention back on me, she says, "Not sure if your dad mentioned it, but one of the cottages is being used by Jack's son, Ethan. In case you see a strange man around, no need to freak out."

My dad's eyes snap open wide, as if until this very moment, the information had slipped his mind.

I swallow harshly, the toast lodging in my throat, and a choking cough attacks me.

"Caleb!" Jenn yells. "Go get Marisa some water."

I swallow again, this time more successfully. My cheeks flame. She mentioned Ethan, and suddenly I felt like she knew something, like she could read the embarrassment from last night on my face.

Caleb sets a glass of water in front of me, and I give him a nod of thanks.

Gulping down the water, my throat slowly relaxes.

"How about you take the next few days to unpack and get settled. On Saturday, if you haven't already explored, we can show you around the vineyard property, and then venture into town. There's the most adorable farmers market that takes over the whole downtown area. I think you'll love it," Jenn happily states. "It'll be a nice little family outing."

Family.

The word tastes bitter in my mouth. Jenn is nice—I can admit that— and the kids seem okay, but these people are not my family.

After breakfast, it's time to face the one thing I've been dreading. Unpacking.

It feels pointless to settle in when I could just as easily be packing it all right back up in a week. Well, maybe not a week. That's more wishful thinking than anything.

But before I can begin unpacking, I need groceries. Badly.

Last night, my growling stomach woke me from my nap, and of course, it was after everything except a questionable-looking convenience store had closed. I didn't even want the food, none of it sounded good, but I was starving and desperate. When that got ruined, I had to scrounge through my work purse, hoping I had a snack or two in there. I was in luck. There was a week-old Ziplock bag of salt and vinegar chips, broken down into tiny pieces and stale. It was great. Super satisfying.

Never again will I let myself be that unprepared. I think what upsets me the most about last night isn't that his dog jumped me and ruined my shitty dinner, or that I was accused of being a criminal, it's that Ethan didn't apologize. Not once. Or offer me food when clearly I was hungry. Aren't small towns known for being able to borrow a cup of sugar from your neighbor? A granola bar would've sufficed.

My nails dig into the steering wheel as I think about my jerk of a neighbor and turn into the parking lot of Harvest Grocers, Red Mountain's only grocery store. I nearly missed it entirely because the faded sign and modestly sized building blend in with the other small storefronts around it.

Inside, the aisles are narrow but well stocked, and the scent of freshly baked bread fills the air, adding a touch of rustic charm. It may not have an overwhelming variety of options often found in big supermarkets, but once I find the freezer section, I'm quickly debating between a single-serve meat lovers frozen lasagna or a chicken Alfredo. I enjoy cooking, but something about cooking for one is incredibly depressing. Thankfully, my appetite has recently started to come back. For a while there, Hillary had to force feed me. I'd take one bite and feel the food slide past the emotional lump in my throat, effectively killing any interest in eating.

Instead of choosing one or the other, I drop both in the cart and move on to the pantry aisles. I stock up on pickles, some canned foods, a decently sized bag of rice, and other random prepared boxed foods, all the while keeping a mental tally on the total, because money is tight.

"Hey!" a familiar voice calls to me from the left, startling me, and I drop the bottle of olive oil I was about to put in my cart.

I bend down to grab it, looking up to see my dad's smiling face. Even though I was just with him, it's weird running into him in public. Standing, I see he's not alone.

"Jack, this is my daughter, Marisa. Marisa, this is Jack Ledger, who I made the cottage arrangements with."

Jack towers over my dad. He's an older man who looks about mid to late sixties, with salt and pepper hair and plenty of fine lines, especially deep in the outer corners of his eyes and around his mouth. He smiles warmly at me, and the lines sink deeper.

"Nice to meet you, Marisa," he says, tipping his head at me like a cowboy in a western film. If he were wearing a cowboy hat, he'd be spot on. He shakes my hand firmly but gentle. "And my apologies about the mixup last night."

My dad rears back, looking confused. "Mixup?"

Jack shoves his hands in his pockets, shaking his head as if he really feels bad. He looks more remorseful than Ethan. "I forgot to tell Ethan about Marisa staying next door, and his dog attacked her." He turns to me. "I feel just awful."

"It's fine, really. I didn't get hurt. No harm, no foul."

"Sweets, why didn't you say anything earlier?" It's been ages since my dad has called me that, and a little corner of my heart pinches.

I force a smile. "It's not a big deal. I didn't think it was worth bringing up." Really, what was I supposed to say? *Thanks for the accommodations, oh, by the way, the neighbor, who's also the owner, hates me.*

"Well, let me or Ethan know if there's anything we can do to make your stay more comfortable," Jack says. He seems like such a nice man, unlike his son, so I hold in my scoff. If I need anything, I'm certainly not going to Ethan for help, unless his personality does a 180 and he actually apologizes to me.

"We should get going," my dad says. "We were just popping in to order some sandwich trays for Caleb and his teammates. There's a big game on Friday, if you're interested?" He waggles his brows at me, as if that may entice me more. I have zero interest in going to a high school football game.

"We'll see," I say noncommittally, but my dad doesn't seem to notice my lack of enthusiasm.

We part ways, and I finish my shopping.

Ten minutes later, I'm unloading a trunk full of groceries as the sun beats down against my back. I can't tell if it's an unusually warm day for fall or if this is normal for the south-eastern portion of the state. Seattle has already dropped down to a rainy fifty degrees, and my body feels out of whack, trying to acclimate.

I retrieve the last bag, feeling way more winded than I should as sweat forms around my temples, and slam down the trunk.

Behind me, someone coughs, causing me to still. It's Ethan. I can sense it's him without even having to look. I muster a forced smile, reminding myself to be friendly. Maybe yesterday was a fluke and I caught him on an off day. But as I turn to look at him, I see he's standing closer than I thought, arms crossed, stance wide and domineering, with an irritated scowl to match.

"Hi, neighbor," I say cheerfully.

His scowl deepens, causing my smile to falter.

Definitely not a fluke.

My smile fully drops, and I suppress an eye roll. What's crawled up his ass now?

"Can I help you?" I ask, because his only response to my greeting was a grunt.

His eyes flick over me, giving me a dismissive once-over. "You can't park here."

Looping my arm through the grocery bag handle, I cross my arms and pop my hip. "And where exactly am I supposed to park?"

He points to the pathway that leads to the sidewalk. "Street parking."

"Where's the sign that says that?" Maybe if he had brought it up nicely, I would gladly park there. But he didn't, so now I'm going to be a bitch.

His jaw hardens. "Don't need a sign," he grits. "No one is supposed to be staying here."

No way in hell am I moving my car right now. I'm hot and sweaty and have way too much to do. "Are you always this rude? Because I'm starting to take it personally. Have I done something to offend you besides exist?"

He huffs, shaking his head. "I'm just telling it like it is. Didn't realize I needed to treat you like a delicate flower."

God! He is the most infuriating man I've ever met. I'm at my breaking point. Lucky for him, my phone rings before I can scream. It's my mom. She's usually not one to call without a reason, especially since we spoke yesterday.

"I should get this." I drop the grocery bag—the one with my canned food—aiming for his feet.

He winces when it lands right on his toes, and his gaze tightens as he tries to look unaffected when I'm sure it hurt like hell. I bite my bottom lip to stop from laughing.

I assumed he would take the hint and leave, but doesn't move an inch.

Ignoring him, I answer the call. "¿Bueno? Mamá. ¿Qué onda?" *(Hi, Mom. What's up?)*

My mom and I have an understanding that if I start a conversation in Spanish, it's intentional. The same goes for her, because for the most part she tries to speak primarily in English. Though when it's just her and I or she's talking to someone else who speaks Spanish, she'll weave in and out of both languages seamlessly.

"¿Me puedes dar la contraseña de Netflix?" *(Can you give me the Netflix password?)*

It's really not a good time. "Espera un momento, estoy ocupada gritándole a mi vecino cabrón." *(In a minute, I'm busy yelling at my asshole neighbor.)*

She sighs, clearly annoyed. "Órale, llámame después." *(Fine, call me when you're done.)*

We end the call, and Ethan eyes me curiously, the corners of his lips tilting. He looks unnatural with a smile. It clearly doesn't belong on him.

"Have a nice chat about me?"

I let out a contemptuous laugh. "Some ego you have. Trust me, you're not that special. That was my mom and she's Mexican, so sometimes we speak in Spanish. Based on your use of grunts, I'm going to assume English is hard enough for you."

His jaw ticks. For someone as abrasive and rude as he is, he sure is sensitive about any little digs I aim his way. He glares down at me, eyes more green than brown today. "So, your car. Are you going to move it?"

Oh. My. God. What is the big deal about parking here? He just wants to pick a fight.

"I'll move it when I'm ready." I pick back up the grocery bag and hit the lock button on my key fob. "I was giving you the benefit of the doubt, but you're worse today than you were yesterday."

His face is unreadable. Hard. Impassive.

It's such a shame that he's the personality equivalent of Oscar the Grouch. He doesn't deserve to look as good as he does in a simple black T-shirt and jeans, with biceps straining against his cotton sleeves and his broad chest looking strong and prominent. He's all thick muscle and hard lines. He looks like the kind of man who could turn a toothpick into a log cabin if you handed it to him in the wilderness. I feel the feminist in me leave my body for a moment while I appreciate how absolutely masculine he looks. It's likely toxic, but a girl can still look.

My cheeks heat, in both fluster and anger that I've become this pathetic, checking out a man who looks at me like I'm gum stuck to the bottom of his shoe.

It seems we're playing the silent game. I thought he would have a quick comeback, but instead, he stays mute and unmoving.

Our quiet beat morphs into an awkward silence. And I hate awkward silences.

Unable to stand it, I continue talking. "Look, I don't want to be here any more than you want me here. But it is what it is. Are you going to keep being difficult, or can we come to an understanding?"

Finally, after what feels like years taken off my life, some of the tightening around his jaw releases and his mouth relaxes. "Fine."

I still. "Fine?"

"Fine," he repeats. "But I have rules."

I stare at him with my brow arched, waiting to hear about these so-called rules of his.

He sighs, as if just being around me exhausts him. "Rule number one, no visitors."

That seems unreasonable. "What about my dad?" I quickly shoot back.

"I'll allow family to visit, but no strange men and no parties. I like my privacy, and I don't need any loud, rowdy noises around."

It's not like either of those things will be happening, but I don't like being told who I can and can't have over. "And if I do?"

"Then you'll have to stay somewhere else, or better yet, go back to Seattle."

"Okay," I agree, begrudgingly. "Any more rules?" I put air quotes around the last word.

"Keep to yourself and I'll do the same. Me and you"—he points between us—"we're not friends."

As if I want to be friends with his grumpy ass anyway. No, thank you. "Works for me," I say, sugary sweet.

I wait for a third rule, but he doesn't continue.

"Is that all, sir?" I smile prettily, daring him to crack.

He doesn't. Instead, he stares at me blankly, eyes dull and mouth flat.

The energy it must take to not show any emotion other than anger and irritation—could never be me.

He turns on his heels and stalks back to his cottage, muttering under his breath something that sounds a lot like *damn city girl.*

CHAPTER 8

Marisa

DROPPED AS AN INFANT

D ays pass in a blur. I make some progress unpacking but leave most of my things boxed up, only taking out what I absolutely need. I'm supposed to start working for the *Red Mountain Herald* on Monday—one of my dad's conditions until I can find a job— but right now, it feels like I'm in limbo. My dad has extended invitations for dinner and offered up his laundry room as a way to get me to come visit. Like a coward, I've lied and said I was busy. Now it's Saturday, and the last thing I feel like doing is spending the day with him and his family.

His family. Not *my* family.

But if I spend one more day cooped up in this cottage, feeling sorry for myself and binge watching reality shows about strangers marrying each other, I'll likely fuse to the couch.

I force myself to take a shower, a good, long everything shower. I put on makeup, something I haven't done since I lost my job. My mom would probably have a stroke if she knew I've been living this way. Rosario Castilla would never be caught dead without a full face of makeup, perfectly curled hair, fresh manicure and pedicure, and just the right amount of jewelry. She raised me to be the same, but with age, I've stopped caring as much about what other people think of my appearance. Something I think she puts a little too much emphasis on.

However, I need to crawl out of this slump I've allowed myself to fall into before it completely swallows me. And the best way I know to do that is to fake it. I pick out a cute outfit and finish the look with some loose curls. Looking at myself in the mirror, I already feel slightly better. More me. More alive. And I did it purely for my own enjoyment and how it makes me feel, not for anyone else.

The drive to downtown is short, with little traffic, but once I get closer, parking lots are overflowing and cars line the streets. Main Street is blocked off, and I'm forced to park on a random residential street and walk.

The farmers market Jenn mentioned is a lot larger than I imagined. There are vendors showcasing everything—local sugar dot corn, homemade soaps and lotions, various foods on a stick, artisan candles, and an assortment of fresh fruits and vegetables. I weave through the crowd, overwhelmed, my eyes darting about like a squirrel, trying to take it all in at once. I could spend hours walking through, looking at each stand, and still not get to see everything.

Further along, the aroma of coffee wafts through the air, guiding me to a coffee shop adorably named Novel Teas and Coffee. Peeking through the windows, I can see it's packed, but not more so than the coffee shop I used to frequent back home. Once inside, I'm met with a wall covered in opened books, the pages creating a 3D effect. As an avid reader, I can't decide if it's cool as shit or blasphemous. I'm the kind of reader who won't even dog ear a book, let alone make a whole wall of pages begging to be ruined. It does contribute to the overall atmosphere of the shop, though, which is very Jane

Austen, romantic with florals, full bookcases, and curated furniture, that feels like a step back in time. Even the menu is on theme, with drinks named The Author, Blank Page, and Typewriter. Naturally, I go with The Writer, espresso with brown sugar and cinnamon.

"Would you like to try one of our chocolate croissants? They just came out of the oven?" the bright-eyed girl, working the register asks me after I place my order.

I can't say no to a fresh croissant. "Sure, I could use a chocolate pick me up."

She smiles, looking pleased with her sale, and grabs a cup and a sharpie. "Name for the order?"

"Marisa."

She scribbles my name across the cup and hands it off to a worker. While swiping my card, she asks, "Are you in town for a wine tour?"

"No, I'm visiting family. My dad." I shouldn't have specified. She doesn't actually care. She's only doing that thing that all baristas do, which is to make uncomfortable small talk while your order is being made.

She hands me back the card with a curious look on her face. "Oh, my gosh! You're Marisa."

I pause midway through returning the card back to my wallet. "Yes...I just said that."

She laughs, but I'm not quite sure what's so funny. "Sorry, what I mean is you're Marisa, as in Marisa, Sadie's stepsister. She's one of my part-timers," she explains.

Stepsister. That's the first time I've been called that. And now I feel bad that I've only spoken to Sadie once.

She hands me over a baggie with the warm croissant. "I'm Ariana Ledger."

It's not a common last name, which means she's likely related to Ethan. Maybe she's a distant cousin—

"I heard about my brother's dog jumping you. He's honestly such a sweet boy most of the time."

Brother? It's becoming more evident that Ethan is the bad seed of his family, because his dad and sister are perfectly nice and normal. He must've been dropped as an infant. There's no other explanation.

I smile tightly, feeling a desperate itch to get away. "Well, it was nice meeting you."

If she senses my discomfort, she ignores it. "Nice meeting you, too."

The line is long behind me, so I'm safely able to find a seat in a hidden corner while Ariana continues ringing up customers. My eyes nearly roll back in my head when I bite into the croissant. *Shit, that's good.*

After devouring the croissant, I decide to stroll through town while I finish my coffee. If I had to guess, I would say Main Street is a mile long, if that. There are numerous tasting rooms and a variety of restaurants, more than I expected for such a small town. The cuisines range from a standard American-style diner, to a French bistro, a Thai restaurant, and a fancy looking brunch spot. There's even a piano bar that I make a mental note to check out one of these days. Shops catering to tourists sell trinkets and clothing adorned with grapes and wine puns. There's an art gallery advertising they will be hosting live music this evening. I'm pleasantly surprised there's plenty of things to do and see in this small stretch.

By now, the farmers market is coming to a close and the vendors are packing up their stations and dismantling their tents. Traffic starts flowing down Main Street again, and parking spots fill up at the storefronts. I catch sight of a tall man wearing a baseball cap in the distance, loading a vendor tent on the bed of an old work truck. He stands out among the crowd due to his imposing height. Even from a distance, I can make out the defined muscles in his arms straining as he pulls down a rope, winding it around his shoulder and elbow. From the way he's standing, I've only been able to get a side profile view, but I'd be willing to bet he's easy on the eyes. Coffee and a show? *Don't mind if I do.* I take claim to a street bench and get comfortable so I can enjoy the arm porn. I'm no better than a man sometimes.

He's chatting with another vendor who's loading up his respective tent. In the middle of his conversation, he turns his hat around so it sits backward—a move that shouldn't be as attractive as it is. It's only after several minutes of gawking that I realize the man I've been staring at is Ethan. My coffee goes down the wrong pipe, forcing me to cough loudly, and the sound travels across the street, like I had intended it directly for him. We lock eyes, mine wide and flustered, his narrow and suspicious.

Shit.

Averting my gaze, I tip my chin down and practically jump off the bench. I think that's enough exploring for today.

CHAPTER 9

Ethan

I'M LIKE A FERAL ANIMAL

T hat was a fucking nightmare. If there's anything I hate, it's having to run the farmers market booth. Normally, Gavin does it, because he loves interacting with people while they try his wines. He's also very good in social situations, something I seem to lack.

And now I have to do another nightmarish thing...ask my little brother Shane for a favor.

"This place is a shit hole." I look around Shane's apartment and try to keep myself from gagging. Every square inch of flooring is covered in discarded clothes, food wrappers, and empty beer bottles.

He snickers at my disgusted face, seemingly proud of his disaster.

"And what the hell is this?" I ask, digging out whatever is poking me from under the couch cushion. I instantly regret it when I find a woman's bra with a high heel dangling from it. My hand drops the items, and Shane catches them before they hit the floor.

His face splits into a smile, and he laughs. "Sorry about

that." He sets the stuff on a recliner, still smiling to himself. "We were wondering where the other shoe ended up."

A full-body cringe starts to set in. "Please don't tell me you fucked some random girl on this couch and now I'm sitting in it?"

"No, of course not."

My shoulders drop in relief.

"She wasn't random," he continues.

I shoot out of my seat so fast the room spins. "What the fuck is wrong with you?"

He shrugs, unaffected by my outburst. "You know Shelby. She's not a random chick."

A vein starts to pulse between my eyebrows. "As in Shelby, your service manager?"

He nods. "Yeah. Hot as hell, right?"

There's no way we're related. Not possible. "You're not supposed to fuck your staff, dumbass."

Shane is the head chef at Flat Stone, our in-house restaurant. His kitchen? Immaculate. Everything else? A total disaster.

"Chill," he says, kicking his feet up on the coffee table and knocking over a stack of mail. "It was her last shift. We were celebrating."

"With how often you stick your dick in someone, I'm surprised there's not a few mini Shanes walking around."

His brows raise. "Bruh, I keep my shit wrapped. Thanks for the advice, though, Dad."

I rub my temples, trying to remember why I came here in the first place. "Are you busy, October thirtieth?"

His shoulders lift. "Fuck if I know, that's forever from now, why?"

"Can you watch Goose? I have an important meeting at the Woodinville tasting room, and I might be gone overnight."

76

He blows out a breath. "And you're asking me? You would actually trust me with him?"

He sounds just as shocked as I feel.

"Mom and Dad will be on vacation, Gavin is busy, Elyse has a wedding, and Ariana is going to be in Pullman visiting Layla for Halloween. It's you or it's no one. Think you can keep him alive?"

He nods, his eyes wandering like he's trying to convince himself. "Yeah, no problem. I got this."

I already regret this decision. Shane is the least responsible of my siblings and probably the least responsible person I know.

After leaving Shane's apartment, I take a full, deep breath. Fresh air never smelled so good. Once I'm in my truck, I cover my hands in a thick layer of hand sanitizer.

On the drive home, I pass by the gas station, the one I'm pretty sure Marisa bought all the food from that first night. Gnawing guilt twists my stomach. I didn't handle that night well. In fact, I haven't handled anything to do with Marisa very well. I don't intend to be an asshole, it just happens. And then I feel even worse afterward.

We came to somewhat of an understanding a few days ago, but I haven't talked to her since. It's exactly what I wanted, yet I've found myself searching for her every time I walk out of my place. My eyes draw to her cottage like they're being pulled by a magnet, looking for any sign of her. And there hasn't been any.

I was convinced she had left until I spotted her at the market earlier. The second she saw me, she up and sprinted away like she couldn't get away fast enough.

I would react the same way if I was in her shoes. I've been a grumpy asshole to her for almost no reason other than she's a distraction. A beautiful, sunny, unpredictable, distraction. And none of that is her fault. It's mine, and my issues, and my baggage, and my terrible anxiety. I'm like a feral animal around her, desperate for her approval and attention, but I snarl trying to get it. I'm a fucking mess.

Even on the very first day when I met her in the vineyard. Sure, I was upset because it was just one more thing I had to deal with, but then she walked out of that dangerous little car of hers, fresh faced and doe eyed, and I didn't know what to do. And then she spoke, that honey-sweet voice of hers. I couldn't peel my eyes off her, even though I wanted to. She had every warning written all over her. A beautiful, tempting, city girl, full of sass and sun, with no patience for my bullshit. It feels like the universe is dangling something I can't have right in my face just to taunt me with it, because why else would that same woman be the very one staying next door to me?

It's a cruel joke.

I make an illegal U-turn and head back toward downtown. At the very least, I owe her a meal. Maybe then I'll be able to put a stop to the guilt and shame eating away at me.

Taqueria Los Volcanes is without a doubt the best taco truck in Red Mountain. There are four other taco trucks in town, and they're decent, but I have a soft spot for this one.

"Hola, amigo," Jose, the owner, says, poking his head out of the order window.

The winery hosts a few evening events in the summer and invites local food trucks to park out front so guests can drink wine and sample the different cuisines. Jose is always invited, and over the years he's become a family friend.

I order my usual and then place an order for one of each taco.

"Big appetite today, huh?"

"Something like that," I mumble.

While I wait for the order to be ready, I take a seat at one of the wooden picnic tables on the patio. If I had been paying attention, I would've noticed the guy with his head bowed and face hidden by a baseball cap seated right across from me. It's not until I feel his stare that I realize who it is.

I knew I was going to run into Laura and Travis when I moved back. It wasn't an *if* it was a *when*. Red Mountain is small—there is no avoiding the inevitable.

You'd think I'd be ready, be mentally prepared, yet somehow I still feel caught off guard. Travis was like a brother to me, my best friend throughout childhood. He was at my house so often, sometimes it felt like he lived there. So of course, when Laura and I started dating, I wasn't surprised at all they were close. In fact, I liked it. I liked that two of the most important people in my life were friends. Looking back on it, there were lots of signs, I was just too blind to see them.

Our eyes meet, and he starts to stand, obviously trying to leave.

"You can stay," I tell him.

He pauses with his leg half swung over the bench, before reluctantly sitting back down.

"It's not like I'm going to pick a fight with you in broad daylight."

He nods and looks away as his Adam's apple bobs in his throat. "I'll leave as soon as my food is done."

I don't respond, instead I let the awkward silence buzz around us like an annoying fly.

He clears his throat and looks at me, opening his mouth a few times and then shutting it, as if he wants to speak but keeps stopping himself.

I shift in my seat, searching for something to break the silence. "I got the wedding invitation. Congratulations." I'm surprised that came out sounding as sincere as it did.

The color drains from his face. "I didn't realize she invited you. I've been letting her handle all that stuff. Sorry about that."

The urge to laugh in his face is so strong I have to clench my fist. That's the thing about Laura. She does what she wants, when she wants to. To hell with anyone else and their opinions.

He shakes his head, wearing the internal conversation going on in his head all over his face. "Seriously, man, I had no idea. I would've never..."

His words die, but I hear the rest. He would've never allowed it to happen had he known.

"Well, like I said, congratulations. I hope it works out for you guys."

"Order for Travis," Jose's wife Marta yells out.

Travis stands and looks at me. "Heard you moved back."

"Yep." I don't provide further explanation.

"Well, that's good, man." The palpable discomfort hangs heavy in the air between us. "So, uh, I guess I'll see you around."

"Yeah, see you."

He grabs his food and quickly leaves.

That was worse than running into an ex, that was like running into someone who's been exiled from your family. I guess at this point, all I can do is hope for the day it no longer feels weird to see him.

CHAPTER 10

Marisa

BEST I'VE EVER HAD

There's something on my porch.

I spot it immediately and then pause, looking around like someone might jump out and try to scare me. I've had my fair share of forgotten online purchases, but I know for a fact this isn't one of them.

I walk up slowly, suspicious. I need to cool it on the true crime podcasts; they're making me think everything is an attempt at kidnapping. As I get up to the porch, I realize it's a plastic take-out bag filled with two styrofoam containers.

That's strange. Strange, but not so strange I'm not going to rip open the bag immediately.

It's tacos.

What?

Tacos, like the kind that come from a taco truck.

In my haste to open the bag, I missed the sticky note attached to it. I reach for it, unraveling it from its crumbled state.

Marisa,
I couldn't in good conscience repurchase your gas

81

station delicacies. Please accept these tacos as an apology for ruining your dinner and being a grumpy asshole. I wasn't sure what you would like, so I chose a variety.

Enjoy,

Ethan

I am absolutely shocked. I'd be less shocked if they had manifested out of thin air. I fight a smile as my stomach does a somersault.

He bought me food.

It's a simple gesture, but it's enough to crack the hardened image of him in my head. Maybe I was too quick to judge and there is a kind human under all that grouchiness after all.

I'm not sure what this means. Are we friendly now? Do we remain passing strangers? I'm full of questions, but there aren't any answers here.

Leaving the food on my porch, I race over to Ethan's and knock on his door. Approaching footsteps sound and a pair of puppy dog eyes greet me through the side window, but no Ethan. Disappointed, I go back to my respective cottage. He may not be home, but I know he was here recently, because the food is still piping hot.

I eat half the tacos, which may be the best I've ever had, and save the rest for another time.

I've barely closed the fridge when my phone rings. It's Hillary calling to FaceTime.

"Hi," I greet, swallowing my last bite.

"Shit, sorry you're eating."

"No, it's fine. I'm done. What's up?"

"Nothing is up with me, my life is boring as hell. You, on the other hand, have the goofiest smile. Do tell."

I have to be careful with Hillary; she latches onto the smallest details and runs with them.

"Remember the guy I told you about? My asshole neighbor."

"Yeah." She sits up straighter. "I thought we hated him."

"He dropped me off some food. That's what I was eating."

"You ate it?" she asks, obviously alarmed.

"Why are you saying it like that? Do you think I shouldn't have?"

She shakes her head, her eyes exasperated. "Sweetie, a man who has been nothing but rude to you since you've arrived woke up one day and decided to bring you food. It's suspicious. I mean how well do you know this guy? He's probably a psychopath."

I get where Hillary is coming from. Honestly, I'm surprised it's not my own train of thought, but I don't see Ethan being any of the things she's accusing him of. He's gruff and grumpy and lacking in manners, but he wouldn't actually hurt me. I'm not sure why I feel so certain of that, but I do. Even in our heated exchanges, I've never feared for my safety. Maybe that's naive of me.

"He's not like that."

She huffs. "That's what they said about Ted Bundy, and we all know how that turned out."

"Anyway," I say, trying to change the subject. "How's the baby?"

"Baby Girl is fine, measuring right where she should be." She rubs her belly and zooms the camera in on it. "Besides getting enormous, all is well in that department."

Her face reappears with concern.

"Now back to this neighbor, maybe you should find somewhere else to stay."

"I'm not packing up my shit again just to move two seconds away. I'm fine."

She rolls her eyes, but her shoulders slump and I know she's dropping the subject. For now, at least.

"Besides Dahmer Bundy next door, any cute boys? Any prospects?"

I snort a laugh. "No, and none of that will be happening. I'm not here to date."

"Who said anything about dating?"

I ignore her not so subtle suggestion. "For all I know, I'll be gone by next week."

"Have you heard from any of the companies you applied to?"

"Well, no." Did she really have to point that out? Dread starts to inch its way into my head. Not one phone call or email, and I've applied for well over a hundred jobs.

"Then it looks like you'll be there longer than that," she says cheerily, unaware that she opened the door to my intrusive thoughts. "Maybe you should get on an app or two and have some fun."

"I'm not doing any of the apps. Hard pass." I dabbled with a few in my early twenties before I met Brandon, but I never took it too seriously, I was trying to have fun. Zoe's horror stories were enough to completely turn me off from giving them another shot.

"You deserve an orgasm you didn't give yourself. Might as well have some excitement while you're there."

"I get that you're the horniest pregnant woman alive, but let's not talk about my lack of a dating life. I'm in my single girl era and loving it."

She furrows her brows at me but doesn't say anything.

"Like today, I went to the farmers market and a cute coffee shop and then I drove around town, giving myself a tour while I listened to a podcast. It was lovely."

Shaking her head, she smiles. "Whatever you say."

I glance at the clock ticking on the wall and notice it's almost one o'clock. "I'd love to continue this delightful conversation, but I'm meeting the stepmother soon and I need to prepare myself."

She exhales sharply. "Fine. Call me later."

We say our goodbyes, and I spend the next thirty minutes touching up my hair and makeup, trying to shake Hillary's ridiculous advice. I'm here to get my life together, not sleep with some random local guy. Irritatingly, Ethan is the first image that comes to mind, and I rapidly shake my head of those thoughts. It's only because I don't know anyone and he's decently attractive. Well, he's more than decently attractive. Still, we're oil and water, and that's reason enough to not entertain those thoughts. And him apologizing with some food doesn't make up for his shitty attitude. It's laughable, really. Ethan would never give me a second look. I'm sure of it.

Jenn found out I went to the farmers market this morning through a friend of a friend, or however gossip spreads around here, and she was a little disappointed I'd gone by myself. So, when she invited me to go wine tasting, just me and her, I couldn't say no, even though it's the last thing I feel like doing. I can already predict how this will go. It will be like an awkward first date, filled with get-to-know-you questions and forced conversation.

I wait for her on the sidewalk, and right on time, she rounds the corner, approaching in a white, soccer mom SUV.

She greets me with a warm smile as I get settled in my seat. We're silent for a moment, an old Faith Hill song filling the void.

"So," Jenn starts, clearing the air. "Thank you for saying yes. I wasn't sure you would, and I'm sure this is probably awkward for you. I don't want you to think I'm trying to be imposing or act like some mom you clearly don't need. From everything your dad has told me about you, you're a smart, accomplished young woman, and I would like to get to know you. And maybe, eventually, we can be friends."

I bite back my sneer. She's either lying or embellishing things my dad told her for my sake. He's not the most forthcoming man, and I can't remember the last time he paid me a compliment. Compliments from him are like unicorns—nonexistent. Even at my own college graduation, where I graduated summa cum laude, rather than congratulate me, he and my mom preferred to deliver little digs to each other in masked happy voices, as if I was a child who couldn't understand.

"Where are we going?" I ask, completely circumventing her attempt to talk about anything deeper than surface level.

Disappointment flashes on her face, but she quickly recovers. "I thought we would start at Ledger and then maybe check out Benton Winery after that. Those are the two most popular ones in town. And I may be biased, since Leanne, Jack's wife, is my best friend, but Ledger wines are the absolute best."

I nod, turning my head like the view from the window is too captivating to do anything but stare at it.

She gasps, and then I feel her head turn to me. "I didn't even ask you. Do you drink? If you don't, we can do something else."

I laugh gently. She looked cool as a cucumber, but I'm starting to think she's just as nervous as I am. "I'm not a big drinker, but I do drink. And I don't know much about wine, so this will be fun." My need to people-please outweighs my disinterest.

She relaxes, easing her grip on the wheel.

While the cottage I'm staying in is on the winery property, I have yet to see the actual winery. Jenn drives along a curved road in what feels like half a circle until a large, open, iron gate appears, with wrought iron lettering reading *Ledger Estate Winery and Vineyards.*

The building is beautiful, clearly modeled after a French Chateau. What strikes me the most is its grandeur. As I lean forward, my eyes take in the intimidating-looking building.

I was not expecting it to be quite so extravagant.

The exterior is solid stone, imposing, yet elegant. The facade is embellished with intricate carving and decorative stonework, giving it an aged look. Tall, narrow windows line the first and second floors, with Juliet balconies adorning the second-floor windows. It's as if someone plopped the south of France in the middle of the Washington State desert.

I look down at my oversize, cable-knit sweater and jeans, feeling entirely underdressed to be within five feet of this place. Jenn, also dressed casually, is seemingly unaffected by the grandiose winery. She parks in the designated parking lot, and we walk in together.

The tasting room isn't busy. There are only a couple different groups seated at high-top tables and others gathered at the marble bar. Whoever designed this building was very detail oriented. Not one area is basic or simple; everything is grand and opulent.

Jenn spots a woman working behind the bar, and the two women embrace excitedly.

"Marisa, this is my dear friend, Leanne." She turns to Leanne. "Leanne, this is Robert's daughter, Marisa."

I extend my hand to her, but she pulls me in for a hug instead.

"So nice to meet you, Robert has told us so much about you."

MICHELLE NAOMI MOSLEY

My cheeks heat. I'm a little taken aback by the affection as I wonder if she's being polite or if my dad really has spoken about me.

Jenn and I hop up on the two open bar stools at the bar.

Leanne rests her hands on either side of the counter. "Are we doing a flight or a glass?"

Jenn and I exchange looks, and I shrug. I'm letting her take the lead on this, seeing as I've never been wine tasting.

"We'll start with a red flight and go from there," Jenn says.

Leanne sets three glasses in front of me and three in front of Jenn and proceeds to fill each one with a few ounces of different wines.

She goes on to explain what each one is, but I'm barely paying attention.

I pick up the first glass and take a sniff of it, because that seems to be what people do when they wine taste, though I have no idea what the reasoning is. It smells like wine, and maybe something spicy. This is so not my thing. If I'm drinking wine, it's usually label-less, two-buck chuck on sale at the grocery store.

Jenn takes a sip. "Oh, this one is good. Very smooth," she tells Leanne.

I follow suit, taking a sip. Unsurprisingly, it tastes like wine. This is going to get embarrassing very quickly if anybody asks me a wine-related question.

"How are you liking the cottage?" Leanne asks me.

"It's great. Thank you so much for allowing me to stay there. I told my dad I was willing to pay."

She waves her hand dismissively. "Absolutely not. We almost knocked them down a few years ago, but at the last minute decided to keep them up just in case. Hopefully, my son hasn't been too much of a bother."

I offer a dismissive shrug. "We've barely seen each other."

Her eyes focus over my shoulder.

"His ears must've been burning." She smiles and then shoots me a wink.

"Ethan, come say hi."

My back goes rigid. I knew I was going to run into him again, but it didn't occur to me that I would see him here.

CHAPTER 11

Ethan

WAITING FOR ME TO FAIL

My mom is working the tasting room, something she rarely does these days. But we had two call-ins, and she was available to fill in on short notice. When I get to the tasting room to check on her, I see she's happily chatting away, totally in her element.

It's not until I'm on the other side of the bar, standing next to my mom, that I realize who she's talking to.

It's Marisa. Marisa and Jenn. And I'm completely unprepared.

Marisa's eyes flick to mine and then flick away, as if she's unsure of how to act. That makes two of us.

My mom clears her throat, rousing me from my stupor. "You remember Jenn."

I blink a few times to try to gather my bearings.

Pull it together.

"Yes," My voice croaks like I'm going through puberty so I clear my throat, trying to mask it. "Good to see you."

Jenn and my mom have been friends for years, but it's been a while since I've seen her.

"Everyone is so happy you're back," Jenn says.

I give her a nod. The last thing I want is to talk about that shit, least of all in front of Marisa.

Marisa's brows furrow, but she doesn't say anything. Instead, she brings the wineglass to her lips and takes a delicate sip. My eyes can't help but track the movement, watching as her throat bobs. How a droplet of red liquid lingers on her bottom lip before her tongue darts out and swipes it off.

My mouth dries, and I swallow roughly, feeling the acidic burn all the way down.

"Has Ethan given you a tour of the grounds yet?" my mom asks, looking between Marisa and me.

Marisa shakes her head and sets down the glass. "No, he hasn't."

The back of my mom's hand smacks my chest. "Show her around. That's your job."

I fail to see how CEO and tour guide fit under the same umbrella. "I think she's more than capable of walking around herself." I didn't mean for it to come out like that, but I would prefer to not spend any more time with Marisa than necessary. If that makes me appear rude, then so be it.

My mom snaps her head at me. To an outsider, she looks perfectly pleasant, but I can tell she's seething. Her flared nostrils say it all. She gives an awkward laugh. "Harvest is so busy, he barely has a moment to himself. I'm sure once things calm down, he would be more than happy to show you around. The estate is a lot larger than it looks."

Marisa's smile falters, and she dips her head, noticeably avoiding looking at me.

Pulling the attention away from me, my mom sighs contentedly and leans over the bar counter toward Jenn and Marisa. "Do you guys want to snack on a charcuterie or anything?"

Jenn eagerly nods, already reaching for the menu on the bar top.

Marisa's shoulders lift. "I'm still pretty full from lunch, but I could do a light snack."

"Did you grab lunch while you were in town?" Jenn asks Marisa.

Marisa's gaze latches with mine, and her lips begin to curve up but never fully form a smile. Instead, her teeth pull at her lower lip and she withdraws her eyes away from me. Her lips are incredibly distracting. "I had tacos."

She had *my* tacos. That *I* bought her. But she leaves that part out.

I start polishing a glass that doesn't need to be polished, feeling the urge to keep my hands occupied.

While Jenn has her head buried in the menu, my mom zeros in on Marisa. "So, Marisa, do you know how long you're planning to visit? Your dad mentioned you're on the hunt for a new job."

My interest is piqued, and I hold my breath, waiting for her to answer. It's not as if I care. It would just be good to know so I can begin counting down the days until I have some of my privacy restored.

Marisa lets out a breathy, humorless laugh. "I'm not sure, if I'm being honest. The job market in my field is over satu-rated, and I didn't part ways with my previous employer on the best terms. Hopefully soon, though, I don't want to over-stay my welcome."

My mom refills Marisa's glass, giving her a very generous pour, more than what is standard for a tasting. "Well, the cottages aren't going anywhere, so don't worry about over-staying your welcome, and I'm sure your dad is happy to have you for a long visit."

Marisa nods, her lips pulling into a tight line. It's a cross between a smile and a grimace. There's a story there, one etched in the shadows of her eyes and the tension in her posture. I'm eager to know more, but I don't dare ask. It's none of my business, and the less I know, the better.

A rowdy group in the corner accidentally breaks a glass, bringing my awareness back to the now-crowded tasting room.

In the time since I've been here, the crowd has nearly tripled in size.

One of the tasting room attendants rushes over to clear up the mess. Multiple conversations mingle together into one loud hum. Forks drag across plates, glasses clink, shouts and laughter blend into a clamor that presses in on me. My heart races, and my breath comes in shallow, rapid bursts. I'm over-stimulated and overwhelmed.

In an attempt to regain some control, I try to focus on one voice, one sound, but it's too late and I can't grasp it. The room spins slightly, and my grip on the glass I was polishing loosens, sending it crashing against the countertop. Glass shards spread across the marble. The sound is jarring, ampli-fying the tight knot in my chest.

My mom, unfazed, simply grabs the small dust pan and brush kept under the counter and cleans up the mess, never pausing her conversation with Jenn. Meanwhile, Marisa's eyes meet mine and she gives me a small, sympathetic smile. It leaves me feeling stripped down and exposed, like she can see everything I'm feeling in one look.

My vision narrows, the noise in the room growing more deafening with each passing second. I need to get out of here. Now.

I rub the back of my neck. "I have a meeting I need to get to." The lie falls easily.

My mom eyes me, aware that I'm teetering on the edge of a panic attack, and simply nods. "Okay, I'll see you later."

Remembering the tasting room is full of scrutinizing eyes, and that there's always someone paying attention, waiting for me to fail, I muster all the energy possible to pull on the mask. "It was nice seeing you, Jenn. And you, Marisa."

With my sweaty palms clenched in fists to prevent the tremor in my hands from being noticeable, I smile and nod to the faces I'm sure I would recognize if they weren't all a blur and calmly walk out. My breath holds until I'm far enough away for the murmur of voices to fade.

Once the exterior door shuts, closing me off from the tasting room, my lungs deflate. Cool air from the northern breeze hits my face, and my heart rate begins to slow.

I can't remember the last time my anxiety was that bad. Usually, I'm able to manage myself better than that. It's been years since it took over so strongly. Had I not been so distracted by Marisa, I would've noticed the growing crowd and made a swift exit before it got to that point. Further proof that keeping my distance from her is best.

"She has to go," I tell my dad the next day at dinner.

He chuckles, looking amused. "Who?"

He knows exactly who I'm talking about. "Marisa. Robert's daughter. You didn't even bother to tell me you and Robert made that arrangement. I don't appreciate you going over my head."

His smile fades, replaced with a pointed look. "I'm still on the board, son. My mistake for doing a favor for a good friend. Would you have said no? Or are you just pissed off about it now because she's a pretty young woman?"

"I didn't— This has nothing to do— Her looks are irrelevant."

His eyes look up at me over the glasses resting on his nose, and his mouth lifts with a *yeah right* smile.

Rather than continue to argue with the man who can't be ruffled, I storm off to the living room.

Marisa is a distraction I don't need. I can't have someone like that living so close to me. I chose the cottages specifically because they were vacant. I could've moved in with my parents or one of my siblings, but I didn't because I like my space. I like solitude. The last thing I need is a woman too beautiful for her own good prancing around. I'm already stressed out enough as it is.

"What's with the face?" Shane asks as he flops down on the couch.

I rub my temples. "Nothing. Dad being dad."

He shrugs, uninterested. "Hey, so I heard the new chick is hot."

From one conversation to the next, I can't seem to escape her. Although this is Shane, he could be talking about anyone.

"What new chick?" I ask, indulging him.

"Robert's daughter. My boy Andy saw her at Novel yesterday. Said she's a sexy little Mexi."

My brain grabs on to that last word. "Don't call her that. It sounds racist as shit."

His eyes widen. "It's not racist," he practically yells. "It's a compliment."

"Who's being racist?" Elyse asks, walking in with Ariana right behind her.

Shane sits up. I can tell by his red, flushed skin that he's getting worked up. "What I was saying before this fucker called me a racist, is that Robert's daughter, who happens to be *Latina,* is fine as fuck."

"Her name is Marisa. Call her by her name," I tell him.

All eyes turn to me. Elyse, in particular, looks way too interested.

"She's my neighbor," I explain. "Dad has her staying in the cottage next to mine."

"Talk about easy access," Shane says. "So, you gonna hit that, or can I call dibs?"

"You've never even met her," I say, my voice rising.

Shane cackles. "So? I will eventually. And I'm calling dibs."

I close my eyes, inhaling deeply. *Murder is wrong. Murder is wrong.* "No one is calling dibs. Keep your dick in your pants. You know how close Mom and Dad are to Robert and Jenn. Have a little respect."

Shane rolls his eyes. "Fine. I won't hit on her. You suck the fun out of everything."

"I met her," Ariana chimes in. "She seemed nice."

Great. That's the problem with Red Mountain. It's too damn small to escape anyone, especially when they're your neighbor.

The front door opens, and Gavin walks in with Lily, effectively moving us on from this ridiculous conversation.

"There's my favorite girl," my dad says, walking toward Lily.

Lily wiggles her hand out of Gavin's and races to our dad, whose arms are wide open for her. "Grandpa!"

He catches her in a hug and lifts her. "Come on, Lily Bear. I need a hand in the garage. You know how to check the oil in a car, right?"

She giggles. "Nooo."

"Sheesh, what's your dad been teaching you?" he says as the door to the garage closes behind them.

"Oh, you know, just how to be a good person," Gavin says, with his head thrown back, looking at the ceiling in frustration. Our dad enjoys teasing Gavin a little too much, because he's the only one of us that's a parent. Gavin hates it. He sits in the leather recliner and leans all the way back in it, looking exhausted. He always looks so fucking exhausted, it's no wonder he turned down the job.

We all hang out in the living room, bullshitting. The only one missing is Layla, because she's away at school. I skipped a lot of Sunday family dinners while I was away, and I'm realizing how much I missed this. My siblings drive me crazy, and growing up with them was total mayhem, but I'm glad to be back and seeing them a lot more often.

"Food's ready," our mom shouts from the kitchen.

"When are you going to let me cook family dinner?" Shane asks our mom as we all take our seats at the dinner table.

She laughs like it's a ridiculous question. "Just because we trust you enough to handle the dinner shift at the restaurant doesn't mean you get to cook in my kitchen. You can cook family dinner when I'm dead and not a day sooner."

Dad and Lily walk back in from the garage, Lily sporting grease and motor oil stains all over her clothes.

"Dad. Come on. She had that outfit on for like five minutes," Gavin cries out.

He shrugs. "Kids get dirty, son, I don't know what to tell you." He shoots Lily a wink, and she preens under all the attention.

Following dinner, I wash the dishes. I've found it's a task that soothes my restless mind. The warm water and rhythmic motion help me unwind, giving me a moment of peace. But that's not the case today. My dad has Gavin and Shane in the backyard, measuring for a new shed while Goose runs circles around them, and Elyse and Ariana are playing dress up with Lily, leaving me wide open for an ambush from my mom. She wanders into the kitchen, the schemer that she is, cornering me while my hands are drowning in hot, soapy water.

"How are you feeling?"

I keep my focus on removing the hardened cheese coating the inside of a casserole dish. "What do you mean?" I know exactly what she means.

"Are you taking your medication?"

"Every day."

She leans against the counter, and I don't miss the concern on her face, despite avoiding eye contact.

"I worry about you." Her voice is quiet. "If it's too much, we can figure something else out."

"That won't be necessary," I say dismissively. I understand that she's concerned, but I'm not interested in being coddled. I also have no desire to discuss options for someone else to take over. Failure in this is not an option.

She picks up one of the washed dishes and starts towel drying it. "Are you still talking to that therapist?"

Jesus Christ. What is this? Interrogate Ethan night? "Yes, mom. Once a week. And I exercise and drink plenty of water and take my medication at the exact same time every day. Why are you bringing this shit up?"

She looks at me through her periphery. "Maybe because of your episode yesterday. You need to stay on top of things."

I keep my head down, focusing on the suds of soap and continuing to avoid her eyes. Her gaze weighs heavily on me, though. "Can we move on from this? I'm managing."

She watches me for a beat before nodding her head slowly and picking up another dish to dry.

We silently work together until we complete all the dishes.

"What was up with you and Marisa?" my mom asks, shattering our peaceful silence. I don't miss the small smile playing on her lips. "You were on the ruder side, but then you kept staring at her, so I figured you have a little crush."

I turn away to fill a glass with water. "I wasn't staring at her." My voice climbs one too many octaves, sounding embarrassingly defensive. Was I staring at her? "And I don't have a crush on her. Just the opposite, in fact."

"She's very pretty. Seems like such a sweetheart. Jenn was telling me that she went through a bad breakup recently."

I still, contemplating joining Shane and Gavin outside. Hell, I'd gladly join my sisters and Lily, even let Lily give me one of her makeovers. Anything to get me away from my mom and that tone she's using. The one that indicates she's conspiring. "It's really none of my business."

"You mean you're not even a little curious about her?"

She's going to keep poking at me until she breaks me.

"Did you not hear me complaining to Dad that I wanted her gone? I don't know where you're going with this, but you're barking up the wrong tree."

"Fine," she sighs. "Forget I said anything."

I glance at the clock and see I still have some time before the sun sets. "I'm going to head out. Go check on my parcel and figure out what the hell to do with it."

She nods, knowing better than to ask too many questions when it comes to my small piece of land. I've all but abandoned it, yet I'm forced to see it every time I come over, because it's nestled between my parents' land and Gavin's. Every time I look at it, all I see is the poured foundation that's now cracked. It was poured for a house for Laura and me, and it started cracking before we even broke up. It was as if the land knew before I did that she and I were never meant to be.

CHAPTER 12

Marisa

DRAGGING A DEAD BODY

"Damn," I breathe, looking around the expansive vineyard. I am so out of shape. Each step feels like a challenge, as I contend with the uneven terrain and my exhaustion grows. Sweat drips down my forehead, blurring my vision, and I squint ahead, searching for any sign of the cottage among the labyrinth of red and orange. The sun beats down relentlessly, casting harsh shadows across rows of vines stretching endlessly before me. That paired with the chilled air makes my body feel both heated and cooled all at once. My heart pounds, a mix of urgency and panic pushing me forward with each careful step. I'm completely turned around. Like, seriously lost.

I thought a Sunday afternoon run would be just the thing I needed to clear my head. I didn't account for how large and expansive the property is. It didn't even occur to me that I could get lost. I've been wandering for over an hour and don't feel any closer to the cottage than I did when I realized I had no idea where I was. At this rate, I'll be lucky if I make it back before sunset.

If only my phone hadn't died, then maybe I would be out of this mess already.

I continue walking, my head on a swivel, as I look for any signs of life. Or even a building, for that matter. My beat-up running shoes rustle against the fallen leaves as I walk. After a while, I'm certain my mind is playing tricks on me. Every time a bird chirps or a ground squirrel scurries, I'm convinced someone is nearby, only to be disappointed to find I'm still out here alone. All I want is to give up, but then what's the alternative? Sleep out here? I'd probably die of hypothermia once the sun sets behind the western ridge. I am so totally and completely fucked. There's a real possibility I won't find my way out of this.

I nearly trip when a rabbit darts out in front of me. It's large, with slim, long legs and tall ears. I think it's a jackrabbit, given how it doesn't look like your standard cottontail. It looks at me and then takes a few hops and then looks back at me again. Either my mind is playing tricks on me—which is more likely—or the jackrabbit is trying to get me to follow it.

My desperation is getting the best of me, but at this point, I'll try anything if it means escaping these circuitous vineyards. It doesn't seem to mind my presence and hops and leaps, moving quicker than I was anticipating.

I've been following the rabbit for several minutes when I think I hear something. I pause, holding my breath and straining my ears. But there's nothing there.

I exhale, about to continue with my ridiculous plan of following the rabbit, when I hear a whistle.

I definitely didn't imagine that. I'm almost positive.

Looking around, I still don't see anyone, but I know what I heard. It was a very faint, distinctly human-made sound. Jackie, the rabbit, looks back at me, probably wondering why I stopped walking. I named it, because it felt wrong to not give my rescuer a name.

I hear it again, and I want to jump for joy. Finally!

Maybe I won't die out here after all.

The sound seemed to come from the left. Without giving myself a chance to second guess it, I start running. My sight becomes blurrier, as more sweat from my forehead drips down and brims in my eyes.

I suddenly collide with something solid, causing me to stumble backward as my footing slips. Two strong hands reach out to steady me, gripping my waist and pulling me back from the brink of a fall. I look up with a gasp, encountering a broad chest encased in flannel, a white shirt peeking through the undone buttons. The scent of laundry and citrus envelops me, and I take a deep inhale of it, relishing in how familiar and relieving it smells. Craning my neck, I peer up to find Ethan's concerned hazel eyes looking down at me.

"Jesus, are you okay?"

I must really look awful based on the expression Ethan is wearing. Instead of his usual scowl, his eyebrows are raised high, his gaze is fixed intently on me, and his mouth is slightly open, as if he's searching for words that won't come. Our chests press together in uneven breaths, drawing attention to how close we are. I'm acutely aware of the way his hands are making contact with my skin, having slipped under the hem of my workout top. His hold on me is firm and steady, yet gentle. Safe.

Simultaneously, we both come to our senses, pulling apart as if equally aware of the intimate position we were in, the unspoken tension still hanging in the air.

Ethan's hardened demeanor returns, his body stiffening and head shaking. "You should watch where you're going."

I scoff, but it comes out sounding more like a hiss. "I've been out here for hours," I shriek. "I went for a run and got lost..." My words trail off as embarrassment floods through me. Of course, it had to be him of all people to find me in this situation.

He shakes his head again, and it only adds to my increasing humiliation.

"Follow me," he says, spinning around with his back to me. He whistles, the same whistle I heard a few minutes ago, and Goose emerges from behind one of the rows of grape vines.

Reluctantly, I follow him, because what choice do I have?

His black truck is parked around the hill. Ethan drops the tailgate, and Goose jumps in the back. Ethan's gaze meets mine as he slams the tailgate closed.

"Get in," he tells me.

I don't like being told what to do, and I really don't appreciate his tone. My arms cross, and I wait for at least a *please* or some other form of basic manners.

He sees me not making an attempt to get in the truck, his eyes surveying me from head to toe, annoyance on his face. "Get in the truck, Marisa."

The way he says my name sends a scatter of goosebumps down my arms. Or maybe that's the cool breeze. Still, it feels like an unspoken invitation, charging the atmosphere between us. We stare at each other, neither one of us moving. We're at an impasse, and someone is going to have to wave the white flag. It's definitely not going to be me. I've walked this far. I can walk some more.

His shoulders sag, and he blows out a breath. Grumbling to himself, he stomps over to the passenger door and yanks it open. "Please," he says through gritted teeth.

I press my lips together, biting back my satisfied grin. "I'm sorry. What was that? I couldn't hear you."

He rolls his eyes, knowing full well I heard him, but he indulges me anyway. "Please, get in the truck, Marisa."

A Cheshire smile stretches my face, and I practically skip

to the passenger side. I sense his eyes on me as I climb into my seat. I'm half-expecting him to slam the door shut the moment I'm in, but he surprises me by closing it gently instead.

Once we're both inside, the cab of the truck seems to shrink. The close quarters amplify his citrusy laundry scent as it mingles with the leather interior. I roll down my window, preferring to not let myself get clouded by the intoxicating smell. I feel his eyes track me as my head leans out.

"You don't get carsick, do you?"

"Nope," I tell him, keeping my attention aimed on the endless rows of vines, realizing how far into the acreage I wandered.

Cool plastic taps against my shoulder.

"Here," Ethan says, nudging a water bottle to me. "Drink this. You look like shit and you're probably dehydrated."

I whip my head toward him. "You're full of charm, aren't you?" I deadpan, grabbing the water bottle. I'm irritated, but not so much so that I'm going to refuse it. He's right, I probably do look like shit, and I probably am dehydrated, not that I'll admit it.

"So...you're a runner?" Ethan asks after I finish chugging the entire water bottle.

"I thought I was," I mumble. "It's been a while."

He nods, his fingers tapping on the steering wheel. If I didn't know better, I would think he's a little nervous.

I turn to look at him, and he regards me cautiously.

"Maybe next time, take a phone with you or run in town."

He doesn't say it in an *I told you so* manner, but I take it that way, regardless.

"Save the lecture. Lesson learned."

"I'm not really a lecture kind of guy."

Sinking deeper into my seat, I shift my face to him. "So, what kind of guy are you?"

The corner of his mouth curls ever so slightly. "The kind

that doesn't feel like dragging a dead body out of my vineyard. Can't have you ruining two vineyards in one season."

My jaw drops, and a giggle escapes. "Har, har. Very funny." I sit up straighter, feeling more energized. "And for the record, I didn't ruin anything and you know it."

His lips pull into a wry grin. It's not a full smile, but it's enough to make me feel like I accomplished something very few do.

"I know. In my defense, I thought you were just some tourist."

"Tourists are your bread and butter. You should be nicer."

He sighs deeply, the picture of resignation. "I'm working on it."

The remainder of the drive is quiet as we ride in comfortable silence.

When the cottages come into view, every muscle in my body releases a sigh of relief. I can practically feel the long shower I'll be taking the second I get inside.

As the truck comes to a stop, something rolls across the floor mat, tapping against my shoe. I reach down to retrieve it, realizing it's an empty prescription pill bottle. Before I can stop myself from invading Ethan's privacy, I read the label and see it's a prescription for the same medication Hillary used to take for her panic attacks in college. I close my palm around the bottle and turn to hand it to Ethan, hoping he didn't catch me reading the label.

Based on the fuming look in his eyes, I'm going to bet he definitely caught me.

"Here you go," I try to say cheerily.

He grabs it from me and swiftly exits the truck, slamming his door.

Uh oh.

I scramble out. "It's not a big deal," I shout to his back as he whistles for Goose to hop out, ignoring me in the process.

Continuing to ignore me, he walks past me.

"Seriously?" I practically shout.

I shouldn't have read it, I know that. It was wrong of me. His reaction, though? Uncalled for.

I groan. Talk about flipping a switch.

I'm almost to my own door when he shouts out, "New rule. Stay out of my way and stay out of my vineyards!"

"Fine by me!" I yell, slamming my door.

CHAPTER 13

Marisa

A SWEET TREAT

I think I may be overdressed. I scrutinize my reflection in the mirror, taking in the black pencil skirt and tucked-in flouncy blouse. The skirt feels like too much; this whole outfit feels like too much. Somehow, I doubt my corporate attire is going to blend in very well around here.

I've never professionally worked as a journalist, despite it being my college major. I was a reporter for my college paper all four years of school, but unfortunately, my college writing experience didn't translate into an actual job.

Post-graduate life was a harsh reality check. Countless rejections slowly but surely killed my romanticized dreams of working for a magazine and living in New York City. My hopes of success were met with disappointment. Eventually, I realized I needed stability, and I let go of the dream entirely, accepting the fact that some dreams needed to die. I grew up and put on my big girl pants and found a job in tech. I was content with my new outlook.

While I wouldn't say working for a small town newspaper is a job I ever imagined for myself, there is something a little exciting about the prospect of getting to write more than technical specifications and work instructions.

"Ready for your first day?" my dad asks, descending the stairs. He's wearing slacks and a polo, and I feel slightly less overdressed than I was anticipating.

"Ready as I'll ever be," I sigh.

"Coffee?" he offers as he works at making himself a cup.

I hold up my travel mug. "Already made one."

I'm currently managing my caffeine addiction with a trusty jar of instant coffee, but I'm this close to caving and buying an actual coffee maker.

He raises his brows, excitement lighting his eyes. "I'll tell you more when we get to the office, but I've got a special project for you."

"Should I be worried?"

"All good things." He chuckles.

Well, that isn't suspicious at all. Now I'm even more nervous.

The drive is short and filled with classic eighties music, bringing me right back to all the times my dad would drop me off at school with Van Halen blasting from the car speakers. That feels like a lifetime ago. He used to say listening to Van Halen was the equivalent of a cup of coffee, and even now, there's usually at least one Van Halen song on my driving playlists.

He parks in front of a brick building that looks like it may have been a factory or warehouse at some point in time. The parking spot he claims has a sign that says *Reserved for the Editor*. I would bet good money he put that sign there himself just to avoid having to drive around the block searching for a spot.

Once inside, my nose is violated by a distinct old building smell, reminding me of libraries and mildew.

"This is where the magic happens," he says, a giant smile splitting his face.

The office is an open space with concrete floors and exposed brick walls. A cluster of desks sit in the middle. Off to the side is a makeshift kitchen area with a fridge older than me and a couple of microwaves. Right off the entrance is a separate office with an *Editor* plaque on the door. The entire space is about five-hundred square feet, if that.

"Well, what do you think?"

"It's...um... It's something."

"Come on, I'll show you to your desk."

We walk the five feet from the front door to a wooden desk that wobbles.

"You're in luck. Edgar left behind all of his supplies and equipment."

If by supplies he means a bundle of old BIC pens held together with a rubber band and some crusty highlighters with missing lids, then yes, there were definitely supplies left behind. And the equipment consists of a paper shredder and a ten key calculator. None of these things are useful.

"Anyway, I'll let you get settled. We do a team huddle at nine. You'll meet everyone else then."

My stomach churns, charged with nerves and caffeine. I fire up my laptop and work on getting connected to the Wi-Fi while also trying my best to not watch the door. What will they be like? Will they be nice? Will they like me? Hillary claims I have a people-pleasing problem and an innate need for everyone to like me. I would argue that most people are like that. Who doesn't want to be liked? It's perfectly normal to want others to accept you. Do I sometimes go out of my way to get someone to accept and like me? Yes. But I'm not over the top about it.

Over the next hour, people filter in. The first is a woman who looks about ten years older than me. She takes the desk to the left of mine and introduces herself as Suzy. Everyone makes it a point to come introduce themselves to me and tell me how much they like my dad. That's no surprise, he's always been well liked by colleagues. Around nine, they all start to gather around the chairs and couch set up near the kitchen, so I follow suit.

My dad stands before the small group in this very casual-looking meeting.

"Okay, team, before we get started, I want to introduce you to our newest reporter. If you haven't met her yet, this is Marisa. Be extra nice to her, because not only is she our newest rookie, but she's also my daughter."

Everyone gives me a wave or head nod of acknowledgment.

"Alright, now down to business. It's a slower week, but as you all know, October is our busy month, so don't get too comfortable."

I learn what everyone's roles are during the meeting. Suzy is the opinion reporter. Bryce covers sports. He's called me kiddo twice, and I'm still determining if it's a term of endearment or an insult. Raquel is the office manager. She brought in a basket of muffins, instantly making me a fan. Then there's TJ, who handles advertising, and Krista is an intern. Mario and Hannah are the other two reporters. Overall, it's a lot fewer people than I'm used to, but also a lot more autonomy. And no one seems to mind that I'm the boss's daughter. I was fully prepared for some animosity.

"For assignments this week," my dad starts. "Bryce, you'll be covering the parks and recreation football tournament. And Marisa, you have your first assignment. You'll be doing a profile on Ethan Ledger and his new role as CEO of Ledger Estate Winery."

He continues doling out assignments, but his voice fades

to the background as my nerves begin to bundle. He couldn't have given me something a little easier? Something simple?

"Let's go chat in my office." my dad says to me after the meeting wraps up.

I walk in, closing the door behind me, and take a seat.

"I—"

"Can—"

We both speak at the same time and then laugh, awkwardness hanging between us.

"You go first," he says.

"About the assignment. The thing with Ethan."

He nods, leaning back in his chair.

"Wouldn't that be better suited for someone else? It's just that Ethan and I didn't get off on the best foot, and I don't think he would be very receptive to me."

I'm putting it mildly. Trying to interview Ethan, especially after what happened yesterday, would be a disaster. We can't seem to coexist without pissing each other off. And it's all his fault. I would be perfectly friendly and stay out of his way, but he's so prickly he can't seem to stop poking me.

"There's a reason I gave you that assignment. It's actually why I called you in here."

This must be related to the special project he mentioned this morning. "Okay, what's going on?"

"A few years ago, we had a quarterly magazine insert called *The Vine* that accompanied the paper. It would highlight the local wine industry, do pieces on community members, advertise upcoming events. It was an enormous hit, but the gal who ran it ended up leaving for greener pastures and it pretty much died with her. I'd like to bring it back, and I think you'd be just the person to revive it."

"But, Dad, I'm not planning to stay here very long. Wouldn't it be a bad idea to start a project when I'm not sure I'll be around long enough to finish it?"

"Sweets..." He pauses, looking at me. "I understand your plans are up in the air, but I think you can handle one edition, and we'll go from there. If we abide by the previous release schedule, you have until the end of October, so about three weeks, to get it together. I imagine that's still within a window where you could manage it if you do get a job offer."

"But I don't know anything about it. I've never even seen it."

He grins. "Check your email. I already sent over the archives."

"But—"

"No more buts. I'm assigning this to you. Not as your dad, but as your boss." He waves his hand, shooing me away. "Now scoot and get to work."

I guess that's the end of that conversation.

After leaving my dad's office, I skim through the archives he sent me, but it's hard to focus. Last week, I was jobless and crying myself to sleep, and now, I've gotten this huge project, which I'm not qualified for, dumped on my lap.

I take a break from looking through old versions of *The Vine* and redirect my attention to actually trying to learn how to do some basic tasks. With the help of Suzy, I spend the better part of the day getting trained on the writing system the *Herald* uses and how to navigate the portal. It all seems pretty cut and dry, but it's nice chatting with her and learning more about the rest of the staff and little tidbits about the town. I also end up word vomiting my doubts about writing a decent article when my subject isn't likely to be a willing participant.

"Welcome to being a journalist," Suzy says. "Unless it's a

fluff piece or something sports related, most people don't want anything to do with being featured in the *Paper*. Heck, I'm not even sure they read it. I think they prefer to get their news through the gossip mill." She laughs at her own joke, and I give her a polite chuckle, distracted by my own thoughts.

If Suzy is willing to divulge as much information as she already has, I may as well take advantage of it. "What can you tell me about the Ledgers?"

"How much time do you have?" she jests. "If Red Mountain had a royal family, it would be the Ledgers. They're one of the founding families."

"Founding families?"

"Yes, as in, they founded the town. The Ledgers and the Bentons."

Small town lore at its finest. "The Bentons own a winery, too, right?"

She nods. "They sure do. Big competitors, those two."

I snort. "You make it sound like the Hatfields and McCoys."

She shakes her head, rejecting the notion. "Oh, no. It's not nearly as dramatic as that mess. Business competitors sure, but they're cordial. Jack Ledger and Bill Benton are co-chairs of the Red Mountain Vintners Association. Around here, if one winery is doing well, it's good for everyone. It ups the local tourism and keeps pockets lined. All in all, everyone wants success for one another."

"That's kind of sweet actually."

Her head tilts, an easy smile lifting the corners of her mouth. "We're a community. I don't know how things are in Seattle, but the traffic alone would turn me into a raging bitch."

Hearing a curse word slip from the proper-looking woman has me stifling a laugh.

"Anyway," she continues. "The Ledgers are the backbone

of this town. Jack would do the interview without question. Ethan on the other hand"—she huffs a laugh— "good luck with that."

If she meant to give me a confidence boost, she did the opposite.

"I take it Ethan has a reputation?"

She rests her chin in her palm, looking to ponder the question. "I wouldn't say reputation. He comes off as abrasive at times, but I think he's more shy than anything."

I give a dismissive scoff. "Ethan? Shy?"

"Well, sure," she defends. "Doesn't talk much, keeps to himself, looks like a deer caught in the headlights when you try to engage him in conversation. Sounds shy to me."

I guess I hadn't thought of it that way. Maybe he is shy. And clearly suffers from anxiety, something he seems to not want others to know about. I'm still pissed about his man tantrum, though. A tad overdramatic, if you ask me.

"But who knows?" she continues. "Maybe he's changed. He only recently moved back. A few years ago, he left. That's a story all its own, though."

Well, now I want to know the story, but I can tell Suzy isn't going to spill. I guess that explains why he's staying in a vacation cottage instead of a more permanent home. But it doesn't explain why he left and then moved back. And why do I care? It's not as if finding out some tragic story—if it even is tragic—would be reason enough to explain why he acts the way he does.

"You know," Suzy says. "I bet if you flashed Ethan a smile or two, he'd definitely be willing to sit down with you for an interview."

I laugh. "I'm not too sure about that." I've already tried that, and it didn't work.

She lifts her shoulders, offering me an encouraging smile.

"There are so many different avenues you can take to make a source feel relaxed and comfortable to speak with a reporter. You need to find what works best for Ethan. Maybe do something nice for him. Even the prickliest of men can appreciate a sweet treat."

CHAPTER 14

Marisa

LIKELY RESEMBLING A CLOWN

I've reached a new low. I'm baking for a man. A man who can't stand me.

Suzy got my mind rolling with her suggestion that I do something nice to encourage Ethan to hear me out and agree to an interview. The first thing I did after getting off work was stop at the grocery store for some supplies.

If there's anything that brightens my spirits, it's baking. I'm of the mindset that sugar is good for the soul. Plus, the smell beats just about anything. Who needs an overpriced candle when there's a batch of snickerdoodle cookies in the oven?

I have the first batch cooling on a cooling rack, one in the oven, some dough chilling in the fridge, and I'm making more dough, because once I get going, I can't stop. Never mind that I only intended to bake enough for one person. When it's all said and done, I'll have enough for an army.

Ethan sounded pretty adamant yesterday about keeping our distance from each other, but I've decided I'm done playing by his rules. I'm not going to walk on eggshells and be made to feel uncomfortable for however long I'm stuck here. I don't care who he is. I'm going to take these damn cookies over to him, and he's going to love them, because everyone loves my cookies. And hopefully that'll soften him up enough to let me do my job. Frankly, he's the one who should be apologizing to me for his outburst. Another man who can't regulate his emotions. Original.

He got home about an hour ago. I wasn't staring out the window, watching for him or anything. Definitely not.

The oven goes off, indicating the second batch is ready. I get them situated on the cooling rack and scoop the first batch into the cute tin container I picked up in the baking aisle.

I quickly glance in the mirror, checking for any food in my teeth and ensuring my makeup isn't smudged. Satisfied, I'm ready to go.

My heart beats loudly in my ears, mingling with the crunch of gravel under my pumps. He's going to say yes. He has to.

I knock, my hands jittery with nerves. Holding my breath, I listen for footsteps between my pounding heartbeat. There's a long pause, and I almost turn away, wondering if maybe I was wrong and he isn't home. I blow out a relieved sigh when I hear the creaking of his wood floors.

He answers, and I'm greeted with a white T-shirt being pulled down from his chest and smoothed across his stomach, providing a peek at the trail of dark hair scattered down his abdomen. His eyes look hooded and heavy, as if I woke him up. There's something so boyishly charming about his sleepy expression and mussed hair that I almost forget about his outburst yesterday. But as soon as he blinks a few times, back is the man I'm more familiar with. Hard lines, tense expression, and ever-present scowl.

I wasn't expecting him to be asleep this early. And I see now this probably isn't going to go well.

He rubs his face, his hand dragging down it slowly. "Yeah?"

His groggy, deep voice gives me a full body tingle, knocking me temporarily out of focus.

"Marisa," he says, his voice more forceful this time.

Right, the cookies.

This attempt at getting him to warm up to me is already going to shit.

I smile, probably too brightly, likely resembling a clown. "Hi, neighbor."

He frowns. "Is there something you need?"

I imagined this going much better in my head. Though I'm not sure why, because nothing has gone smoothly with Ethan since we've met.

I hand him the tin, and he looks down at it like I'm handing him a bag of garbage. It hangs between us awkwardly as he makes no attempt to grab it. I give it a shake, hoping that makes it more enticing. It doesn't.

"I baked you some cookies."

His face scrunches. "Why?"

I laugh, and it comes out breathy, desperate. "To thank you for rescuing me yesterday. I also feel really bad about... well, you know... Anyway, I thought I would make it up to you with some homemade cookies. Seeing that we're neighbors and Red Mountain is so small, I was hoping we could start over. Get to know each other, maybe even try to be friends?"

"What's rule number two?"

My skin heats, embarrassment washing over me. "You were serious about those?"

His dull eyes meet mine.

"I know a bribe when I see one. What do you want?"

When I don't answer, he continues. "I'm not even into sweets, so there's your first mistake."

I fold my arms, hating the raw, unsettled sensation building in my chest. My determination from earlier slips away more and more by the second. I take a deep breath, hoping I can turn this back around. "Here's the thing, I don't know if you heard, but I'm temporarily working at the *Herald*, and my first assignment is to do a piece on you. I couldn't get out of it. I tried."

His eyes narrow. "Not my problem. And I don't do personal interviews. You're welcome to write about the winery, but that's it. Leave me out of it."

He starts to close the door on me, but I put my hand out to stop him.

"Please, I promise it won't be invasive. And I really would like to be friends. Really." I'm begging now, and it's not a good look.

He crosses his arms and takes a step back. Goose's face peeks at me between his legs.

"So, is that a yes? A maybe?" I chuckle, nervously.

"The answer is no." He laughs, but there's no humor behind it, and rubs between his eyes. "We're never going to be friends."

What?

My chest sinks, and my face burns in mortification. He's proven exactly the kind of person he is time and time again, and I keep expecting a different outcome. I'm done making excuses for him. He's shy, he has anxiety, he's stressed. News flash, we're all suffering. It's not justification to treat me like I'm less than. Silly me for thinking tacos and a ride home meant there was a nice guy buried somewhere in there. He wants to keep to ourselves and avoid one another? Well, he's sure as shit going to get exactly what he wants now.

"Oh, well, okay then." I bend and drop the tin of cookies on the doormat. "I'll just leave these here and fuck right off. Don't mind me."

I turn and walk down the steps. I can't get out of there fast enough.

"Marisa..."

Without turning, I keep walking. "No, it's fine. I heard you loud and clear."

Right before my door closes, I swear I hear him grumble *fuck*, but I don't care enough to check. Or speak to him ever again. I've had enough. There's only so many times I can humiliate myself in front of him.

CHAPTER 15

Ethan

F uck.
   I lean my forehead against the door, closing my eyes as an overwhelming feeling of regret floods my senses.

Why am I like this? That was really fucking mean of me. I told myself the next time I saw her I was going to be cordial, act like a normal fucking person, especially after yesterday.

But then she shows up on my doorstep dressed in one of her sexy skirts, smiling so brightly, like the damn sun. Her eyes were wide and excited, if not a little nervous, too. And it pissed me off. It also didn't help that I was already asleep and I'm not exactly the nicest guy when I'm abruptly woken up.

I had to rush in earlier than usual this morning due to an emergency with the harvester, and by the time I got home, I was dead on my feet, ready to crash.

There's still no excuse good enough to justify why I continue to be my worst self in her presence. What the fuck is wrong with me? A beautiful, kind woman baked me cookies and tried to befriend me, even after all I've done, and I still rejected her.

Goose looks up at me, his eyes saying so much. I'm an asshole. He knows it. I know it. And I'm ashamed of myself.

I start to walk further into the living room, but Goose blocks me and whines, and then tips his head to the front door.

"What?" I ask as if he's going to be able to provide an answer.

When all he does is cock his head, I shake mine and try to push past him, but he whines again.

"What?" I repeat.

He starts pawing at the door, his nose sniffing all around it.

"Is this about the cookies?"

At the word "cookie" he grunts and whines, circling around me.

Jesus Christ.

I take a quick peek through the window at Marisa's cottage to make sure she's not outside. Quietly, I open the front door enough to crouch down and grab the tin. It feels wrong to take them after I so rudely refused them, but it also feels wrong to not take them.

I set the tin on the kitchen counter, Goose's nose bumping into the back of my thigh as I stop. He stares at me, his brown, pleading puppy dog eyes boring into me.

"Fine." I give in and pluck the first cookie off the stack to hand to him.

They're fairly small and look like a sugar cookie or cinnamon. Either way, they're safe enough for Goose to have one.

He gobbles it down in one bite and happily trots away to lie down on his bed.

The tin is still open, staring at me. I wasn't lying, I'm really not a sweets guy. Still, they do look really good, and the cinnamon-sugar aroma swirls in the air, tantalizing me. It would be a waste to not at least have one.

Fuck it.

I plop one in my mouth, and it melts on my tongue. Soft and moist, still warm from the oven. Fuck me. Of course they're delicious. I find myself reaching for another before I've fully swallowed the first. The warmth of the cookies spreads through me. They're the perfect balance of crisp edges and tender center.

Maybe I am a sweets guy after all, but only if they're coming from Marisa.

Only allowing myself the two cookies, I close the tin and put it away in a cabinet. It doesn't matter how good they are, I'm not deserving of them and it feels wrong to allow myself to indulge too much.

Wide awake now, I feel restless. I try to find something to do until I can go back to bed. The cottage is clean, but I sweep and vacuum it again and wash the two dishes in the sink, all the while my gaze continues to drift out the windows, looking for a sign of the beautiful brunette next door.

Over the next hour, the guilt stews—my stomach starts to curl in on itself at how much of a dick I've been to Marisa. This isn't me. Sure, I'm rough around the edges, but not like this. I've been an absolute asshole to her, and she's done nothing to deserve my poor treatment.

Dammit. She's getting under my skin, and I'm going to let her. I can't keep acting like an immature idiot. It ends now. I'm probably too late, the damage has been done. I can't take back my words, but I can at least apologize.

The sun has set, but it's only eight.

Though the outside of Marisa's cottage is dark, I hear the

low murmur of voices coming from the TV and it's enough of a sign to tell me she's still awake.

I knock twice and hear rustling before she opens the door.

Her eyes are unblinking, shocked even. But that's not what catches my attention. It's the red rims around them. It's the puffy nose. It's the moisture on her cheeks.

She's been crying.

And I feel like an absolute piece of shit. I *am* a piece of shit.

"What do you want?" she says, sniffling and wiping her cheeks with the sleeve of her sweatshirt. Her voice is garbled and trembling.

Those tear-soaked brown eyes will haunt me for the rest of my life. And knowing I'm the one who made them that way creates an ache that throbs in my chest.

"I'm... I'm—"

"Here to keep being mean to me? To keep throwing your man tantrum?" she says, cutting me off.

Man tantrum? "No... I—"

"Spit it out already. I don't have all night. And you're about two seconds from getting this door slammed in your face."

I deserve that. I deserve worse, honestly.

She shakes her head, eyes rolling as she starts to close the door.

I put my foot over the threshold to stop it from fully shutting. "Wait."

Her shoulders drop, her head cocks, and she looks up at me through furrowed brows. "Why should I?"

"I'm sorry."

Her expression remains. "Is that all?"

I'm not sure what else to say. Clearly, my simple apology hardly made a dent in the damage I caused. "I'm really, really sorry."

Her lips pull into a thin, fake smile. "Good to know." She starts to close the door again, but again, I stop it.

Blowing out a frustrated sigh, she says, "I'm going to have to ask you to leave."

My heart races as panic grips me tightly. I'm struggling to catch my breath, and my chest tightens with each inhalation. My thoughts scatter. I search for anything I can say or do to make this right. And I know what I have to do.

"I'll do it," I nearly shout.

She freezes, her forehead scrunching. "Do what?"

"I'll do the interview."

Her arms cross, and she leans against the door frame, eyeing me suspiciously. I get it. She has no reason to trust me or my word.

"I'll do the interview," I repeat. "Anything you want. A full exposé. Pictures. The works."

"Okay."

"Are we good?"

A sharp, humorless laugh escapes her lips. It's a harsh, biting sound, tinged with irritation. "No, we're not good. It's going to take a lot more than a half-assed apology and an interview to get me to forgive you."

I nod, my shoulders slumping. "I understand." I start to leave, but then pause. "For the interview, call tomorrow and my admin will make the arrangements. And I really am sorry. The guy you met and that you've been dealing with, that's not me. I'm under a lot of pressure, and it's flipping me upside down. My anxiety has been getting the best of me. I overreacted when you found the bottle, I just hate people knowing that I need to take meds—it makes me feel weak, which I know is counterintuitive. I'm not the asshole you think I am, and I'm going to prove it."

Her eyes hold mine, giving away nothing. What I

wouldn't give to know the thoughts behind those impene-trable pools of dark honey.

I know she needs more than words from me to atone for all the ways I've treated her. It's mortifying, the depths to which I've sunk in the short time we've known each other. I'm ashamed of myself.

As I walk away, she stays unmoving, but halfway down the porch steps, her voice brings me to a stop.

"Ethan," she calls, and I look back at her over my shoulder. "Beg."

Beg? "Excuse me?"

The edges of her lips lift and delight dances in her eyes. "You heard me. Beg."

The weight that's been sitting on my chest since I arrived to see fresh tears in her eyes eases slightly. I'll take her mischie-vous smile over crying any day. It's downright sexy. The last thing I should be doing right now is checking her out. I force my eyes to remain on her face and not travel down to her tan, bare legs in barely there shorts. From my position on the bottom step, they're closer to my eye level and damn-near unavoidable. Climbing up the steps, I rejoin her on the porch.

"If you want me to *start* to forgive you, I'm going to need some begging, a little groveling." Her tone has pivoted. There's a playfulness that wasn't there before.

If begging is what she wants, then she's going to get it. "I can do that."

The pink tip of her tongue darts out, wetting her lips and leaving behind a shiny sheen. My thoughts drop down to the gutter, wondering what else that tongue can lick. I shake my head, forcing away the image. I go from making her cry to checking her out; something is seriously wrong with me.

Her eyes are full of challenge. "Prove it."

"How?" Nerves swirl in my stomach. I'm positive she'll

have me do something that will no doubt embarrass the shit out of me.

Her smile is devilishly mesmerizing. I fear I'll be doing anything she asks of me.

"On your knees."

I cock a brow at her. "You want me to beg for your forgiveness on my knees?"

Based on the way my body is reacting to her bare legs and the way my heart is thumping in my chest, there are other things I'd gladly do on my knees for her. I toss the thoughts aside. Clearly, my unintentional celibacy streak is clouding my brain.

Her shoulders bounce as she bites down on the corner of her plump bottom lip. "I'm short, and you've been an ass. We need to restore the balance of power, which means you need to come down to my level and tell me that you're sorry. And mean it."

I can't believe I'm really going to do this. "If you want me to beg on my knees," I tell her, already dropping one to the wooden planks. "I'll get on my knees." I'm now fully knelt before her, completely at her mercy. I look up at her, the air between us inflating with tension. "Only for you."

She swallows audibly, staring at me wide-eyed, like she didn't think I'd give into her. She clears her throat. "Whoa, you're really doing it, huh?"

"Marisa," I start, my hands pressing tightly together. "I'm deeply, regretfully, incredibly sorry for my poor behavior."

Her full lips stretch into a radiant smile, revealing rosy cheeks. It's a beautiful sight, and it's directed at me. For a moment, the world slips into slow motion, my brain mentally capturing the image to keep as my heart thunders in my chest. I make a silent promise to continue giving her reasons to reveal that gorgeous smile.

Her eyes playfully roll. "Fine. You're a quarter forgiven." She giggles, a sound so bright it feels like the sun has come out and replaced the moon. "Get up. Before you hurt yourself."

I stand, my knees cracking. Our gazes lock, and I'm pleased to see all evidence of her crying is long gone.

"I really am sorry," I say more seriously, so she knows I meant what I said. "Especially for making you cry."

Her brows knit, and she shakes her head. "You didn't make me cry."

"But you were crying when I got here?"

She tosses her head back and snorts. "I was crying because of the movie I'm watching."

That can't be right. "You were crying that heavily over a movie? What kind of movies do you watch?"

Her head gestures to the TV screen inside that's paused on a young Tom Hanks. "*Sleepless in Seattle*. You know, it's the part when he's on the phone with the radio show talking about how the moment he first touched his wife, that's when he knew."

I've seen the movie, but only once or twice and it's been years. "Knew what?"

Her eyes brim again with tears, and I want to laugh, but it wouldn't be appropriate given the circumstances. "That she was home. It was like magic."

A single tear slides down her cheeks, and the corner of my mouth starts to twitch.

"Don't laugh," she says, a mix of tears and laughter. "It's not funny."

I put my hands up in defense. "I'm not laughing."

"What? Like you've never cried over a movie?"

"My eyes may have gotten a little misty watching *Band of Brothers*." I'm not so emotionally stunted that I don't cry. I just don't cry very often, and it's usually not over something fictional.

"You're such a guy," she says, shaking her head.

I shrug. "Can't argue that."

Quiet settles between us. It's a comfortable silence, not awkward like the ones we've shared before. We exchange gentle glances, her eyes soft and jaw relaxed. I feel lucky to have this moment with her, to even have the opportunity to be in her presence after the way I've behaved. It's going to take a lot more than begging on my knees to earn her forgiveness, but I'm up for the challenge.

"It's getting late," she says with a sigh. "I think I'm going to start getting ready for bed."

A tinge of disappointment creeps in. I didn't intend to stay here long. Truthfully, I'm surprised I made it this far without fucking things up even more. But now that I've spoken to her and made a small amount of progress toward repairing the destruction I caused, I find myself not wanting the night to end.

I nod in agreement. "Yeah, same." I turn to leave. "Goodnight."

"Goodnight," she echoes.

As I take the final step off her porch, my shoe catches on the corner of the railing and I have to do a hop-skip dance to catch myself from falling. It's the opposite of subtle.

Please be inside. Please be inside.

"Watch your step." I can practically hear her shit-eating grin.

She's not inside.

I turn back to face her, positive my cheeks are flaming red. "I'll keep that in mind."

Her eyes shimmer, reflecting the half-full moon. She covers her mouth with her hand, suppressing a laugh. "I'm not laughing at you. I'm laughing with you."

Her laughter spills out despite her best efforts.

"If you keep laughing at me, I might just cry."

She scoffs. "Liar."

Warmth climbs into my chest. I like this side of her, and I like being on the receiving end of it even more.

"Goodnight, Marisa."

"Goodnight, Ethan."

CHAPTER 16

Marisa

ADAM SANDLER GETUP

T he work week flies by. Between getting trained at the *Herald*, scouring job postings for anything that fits within my skill set, and making a better attempt at spending time with my dad and Jenn and the kids, I'm very ready for the weekend.

I've only run into Ethan twice since Monday night, just in passing. So far, we've managed to get along, to be friendly even. A win, if you ask me.

My plan for this very wild Friday night is to wear the largest, baggiest sweats I own, eat an entire box of Cheez-Its for dinner, and binge watch some trashy reality TV.

I get bundled up on the couch, set up with all my needs for the evening, when my phone decides to be a total buzz kill and go off. I look to see who's calling me. I'm a little surprised and more than curious.

"Hello?"

"Hey, girl!"

I sit up straighter, my mind slowly wrapping itself around the familiar voice. "Zoe?"

"Yes, girl, did you forget about me already?"

"No, I'm surprised to hear from you, that's all."

"Did I catch you at a bad time?"

"Nope, I was about to do a little Netflix and chill by myself."

She laughs. "Sounds like my kind of night."

I like Zoe. She was my work bestie, but we never really spoke or hung out much outside of work, save for the occasional happy hour.

"So, what's up?"

"I'm calling to let you know the new company I'm at is going to be hiring a technical writer after the holidays, and I think the role would be perfect for you. This place is so much better than *you know where.*"

My heart jumps. A job. A real fucking job may have just landed in my lap.

The possibility of a job is exactly the kind of motivation I need to keep going. The holidays are right around the corner, and soon enough they'll be done and over with. A light at the end of the tunnel starts to flicker. Finally, some good news.

Zoe goes on to explain what happened after they let me go. It turns out Brandon wasn't totally lying about everything like I assumed he was, and she, along with twenty other staff members, got laid off. And because she's a networking queen, she was unemployed for all of five minutes before she landed herself at a better company with better pay. Some people have all the luck.

I'm about to say something, to thank her for thinking of me, but she cuts me off.

"Anyway, I wanted to tell you, because I noticed you hadn't updated your LinkedIn to show you were working somewhere else. I figured you were probably still looking. Check your email. I sent you all the details. We'll talk soon. Okay? Bye, girl. Love you."

She hangs up before I can get another word out.

A rush of adrenaline courses through me. Soon enough, I'll be back to my old life. I can feel it.

I'm too excited to continue on with my show, so I Face-Time Hillary instead.

She answers right away, dressed similarly to me and also splayed out on the couch. "I see we both have very exciting Friday night plans," she says with a giggle.

"I'll take this any day over standing in the pouring rain, waiting in line outside some club or bar on Capitol Hill."

Snorting, she nods in agreement.

"I might have some news," I tell her. "Nothing concrete yet, but there's hope."

She sits up straighter. "Spill, tell me everything."

I repeat the phone call from Zoe.

Hillary claps excitedly when I finish. "See, I told you everything would work out."

"I don't have the job yet. I don't even have an interview."

"Pshh, semantics. You're going to get that interview, and you're going to nail it, and then you'll be back in Seattle in no time. And then we can go back to have girls' nights and the occasional brunch. I mean, I know I'll have a baby, but I still need time with my bestie."

I should feel relief at the thought of going back home, yet a shot of panic grips me, leaving me uneasy. This feeling must stem from worries about finances and the stress of packing once again to move back across the state. It has nothing to do with the charming little town that's grown on me, or getting to see my dad again and slowly working on repairing our relationship, or actually enjoying my job at the *Herald*. I knew coming here was temporary, yet I find myself getting attached. My mother's warning replays in my head. *Don't get distracted and end up stuck there.*

My mom is right. I need to focus and not let my fears

prevent me from going forward with the plan. And the plan is to go back to Seattle, where I belong.

Hillary and I chat a while longer, her eyes growing heavier and heavier before we call it and say our goodbyes.

I dig out my laptop from my work bag and see Zoe's email at the very top of my inbox. It goes into greater detail, explaining day-to-day duties and responsibilities. What really catches my eye is the pay. It's significantly higher than what I was making. So much so that I'm questioning whether Brandon was underpaying me. I wouldn't put it past him. The application takes me no time. I'm a pro at them now that I've applied for more jobs than I can count.

I continue watching my show, but it feels like trying to read while distracted—re-reading the first sentence over and over without it ever sinking in. The job is everything I could want, so why is my gut telling me it's not the right move? I wish I could trust myself and my instincts more, but they need to be recalibrated. I trusted Brandon implicitly, and look how that turned out. Evidently, I'm off kilter, and my gut is just as wrong as my heart, putting trust where it doesn't belong.

The following morning, I'm woken by a knock on my door.

I assumed it would be my dad, trying to drag me on some "family outing" he was hinting at the other day, but instead a tall brunette woman is standing on my doorstep. She looks about my age and like a literal supermodel. Her body is tall and lean, and she has the most stunning light-green eyes. They look like they're lit from within. She's wearing an effortlessly cool, all-black outfit. Meanwhile, I answer the door in an Adam Sandler getup.

"Hi." She smiles. "I'm so sorry. Did I wake you?"

I shrug. I should've been up, anyway. It's after nine. "No worries. Is there something I can help you with?"

"I'm Elyse. You're Marisa, right?"

I've become accustomed to everyone automatically seeming to know who I am. I suppose it's a side effect of small town living.

I nod.

"I'm Ethan's sister," she continues. "I was wondering if you have a key to his place or know where he might keep a key?"

Of course she's his sister. Either the entire family won the genetic lottery, or someone made a deal with the devil. I have yet to meet a Ledger who isn't gorgeous. It's bizarre. And how many of them are there?

I shake my head. "Sorry, I don't have a key. And I have no idea if he keeps a spare."

She frowns. "I'm supposed to let Goose out for a potty break and I lost my key."

She looks genuinely upset, so I try to think of something that may be comforting. "Worse comes to worst. He'll have a little accident inside, but he'll be fine."

Picturing burly Ethan wiping up a pee stain, or worse, a giant pile of dog shit right in the middle of his living room makes me want to laugh. It would be karma, really.

Her shoulders sag. "You're probably right. I just feel bad."

She stands with her hands on her hips, contemplating something. And then she looks at me, eyes bright with an idea. "You have a key to this cottage, though, right?"

"Yeah..."

"They were all built at the same time. Maybe they all take the same key?"

I doubt it, but it's worth a shot, I guess.

I grab my key and hand it over to her, and we walk next door to give it a try.

She inserts the key, and it easily turns, unlocking the door. You're kidding me. That actually worked?

The cottages were built at least twenty years ago, if not more. And this entire time, they've all taken the exact same key. Isn't that a safety hazard?

"I can't believe that really worked," Elyse says.

"Me either," I muse.

Once she's inside, I start to turn around, but her voice stops me.

"You can come in with me. I like the company."

She offers me a hopeful smile. Ethan may no longer despise me, but I'm not too sure how he would feel if he knew I was in his place without his permission. Before I can decide if it's a bad idea or not, my feet are already dragging me in.

His cottage is a mirror image of mine. Completely the same, but flipped around. There's nothing personal on the walls, and it's tidy and bare, no indication that anyone actually lives here. I feel a touch of self-consciousness when I think of my place and the clothes I have scattered everywhere, the unpacked boxes, the mess of snack boxes on the counter.

Maybe I'll add cleaning to my list of things to take care of today.

"Goose," Elyse calls and then does a whistle. "Come on, boy."

A sleepy looking Goose emerges from the bedroom.

"Time for a potty break." She opens the door for him, and he slowly walks out.

"Doesn't he need a leash?" Apart from the time I was lost, I've always seen Ethan have Goose on a leash.

She shakes her head. "Nah, Ethan is just paranoid about his precious child. That dog isn't going anywhere." She leans against the kitchen counter. "He's always been super overprotective and worries about everything. I love my brother, but when you look up anxiety in the dictionary, there's a picture of him right next to the definition."

I give her a polite chuckle, but it feels wrong to even do that. From what Ethan shared, it's clear his anxiety is a sensitive topic for him. Despite being his sister, I don't think it's something she should be making light of or joking about. If I knew her better, I might say something, but I ignore it for now.

"So, how are you liking this small-as-shit town?"

To that, I do genuinely chuckle. "It's growing on me."

"Yeah, I tried to leave, but it sucked me back in." There's no regret in her voice; she says it like she's happy to be sucked in. "Growing up, I was so ready to leave. I hated it. I hated how everyone knew everything about me. When I got into the University of Washington, I was beyond excited. A fresh start with fresh people, people that haven't known me since I was in diapers. I was ready for city living. And then, shocker, I hated it, but I toughed it out and graduated, and moved back not a second later."

"I can see the appeal."

She nods, agreeing. "The only thing that is shitty is a lot of my friends left and didn't come back. My best friend, Scottie, she's all the way over in Chicago, so I rarely get to see her."

"Since moving here, I've been doing long distance with my best friend, too. It really does suck."

Goose scratches at the door. She gives me an *I told you so* look, and we share a laugh.

She opens the door, and he happily trots back in.

"Well, not to sound like a kid on the playground, but if you ever need a friend, or a girls' night, or anything like that, we should totally get together."

I might need to take her up on that. Based on the information from Zoe, my stay here is going to be slightly longer than I was anticipating.

"I would like that."

Later in the afternoon, I make the drive to Badger Canyon to pick up a very important and much needed item. A coffee maker. I decided I deserve it. I got my first paycheck and could really use the dopamine boost.

Not wanting to be tempted by everything else in the store, I opt for curbside pickup and then drive straight back to Red Mountain. I can't let myself go too crazy with the spending after only one paycheck.

It's not until I'm staring at the oversize box crammed in my trunk that I realize I probably should've ordered it online, because I don't think I can get it inside.

It's not that it's too heavy, it's that it's too wide, and my arm span can't handle it. I stare at it, trying to figure out what the heck to do, when I hear the familiar crunching of boots walking on gravel behind me.

"What are you staring at?" Ethan asks, his shadow looming over me.

Though we've come to a truce of sorts, I still tense slightly, waiting for him to flip the switch. Slowly, I turn to face him, unsure what expression I'll find.

The expression I do see leaves me feeling more tense than if he wore the familiar scowl I've grown accustomed to. He's looking at me with amused confusion. I don't know what to do with that.

Flipping back around, I return my attention to the large box. "I bought this coffee maker and underestimated the size of the box," I tell him, feeling much more comfortable with my back to him.

He chuckles, and the puff of air that releases with it fans

across my neck, sending a trail of goosebumps down my spine. I thought I was uncomfortable around grumpy Ethan, but friendly Ethan has him beat.

"I was wondering what you were staring at. I assumed you hit something with your bumper and were assessing the damage."

My head whips back at him. "I'm not that bad of a driver."

He tilts his head at me. "Yes, you are." He's not standing particularly close, but the heat of his body is crowding me, increasing mine by a few degrees. A muscle in his cheek twitches as he tries not to smile.

I look down, not ready to see it fully bloom. "Anyway." I cough then rapidly blink. "I was trying to figure out the best way to get it inside. I might unbox it here and bring it in part by part."

"No." He shakes his head. "You're not doing that." His brow arches with an expectant stare, but I don't understand what he wants from me. His eyes flick to the box in my trunk. "If you could get the door, I'll bring it in."

"Oh... right."

I step aside, and Ethan comes forward, his hand grazing my thigh. I look down at where his hand brushed, convinced I imagined it. There isn't evidence to show one way or the other, so I shake the ridiculous thought and unlock the cottage door. I lean against it, watching as he effortlessly carries in the box. He holds it with flexed arms, and I force myself to focus on his face so I don't ogle him.

His eyes slide to mine as he crosses the threshold with a silent thank you for keeping the door propped open. As he passes, his scent penetrates my senses, leaving me dizzy and glued to the entry.

He sets the box on the counter. "Where do you want this thing?"

I give myself an internal shake and join him in the kitchen. "There's fine."

The kitchen is small, but I'd already determined I would set it on the end of the counter next to the fridge.

"Fancy," he comments, admiring the picture on the box.

"It was on sale," I defend.

He shrugs, opening a drawer as if he owns the place—which I guess, technically, he does. Still, it catches me off guard. Had I known he'd be coming inside, I would've tidied up a bit. While he digs through the junk drawer, I discreetly try to clean up. A box there, a wrapper here, slowly picking up and discarding pieces of packaging. There are dishes in the sink, a musty towel on the bar counter, crumbs piled where I make my morning toast. My cheeks flush as I take in the mess. And that's only the kitchen. There are laundry piles on the couch, shoes scattered, boxes stacked. What must he think of me?

When I look over at Ethan, I expect to see judgment, or disgust even. Instead, he's reading the paperwork that came with the coffeemaker, not paying any mind to my mess.

"What are you doing?"

"Hmm," he hums, distracted.

I join him in the kitchen and roll my lips, holding back a smile at the winsome, pensive look on his face as he reads. He meets my eyes briefly and then returns to reading.

"I'm looking over the instructions," he says quietly.

I freeze, a little stunned. Some of the worst fights I had with Brandon stemmed from his refusal to read instructions. He would always repeat the same sexist line to me. *Instructions are for women.* A red flag if I've seen one.

I didn't expect Ethan to stick around any longer than it took to drop off the box, let alone set up the coffeemaker for me. But that's what he does, removing it from the box and then connecting all the pieces. It's not complicated. I could've easily done it myself, but not having to do it at all and stand back and watch is nice. It's more than nice.

"You didn't have to do that."

His shoulders rise, and he lets out a breath as if it was nothing. "I'm still groveling, remember?" He moves to put a pod in and sets a coffee cup under the drip. As he hits the start button, he shoots me a wink.

My mouth falls open. Who is this man?

The coffee presses out of the coffeemaker loudly, and Ethan works to clean up the plastic and packaging, but I'm still stuck on the wink.

He sets the box aside and hands me the cup of coffee. "Why are you looking at me like that?"

I take the cup from him and turn to grab my creamer out of the fridge. With my back to him, it's easier to conceal the blush that's heated my cheeks. When I turn back to face him, he's waiting. His gaze is steady. Patient.

"It's just a little weird, that's all."

His forehead crinkles. "What's weird? The coffee?"

I haven't tried the coffee yet. It's honestly the last thing on my mind right now. I'm too distracted by the tall man, swallowing up my kitchen, shooting me winks, and making me feel flustered.

"You're being nice and it's weirding me out," I blurt.

His head tips back, and a deep laugh rumbles out of him. My body jolts, completely unprepared. When our eyes collide, I find his vivid and strikingly clear as they regard me.

"First I'm too much of a dick and now I'm too nice?" He laughs again, shaking his head. "I told you I was going to be nice to you."

"I know." My voice is girlishly high. "I wasn't expecting... I don't know what I was expecting."

He narrows his eyes playfully. "I'm *trying* to be nice."

I pout. "Try less. I don't know how to handle it."

His eyes drop from mine, and his attention moves to my lips then lower, lazily tracking down, before coming back to my eyes again. "You can handle it."

I swallow, and it feels like sand going down. The way he's looking at me paired with this alternate personality I can't seem to wrap my head around is setting me off balance. My body feels jerked into a heightened awareness, and a shiver runs down my spine, making me take a step back. I'm confused by what's happening. Am I imagining an innuendo where there isn't one and mistaking his stare as being more than friendly? I decide it's in my head. It has to be.

Ethan watches me with curious intent. The weight of his observation makes me acutely aware of every small movement I make.

I take another step back, putting more distance between us. "Well, thank you for setting everything up for me. It was a very *nice* gesture."

His lips tick up to a soft, barely there smile. "I should get going.

With a parting nod, he leaves. I take a deep inhale, breathing in the last of his lingering scent. A mistake I wish I could take back, because it's already infiltrated my senses, rendering me more unsteady and uncertain than ever.

CHAPTER 17

Ethan

I LOOK LIKE A BARN ANIMAL

I used to consider myself a morning person, but a steady schedule of waking up at 4:00 a.m. has me thinking otherwise. Thankfully, we're now on the tail end of harvest, with less than three weeks left. It's been a few years since I've actively participated, having stayed in Woodinville, so I'm a bit rusty, and it shows. It's what the entire year is about. Everything leads to these few months, and there's a certain pressure that comes with making sure it's a success. With the late nights and early mornings, now paired with an added layer of stress as CEO, I'm going to need to sleep for a month when this is all over.

Though I hate to admit it, some of my sleep loss might be attributed to the brown-eyed girl next door. Ever since I managed to turn things around with Marisa, she's been occupying my thoughts a lot more than I'd prefer. I have no business looking at her as anything more than a temporary neighbor, someone to be cordial with. At least that's what I keep reminding myself of. I was doing fine, great even, until I bumped into her the other day while I was walking Goose. She ran out of her cottage as if she had been waiting for us and offered Goose a treat. It was a quick exchange, a hi and a bye before she skipped back. But the whole time I felt like a tongue-tied idiot, rendered speechless because she thought of my dog. That's how easy I am apparently. It didn't help that she was wearing a thin tank top that did nothing to hide her hardening nipples as they battled the chilled air.

I'm aware that she's pretty. She's more than pretty; she's fucking beautiful. But she's also sweet and has a sassy bite when she's provoked. I want to know things about her, I want to ask questions. It's fucking terrifying.

When I helped her set up that ridiculous coffeemaker, that's when I knew I was in trouble. I pathetically tried to flirt with her, which completely threw her off. She even called me out on it. Of course she was confused; hell, I was confused. It was as if her cloud of vanilla drugged me into thinking I was someone else. Someone who wasn't a total asshole.

The last thing I want or need right now is to start catching feelings for someone whose time here is limited. Not to mention the fact that there's no way she would ever think of me like that. A woman like her wants a refined guy, not some rough around the edges, anxious mess.

It's still dark when I get to the winery. The windows on the second floor, where the offices are, illuminate the front of the building. Tawny beat me to the office.

"Happy hump day," she says, entirely too chipper for this God-awful hour.

"You're here early," I mumble. Typically, she gets in around 6:00 a.m.

Her eyes perk up. "Never went to bed. I was up all night with Charlie, he caught some stomach bug at school, so I snorted a line of coke to keep me going."

I jerk my head at her, hoping she's joking.

"Kidding." She smirks. "I made a quad-shot latte." She

144

shakes her tumbler at me, the ice rattling against the glass straw.

"That's good. I'm not above firing family."

She laughs like I said a joke. "You can't fire me. You'd be lost without me."

I quickly run through my emails, ensuring nothing major has come up since last night. Thankfully, nothing has, and I make my way downstairs and out to the back parking lot to grab one of the buggies. The Syrahs are scheduled to be harvested today.

Alex, the foreman, and Miguel, the vineyard manager, along with the permanent and seasonal staff are already hard at work. Miguel is overseeing the picking process, and Alex is gathered with a group at the sorting tables. Workers are picking up the clusters of grapes and inspecting them for imperfections, discarding the ones that are below standard. The smell of fermenting fruit sits heavy in the air, mingling with the earthy aroma of the vines and soil. It's a familiar, comforting smell. Despite not having any energy earlier, one whiff of this has me ready for the day.

"How's it going?" I ask Alex.

He peels off his gloves and stands off to the side of the sorting tables to get out of the way. "We're ahead of schedule. I'm thinking we'll be able to hit the cabs after lunch."

"That's good, man, good work. I'll have Tawny get you guys set up with water and coffee before first break. Shane is stopping to get pan dulce, too. You guys have been working hard. I want to make sure everyone feels appreciated."

After Tawny pointed out that I have not been as approachable as I should be, I've been trying to make more of an effort to be friendly.

Alex chuckles. "Trying to buy our love with food?"

I laugh. "Whatever works, right?"

After making sure the crew is set up with their break

supplies, I check in with Gavin at the crush pads, and from there the day continues at a rapid pace. There's an equipment issue with the grape harvester, a pipe leak with the irrigation system, and one of the transport trucks breaks down halfway to the warehouse.

By two o'clock, I'm tired, I smell, and I'm starving.

"Did you check your calendar for the day?" Tawny asks as I walk by her desk, heading to my office.

"No, that's what you're for," I snap.

She lets out an exaggerated exhale, trailing behind me. "There's someone from the *Herald* coming by in about thirty minutes to interview you."

I halt immediately. That's today?

Fuck!

Dirt covers my worn jeans, and crusted sand cakes my work boots. My shirt is disgusting, stained with sweat. I look like a barn animal, and I probably smell like one too. Marisa is going to show up here in one of those little business looks I catch her in when she's coming and going to work. I wonder if it'll be a skirt. I really enjoy the days she wears those tight skirts that hit below her knees, the way they hug her ass—

"Did you hear me?" Tawny asks.

"Yeah." I flick my wrist to check my watch. "I have thirty minutes, right?"

Her arms cross. "That's what I said."

Digging in my pocket, I fish out my keys. "Here." I hand them to her, and she reluctantly grabs them. "Go to my place and bring me back a change of clothes."

Her eyebrows raise. "You're going to let me dig through your things?"

She's wasting time, and she knows it.

"Yes. Can you do it or not?"

A smile splits her face. "What's wrong with what you're wearing now?"

I knew I should've fired her. "Look at me," I deadpan.

Her eyes narrow and lips lift to a questioning smile. "Does this have something to do with a girl?"

Definitely getting fired. "Tawny! Can we talk about this later?"

She smiles, pleased. "Alright, alright. Don't get your panties in a twist."

"Make it quick," I snap.

At the pace of a sloth, she starts to walk out of my office and then lingers in the hallway outside of it. "Any preference in clothing?"

Jesus Christ. I could've been there and back by now with how long this is taking. "Something clean. You know what I wear."

"Okay, be right back," she says, practically bouncing with glee.

While she handles that, I take inventory of my office, meticulously scanning for anything that looks messy or out of place. Except for a few stray stacks of paper, everything looks to be in order. I tend to keep my office organized.

I pop a beta blocker for good measure and attempt to deal with my mussed hair. I look like hell. Bags hang heavy under my eyes. My hair is a lost cause from sweating on and off all day. A hat it is.

Slathering on a thick layer of deodorant, I continue to glance at the giant clock that hangs on the wall, praying time will slow down enough for Tawny to get back here with my change of clothes before Marisa shows up.

I try to not allow myself the time to overthink the nerves taking hold of me at the thought of Marisa coming into this space. It's one thing to see each other in passing. It's quite another to let her infiltrate this version of me. Though I try my damndest to maintain a facade of composure around the staff, the cracks begin to surface when I'm forced to engage one on one with someone. Given how often Marisa has seen the worst parts of my personality, it shouldn't be hard for her to see past the image I work so hard to uphold. It's draining, actually, the energy it takes to keep my overactive, racing thoughts from being written all over my face.

Tawny made quick work of her task and is back to the office with time to spare. I suppose she can keep her job. I use the private en suite to change into the fresh jeans and flannel she packed me, my heart hammering against my ribs like a trapped bird. So much for that beta blocker. My clammy, trembling hands can hardly button and zip my pants. This is going to be a disaster. I'm already a mess, and the interview hasn't even begun.

CHAPTER 18

Marisa

A NEPO BABY

otebook? Check. List of questions? Check. Phone? Check. Pens? Double check.

    I get to Ledger Winery with three minutes to spare before 2:30, which is when I scheduled with Ethan's admin to conduct the interview. She was perfectly sweet on the phone. Part of me was expecting him to back out, but he stayed true to his word. So far, at least. We'll see how the interview goes. There's still a fifty percent chance it'll end in a standoff.

There's a hostess standing at a podium off the entrance. "Hi, are you here for a tasting or to dine in?"

"Oh...um...neither. I have a meeting with Ethan Ledger. I'm with the *Red Mountain Herald*."

She gives me a customer service smile. "Okay, let me call up. Just a moment." As she's punching in the number, she points to a chaise lounge-style sofa. "You can have a seat while you wait."

I take a seat and eavesdrop on her call.

"Hi, Tawny, this is Gwen from the hostess station. There's a reporter from the *Herald* here to see Ethan..."

mm-hhm…okay…will do…bye, thank you." She hangs up and says, "Someone will be by shortly."

A few minutes later, a woman with a jet-black Anna Wintour bob and thick, black-framed glasses comes down the curved staircase.

"Hi, Marisa?"

"That's me." I hold up my notebook, as if it somehow makes me look more official.

"I'm Tawny. We spoke on the phone. Come on up."

I follow her up the curved, wrought iron staircase.

When we reach the top, she turns back to me. "His office is down the hallway, straight ahead. Can I get you anything? Water? Coffee? Wine?"

"Water would be great, thank you."

The nerves tickling my throat as I walk toward Ethan's office make me thankful I asked for water; though wine would've done wonders for my overactive heart rate.

I'm even more thankful I asked for water when I catch sight of Ethan. Seated behind an intricately carved wooden desk, he's wearing a button-down flannel and backward cap.

A backward cap.

It's my kryptonite. And wow, does he wear it well. I swallow the nonexistent saliva in my mouth, my throat burning from the action.

Sweat forms a sheen over his face, causing his flushed skin to glisten under the overhead lighting and highlighting the contours of his high cheekbones. It's evident that he's been outside most of the day. The stubble lying outside of his shave line creates a shadow around his normally trim beard, giving him a slightly undone look. A bead of sweat slides down from his temple, rolling down the curve of his neck before disappearing under the collar of his shirt. My tongue slips between my lips, and the desire to lick that trail catches me completely off guard.

"Is everything okay?" Ethan asks, a crinkle of concern resting between his brows.

Of course he's concerned. I've just been standing in silence, staring at him.

I recover with a nod and an attempt at an easy smile. "Can I have a seat?"

"Yeah, come on in." He gestures his arm, welcoming me to take the chair across from him.

As soon as I'm seated, Tawny walks in with a glass of water. "Can I get you anything else?" she asks me.

"I'm good, thank you."

"Anything for you, Mr. Ledger?"

A sharp burst of air hisses from Ethan's nose, followed by a guttural chuckle. "What the fuck did you call me?"

She busts up, roaring with laughter. "Sorry," she says between bursts. "I was trying to make you sound important for your interview."

My eyes ping-pong between the two as they exchange humorous looks. Clearly, there's familiarity between them. Ethan looks relaxed in her presence, displaying a noticeable ease.

In fact, I'm not sure if I've ever seen him look this relaxed with another person. And she's a woman. A hot, green slurry begins to simmer below the surface of my skin. Ignoring it, I force a smile and try to join in on their shared joke, but my smile strains, and my eyes wander over to Tawny, immediately playing the comparison game. Is she his girlfriend? Has he had a girlfriend this entire time and I didn't notice? My stomach tightens, and my lunch rolls, turning sour. I've flirted with him. It was innocent, but still. I never would've had I known. And he's kind of flirted with me, too. He literally got down on his knees for me. Did I imagine how sexually charged that moment felt? Maybe it was just me.

Willing myself to stay composed, I fist my hands, the sharp daggers of my nails digging into my palms.

Even when they seem like they're not the type, they are.

Ethan, still gleaming from laughter, looks at me, seeming to suddenly remember I'm still in the room. "Marisa, this is Tawny, my cousin."

Cousin.

I'm an idiot.

"Your cousin!" My body jolts, shocked by the screech of words that flew out of my mouth.

Tawny does a half wave. "Only a relative would put up with his cranky ass."

I feel silly, stupid, honestly, for allowing myself to get jealous. And for what? I have no claim to Ethan. I hardly know the man, and up until a few days ago, we couldn't tolerate each other. I'm not even the jealous type. Brandon used to brag to his buddies that I was such a cool girlfriend because I never minded if he went out without me. He was always the only guy in his friend group who didn't have a wife or girlfriend blowing up his phone trying to keep tabs on him during long trips and guys' nights out. It truly never bothered me. I'm starting to wonder if it's because I blindly trusted him that much or if I didn't like him enough to care. Evidently, I'm still carrying around the trauma of my ex cheating on me with his admin; I automatically assume all men behave this way.

"I'll leave you two to do your interview thing." Tawny turns her attention to me. "If you need anything, give me a holler, and if he's being an ass, come grab me and I'll put him in his place." She winks and then leaves us alone, the door closing behind her with a loud click.

"She seems nice."

He snorts. "Me, her, and my older brother Gavin are the oldest kids on my dad's side. We've always been close."

"Must be nice having such a large family." I can only imagine how much brighter and less lonely my childhood would've been had I grown up surrounded by siblings and cousins.

His chin dips, and his lips pull to a tight smile. "Chaotic, but a good kind of chaotic."

I look away, worried he'll notice the wistful look in my eyes, and bury my head in my bag.

"Do I have your permission to record this interview?"

When I glance up for confirmation, he nods stiffly, and then rolls his neck like he's getting ready for a match in a boxing ring.

I set out my supplies in front of me, turning my phone on to record, and ready myself with my pen and notepad to write down additional notes. Thanks to Suzy, I have a pretty solid question set. "Should we get started?"

His face contorts, and I feel like I'm catching a glimpse of what he must've looked like as a petulant child. "I guess," he groans.

Pressing my lips together, I bow my head slightly to mask the giggle I'm holding in. That was kind of adorable.

"I promise not to bite."

His eyebrows raise, hazel eyes darkening in a flash before he clears his throat. "I'm pretty private, so this is a big deal for me."

I note the catch of breath in his throat, the fidgeting of his hands, and feel an overwhelming need to reassure him that everything will be okay.

"We'll start with questions about the winery. Get some history and background. I'll save personal questions for the end. You don't have to answer anything you're not comfortable answering. I'll even make sure you get the first copy, fresh off the press. You'll be the first one on the delivery list, if that would make you feel better?"

The creases around his eyes soften. "Really?" He looks genuinely surprised.

"Sure, I'm not trying to get on the bad side of one of the founding families." I waggle my eyebrows at him, trying to lighten the mood.

He angles his head, not smiling, but definitely looking less pensive than he was a moment ago. "I see you've been getting your fair share of gossip from the nosy townies."

"It's called research."

"Riiight," he drags. "Trust me, it's not as fascinating as it sounds. Just because my great great whatever decided to build his pioneer shack in the middle of the desert doesn't make me or my family all that special."

I make a show of my eyes looking around. "I wouldn't call this a pioneer shack by any means."

He chuckles. "This is ostentatious as hell." His jaw slacks slightly. "My mom has a thing for France. Naturally, my dad took that into consideration when they built the estate."

This is exactly what I wanted to happen. I didn't want to sit here and ask him question after question. I wanted the information to flow naturally. Just two people having a conversation. "Is this not the original winery?"

"No, the original winery was an extension built off the house my parents live in. It used to be my grandparents' house, and when they transitioned from wheat farming to growing grapes, they started with using their home and eventually built a separate addition."

"I'd love to see it. Maybe take some pictures. That is, if it's okay with your parents."

He nods. "I'll talk to my mom about it. She would love to show you around. It shouldn't be an issue."

"So, how did the winery begin? What's the story there?"

His lips compress, and his head tilts. "My grandfather started the winery in the late seventies. Wheat wasn't providing well enough for the family, and he was willing to try anything to start turning a profit. Around this time, there were already whispers about the unique soil of Red Mountain and being in the rain shadow allowed for an easier control of water. He took a gamble and planted the first vineyard on some fallow land, which is land left unplanted so the soil can rest. From there, he learned everything he could, and it took off. He replaced all the wheat with vineyards the following year, and the winery was born."

"Smart man," I comment.

"Very smart."

"That makes you a third generation, then?"

"Yep, a third-generation vintner."

"So, you're a nepo baby."

His face twists. "A what?"

I can barely contain the laugh that wants to escape. "Nepo, as in nepotism. It's a fairly common term these days, Grandpa."

He gives me a good-natured eye roll. "You sound like my little sister, Elyse."

I perk up slightly. "Oh, yes, we've met. We're actually going out this Saturday for country night at The Jackalope."

His eyes nearly bug out. "You're going out with my sister? That's a recipe for disaster." He rubs the bridge of his nose, looking undoubtedly stressed.

"What's wrong with your sister?"

"For starters, she finds trouble everywhere she goes."

"How much trouble can one find in a small town?"

He cocks his head, eyes leaving mine and landing on my lips, where they linger for a moment before he clears his throat. "You'd be surprised."

I shift in my seat, ignoring the heat starting to coil in my stomach. I continue, asking about how much of his family is involved in the winery. Apparently, nearly all of his family works for the winery in some capacity. All of his siblings, a majority of his cousins, and his aunts and uncles are on the board. It's a complete family business.

It turns out Ethan can string together quite a few words and speak in great detail when he's not the focus of the topic. The further into the interview I get, the more relaxed he becomes.

I learn a little of the winemaking process, and he has Tawny schedule a time for me to take a look at the original winery tomorrow. He explains the grape varieties and why they're chosen and how they manage sustainability. He tells me about successes and failures they've experienced over the years and how they're constantly having to adapt to keep up with competitors.

By the time we're through, my brain is in overload mode. I feel like I got a crash course in starting my own winery.

"And now for the personal questions."

He blows out an exhale. "I was hoping you'd forgotten."

"Like I said, you don't have to answer anything you don't want to, and these questions are mild compared to the ones on dating apps."

He shrugs. "I wouldn't know."

My pen slips, dropping and rolling across the floor, under the desk. Ethan bends in his chair to retrieve it and hands it back to me. The very slightest contact of his skin touching mine, fingertip-to-fingertip, has me nearly dropping the pen again.

"Thanks," I mumble.

Re-straightening in my chair, I ask the question that's begging to jump out, even though it has nothing to do with the interview. "You've never been on a dating app?"

He shakes his head. "Nope, never felt the need to."

Oh, right. Of course. When you're ruggedly handsome

with a job, that ticks off a majority of the criteria most women have.

"I get it. The women come to you. That makes sense."

He barks out a laugh, shaking his head like what I said is ridiculous. "Just the opposite. I'm awkward enough in real life. I don't need to add to that by being even more awkward behind a screen."

"So, you don't date?" The question falls out of my mouth before my brain can think twice at holding it in.

His head jerks back a little, eyes wide. "Uh, not really. I was with someone for a while, but it didn't work out. I haven't been serious with anyone else since."

The once comfortable flow we had going is long gone, replaced with palpable tension.

Way to go, Marisa.

"Is this part of the interview?" he asks, jaw tightened.

"Oh, um, no. Sorry about that." I giggle and it sounds dolphin-y. Great. "Anyway," I say, trying to recover. "I'll just read off my handy notebook."

Handy notebook? Ugh, kill me now.

I decide to start with an easy one. "What's your education and background?"

Some of the tension in his jaw releases. "I studied finance in college. I had always planned to work my way up in the accounting department. That's what I was doing before I started this position."

I can see him in that role. Something behind the scenes, not quite so front and center.

I set down my pen and close my notebook. It doesn't feel right to continue. He doesn't like to be the center of attention, and I have the ability to make the article less about him and more about the winery.

His brows furrow, and his eyes dart between me and the closed notebook.

"I think I have enough information."

"But you only asked one question?"

I shrug. "Yeah, and I think I have enough information about the winery that it's not necessary to ask you a bunch of personal questions that you'll hate answering."

"Really?"

"Yeah, really."

His shoulders visibly relax. "You have no idea how relieved I feel."

"Do you mind if I walk around the property and take some photographs for the article?" I ask now that we're through my question set.

"Go for it."

I get up from my seat and feel him moving behind me. "What are you doing?"

"I'm going with you. Like I'm going to let you walk around by yourself. We both know how prone you are to property damage, and getting lost."

Oh, so now that the tension between us isn't so awkward, he's got jokes.

"That was so funny, I forgot to laugh."

He smirks, looking pompous, and a little zing zips up my spine. Hillary was wrong about my type. It's definitely not tech bros.

Heat radiates behind me as he follows me out of his office and down the stairs to the lobby.

"Let's go this way." His hand practically brands the middle of my back as he steers me in the opposite direction from where I was heading. It made contact for a second if that, but I continue to feel it long after it's gone. Meanwhile, he's fine. It's not like he stopped my heart and gave me a third-degree burn or anything.

"Where are we going?"

Rather than answer, he steps in front of me, taking the

lead. I have to half-jog to keep up with his long strides. He looks back at me and notices, so he slows his steps.

"The crew should be harvesting the cabernets. I figured you'd want some pictures of the action."

"Good thinking."

He signs a clipboard and grabs a jacket hanging on a hook and leads me out to the back parking lot.

"We'll take a buggy. It's quicker than walking."

"What's a buggy? Is that like a horse-drawn carriage?"

A loud, boisterous sound comes out of him, and it takes me a second to realize it's a laugh. He's laughing. Full on, bent over, laughing.

A smile tugs at my lips. "Did I say something funny?"

He takes a few seconds, his breath catching in the cusps of dying from laughter. "I don't think anybody has ever asked me that before. Caught me off guard." He walks further into the parking lot along a sidewalk lined with golf carts. "A buggy is a golf cart."

"Why not call it a golf cart then?"

He shakes his head, the remenance of laughter pulling at the corner of his mouth. When he's smiling and laughing so freely like this, he makes it hard to look at anything else but him. If he was like this all the time, I would be done for. "We just do, couldn't tell you."

I stare at the old-looking golf cart. "Is this thing safe?"

He's already seated, the soft whirr of the motor sounding. "Are you scared or something? You'll be fine, I can't be any worse of a driver than you."

Is that his second joke in less than a few minutes?

"Okay, if you say so."

"Wait!" He jumps out of his seat and comes around to my side. "You're going to get cold once we get moving."

He takes the flannel-lined canvas jacket he grabbed from the backroom and drapes it around my shoulders, the size of it swallowing my slacks and silk blouse. I'm immediately engulfed in a smell I'm beginning to associate with Ethan—citrus and laundry and something unidentifiable, completely unique and distinct. I resist the urge to bury my nose in the fabric. I should protest and tell him that sixty-five degree weather isn't what I would consider cold, but I find myself too entranced by the small gesture to care about getting over-heated. Our eyes meet as he settles the jacket collar across my clavicle, his touch lingering a moment longer than necessary. The faintest brush of his thumb along the exposed skin near my shirt collar sends my stomach into a dip, and my breath hitches at the contact. He smiles, a small, subtle smile, but it feels like it's just for me.

"There," he murmurs softly. "All set."

I nod as I try to steady my racing heart. "Thank you," I manage to whisper, my voice barely audible over the air caught in my throat.

He steps back slightly, his gaze never leaving mine. For a moment, it feels like we're the only two people in the world. The air is thick, charged with something unspoken. Something neither of us is quite ready to acknowledge. Or maybe I'm imagining the electricity buzzing between us.

"Ready?" he asks, breaking the spell. His tone is hesitant, as if he, too, isn't sure of what's happening.

I break eye contact first, feeling like if I stared into his forest eyes much longer, I may get drunk off of them alone. "Yeah, let's head out." I take my seat and keep my attention focused on the surrounding landscape.

A squeal flies out of me when his foot hits the pedal and the cart jerks into motion. Soon we're racing down acres of vineyards. The terrain is hilly and rough, but the sight is breathtaking. I feel like I'm being transported into some kind of dream sequence, where clouds sit low in the autumn air and plump grapes hang from the vines. It's too beautiful to be real.

CHAPTER 19

Ethan

IT HIDES YOUR PRETTY EYES

M arisa's eyes are stuck on the view, and mine are stuck on her, biting her lip in concentration. It's wildly distracting. It's a miracle I didn't crash, because I don't think I looked at the road once the entire drive.

"We're here," I announce, even though it's obvious since we came to a stop.

She sits back and sighs, wrapping my jacket tighter around her. "I actually did get a little cold." Her eyes shift to mine, and she smiles softly. "Good call on the jacket."

I nod, getting out, unsure if my voice will crack, so I don't say anything. I like seeing her in my jacket way too much, as if I've staked some claim on her. A fleeting moment of possession.

She slips it off, leaving it on the seat, and joins me by the sorting tables. Alex and his crew are hand-picking the grapes nearby. This variety of grape is too delicate for mechanical harvesting and requires more of a careful selection. Miguel and his crew are at the sorting tables, meticulously inspecting each cluster to ensure only the best grapes make it into the final batch. They examine every grape, removing any that don't

161

meet the high standard necessary for the wine. Miguel removes his gloves and comes to greet us.

"We should be done in a couple of hours," he tells me. He looks to Marisa, curious. "¿Y quién será esta hermosa señorita?" (*And who might this beautiful young lady be?*)

Marisa smiles brightly at him, shaking his hand. "Soy Marisa, mucho gusto." (*I'm Marisa, nice to meet you.*)

He chuckles, delighted. "Así que hablas español, qué padre." (*And you speak Spanish, how wonderful.*)

Miguel's eyes meet mine. "Ya me cae bien." (*I like her already.*)

"Sí, ¿verdad" (*I know, right?*)

Marisa gasps, taking a step back. She stares at me, her eyes wide with disbelief. "Are you fucking kidding me right now! You speak Spanish?" Her voice is a mix of surprise and barely contained laughter. She playfully pushes my chest, giving me a little shove. "Why didn't you tell me?"

I shrug, my lips curling slightly at the edges. "Never came up, I guess."

Her head shakes as she struggles to keep a straight face. "You're just full of surprises, aren't you?"

My chest puffs slightly. She almost looks...impressed with me. And it makes my heart thunder right under the searing handprint she left behind.

Miguel gets called over for a question and waves his goodbye, tipping his head at Marisa as he leaves.

"Anyway," I change the subject, before I get too comfortable enjoying Marisa looking at me like she doesn't completely hate me anymore. "You should get your pictures. The sun is in the perfect spot right now."

She nods in agreement, already pulling out her phone.

The sun really is in the perfect spot, as if it knew Marisa needed it to peek through the cloudy sky just enough to shine down over the gloomy autumn day we're having.

I leave her to check on Alex.

"Who's she?" Alex asks, nodding his chin in Marisa's direction. "New girlfriend?" He nudges my arm jokingly.

I give him a flat look. "You know she's not. She works for the *Herald*."

He laughs, his shoulders lifting. "Jefe, don't be so sensitive. I'm just asking."

I let Tawny convince me to get the guys to like me, and now Alex is comfortable enough to tease me. And I'm not sure if that's a good thing or a bad thing.

"Hey, Ethan," Marisa yells. "Come here for a second."

"Your novia is calling you," Alex says with a snicker.

"Shut up," I whisper under my breath, feeling my cheeks heat like a pubescent boy.

Marisa stands in the section of the vineyard that has a direct view of Red Mountain, the town's namesake.

"What's up?"

Her already large eyes somehow look even larger as she looks at me with her chin down and head tilted. She's giving me the female equivalent of puppy dog eyes, and I know I'm about to be talked into something I don't want to do.

"Would you be totally opposed to a picture?" She smiles cautiously, almost wincing, as if she's worried. "Just one?"

I hate the pang of guilt that hits me because of the tiptoeing she feels she has to do around me. I don't want her to be afraid to ask me for anything, let alone a silly picture.

"Sure." I hate pictures. The last thing I want to do is take a picture, given how much I sweat my ass off today, but I'm not saying no to Marisa. I'm not sure I'm capable of it.

"Really?" she squeals. "I thought for sure you'd stomp away from me, pissed that I even asked."

The guilt transitions to full-fledged shame. Of course she expects that. It's how I've been behaving, and I wish now, more than ever, that I could restart the clock and go back to our first meeting. I would do it all differently.

Her eyes squint, assessing the space. She grabs onto both of my arms and guides me a few inches right and then steps back, taking it all in.

"Stay right there," she commands.

I do as she says and remain unmoving, save for my eyes. They bounce from where she sucks in her bottom lip, deep in concentration. To the floppy strand of hair sweeping across her forehead that I itch to touch. To her completely out of place professional attire. The juxtaposition of it all has me biting back a grin. I can't tear my eyes away.

Her lips purse, and she stares at me as she walks closer. Close enough that I can smell her signature vanilla scent.

"Mind if we lose the hat? It's just that it hides your pretty eyes."

I snort. "My eyes are pretty?"

"Yes," she practically yells. "I would trade eyes with you in a second. Anything besides my boring brown ones."

We share a lingering stare. I can't believe she would think any part of her is less than perfect. And even though her tone is humorous, it still bothers me. "Your eyes are beautiful." I didn't mean to let it slip, but the truth tumbled out before I could stop myself.

With our gazes still locked, I can't help but notice her bulging eyes and raised brows. She's stunned. Astonished. And I get the feeling no one has ever said that to her before.

I swallow, my attention wholly on her, but she quickly looks away, dropping her head and backs up.

"Thanks," she murmurs, not looking at me.

I probably crossed the line. I should've worded it differently. *Beautiful.* It's not a friendly word; it's an intimate one. And I think I fucked up everything.

She's backed up to the pathway, lifting her phone and looking at the screen. "Your hat," she reminds me.

I take it off, tossing it a few feet away, out of frame, and attempt to smooth down my hair.

"Here, let me," she says, coming back and rewarding me with a cloud of vanilla.

I squat down to her level and get a flashback to being a little kid about to get his hair fixed by a spit-wielding grandma. Thankfully, Marisa doesn't hock one. But she does use her dainty fingers, running them through my hair and scratching at my scalp. It takes Herculean strength to not let my eyes roll back in my head and moan. Meanwhile, my dick doesn't have the same levels of restraint and starts to harden.

"There," she whispers."

I tense at her closeness. Her warm breath grazes my forehead, a jolt of heat that sharpens my senses. The contact feels too visceral. Her presence is overwhelming, intoxicating.

"All better."

She goes back to the edge of the path, but I'm still reeling. She starts taking pictures, and I couldn't tell you if I looked at the camera, if I smiled, if I even stood straight. Mentally, I wasn't there. I was still living five minutes ago when she was close enough to hear her heartbeat, completely dazed.

"I think I got it," she says excitedly.

I'm so fucked.

CHAPTER 20

Marisa

MINUS THE CULT PART

"Come in, come in," Leanne Ledger gestures her hand at me to come inside.

My eyes flick over the colonial-style exterior of the home before I step in. The house is tucked away deep within the vineyard property, nearly hidden unless you know exactly where you're going. If Jenn hadn't drawn me a makeshift map, I'm not sure I would've found it.

"I hope it wasn't too hard to find," she tells me, looking over her shoulder as I follow her down the long hallway lined with family photographs and art pieces.

"Jenn gave me directions." I hold up the napkin with black ink scribbles that Jenn drew for me.

She smiles warmly. "It's a bit of a maze out here."

As we pass the kitchen, she pauses and turns to me. "Would you like something to drink? I made a fresh batch of lavender lemonade."

"That sounds amazing."

While she works on pouring two glasses, I continue to look around. The home reminds me of something out of a Nancy Meyer's film, with its mix of new finishes and antique-looking furniture. My focus sweeps around, trying to take it all in. Maybe it's the reporter in me or maybe I'm just nosy as hell, but all I can think is this is the home Ethan grew up in. He probably ran through this kitchen as a kid or watched TV on that couch or walked down the stairs near the foyer for dates. I'm imagining him everywhere.

In the living room near the kitchen, there's a credenza full of framed photos. I glance over at Leanne and see she's still busy, so I quietly wander over.

The pictures are an array of posed family portraits and candids, all taken over the years. My gaze catches on one of a middle school-aged boy with braces and hazel eyes. It's a school photo and clearly, it's Ethan. He's smiling a closed-mouth, forced smile, and the corners of my lips lift imagining what he was like at that age.

"Find anything interesting?"

I jump, caught off guard by Leanne's sudden appearance. I didn't even hear her footsteps. Thankfully, I'm able to recover with a smile as she hands me my glass.

"I was snooping," I admit. "You have a beautiful family."

She breathes a laugh and takes a sip of lemonade. "Thank you. Sometimes they drive me bananas, but most of the time, they're pretty amazing."

Her smile slips into one of longing as she looks at all the pictures, almost as if it's not something she does often. "They grew up so fast. It's like I blinked and all of a sudden my kids are adults."

I wonder if my mom thinks of me that way? If I grew up too fast, or if I didn't grow up fast enough? Based on how quickly she leaped at the opportunity to get as far away as possible, I'm going to go with the latter.

A quiet laugh slips out of Leanne, almost to herself. "We didn't plan on having so many children. Gavin was our honeymoon souvenir," she says while pointing to a picture of a teenage Gavin. "Ethan and Elyse were planned because we knew we wanted at least three. Then came Shane. He wasn't planned, but we were ecstatic. Now the twins" —her gaze meets mine with raised brows— "total surprise."

Exhaling a smile I say, "It seems like it all worked out for the best."

"It did." She shakes her head like she's pulling herself out of a memory. "Ethan said you wanted to see the original winery and get some pictures?"

"Yes, if you don't mind. I'm doing an article on the winery."

She claps excitedly. "I know, and I can't tell you how happy I am that you managed to get Ethan to do it. I'm not sure what you did or said to get him to agree, but I'm sure it was something close to magic." She winks at me and something about it makes me blush. I turn my head, pretending to admire the décor before my skin becomes completely red. "He must think pretty highly of you."

A nervous giggle nearly surfaces, but I clench my jaw to trap it. "I'm assuming it's down this way," I point, trying to escape this conversation.

If Leanne notices, she doesn't say anything. Instead, her lips press into a smile. "It's down these steps."

I follow her as we walk through another long hallway. At the end of it, we take two awkward steps down to a different level.

"This used to be a breezeway, but Jack had it enclosed," Leanne explains as we trail across the long stretch until we go through a door of a shed-like building. "This is it."

Inside, the smell of aged wood and something sour penetrate my nose. It's not a bad smell, it's almost familiar.

"Decades later and this place still smells like fermenting wine," Leanne says.

The space is bare, the furniture no longer in place, but it's clear where the bar once was.

I snap a few pictures, going for a moody effect.

"It's not much to look at these days, but we don't have the heart to tear it down." She wanders over to a separate room, closed off by a barn door. "Through here is where everything happened."

It's hard to tell what it once looked like, and apart from some old barrels stacked in the corner, the room is empty.

"Can you believe they did every process in this little room? Crushing and fermenting and aging, even bottling. Now we have multiple warehouses for that."

I manage to capture some great pictures I think will beautifully compliment the article, and Leanne tells me more about the earlier days of the winery, which I make sure to take note of. As she's walking me out, an overgrown lot between the Ledger home and another house catches my attention. Leanne notices me staring.

"Bit of an eye sore," she muses.

"Is it meant to be more land for a vineyard?"

She smiles wistfully at the lot before returning her focus back to me. "No, it's Ethan's. He was supposed to build a house on it, but life had other plans. I keep hoping he'll finish it one day. Call me crazy, but my dream is for all of my children to live on the land, like a giant commune. Minus the cult part, of course." She releases a soft chuckle and points to the other house. "That one is Gavin's."

Leanne continues talking, but I find myself distracted, wondering why Ethan abandoned the lot. I can't imagine he actually prefers living in a vacation cottage over a real home.

CHAPTER 21

Marisa

HOES DON'T GET COLD

I often look my best when everything seems to be going wrong. The pesky five to ten extra pounds I tend to carry? Gone. The glowing skin I'm always trying to attain? Happening. I can't explain this phenomenon, but it's like the universe is balancing everything out for me. *Oh, your life is shit? Might as well look good.*

And because all the stars are aligning, Layla—Elyse's little sister and Ariana's twin, who's visiting for the weekend—happens to be the same shoe size as me. Meaning I'm wearing my first pair of cowboy boots, ever. When it comes to country music—well, country anything—I'm a bit of a virgin. The closest I've come to listening to country music is Carrie Underwood singing about shooting whiskey and hating pretty little drinks. That song still offends me. I happen to love pretty little drinks, and I'll never stop.

"Those white boots look so good against your tan legs. You definitely need to wear something to show them off." Elyse holds up a short black dress covered in a small floral print. She places it up against me, covering the lounge shorts and crewneck I'm wearing. "Okay, hear me out. This dress with a tight denim vest?" She looks at Layla and Ariana. "It would be so nineties, right?"

They both nod in unison.

"Wait, I actually love that," Layla says.

"Is that a good thing?" I ask.

"You're going to look hot, just trust us," Elyse says.

The three sisters get to work on me, primping and prodding as if I'm their own personal doll. Ariana styles my hair in big, bouncy waves, each strand cascading in a perfect loose curl. Layla adds some finishing touches to the makeup I already applied, layering on more blush and swiping some gloss over my lips. Meanwhile, Elyse is working to suck me into the little denim vest she insists pulls the whole look together.

I stand still, overwhelmed by the whirl of activity around me. Once they're done, I have to admit, I actually look really good. The outfit isn't one I would've chosen for myself, and it does look a little like I should be an extra in a country music video, but it's flattering, highlighting my best features. One part in particular is highlighted a little more than I would typically allow. Because the vest is a snug fit, it's pushing my breasts up high, and they're practically spilling out over the top.

Elyse steps back, examining me from head to toe with a critical eye. "You're going to get so many free drinks tonight."

I smile, feeling a surge of confidence. "You think so?"

She nods. "Definitely."

Ariana opts for a flowy white dress that cuts off above her knees and some brown cowboy boots that actually look like they've walked through dirt a few times. Layla is wearing cut-off denim shorts, a cropped denim jacket with a white tank top that bares her midriff, and white sneakers. It's giving sexy Canadian tuxedo, something I could never pull off. And Elyse is wearing a simple black, body-hugging dress with an elaborate belt sitting low around her hips, paired with teal cowboy boots. She's always dressed in a way that says *I didn't try, but I still look amazing*.

"Won't you be cold?" I ask Elyse because she's the most scantily clad of us.

She shrugs. "Hoes don't get cold."

I wasn't expecting that answer, and laughter bubbles out of me.

Hillary would like Elyse.

I was surprised when Elyse invited me over to her place to get ready with her and her sisters. I appreciate the gesture, because despite myself, I am a little nervous about going out tonight. It's not the same as going out in Seattle where there are so many people there's a comforting layer of anonymity. Here, it seems everyone knows each other and will definitely remember drunken embarrassments.

"Are we taking a ride share? I can order it." I start reaching for my phone.

Elyse snorts. "Unfortunately, we don't have any of the fancy apps, but I called Tony at Rad Cab, and he'll be by in about ten minutes." She tugs at my arm. "Whatever you do, don't mention his glass eye. He gets super sensitive about it."

Is she serious right now? "The cab driver only has one eye? Is that safe?"

Elyse nods. "Oh, yeah. It's totally fine. He's been driving that cab for like thirty years. We're good."

Are we though?

Tony rolls up outside Elyse's—hitting the curb, might I add. Reluctantly, I get in, making sure to buckle up. I clutch the door for an added safety measure. Logically, I know it would do nothing to save me in the event of an accident, but I'm not really feeling like being logical. I'm more interested in peace of mind.

Thank goodness Elyse warned me about Tony's eye,

because it's not a regular glass eye—well, as regular as a glass eye can be—it's a snake eye. It reminds me of the contacts people wear around Halloween. Why on Earth would he have a snake-style glass eye if he didn't want people to stare? I can't seem to look anywhere else but the reflection of his face in the rear-view mirror. I'm in the back with Layla and Ariana, and Elyse is up front, happily chatting away with Tony. She even has her phone connected to his bluetooth, playing poppy sounding country songs.

It's a quick drive, and we make it in one piece, but not before he promises to come by and pick us up at the end of the evening. I think I'd be safer walking the short distance.

The Jackalope has no qualms about its name. Their sign is designed to look like one of those yellow road crossing signs and reads *The Jackalope* with a giant jackrabbit sporting antlers at the center. A bouncer stands out front and waves us right in, not bothering to check our IDs.

Once inside, I'm hit with the pungent smell of body odor and sweet liquor. It's a lot busier than I thought it would be. Large groups of people are crowded together and drinking, shoulders touching. The bass of the music vibrates the rickety wooden floor, and my shoes stick to years of caked-on liquor as we walk through. Elyse leads the way straight to the bar, where every liquor and beer I can think of lines the shelves. The bartender, a woman with harsh makeup and a smokes-a-pack-a-day look, asks for our order.

"What can I get you, princesses?" Her voice could saw wood with how rough it is.

Layla orders us a round of lemon drop shots. I want to protest, but I don't want to be that person. Starting off with shots is a horrible idea, especially when I've barely eaten today. I'm a lightweight, so I'm going to be drunk in no time.

"Bottoms up, ladies," Layla yells over the loud music, and we clink our glasses together.

Ariana, who looks as reluctant as I feel, meets my eyes and then shrugs, slinging back the shot in one gulp. Well fuck, if she did it, I have to. The three sisters watch me as I take a few deep breaths and down the shot. It takes me two gulps. I've never been any good at taking shots. I must've missed that course in college.

"Come on, let's go find a spot," Layla says.

We end up in a section with high-top tables and gather around one, placing our drinks on it while we stand and look around the crowd. I can feel glances and whispers as people take notice of my presence. Clearly, I stand out, since everyone knows each other around here. The Jackalope is one of the few businesses in town not frequented by tourists, making it painfully obvious when there's a new face in the crowd. It's never fun being the new kid, no matter how old you are.

"Are the boys coming?" Ariana asks Elyse.

Elyse nods. "Yeah, Mom and Dad are watching Lily, so Gav and Shane are coming and somehow they convinced Ethan to come out, too."

Layla's eyes widen. "Ethan is coming? That's interesting. I wonder why."

Elyse sways her shoulders to the music. "I can think of one reason," she singsongs and looks right at me.

I force a laugh, trying to dismiss her. "Your brother does not see me that way. And neither do I." *Liar.*

"I don't know about that," she says with a smile that tells me she knows something I don't. "Me thinks the lady doth protest too much."

Ariana's focus is on the front. "Speak of the devil. They're here."

The three brothers, who look so similar, yet incredibly different, are gathered at the entrance. One is completely tattooed, looking like a bad boy version of Ethan, and wearing a T-shirt, his ink-sleeved arms on full display. The other is

174

swallowing the doorway with his viking-like size. And then there's Ethan, his hands shoved in his pockets, eyes scanning the crowd with a weary expression, stopping when they lock onto mine. I try to look away and break the connection, but I can't. The familiar tension tethers us together, undeniably complicated.

CHAPTER 22

Ethan

SMALL DICK ENERGY VIBES

"First round is on me, fuckers." Shane sandwiches himself between me and Gavin, his arms around our shoulders, and pushes us into the bar, forcing me to tear my eyes off Marisa. But not before the image of her burns into my mind. The way her black, breezy dress skates across her perfect thighs. The way the little vest she's paired with it has her perky tits spilling out over the top of the deep V. The way her tan, toned legs are on full display in white cowboy boots that shouldn't look nearly as sexy as they do on her. The way her long, thick hair flows down her back in loose waves, and my fingers rub together as I imagine how it would feel to slide my hands through those silky strands.

She looks good. Too good. And it pisses me off, because I'm not the only one who notices. Heads turn like dominos falling over as my sisters pull her deeper into the bar and farther away from me.

I knew she was going to be here tonight—hell, it's the only reason I agreed to come. I don't enjoy this shit. Dive bars, crowds, drunken idiots—it's my personal nightmare. But I'd

176

rather suffer through this than stay at home and wonder if some asshole is hitting on her, making her smile, buying her drinks. No, I guess I'd rather torture myself by witnessing it instead.

If I had walked in alone, no one would have paid me any attention, but with my brothers on either side, the attention is unavoidable. Gavin is everyone's favorite DILF—not my words, just what I know to be true. If he had any interest in dating again, he wouldn't lack for options. It continues to surprise me how brazen some women can be, cornering him after PTA meetings and using their own kids to orchestrate some alone time under the guise of playdates. He's a good sport about it, though. Unlike me, Gavin is actually nice, and likable, and so goddamn patient he deserves a medal.

Shane is a man whore—a title he owns proudly. We're opposites in nearly every way. Where I'm brusque, stand-offish, and tongue tied, he's all smooth lines and charisma. I'd think we weren't blood related, but we look nearly identical, minus the seven years I have on him and the thirty plus tattoos he has on me.

I'm just the weird one. The quiet one. The one people tolerate in hopes that my brothers are part of the deal.

Gavin and I find an open booth, and Shane splits off to get us drinks. I try my damndest to not let my eyes search for Marisa. I didn't come here to bother her. I just can't seem to stay the fuck away.

Despite the fact that I recognize nearly everyone, my anxiety festers below the surface. A stray laugh, a drunken yell, a glass breaking; all sounds that weave around my nerves. Each noise causes my heart to pound harder in my chest, loud and insistent. I purposefully didn't take a beta blocker because I knew I'd be drinking, and until some alcohol numbs me, I'll have to ride out this raw feeling a while longer.

Shane returns with cold beers and shots. Skipping the beer, I go straight for the hard stuff and down the whiskey in one gulp, hoping the burn of it will tamper down my spiking pulse.

An hour. I can do an hour of this. If I set a clear, tangible goal, the competitor in me has to achieve it.

Shane is quick to abandon us for Shelby, who's fluttering her eyes at him at the next table over, and a few of Gavin's buddies join our booth to catch up. He rarely gets a night out like this, so when he does, he makes the most of it. Their conversation fills the void around us and enables me to relax slightly.

When my eyes scan the crowd again, they land on Marisa, who's standing at the bar, laughing with none other than Cole Benton.

Fuck me.

Contrary to popular belief and small town gossip, the Ledgers and the Bentons get along just fine. We're competitive in business, but it only makes us better in the long run. We all grew up together, and in most circumstances, I would even consider Cole a friend. But right now? I'm not feeling very friendly. Right now, I want to punch Cole square in the jaw.

He must be fucking hilarious because her head tips back as she giggles. My veins ignite with a rush of heat. It's like a slow burn that starts in my chest and spreads out to my fingertips, which clench into fists at my sides.

I can't take my eyes off them. Marisa's smile is radiant, her eyes sparkling in a way that makes me wish I was the reason they shined. And Cole—damn him—leans in closer, his hand resting casually on the bar, inches from hers.

A wave of jealousy crashes over me, almost knocking me off balance. I have no right to feel this way. Marisa and I are friends, barely. And we need to stay just friends, because she'll be back to Seattle in no time and I'll still be here. But with the way my heart is hammering in my chest, you'd think it's a different story.

I force myself to look away, trying to focus on anything else. Gavin abandoned his beer for another whiskey, and even though it's lukewarm and flat now, I drink it down.

I told myself I wouldn't keep watching her, but I'm unable to resist. I feel more and more like a stalker the longer I watch. Eventually, she leaves Cole and returns to my sisters. I almost relax enough to look away, but then my sisters take her from group to group around the bar, introducing her to the whole damn town.

She doesn't realize it, but she's the center of attention tonight. Like the little social butterfly she is, she's been giving them her cheerful smile and warm laugh, and I slowly watch everyone fall in love with her.

It's going to be a long night.

I tried so hard to dislike her, tried to avoid her. Maybe because I scare easily around a beautiful woman, or maybe because some primal part of me knew she was different. That from the moment I laid eyes on her, I was done for.

Forcing my gaze straight ahead, I try to pay attention to the story one of Gavin's friends is telling, but my periphery follows Marisa's every movement. My ears are so trained on her laugh, it seems to overpower all other sounds, even the blaring music. All I hear is her. All I see is her. I'm an absolute masochist for coming tonight.

The waitress comes by, and instead of continuing to drink my sorrows away, I opt for a water so I can sober up and get the hell out of here.

"Fuck," Gavin grumbles, his eyes on the bar.

"What is it?" I ask, following his line of vision.

I'm about to ask him what I should be looking for when my eyes pause on a familiar golden-blonde mane. It's Laura. And she's not alone. She's ordering at the bar, and Travis has his arms wrapped around her from behind, his hands resting low on her torso. They look right together, comfortable. It reminds me of a time when it was my arms she was in. The unwelcome image hits me, and I squeeze my eyes shut, pushing it out as quickly as it popped in. That was someone else entirely. It wasn't me. At least not the person I am today. I wait for the stabbing pain to start in my chest, but it never comes. The jealousy I should feel at seeing them standing intimately with each other never surfaces.

"Oh, shit." Gavin dashes out of his seat.

It takes me a brief moment to catch on, but then I'm seconds behind him. Elyse has spotted Laura, and she's making a beeline straight for her.

We practically sprint to get there before her, but we're too late. Elyse reaches Laura first.

"You fucking bitch! I can't believe you have the balls to show your face around here!"

Elyse screams in Laura's face, and rather than Laura looking angry or scared, she's smiling, which in turn only riles up Elyse more.

"Get over it already." Laura laughs her perfected, condescending laugh.

Elyse stiffens, and her eyes narrow into thin, darkening slits. She's about to lose her shit. "You dumb fucking whore—"

Gavin swoops between the two women, picking up Elyse mid-insult and hauling her away.

"Come on. One hit!" Elyse screams, trying to wiggle out of Gavin's hold. "Just one really good one. You know she deserves it!"

Gavin, unrelenting, continues walking with her in his hold until they're both outside, leaving me behind to deal with the aftermath. The crowd that had gathered due to the commotion disperses, uninterested now that there won't be a fight. The bartender shakes her head at me, as if I'm to blame, and then returns to wiping down the counter.

Laura's amused eyes meet mine, and Travis awkwardly coughs. Her mouth quirks up in what I think is supposed to be a smile, but it looks fake as shit. "Ethan. So nice to see you. Looks like Elyse still hates me, huh?"

Her voice is like the high-pitched whistle on a teakettle. Fucking annoying.

"Laura," I say, tipping my head slightly.

She frowns at my dismissive greeting. What was she expecting? Me to beg for her back?

"Good to see you," Travis says.

Fuck, this is uncomfortable as hell. Gavin should've let Elyse get one hit in. At least that would have saved me from having to interact with these two at all.

A tingle of heat singes my shoulder as someone taps on it.

"Hey, have you seen Elyse?"

I turn to face the woman I've had my eyes glued to the entire evening. Her brow is furrowed, looking confused, and it's cute as hell.

I like her. More than I should. More than I should allow myself to. Up until recently, I was convinced it was simply a physical attraction. But with the relief I feel just being in her presence, the way she changed the beat of my anxious, overactive heart, I know it's more than that. And the worst part of it all is that it's been so long since I've felt anything close to this. It's just my luck that it's for someone who doesn't live here. She's only temporary, and it would do me some good to remind myself of that every time I see her. She's temporary.

"Ethan? Did you hear me? I can't find Elyse," Marisa repeats, louder.

I would rather not explain the entire situation. At least not now. "She got a little out of hand, so Gavin took her to cool off."

"That's kind of strange," she says.

Marisa, noticing Laura and Travis, flashes them a sweet, sunshine smile. "Hi, I'm Marisa," she says, tapping on her chest, slightly leaning and yelling over to them so they can hear her over the music.

"I'm Laura, and this is my fiancé, Travis." She encircles him, blatantly setting her left hand on Travis's stomach to show off her gaudy ring. Laura's eyes dart between us. "Ethan, I didn't realize you were seeing someone."

"Oh— No— I..."

Marisa slides her hand through the crook of my arm and clasps on to me, pushing her body in closer, her breasts rubbing up against my arm.

I nearly groan at the contact.

What is she doing?

Marisa is more than a foot shorter than me. She shouldn't fit at my side as well as she does, yet I can't help but notice how perfectly snug she feels, like a missing puzzle piece effortlessly slotting into place.

Glancing down at her, I catch her eye, and there's pure mischief dancing behind those molten chocolates. I have a feeling she knows exactly who Laura and Travis are.

"It's still new," Marisa dreamily says to Laura. "We're still in that can't-keep-our-hands-off-each-other stage."

I will my face to not burn. If we're going to get caught in this lie, it's going to happen now, because Laura knows I'm not the most affectionate. At least I never was with her.

Laura's eyes pinch, landing directly where Marisa has her hands wrapped around my arm. Normally, I would overthink this, cipher through various options and hope to land on one that appears the most natural, but there isn't time for that. I need to make a quick move that doesn't look robotic to shut down any doubts Laura may have about the legitimacy of this very illegitimate relationship. I'm sure I'll be paying for this when the gossip spreads around town.

It will be worth it just to touch her. Even if it's only once.

Marisa angles her head and rests her chin on my chest, and as if we've done it a million times, I tuck a stray strand of her long hair behind her ear, indulging myself more than anyone else by letting my hand graze her jaw and travel down her neck before slipping my fingers around the silky, dark, curled tendrils. In the time since I arrived, it's taken on a more messy, disheveled appearance. It's the way I imagine her hair would look after she's been thoroughly fucked. I fight the desire to wrap the thick strands around my knuckles and instead smooth it out for her, untangling the knots with gentle slowness. I think she moans, but I can't be too sure if I imagined it or if it was the music messing with my head. Her eye lids slant, turning hooded, and I feel her chest rising and falling much quicker than it was just a moment ago. It's not a big show of affection, but it's intimate. It's the way I would touch her in public if she were mine.

Our gazes latch. If things were different—if *I* was different—I would take advantage of the opportunity and kiss her right here and now. But I'm still me, so I don't.

I finish smoothing one final piece around her temple. "There," I say quietly.

Her eyes are soft and almost sad as they stare into mine. It's as if she's in disbelief that I fixed her hair—or maybe I'm reading the situation wrong, and she's weirded out.

She swallows harshly and takes in a lung full of air. "Thanks." Her tone is low and hushed, just for me to hear.

"Should we go sit down?" I ask her, saving us both from continuing this charade.

She nods, her chin still resting on my chest, eyes looking dazed, likely from one too many drinks.

"Nice seeing you guys," I say, not bothering to even look at them as I spin Marisa around, pressing my front to her back and keeping her in my arms as we move together.

God, she feels good. And she smells good, like sweet, warm vanilla. I would've stayed planted in front of Laura and Travis the rest of the night if it meant I could touch Marisa this way. But even that small bit was too much. Marisa is someone I would drown in if I let myself. It's better if I keep swimming.

Once we're out of sight, Marisa walks out of my embrace, and I immediately miss the feel of her, but the moment has passed and we're back to reality.

She turns to face me, her face bright with laughter. "Oh, my God! Did you see the look on her face? She wanted to murder me."

"How did you know?" She had to have known. Someone must've told her, or else she wouldn't have started that little display.

She lifts her chin toward Shane, who's standing by the retro jukebox. "Your brother with all the tattoos. Shane, right? He stopped me when I walked out of the restroom and told me to go save you from your, and I quote, 'cunt of an ex and her pussy fiancé.'"

That sounds like Shane. "Thanks, but you didn't have to do that. You'll be the talk of the town if anyone noticed."

She shrugs, unaffected. "Meh, who cares. If I was given the opportunity to do that to my ex, I totally would. Gossip be damned just to see the look on his stupid face."

Marisa slides into the booth near us, and I follow suit, sitting opposite of her.

"Bad breakup I take it?"

She blows out a groany breath. "The worst. He's the whole reason I'm here. Cheated on me, evicted me, fired me. It was a mess."

Jesus. And I thought I had it bad. Now I feel even worse than I already did about her first couple of weeks in Red Mountain. She was going through all of that, and then had me to deal with, too. I don't deserve her friendship—hell, I barely deserve to be speaking to her at all.

She shimmies her shoulders absentmindedly to the upbeat country song playing. "I showed you mine. Now you have to show me yours. What's the story?"

I take a deep breath. It's been a while since I've had to rehash everything. "Laura and I were engaged."

Marisa's smile drops, and her back goes rigid. "Oh. Shit. I had no idea. That's like—wow. That's serious."

With time having dulled the sharpness, it's easier to talk about than it used to be. I give her a nod. "It was serious. For me, it was at least."

"What happened? Unless you'd rather not tell me, that's totally fine too. It's really none of my business and I—"

"Relax." I chuckle, cutting off her adorable rambling. "Everyone else around here knows, you may as well, too."

Her shoulders relax slightly, but her eyes remain soft and expectant.

"The guy she was with, Travis. He was my best friend."

Her eyes become saucer-like, but she remains silent.

"Anyway, I'm sure you can put the pieces together. She was cheating on me with him. He was my best man. I caught them about a month before the wedding, going at it like a couple of horny teenagers, parked in the driveway of the condo Laura and I shared. They thought I had gone to bed."

Marisa's jaw drops. "Excuse me? I'm this close"—she pinches her fingers together for emphasis—"to putting on my thick cocktail rings and slapping her around. She seriously cheated on you"—her hand waves up and down like I'm a prize on *The Price is Right*—"for that below average, crusty man?"

"The heart wants what it wants, I guess. Besides, Travis probably saved me from what would've been an unhappy marriage. We weren't a good fit, and I think I thought getting married would fix all of our problems. I know she seemed awful, but that's her defense mechanism. She's not a bad person and neither is he, they just did a bad thing."

Her face scrunches. "You're a much better person than me. I hope the wires in her bra always poke at her, and I hope he misses her clit by millimeters for the rest of their lives. And I hope he has a small penis. Which I'm sure he does. He gives small dick energy vibes."

I laugh, listening to her basically curse them. "You're not some kind of witch, are you?"

She throws me a teasing look. "No, but I know how to find a bruja if necessary."

This woman never fails to surprise me. Anyone else, and this night may have been ruined, but with her, it keeps getting better.

Elyse returns with Gavin trailing behind her. I forgot where we were for a while there. The crowded bar faded away, and all of my focus went to Marisa. That's a first. Usually, with this much surrounding commotion, my anxiety would be floating beneath the surface, threatening to jump out at any moment.

Elyse slides in next to Marisa, and Gavin takes the seat next to me.

"I can't believe you missed my almost bar fight," Elyse tells Marisa, retelling the events from earlier.

While they chat, I turn to Gavin. "You think she's calmed down enough?"

He snorts. "Is she ever calm enough?"

I guess not.

Gavin starts telling me a story about Elyse trying to bum a cigarette off someone, but I'm only half-listening. Marisa's eyes flick to mine while Elyse talks her ear off. It's brief, but it feels like a silent acknowledgment that the rest of the evening will be spent apart. As it should be. Because we're just friends, and friends don't hang out in a secluded corner of the bar, getting lost in each other. No, *friends* definitely don't do that.

CHAPTER 23

Marisa

FULL ON, PRINCESS-STYLE

"**O**pen up your throat! Wider!" Elyse yells at me.

Elyse has the drinking capabilities of a twenty-year-old frat boy. She's also a master at peer pressure and is trying to teach me to properly take a shot. We're four shots deep, and I haven't gotten any better, only drunker.

"I sure hope your throat can open up for other activities. I feel bad for your future husband."

I hate being underestimated, even if it is for something as ridiculous as taking a shot. "Can I get another?" I call to the bartender on the other end of the bar. I'm going to take this shot and prove her wrong. I happen to be very good at other throat activities, and I won't have her implying otherwise.

The bartender pours the tequila and slides the shot over to me.

"Attagirl," Elyse whoops, Layla joining her. Ariana snuck out of here the first chance she got, leaving me alone with these crazy women.

I haven't seen Ethan since Elyse pulled me from him. A pang of disappointment hit me when my eyes scanned for him and he wasn't anywhere to be found. He probably left. The Jackalope doesn't seem like the kind of place he would frequent. Still, part of me had hoped he would stay. Maybe then he'd be here to save me from his wild sisters.

I take the shot, swallowing it in one big gulp, and it burns so painfully I'm afraid it's going to come right back up. Elyse shoves a lime in my mouth, and if I wasn't loosened up from alcohol, I'd worry where the lime came from and how many germy hands have touched it.

A song I don't recognize starts playing, and Layla gasps. "I love this song! Let's go dance."

She doesn't wait for an answer before grabbing mine and Elyse's hands and dragging us out into the middle of the bar. The Jackalope isn't really a dancing kind of bar. I feel eyes on us from all around as my hips move to the beat of the music. More people join us on the makeshift dance floor, and I relax slightly.

Once the next song starts, the alcohol has fully hit. The room sways around me. Colors bleed together, forming dark shadows in the fringes of my vision. It's incredibly loud, but everything sounds like one constant hum, a distant echo as I try to focus.

Water.

I need water.

Abandoning Elyse and Layla, I walk back to the bar in search of anything other than alcohol. On the trek there, my boot catches on the sticky floor and I stumble slightly, but a firm hand steadies me.

"Whoa there, you okay?"

I first look at the hand grasping my shoulder, and then my eyes travel up his arm and neck to meet his face. A pair of cloudy blue eyes are looking at me, crinkled at the corners from a smile. They're familiar, yet I can't place him. It starts with a C. Conner? Chris? Cody?

189

"It's Cole," the man says, pointing to himself. "Remember? We met earlier."

I hope I didn't try to guess his name out loud.

"You're smashed, aren't you?"

I giggle, but it sounds foreign to my ears, like I'm outside of my body, listening in. "Just a little."

Still holding my arm, he snakes his hand up and around my shoulder, dragging me against him. "Come on, drunky, let's get you some water."

He smells of cinnamon, and a wave of nausea rises as I'm reminded of the cinnamon whiskey shots we took before we switched to tequila.

In the far reaches of my memory, I recall introducing myself to him when I arrived because I'm scheduled to interview him soon. Like Ethan, he's also running his family's winery.

Cole lets go of me to chat with the bartender, and my body unfurls in relief that we're no longer touching.

"Here, drink up," Cole tells me, handing me a water bottle.

I may be drunk, but I'm still cognizant enough to listen for the crack of the seal to break on the water bottle before bringing it up to my lips for a drink. I don't know if it's paranoia trickled in from the smell of weed wafting around or the cool water has slightly sobered me, but I'm now keenly aware that I don't know this man. I should go back to Elyse and Layla.

I turn to leave, and the water in my bottle sloshes over the top due to my unsteady steps.

"Sit down for a second. Before you get hurt," Cole says, tugging on my arms until he's gently guided me into a barstool. His eyes dance with amusement as he watches me. "You gotta watch out for the Ledger girls, they'll drink you under the table."

"I had no idea," I say more to myself than to him.

He hops on the barstool next to mine, looking completely content and relaxed. In fact, he looks sober.

"Have you had anything to drink tonight?" I blurt out.

He chuckles. "Just a beer."

My already flushed skin heats even more.

I drink more water and start to feel my eyes growing heavy. I could fall asleep right here if I let myself.

"Maybe I should take you home," he says, his brows scrunching in worry.

My head feels too heavy for my neck, so I let it tip back to relieve some of the tension. Unable to stand the vest any longer, I work at the buttons, fumbling slightly because the tips of my fingers feel numb. Eventually, I get it off and take a deep breath, my first all night, and I feel so much better already. When I sit back up, Cole is watching me with an odd look.

He smirks. "Even drunk off your ass, you're easily the sexiest woman in the room."

Oh.

My brain grabs hold of his suggestive words, bouncing them around. It's not that I think Cole is bad looking, it's that I don't think of him that way. In fact, I can only think of one person who's suggestive words I want and it's—

"Ready to go home?" a voice says, sneaking up on me.

My head whips, trying to find the source, even though I know exactly who it is because I'd recognize that deep timbre anywhere.

"Ethan!" I yell excitedly and fling myself at him, my arms wrapping around his neck.

A whoosh of air leaves him as he grunts from my forceful leap.

"I thought you left."

"Nope," he whispers against my head, his warm breath caressing my ear.

I fight the urge to burrow into him at the same time that he starts to peel me off, taking a noticeable step away from me. I avert my eyes, trying to mask my disappointment. He clearly doesn't like me touching him.

"Ledger." Cole assesses Ethan, standing and squaring up against him.

"Benton." Ethan mirrors Cole's stance.

My eyes bounce between the two men. Are they going to fight? What's happening right now? Their eyes are locked in what looks like a deadly stare-off. Tension crackles in the air, and a bundle of nerves tightens in my stomach. Positioned in the middle, am I the only thing keeping these two from pouncing on each other?

Cole cracks first. A grin splits his face, and before I can fully register the shift, he bursts into laughter, doubling over and slapping his knee. I look over at Ethan, he's not laughing like Cole is, but the corners of his lips are twitching and the edges of his eyes are creased with a hint of humor.

Am I missing something?

"What just happened?" I ask Ethan, still trying to wrap my mind around their interaction.

Cole wipes a tear from his eye, still chuckling. "Good to see you, man."

Ethan nods, moving around me and clapping Cole on the back. "What are you two up to?" Ethan asks us, but he's looking directly at me, his expression unreadable.

"I was about to take her home. She can barely stand," Cole says, like I'm not right next to him. He points between us. "How do you guys know each other?"

Ethan stiffens slightly, and his eyes grow darker. If I'm not mistaken, there's a challenge there, unspoken but clear.

"Marisa is staying in my cottage," he tells Cole, eyes still fixed on me.

The way he worded that made it sound like I'm literally staying in the cottage with him, but I don't correct him because part of me wants his claim. Ethan's probably trying to save me from his playboy friend and doesn't actually mean anything by it, but I can't help the gooey feeling coating my insides like warm honey.

"Ready to go home?" Ethan repeats, and I melt.

Home.

Everything about that felt electric, like a current is running through me.

I nod, and Ethan's hand grazes the small of my back as he guides me to stand before dragging around to my side, splaying out to grip between my ribs and hip.

"See you around, Cole," Ethan says, as he walks me out of the bar

I was starting to sober, growing more sleepy than anything, but now that familiar drunk feeling has returned and it has nothing to do with alcohol.

As we step outside, the cool night air hits my face, causing my breath to fog.

"Wait," I gasp. "I didn't say bye to anyone."

He glances down at me and laughs quietly. I love that sound. In fact, I think it's my favorite sound. "I know. Something tells me they'll live."

We walk a few more paces until he abruptly stops. Before I can gather my bearings, his palm is sliding under my thighs and my stomach dips as my feet lift off the ground.

He's carrying me.

Like full on, princess-style carrying me.

"What are you doing?" I screech.

"I'm carrying you," he deadpans.

Well, no shit. "Why?"

He keeps walking, his hot breath heating my chest. "Because at the snail's pace you were walking, we wouldn't get to my truck before sunup."

I like this a little too much. I've never been carried by a man before. Ever. A swarm of butterflies has taken flight inside me, so powerful I'm certain he can hear the flapping of their wings. If I turned my head slightly, I could nuzzle his neck, feel his warm skin against my lips. I just might. What's the worst he could do?

Would he like it? Would it be his undoing? I know I said I wouldn't let myself get distracted, but that ship has sailed. I'm distracted as hell; by his scent, and his scruffy beard, and the way his rough hands gently touch me. I bet they would feel even better—

"Here we are." Ethan slowly places me back down, ensuring I have my footing before letting go. The moment he's no longer touching me, my body shutters at the loss of contact.

He opens the passenger door and grabs hold of my hand to help me up. The hand hold is brief, but the lingering heat he leaves behind sears my palm. Just when I think he's going to shut the door, he catches me by surprise and buckles me up. My breath hitches as he clicks the belt in place and his heavy-lidded eyes hold mine.

I lick my lips and watch his eyes track the movement. His normally mossy eyes have gone dark, fully dilated and shining from the overhead streetlight. Risking my pride, I lean forward, blurring the invisible line we've drawn. I can't remember the last time I wanted so desperately to be kissed.

He inches closer, and my entire body stills, save for my erratic heart threatening to leap out of my throat. I want to know what he tastes like. I want to know if his beard will scratch against my skin like I've been imagining it would. I want his gentle touch to be a little not so gentle, unrestrained and unguarded, just for me.

He's close enough to me now I can feel the ghost of his lips, the soft heat of them invading my senses. Just when I think he's going to crash his mouth to mine, the heat dissolves, replaced with cold air.

He pulled away.

He rejected me.

My face burns, and I turn away from him so he doesn't see the impact he has on me.

He closes the door and walks around to his side. Not looking at me he starts the truck and silently cranks up the heat. I feel like a fool. Like a silly, stupid girl. Of course he doesn't want me; he's done nothing to make me think otherwise. I built something up in my head that wasn't real. As we drive away from the bar, I pivot myself away from him, curling my body against the door and closing my heavy eyes. Never again. Never again will I let myself go there.

CHAPTER 24

Marisa

OH, GOOD, YOU'RE UP

C an someone turn down the sun?

Dry and crusted with last night's makeup, my lashes stick together as my eyes peel open. I wince at the harsh light. My head throbs relentlessly, pounding with the rhythm of my heartbeat. I crank my neck, feeling the dull pain of a strain. I slept on my stomach, and I never sleep on my stomach. Moaning, I roll over, reaching for my lumbar pillow, but I don't feel it. My hand pats along the opposite side of the bed. It's not there. Forcing myself to sit up slightly, I turn to find it.

None of my pillows are here. Neither are my blankets.

Something isn't right.

Everything is backward.

I rub my eyes, trying to get them to adjust. I'm definitely in a cottage, but it's not *my* cottage. Did I go inside the wrong one last night?

A burst of panic hits me, and I pat down my body. Relief floods through me when I find I'm still wearing last night's clothing, minus that nightmare of a vest. I slide my thumb under the band of my underwear and I'm relieved to find they're firmly in place. Nothing like *that* happened, thankfully.

The events of last night start to flash through my head like a montage of fuzzy photographs. I remember taking the lemon drop shots, seeing Ethan, dancing a little, and then it starts to get a little hazy. There were tequila shots and that guy, Cole, and then it's all a blur. The last thing I remember is a man's warm, callused hands sliding under my thighs, carrying me, and putting me in a truck. I remember they were callused because of how they scraped across my skin. And I remember feeling like I was being cocooned in a warm blanket, like I was safe.

Cole must've taken me home, but not knowing what cottage I was in, he let me into the wrong one.

The slapping sound of skin padding against hardwood, slow and quiet, approaches the room. Whoever it is, they're being intentionally quiet, as if they don't want to wake me. Before my brain can wake up enough to start filtering through whoever is in this cottage with me, Ethan appears in the doorway with bare feet, well-worn jeans, and a white T-shirt. His hair is still wet from a shower.

"Oh, good, you're up." He says it so casually. Like it's not weird that I woke up in his bed.

Oh, my God. I slept in Ethan's bed.

He must see the panic on my face, because he chuckles. Ethan chuckles, smiling freely.

That's even weirder than sleeping in his bed.

"Calm down," he says. "I couldn't get your drunk ass inside your place last night, so I put you to sleep in here. I slept on the couch."

That's strange. Because all of these cottages take the same key. Either he doesn't know that, or he *does* know that. I'm struggling to process it, so I push it down. I'll deal with that detail later. When I'm not foggy from alcohol.

He hands me a glass of water and sets a cup of coffee on the nightstand. "Water first then you can have some coffee." Then he reaches into his pocket and produces a small pill bottle. "And some ibuprofen in case you're feeling like shit."

My eyes dart between the three items. This is a surprisingly sweet gesture. I'm not sure what to make of it.

My mouth is dry and cotton-y so I chug the water and take two of the pills. All the while, Ethan remains in the room, watching me, amusement in his eyes.

Laugh it up.

I can only imagine what I look like. My hair sticking up on all ends, a tangled rat's nest. My makeup is probably smudged and clown-like. Basically, I'm pretty sure I look the worst I ever have.

"Thank you...for...all of this."

He nods with a gentle smile. "I have to go in to work, but you're welcome to stay as long as you'd like."

"Isn't it Sunday? And where's Goose?" I look around, waiting to see his nosy big eyes, but he's not around.

"It's not really a nine-to-five job." He laughs. "And Goose is at my parent's house. It's just you and me."

I swallow, trying to ignore the way my stomach is dipping.

"Anyway," he continues. "I'll see you."

I remain sitting up at the edge of the bed, still in shock, as I hear Ethan move through the cottage.

The front door creaks. "Bye, Marisa," Ethan calls out before I hear it lock into place.

More memories of last night flash to me. Pretending to be Ethan's girlfriend, Elyse bullying me into more shots, and then another one hits me. I jerk forward and my head spins. Shit!

He carried me out of the bar.

Oh, God. My body winces. I'm not sure why the thought of Cole carrying me out doesn't really phase me, but imagining myself in Ethan's arms sends me into a spiral.

I hope that's the worst of it. I might die of mortification if there's more.

According to Elyse, brunch is a must when nursing a hangover.

After leaving Ethan's, I hop in the shower. Between that and the water, coffee, and meds, I feel like a brand new person. Still a little shaky, and occasionally nauseous, but not like the dumpster fire I felt like this morning.

Elyse said to meet her at Flat Stone at 10:30 a.m.

The restaurant is an extension of the winery, with its own entrance.

When I get inside, Elyse is already at a table, wearing sunglasses and very clearly still hungover.

"Why do you look so pretty and alive?" she grumbles. "You're supposed to look like garbage, like the rest of us."

I take the seat across from her. "I feel like garbage, if that helps."

I can feel her eyes roll through her sunglasses. "I already ordered us some Bloody Marys."

"More alcohol?" I wince.

"Hair of the dog, duh."

"Remind me what that means again?"

She smiles deviously. "It's when you keep drinking to avoid a hangover."

My stomach rolls, and acid trickles up my throat. I think another sip of alcohol would be my undoing. I'm pretty sure it's a myth anyway. I already did the wild, drunken nights out in my early twenties. As much fun as I had last night, that was a rare occurrence for me. I'd much rather have a night in than drink the night away and spend the remainder of my weekend feeling like I got hit by a truck. Elyse is obviously someone who enjoys going out a lot more than I do.

The waitress arrives, setting a Bloody Mary in front of each of us, and takes our orders. Elyse orders two breakfasts, one sweet, a Belgian waffle, the other savory, a breakfast scramble. I stick to my usual, safe order, and get an omelet.

"I heard my brother carried you out of the bar last night." She's smiling wide, giving me a suggestive look.

A blush skirts across my cheeks. "Apparently he did. I have no recollection. But he got me home safely, so that was nice."

I leave out the part where he actually got me to *his* home safely. And that I slept in his bed. It's really none of her business. Besides, nothing happened.

"He never goes out. I was kind of surprised he did."

I shrug, not sure where she's going with the conversation.

"He left his card at the bar last night, and I was going to run it over to him after we finish eating. Want to come with me?"

"Sure. I guess so."

She smiles, looking pleased with herself.

While we're eating, I tell her about my upcoming job interview. The Monday after I applied, I got called and asked to come in for an interview on the thirtieth. I'm still shocked they called me. I thought I would be more excited, but I think it hasn't fully hit me.

"I'm happy I finally landed an interview, but I'm nervous about the drive."

She looks at me, confused. "Why?"

"According to the weather predictions for Snoqualmie

Pass, there's supposed to be heavy snow, and my car does not do well in snow."

She slides her sunglasses down, revealing bloodshot eyes. "Snow? Already? But it's October."

"I know, I was surprised, too."

A small smile plays on her lips. "I think everything will work out. You'll see."

CHAPTER 25

Ethan

SOAKING MY FACE

"I come bearing gifts."

Elyse waltzes into the empty tasting room, looking hungover as shit, with Marisa walking behind her. The corners of my lips tug at the memory of Marisa waking up in my bed this morning.

My fucking bed.

Seeing her in it did weird things to my head.

When I laid her down last night, I stood and stared like an absolute creep, marveling at the way her hair fanned out across my pillows. The way she immediately curled herself into the fetal position, as if she was craving the comfort of being held so much she had to hold herself. My heart seized in my chest, and for a moment, I let myself imagine things I had no business imagining. What it would be like to see her in not just my bed, but our bed. What it would be like to wake up with that long hair of hers tangled and splayed out on my chest, her body molded against mine. What it would be like to nuzzle the pillows and smell her sweet vanilla scent. I watched her stir and bury herself deeper in my blankets, a small smile resting on her sleeping face. I wondered if she could smell me on the bed and that's why she smiled, or if it was the alcohol still working its way through her. It was probably the alcohol.

My thoughts of Marisa are dangerous. They're deeper than attraction. They're weighted, almost tangible. She's like the bright sun I can't seem to stop staring into, even though I know if I stare long enough, I'll go blind. It would be irreversible. Permanent.

I forced myself to leave her, closing the door as an added barrier, and slept on the couch. I was already crossing too many lines. She could've easily been in her own bed, seeing as I have the key, but I convinced myself it was safer for her to be with me in case she got sick. I'm an expert at convincing myself of false truths to justify my actions. The actual truth is that I selfishly wanted her in my space and in my bed, if only for one night.

This morning, I took one look at her and could see the hangover was in full effect. Her hair was a mess, clothes twisted, makeup smeared, but none if it mattered, she still took my breath away. And if I were a different man—a man who wasn't afraid to go for the things he wanted, I would've crawled into that bed with her and taken care of her hangover a different way. I could just imagine spreading her perfect thighs wide and slipping off those lace panties I got a good look at last night. I would've buried my tongue in her warm pussy until she was soaking my face, shaking in orgasm, and then I would've slid my co—

"Earth to Ethan," Elyse sings. "Still waking up, I see."

My eyes dart to Marisa. I expect to find a look of repulsion from my inappropriate daydream, as if she had been able to see the fantasy I was playing in my head. Instead, she blushes and rewards me with a shy smile.

I've never seen that smile.

Fuck, it's cute.

I wonder if she remembers what almost happened in my

truck last night, because I haven't stopped thinking about it. It would've been wrong to allow it to happen. No matter how badly I want her, I don't want her when she can't consent. She was drunk, beyond drunk. And I'm fairly certain sober Marisa would never try to kiss me. In fact, she passed out not even five minutes later.

Based on her shy smile and content eyes, I'm going to bet she doesn't remember any of it. At least I know I did the right thing, because if we ever do kiss, I want her to remember every detail.

"Here's your card." Elyse hands me my credit card. "You left it at the bar like an amateur."

"Thanks," I take it, still distracted by thoughts of Marisa.

I begin polishing glasses to keep my hands busy. I'm one-hundred percent certain they're already polished, but if I don't keep myself busy, I'll do or say something stupid.

Elyse takes a seat, and Marisa joins her.

"You know," Elyse starts. My sister has a scheming look in her eyes, so I know something is up. "Marisa was telling me she has a job interview coming up."

I look over at Marisa, and she's wearing the happiest expression. "Congratulations," I tell her.

"Anyway," Elyse continues. "The thing is, it's in Seattle."

My chest sinks. Obviously, I know her time here is temporary, but I didn't realize how temporary until right now. I shouldn't care. I knew she was never going to stay. But I guess now I might be starting to care. What a fucking mess.

"Okay," I say hesitantly, not sure where she's going with this.

"Well, her car isn't the greatest, and the pass has such unpredictable weather." Elyse is looking at me like I should be connecting the dots in this conversation. I have no idea what she's trying to get at.

"Spit it out already, Elle."

She glares at me, annoyed. "Don't you have to be in Wood-inville on the thirtieth?"

"Yeah." I shrug.

"What a coincidence. That's the same day as Marisa's interview. You two should ride up together, since you have all-wheel drive."

Marisa's eyes meet mine, and she's already shaking her head. "Oh, gosh, no, it's totally fine. I don't need a ride. Seriously. My car will be fine. Really, Ethan, it's fine I—"

My head is already nodding before my mouth can catch up. "Yeah, I'll take you. But I'm going up the night before. Do you have somewhere to stay? There's room at the apartment above the tasting room, but you probably wouldn't be comfortable."

Her eyes blink rapidly, flooded with disbelief. Did she really think I wouldn't take her?

"Oh, um, wow. Thank you. I can stay with my friend Hillary. I haven't seen her since I moved here and it would be nice to catch up."

"Okay, sounds like a plan."

Our stares anchor together, and something about this moment feels like the turning of a page, so many unspoken words hanging between us.

"I'm such a genius. What would you guys do without me?" Elyse says.

I know exactly what that was. For whatever reason, Elyse is trying to push Marisa and I together, and for once, I'm not mad about my little sister's meddling.

CHAPTER 26

Ethan

I HAVE A MARISA FETISH

I didn't think this through. There's no way I'm going to survive hours alone with Marisa, cramped in the tight quarters of my truck.

I just know she's going to be wearing that sweet vanilla perfume I always smell coming off her skin, and some little outfit that will be beckoning my eyes off the road the whole drive there. Being alone with her that long, I'm bound to say something stupid and get tongue twisted and make a fool of myself. She may have accepted my friendship, but we're still on shaky ground. I denied it for long enough, pushed her to the point I thought she would hate me for sure, but the jig is up. I can't seem to stay away from her. And now that I've gotten to this point, there's no going back. I'm in deep, whether I like it or not. If this ever evolves past friendship is irrelevant. I'll take whatever she's willing to give.

We planned to be on the road no later than 10:00 a.m. since snowfall on the pass was predicted to start later in the afternoon, but I got tied up with the final details to wrap up harvest for the season, and Marisa had a deadline to meet to release the first edition of *The Vine*. Now, it's nearly three o'clock. I've just put the truck in park outside Marisa's cottage when I see her trying to lug a giant suitcase out the front door. The thing is almost as big as her, and it's comical watching her try to maneuver it.

I jump out and get to her just before the two steps on the porch. "Trying to throw out your back?" I grab the suitcase from her and lift it, taking it down the steps to my truck. It weighs a shit ton, and I am not exaggerating. "You do know we're only going to be gone one night, right?"

She shoots me a glare. "This interview is important, and I needed outfit options. For a guy that has sisters, you should know these things."

I was right about the distracting little outfit. Although by most standards, it's not distracting at all. She's wearing leggings and a hoodie with some open-toed sandals. Her white painted toes stand out against her olive skin. Who knew toes could be so sexy? Do I have a foot fetish? I think about it for a moment and decide it has nothing to do with her shoes or her clothes, it's her. I have a Marisa fetish, plain and simple.

We get loaded up and on the road. On our way out of town, I stop at the gas station before we get to the highway.

"Want anything from inside?" she asks me before I start pumping gas.

"Surprise me."

An excited grin splits her face. "Okay."

As the gas pumps, I run through the mental checklist I always do before a longer drive. I already checked the oil last night, and that's good to go. The tires all feel good. There's plenty of water and roadside supplies underneath my back seats for emergencies, and all the windows are free and clear.

Marisa emerges from the Pit Stop carrying a bag full of junk food. It's rude of me to assume it's junk food, but I know for a fact that the Pit Stop doesn't so much as carry apples. It's all pure gas station trash food. And for some reason, this woman loves the stuff.

We both get back in at the same time, our doors closing in sync.

"Find anything good?"

She buckles up and sets the bag on the floor. "Only the best of course. I got nachos, corn nuts, two pops, a variety of candy bars, and some questionable-looking corn dogs. As I'm sure you remember, I'm quite the gas station food connoisseur."

"Which one is for me?"

She laughs, handing me a corn dog. "In case it has food poisoning, you can eat it first as the test dummy. It's the least you can do for ruining my dinner that night."

I take an exaggerated bite. I'm not too worried about it. I lived off of these as a kid and know for a fact that as stuck up as Shane is about food, these are still a frequent part of his diet.

She grabs a red box out of the bag. "Want some Cheez-Its to go with it?"

I audibly gag. "No. Those are the worst. I hate Cheez-Its."

Her head snaps at me. "What?! I think this friendship might be over."

A huff of a laugh falls out of me. "Think of it this way, more for you."

My answer seems to please her, because she happily shrugs and pops an orange cracker in her mouth.

Once I get onto the highway toward I-90, Marisa is already on her third Taylor Swift song.

"Got anything else on that playlist besides the entire *Reputation* album?"

She laughs. "I'm surprised you know what album this is."

"I have sisters. And I like the occasional Taylor Swift song. Plus, it's one of her more upbeat albums."

She stares at me, openmouthed.

"What?" I smile. "Should I hand in my man-card or something?"

"Just the opposite. I couldn't be more attracted to you than I am right now."

Heat creeps up my neck and flames my cheeks. There's humor in her voice, so I know she's only fucking with me, but damn do I wish it was true. I want her to find me attractive. I want her to see the good parts of me. It's delusional of me to think she would ever see me the way I see her, especially after I treated her the way I did, but it's nice to think that maybe we're on the same wavelength, if only for a moment.

After the song ends, she puts on an Arctic Monkeys song, which is a lot more my speed.

"Do you think we'll make it there before it gets dark?" she asks, her voice tense and worried as she looks out the window.

"I'm not sure. I guess we'll see."

CHAPTER 27

Marisa

THE BATES MOTEL

I fell asleep shortly after our trip began. I don't know what it is about long car rides, but they put me to sleep faster than anything over the counter ever could. I must have been deep in sleep, because when the voice of a man pulls me out of my slumber, I gasp in shock, completely disoriented. It takes me a second to gather my bearings and realize, for some reason, we're at a standstill, pulled off to the side of the road. The man is wearing a high-visibility jacket and has his head poked through the driver's door window, chatting with Ethan. The last thing I remember is looking out the window at a sunny day, and now it's dark, with white snow falling in huge flakes, blanketing the ground.

"You're going to have to turn around or find somewhere to stay, because DOT is shutting the pass down. The snowfall is pretty heavy up there, and we're predicting some avalanche activity."

"When do you think you'll reopen it?"

"Probably not until tomorrow morning. Where did you folks come from?"

"We're coming from Red Mountain. It's about three hours east of here."

"Oh yeah, I've heard of it. Wine country right?"

"Yes, sir."

"Well, I wouldn't recommend heading back. I heard the canyon outside Ellensburg had a series of accidents and car pile ups. Your best bet is going to be taking the next exit and hoping Roslyn or Cle Elum have some hotel vacancies for the night."

Ethan and the man chat a bit more. Once we're back to driving, Ethan apologizes.

"Sorry you had to wake up like that."

"I'm the one that's sorry. I was *that* person, falling asleep on you. And now we're going to be stuck here for the night."

He turns up the dial on the heater. "I'm not upset about any of that. I would be more upset if I was all the way back in Red Mountain hearing about you having to find some road-side motel in the middle of a snowstorm, completely alone."

"I'm a big girl. I'm perfectly capable of figuring things out on my own." I can't help the attitude that slips out of me. I don't appreciate being underestimated simply because I'm a woman. And I just woke up from a nap, which is when I'm at my bitchiest.

"That's not what I mean," he says gently. "Of course you're capable, you just shouldn't have to do it alone. I'm glad I came."

Warmth surrounds my body, and it has nothing to do with the heater. I shouldn't have snapped at him. He's been nothing but sweet lately, going above and beyond anything any other guy has ever done for me.

He takes the exit to Roslyn. I've passed the sign countless times but have never actually ventured into the town.

"Cute town," I comment as we drive through the main stretch.

The town looks like it has a bit of a magical flare as the heavy snowflakes fall, veiling everything in soft white.

Ethan points to a grocery store parking lot. "I'm going to pull in here and make some calls. See if we can find a couple of rooms for the night."

While he does that, I send some texts to Hillary and my dad, updating them on the situation. I also fire off an email to the HR rep who sent me the interview invite, warning them that weather may prevent my ability to get to the interview and that I will update them if I'm no longer able to make it.

"I was really hoping Suncadia would have vacancies," Ethan says. "But they're all booked up and so is the rest of Cle Elum. I called a few hotels here in Roslyn and they all directed me to the Huckleberry Lodge. I called them and they have one room available. So, what do you think? Stay there or drive back and see if we can at least make it to Ellensburg?"

I look around, watching the snow fall heavier by the minute. "Let's try the huckleberry place."

Ethan types it into the GPS, though we soon find out that wasn't necessary, since it's down the road.

The Huckleberry Lodge is everything you would imagine a crappy roadside motel to look like. In fact, I'm surprised it's not called *The Bates Motel*.

"Sure you don't want to try Ellensburg?" Ethan asks, his face scrunching as he looks at the ramshackle building.

"With the luck we're having so far, we could end up at a shittier place than this. Let's stay here. It can't be any worse inside."

Ethan leaves me with the engine running while he runs to the front office to take care of the check in. When he returns a few minutes later, he moves his truck in front of the room marked with the number eighteen. While he unloads our bags, I go inside.

I was wrong. Somehow, the inside is even worse. The

carpet is an interesting shade of brown, shaggy and worn, and the walls are paneled. I feel like I've stepped into the 1970s, and not in a good way. Taking a deep breath, I'd guess that was also the last time it was properly cleaned.

"This place is a dump," Ethan says behind me, rolling in my giant suitcase.

"You took the words right out of my mouth."

In the distractions of getting here and the snow and the detour, I'm now realizing I'm going to have to sleep in this room with Ethan. I've slept in his bed and I was napping in the car with him an hour ago, so it shouldn't be a big deal, but it feels like a really, really big deal. There's something so intimate about beds and changing into pajamas and brushing your teeth alongside someone. It's all very couple-y, and we are not a couple. We're friends.

Thank God there are two beds, because I wouldn't let an animal sleep on this carpet, let alone a person, so we would've definitely been stuck sharing a bed. My face reddens at the thought.

With my head down and gaze averted, I claim the bed furthest from the door. If this happens to be one of those murder motels, at least I'll get a fair warning when the killer goes after Ethan first.

I sit on the bed, fully clothed with my legs stretched out in front of me. Even like this, I can smell the musty bedding, feel the itchy fabric rub against my leggings. I only brought skimpy choices for pajamas because Hillary keeps her house as hot as a sauna. Thinking about all this bedding making contact with my skin somehow makes me feel even itchier. Meanwhile, Ethan is working on latching the door, pulling it, making sure it's actually locked. I watch as he moves the lone chair in the corner and wedges it under the doorknob. I can't help but smile, because it's exactly what I would've done.

Brandon used to make fun of my obsession with locking

doors. When we lived together, every evening I would run through my routine of checking the doors and windows, making sure they were all locked. That's how I grew up. It's not like we lived in a bad part of town or there were ever incidents that made us question our safety, but my dad made it a habit to lock up the house before we all went to sleep and it always made me feel safe. As an adult, I carry on with that practice. Brandon grew up with nannies and vacation homes—or as he would put it, "comfortable"—meaning the thought of someone breaking into his home in the middle of the night never even crossed his mind. I'm glad Ethan is a lock up the house kind of person. I feel my shoulders relax knowing we're safely locked in here for the night, even if it means being in this shitty room, pretending I'm not wondering what Ethan sleeps in.

"Mind if I use the bathroom first?" Ethan asks, cutting through the silence.

"Nope, go ahead."

He rifles through his bag and pulls out what I'm assuming is his toiletry bag. I can't stop my mind from the journey it's now on. Will he shower? What body wash does he use? Will he shave or brush his teeth? *Gahh!* This is too intimate.

I simultaneously feel like I absolutely need to know the answers to all my nosy questions and like this is a side only a girlfriend or wife gets to see, and I'm getting a front-row seat.

While he does his thing in the bathroom, I turn on the TV, because I desperately need noise. If I hear him pee, I'll spend an embarrassing amount of time thinking about his penis. There is something seriously wrong with me. I shouldn't be thinking about Ethan's penis.

He's out a lot more quickly than I thought he would be. He goes back to his corner of the room, so I grab my own toiletry bag and pajamas and barricade myself in the bathroom. Halfway through washing my face, it hits me that it's still fairly early. How will we pass the time? And will there be food? I'm not hungry now, but I will be soon, and Ethan does not need to meet my hangry personality, because she's a bitch and I do not claim her.

I do my skin care routine and change into my pajamas. They're the most modest pair I brought, pink short shorts covered in little red cherries and a matching tight-fitted tank top. Normally, I wouldn't wear a bra, but I am not about to go braless in front of this man. I may be able to hide my attraction to him pretty well, but my nipples would betray me instantly.

My hand lingers on the doorknob. I'm actually very nervous for him to see me like this. I've never been the type to be uncomfortable being seen without makeup or in my hideous baggy sweats. Hell, we met when I looked scrubbed out from the drive to Red Mountain. He's seen me looking less than dressed up several times since we've met, so this shouldn't feel weird. Yet it does. This is vulnerable. Taking a deep breath, I force myself to look unaffected and step through the door.

My gaze avoids even so much as looking in Ethan's direction, even though I swear I can feel his eyes on me. When I sense him turn his head in the opposite direction, I sneak a peek at him, hiding my face with my mass of hair, and I swear his cheeks are tinted a light shade of pink.

Ethan clears his throat, slicing through the deafening silence between us. "Are you hungry at all? I was going to try to find something to hold us over until morning."

His eyes hold mine, almost to the point that I feel like they're unable to look anywhere else.

"Sure. Do you want me to come with you?"

The heat of his stare has me thanking the universe I kept my bra on.

"No, you're already dressed for the night. Any food aversions I need to be aware of?"

"Olives. I hate them in all forms."

He smiles and then nods before he starts the task of moving the chair and unlocking the door. "Put the chair back against the door after I leave." He pulls out his phone. "Give me your number so I can text you before I come in, that way you know it's me."

A sudden bout of shyness hits me as we exchange numbers. I bite the inside of my cheek to distract from my rapid heart rate and the fluttering in my stomach, hoping he doesn't notice the nervous energy coursing through me.

Ethan returns with tacos.

"I figured tacos were the safest bet. You seemed to like them last time."

We share a look, and it makes my stomach somersault.

"Fair warning, though," he continues. "It didn't look like the most authentic place, so don't come for me."

He sets the bag on the table by the corner, and we work to unload the foil covered paper plates. The scents of seasoned meats and cilantro waft from the tacos.

"It smells good, so I'm sure they're edible."

Since the table is too small to eat at, we decide it makes the most sense to eat in our respective beds.

"Any TV requests?" I ask him.

I get the feeling Ethan isn't much of a TV watcher. He shrugs while I scroll through the channels, confirming my suspicions. As I'm scrolling through like it's 1995, since there's no guide on this thing, I randomly land on a Spanish-speaking channel playing a telenovela. I pause for a moment, trying to figure out if it's one I recognize.

"My mom lives out of the country, so sometimes we'll try to watch a show together to stay connected even though we're so far apart. Usually, it's a novela of some kind, but right now we're not watching anything."

I'm not sure why I decided to volunteer that information to him. I'm sure he has no interest in mine and my mom's TV habits.

"You miss her?" he asks hesitantly, while chewing softly.

"All the time. Especially lately. She's out there having the fun she missed out on."

He's stopped eating and is watching me, giving me time to continue.

"My mom had me at nineteen and my dad was twenty," I explain. "I think they tried their best, but you know, babies raising a baby isn't ideal."

Ethan gives me a cautious expression, opening his mouth a few times before he decides to speak. "I have a question," he starts.

His face twists, and I can tell he's worried he's going to upset me, so I give him a nod to continue.

"Why don't you have the same last name as your dad?"

I breathe a smile, relieved it's an easy question. "It's really not that controversial. My parents weren't married yet when I was born, and my mom thought I should have her name, I guess. And then weirdly enough, when they got married, she took his last name, and I was the only Castilla, until she changed her name after the divorce. I've thought about changing it, but it feels too late now. Plus, I'll probably take my future husband's last name."

I turn my focus back on trying to find something to watch, but I feel Ethan's stare stay on me a few beats longer.

I stop on another novela, pausing to see if it's one I've watched before.

He points to the TV. "Is this one any good?"

I shrug. "I'm not sure, but we can give it a try. Is the Spanish going to be too fast for you? Even though you somehow secretly know Spanish fluently."

"It's not really a secret. You assumed I didn't know it. My mom wanted us all to know a second language, so we all speak something else besides English. I picked Spanish because I knew I was going to work for the winery in some capacity and a lot of the workers speak Spanish. It made sense. Plus, now that I'm the boss, I can communicate easily and I feel like they respect me more because I try."

A teasing smirk crosses my lips as I look at him. "You think they respect you, but really it's because they have to wait until you leave the room to talk shit about you, because they know you'll understand."

He gives me a sad little pout. "Probably."

We start watching the novela, and even though we missed the first ten minutes, and it's clearly not the first episode, we're quickly sucked in.

"Do you think she knows that he's secretly her father and she's acting like she doesn't know?" Ethan asks. He's so engrossed in the show it's actually cute. It's like the time Hillary and I introduced Archie to *Love Is Blind*. He still pretends he hates that show but will actively watch every episode and then need to discuss it afterward.

"There is no way she knows. I think she's suspicious about him in general. He's not a good guy. Obviously, she's not going to trust him."

The show must be airing a marathon. We get two more episodes in, but when the next episode is about to start, my eyes feel heavy with sleep.

"We should get to bed. We'll leave first thing in the morning so you can make it to your interview."

I yawn, slinking under the scratchy sheets. "Sounds good."

Ethan shuts off the TV but leaves the lamp between us on while he uses the bathroom.

A heavy weight sits on my chest, making it hard to breathe as I wait for him to finish his nighttime routine. The intimacy I felt earlier returns in full force. It's more intense now that we've shared food and bonded over a TV show and I've been lying around in my indecent pajamas for most of the evening.

Ethan emerges from the bathroom in low-slung flannel bottoms and a white T-shirt. I watch as he walks from the bathroom to his bed, lightly tugging on the collar of his shirt.

"Sleep however you usually sleep. No need to keep on a shirt or something if it's uncomfortable." I blurt it out before my brain can stop me. I immediately want to swallow back all the words. My cheeks are surely bright red, and I'm hoping the glow from the lamp masks it.

Ethan merely nods and then starts lifting the hem of his T-shirt. I should look away. I should look anywhere else than at the man in front of me, playing into my strip tease fantasy. The higher the shirt lifts, the more I feel like I'm in a free fall. His toned stomach comes into view. It's not the kind of body that spends hours in the gym, more like the kind that takes an active role in the labor of his vineyards. Sturdy and solid, dusted in neatly trimmed dark hair. My hands itch to touch him, to run along every groove, trace every line, and feel that prickly hair scrape across my fingertips. When his shirt is fully off, he turns and folds it, returning it to his suitcase, completely unaware that I'm drooling like a dog, practically panting. My skin feels overheated and restless, like I could combust at any moment. And I just may with the ache building between my thighs.

"Are you done checking me out?"

I jackknife in bed, sitting up. "I was not checking you out." *Deny, deny, deny.*

"Liar." I can practically feel his smirk. He wrestles in the bed and then turns to switch off the lamp, cloaking us in darkness.

"Goodnight, Marisa."

"Goodnight, Ethan."

CHAPTER 28

Ethan

I BELIEVE IN YOU

I f it was possible to die from blue balls, I would be a dead man.

Who knew little cherries could be so sexy, especially when they're scattered across that scrap of fabric she called shorts. I could practically see her pussy, and I know for an absolute fact she wasn't wearing underwear. There wasn't a line or indent of a thong anywhere across her ass. And believe me, I was looking. I could hardly look anywhere else. My eyes kept coming back to her like there were magnets all over her body. It's a miracle I didn't come in my pants the moment she came out of the bathroom in those sinful pajamas.

I hardly slept, my mind working in overdrive, fantasizing about Marisa in more ways than I can count. I can barely look her in the eye this morning. Thank goodness she's in the bathroom getting ready, it gives me a moment to wrangle my racing thoughts.

As soon as day broke, I hopped into the shower. The water barely started beating down on my back before I curled my fingers around my painfully hard cock. I thought I had self-control, that I had better restraint than this, but I was wrong.

With my palm braced on the tile wall, I pictured her. I pictured her on her knees, those doe eyes begging for me, pouty lips in a perfect O. I pictured her bent over, me sliding my cock between those delicious ass cheeks. I pictured pulling on her long hair and wrapping it around my fist while I fucked her from behind. I pictured picking her up and feeling her bitable thighs wrap around my waist as she sunk down on my cock. Her smell was everywhere, infiltrating the bathroom and tangling with my fantasies. I came hard, my cum jetting out and splattering across the shower tiles. After my blinding orgasm faded, realization hit me. I was beyond fucked. It doesn't matter how many times I picture her while I fuck my own fist, it'll never be enough. I want the real thing. I want her, and I don't think it's a one and done kind of want. It's consuming and visceral.

As I'm seated on the edge of the bed, trying to keep my thoughts in line, she walks out of the bathroom dressed, wearing a form-fitting skirt with a blouse tucked in. She comes up to me and does a spin.

"Well? What do you think? Does it say *hire me*?"

"I would definitely hire you." *I would also fuck you, but I'll keep that to myself.*

She stares at her reflection in the mirror. "Is this skirt flattering? I feel like it makes my stomach look weird."

Is she seeing something I don't?

"You look gorgeous." I have to hold in my wince for letting my mouth speak before my brain could intercept the compliment from me.

Her hands that were smoothing over the fabric of the skirt stop mid-stroke, and her eyes meet my gaze in the mirror. "You really think so?"

Her voice sounds so vulnerable it almost doesn't sound like her. Marisa usually comes off as very confident. I would never guess she sees herself as anything less than beautiful.

"Have I ever lied to you?"

"No. I don't think so."

"Well, I'm not about to start now."

I already checked the pass report, but we double check it again and thankfully it says it's clear. There's still snow covering the ground, but the sun is out and slowly melting everything. All the roofs are dripping in melted snow.

"I hope we make it on time," Marisa says as I pull out of the parking lot of the shittiest motel I've ever stayed in.

"We will. We have plenty of time."

Marisa grows quieter and quieter the closer we get to Seattle. By the time we're downtown, she's completely silent, her mouth drawn in a thin line, hands clenched in tight fists. I can practically feel the nervousness coming off her.

"Nervous?"

"Just a bit." She lets out a breathy laugh.

I pull into the loading zone outside the building her interview is in. It's one of the various skyscrapers that's part of the Seattle skyline.

"You're going to do great."

She takes a deep, shaky breath. "You think so?"

Every instinct in me wants nothing more than to pull her into my arms and try to give her comfort. I hate seeing her like this, so unsure of herself. The confidence she usually wears seems to have left her. Despite wanting to hold her, I can't. That would be weird. So I do the one thing I hope she won't pull away from, even if it is crossing a line that shouldn't be crossed. I grab her hand in mine, lacing our fingers together.

Her small, smooth hand fits nicely in my rough palm. For a moment, time suspends. My heart beats in fast succession, pounding the blood in my ears to the point that all noise dulls. It's just me and Marisa, holding hands, and nothing has ever felt more right.

Through thick lashes, she looks down at our intertwined hands and then meets my gaze.

I give her hand a squeeze. "You've got this."

"You sound so sure."

"I've only known you for a short while, but it's abundantly clear that there's nothing you can't do. I mean, look at you, writing for the newspaper and killing it. You've been in town for five minutes and you're already the town sweetheart. You're smart and kind and completely relentless. I believe in you."

Her eyes turn glassy, and she gives me a fragile smile, the corners of her mouth barely lifting.

I'm so gone for this girl. And I'm not sure how much longer I'll be able to keep it to myself, seeing as I can barely look away from her. I knew this trip was going to test me, but I didn't realize it was going to push me over the edge and down a free fall.

I don't stand a chance against those deep-brown eyes and sweet, sunshine smile. I never did. I was a fool for thinking pushing her away would diffuse my feelings for her. If anything, it made them stronger, and now, I'm aptly in the friend zone.

She reaches for the door, and I give her hand one final squeeze before letting her go.

"Break a leg."

Woodinville, a small, destination wine town, is a quick, thirty-minute drive north of Seattle. The meeting goes smoothly.

And truthfully, I could've done it over video chat. I won't tell Marisa that, though.

When I get back to Seattle, I wait in the loading zone for her to come out. I already sent her a text explaining where I was. A few minutes later, she emerges from the building with a beaming smile.

She slides into the truck, her wide smile still splitting her face.

"I take it the interview went well."

She throws her head back, sinking into the seat, and sighs. "It was amazing. I mean everything is mountains above the last company I was at, and their benefits package was amazing, and everyone seemed so nice. I couldn't ask for a better work environment. Plus, Zoe, my former coworker, works there, so I know it wasn't a bunch of smoke and mirrors."

As happy as I am for her, I can't help but feel the seed of anxiety plant and take root. If she gets this job, then that's it. She's gone. It's everything she wants, and I want that for her, but selfishly, I don't want her to leave before we have a chance to explore what this is. Right now, it's friendship, but I've caught her giving me the same longing stares I give her when she thinks I'm not paying attention. I hope to hell my feelings aren't one-sided. Maybe I was imagining the way she practically drooled watching me take off my shirt. Did I do it purposefully slow? Yes. But I also thought she wouldn't have a reaction to me. Still, a physical attraction and real feelings are completely different.

"That's great. I bet they'll give you an offer."

"I hope so. It's the waiting that's going to be torture. They also said the position wouldn't start until after the holidays. So, even if I get the job, I'll still be waiting around for a bit."

My blood pressure spikes. Two months. I have two months to explore if there actually is something between us. Or at least attempt to. I fully expect to be shot down the second I move past a line she isn't ready to cross. She hasn't spoken about it much, but I know her breakup is fresh, and she's probably not interested in getting involved with someone else so quickly. Least of all a guy still working toward earning her forgiveness.

"What time are we meeting up with your friends?"

"In thirty minutes. We're meeting them at Buckley's. And just to warn you, the place is a dive bar and incredibly loud. They're usually playing some sports game on the TVs and the crowd chants loudly. So, if it gets to be too much, let me know and we can go take a breather or walk around the block."

She busies herself, typing in the address for me on the screen, but I can hardly focus on that when I feel shocked by her consideration for me. She seems to know I get anxious in large crowds despite never having spoken about it. Rather than making me feel small for it, she weaves it into the conversation, offering me solutions if my anxiety gets to be too much. She really is pure sunshine. She has no idea that what she said means so much to me, and I have no way to truly express it.

CHAPTER 29

Marisa

GOOD ON PAPER

As I predicted, Buckley's is bustling with large groups and loud conversations despite it being two o'clock in the afternoon. Since my plans to stay with Hillary got squashed, we compromised and made plans to meet up for lunch before Ethan and I drive back to Red Mountain.

Ethan paid an exorbitant amount for parking, so we didn't have to walk further than a block. When we get in, Hillary and Archie are already at a booth waiting for us. I've only gone a little over a month without seeing Hillary in person, and her belly looks like its tripled in size, which I didn't think was possible.

"Yes, I look like a whale," she says, as she pulls me in for a hug. "I feel like Regina George." She releases me and sits back down.

"Why's that?"

"Because sweatpants are all that fit me right now." She points to her outfit as if that explains why she's in a cashmere lounge set instead of something dressier. She focuses her attention on Ethan. "Oh, gosh. I'm being rude." She extends her hand out to him. "I'm Hillary. You must be Ethan."

They introduce themselves, and then Archie and Ethan shake hands.

Archie is quick to warm up to Ethan, and the two end up in a riveting conversation about pickleball. Well, riveting for them. Hillary and I couldn't care less.

The entire meal, Hillary darts her eyes between me and Ethan with a curious look on her face. I'm not sure why, since we're doing an exceptional job of sharing one side of the booth without so much as touching our shoulders. It's a lot harder than it looks.

Our late lunch goes by way too quickly, but I know we can't linger because a ton of snow could easily dump on the pass again and leave us trapped for another night.

Ethan and Archie head to the bar to pay the bill, but before they do, I try to slip Ethan some cash. He refuses, like he has every other time I've tried to pay for something on this trip. Hillary watches our interaction with a knowing smile.

"You like him." Her smile is so self-satisfied, if she weren't pregnant, I'd kick her under the table. "And he doesn't seem anything like the serial killer I was expecting. In fact, he's stupid good-looking."

She gives me an exasperated look, and I fiddle with the remaining fries on my plate, ignoring her.

"I don't like him. We're friends."

She takes a long, loud slurp of lemonade. "If I looked at my male friends the way you look at Ethan, then I never would've married Archie. There's something there between you two, whether you want to admit it or not."

I cross my arms, suddenly feeling defensive. "It's too soon. I'm still processing the whole Brandon thing."

Hillary twists her mouth, grimacing. "Oh, please. That's bullshit and you know it. You were already falling out of love while you guys were still together. The only reason you were still with him was because you thought it was time to settle down and Brandon sounds good on paper."

Was I really with Brandon because he sounded good or because I loved him? Where was all this advice when I was still with the guy?

"Either way, it doesn't matter because if I get this job, then I'm moving back to Seattle, and Ethan has to stay in Red Mountain because the winery is there. So, what then? I give into the feelings only to fall for him and then have to move? I'm not doing long distance just to get broken up with months later over a text message."

"Wow, you've really thought about this, huh?"

"I'm being a realist."

"Whatever you say. All I'm saying is it might be worth it. Even if it's just for fun, he's hot and you're hot. Two hot people should be having wild sex."

"I see you're still horny as ever."

"Always," she says with a wink.

"Do you think you're going to get the job?" Ethan asks as we begin our journey back to Red Mountain.

I look down, twisting my fingers in my lap. I was so caught off guard to hear from Zoe and get called in for an interview, I haven't had time to sit in my thoughts and really mull it over. It's exactly what I said I wanted. This was the plan. But now, when I think of actually getting the job, and leaving, it doesn't feel like I thought it would. I'm starting to question what I even want anymore. In truth, I'm feeling lost.

I smile, but it's not genuine. "I guess we'll see."

"I like your friend Hillary," Ethan says, changing the subject. "She was looking at me a little odd, though."

A laugh bubbles out of me. "I swear she's usually so normal. The pregnancy has made her weird."

He nods, taking in my words. "How did she and her husband meet? Seems like kind of an odd pairing."

Hillary and Archie have a love story for the ages. It honestly sounds like the plot of a movie.

"Hillary was dating this rich app developer douche and, like, three months into dating, he whisked her away for a European vacation. They started in Spain and then hit France and eventually made their way up to the UK. At some point things started to take a turn. He started showing his true colors, and they began arguing a lot more. They were in a pub, and he was drunk off his ass and got handsy with her. Then he straight up slapped her across the face."

Ethan's head whips to me, his face painted with shock.

"I know," I continue. "It was so bad. Anyway, emerging from the shadows comes Archie, her knight in shining armor. Him and his buddies roughed him up and threw him out of the pub, and Archie swooped in to make sure she was okay. He couldn't let her go back to him, it obviously wasn't safe, but Hillary had almost no money on her. She was screwed. She ended up crashing at Archie's, and he basically saved her. He helped her get another passport, which the douche was holding hostage as a tactic to get her back. It was a whole thing. And then I don't know, they fell in love, and he flew back with her. And then she flew to him. They went back and forth for a bit, and eventually, he decided to move here."

"That's quite the story."

"I told her if I ever write a book, I'm stealing their story." I smile, suddenly feeling tired, the trip finally hitting me. "I think some people are meant for epic love stories while the rest of us have to settle for mediocre."

Ethan swallows audibly, his throat bobbing. "Do you

think you're someone that's going to have to settle?" His voice is quiet, almost a whisper.

I yawn, wiggling further into my seat. "That's all I've ever done. I settle." My eyes start to feel heavy. "I don't even think I know what it feels like to not settle."

I wake up as we're passing through the Yakima River Valley, the very same road I was on almost a month ago, full of nerves and worry. It's hard to believe it wasn't that long ago when it feels like another lifetime. My time in Red Mountain has felt a lot fuller than I anticipated, and the longer I stay, the more I think about not leaving. Which is crazy. Leaving has been and will continue to be the plan. Seattle is my home, this is limbo, this isn't real life.

"Morning, sleepyhead," Ethan says quietly when he notices me stir.

My eyes glance at the clock on the dash. Seven o'clock in the evening is far from morning.

I give him a small smile but stay quiet.

The remainder of the drive is silent, only the murmur of throwback 2000s songs plays low in the background. There's a noticeable tension, not electrically charged, but sad. It feels like a conclusion. The adventure is over. Back to reality. I lean my elbow against the window and let my chin rest in my palm as we pass darkened vineyards. I feel Ethan's stare on me, but I can't bring myself to meet his gaze.

"Hey." Ethan pulls his truck between our two cottages, puts it in park, and turns off the ignition, hitting the dome light as he turns to me. "What's wrong? You seem upset?"

"Nothing," I respond automatically but don't turn to look at him. "I'm fine."

"I wish I believed you." His hand reaches out and gives my knee a gentle squeeze, forcing my attention to his face. "I know something is wrong. Talk to me."

I look down at his hand still resting on my knee, and he quickly removes it, but my eyes remain fixed on the spot.

"I think I'm feeling conflicted about the job."

"You were so excited earlier."

"I was... I am—" I break off, trying to find the words to explain this melancholy feeling. "I want the job, don't get me wrong. But it's been nice seeing my dad again, feeling like I have someone to lean on. Hillary is great. She's always there for me, but she has her own family now, and with my mom always gone and being single, I don't know. Sometimes it feels incredibly lonely. I don't know what's worse, actually being alone, or feeling alone even around those who love and care about you."

Ethan nods, giving me the space I need to voice my thoughts as he listens.

"When I was with my ex, it was easier to distract myself. There was always some errand to run or event to get ready for. I never felt the gaps in my life. And I'm not saying I miss him —because no, fuck that guy—I just know that when I go back to Seattle, it's only me, and that's a little scary. Am I making any sense, or do I sound like some emotional girl?"

I didn't mean to spill my intrusive thoughts all over Ethan. Embarrassment settles deep in my chest, spreading to my heart and squeezing. The longer Ethan stays silent, the more it constricts.

He unbuckles and turns toward his door. I'm not sure what I was expecting him to do, but it wasn't him completely ignoring me. I'm not someone who opens up like that often. Being vulnerable and talking about real shit is something I usually avoid. I feel foolish for dropping my guard. I should've kept it surface level and not let him pry.

Ethan clears his throat, stilling me from making a quick exit.

When I face him, he's spinning a white envelope between his fingers.

"Laura and Travis invited me to their wedding," he says, looking straight ahead, still fidgeting with the envelope.

"That's..." I try to find the appropriate word but nothing feels right. "Unexpected."

He chuckles dryly. "Yeah, unexpected." He pauses, tossing the envelope on the dash and twists to face me. "So, believe me, I get it. It's not that you miss them, you miss the comfortable bubble. You miss feeling like you had someone that would always be there. You miss the plans you had for a life and a future that no longer exist. And worst of all, you start to question your judgment. How you couldn't see all the obvious signs that something wasn't right."

I let my head fall back against the seat, rolling my neck to meet his gaze. Ethan's expression is wary, like he's worried he revealed too much. A sense of camaraderie falls over me. It's as if he's voicing everything I felt in the aftermath of Brandon. I feel seen, understood. I suspect he doesn't reveal this side of himself often, and being entrusted with his vulnerability is a precious gift.

"Should we go to the wedding?" I joke, trying to lighten the mood.

Ethan huffs a laugh. "As much as I would enjoy seeing the look on her face if I showed up with a stunning woman on my arm, I think I'll be nice and let them have their day."

My cheeks warm. Am I the stunning woman he's referring to, or was he speaking more abstractly?

A spark of bravery lights within me, and I decide to push against the boundary. "Darn. We could've made out in the church. Now, *that* would ruin the wedding." I end on a giggle so it comes off as humorous despite my pulse having picked up speed at the thought of kissing Ethan.

His playful eyes shift into a darkened stare as they drop to my lips.

The cabin of the truck compresses, closing us off from the outside world. A sanctuary where only we exist. Us and this moment.

I lean forward. Or maybe he does.

"Marisa," Ethan whispers.

"Hmm," I sigh, getting lost in the flecks of gold in his eyes.

"Do you remember last Saturday when we were leaving the bar?"

My heart jumps, and I rear back slightly. "No. Why?"

"You— We— You almost—"

I cover my face with my hands. "Do not tell me I drunkenly kissed you."

His hands grab hold of mine and he peels them away from my face, and I'm met with his twinkling irises. "We didn't kiss."

I release a breath. "Oh, good. Not that I— I mean not—"

"You tried." He cuts me off, his smile wider.

I try to rebury my face, but he still has a hold on my hands. This is mortifying. And to think he's been walking around for days acting as if nothing happened. Even more embarrassing is that I tried and he rejected me. I don't know what stings worse. The rejection, or the fact that he's laughing about it now.

I try to pull away from him, but he's firmly holding me in place.

"I wanted to." His eyes bore into mine, all hints of amusement gone. "But you were drunk and it would've been wrong."

My embarrassment eases slightly.

"Besides." His thumbs begin to draw lazy circles on my

palms, a motion that shouldn't feel sexual at all, yet I feel it all the way to my core. "When I do kiss you, I want you to remember it."

When. He said *when,* not *if.*

My breath catches as butterflies take flight in my stomach. His left hand comes up to cup my jaw, and his thumb slides across to brush over my bottom lip, causing my pulse to spike. I melt into his hand, my body going slack.

His face inches closer, close enough that I would only have to lean into him slightly to feel his lips on mine.

"Marisa," Ethan whispers, his warm breath fanning across my face.

"Yes," I breathe, barely audible.

His eyes look down at my lips and then back at me. "Have you had anything to drink?"

His tone is teasing. Seeing as we haven't been apart for hours, he knows I haven't had a sip of alcohol, but I play along.

"Nope." I pop the P.

"Good," he replies, his voice low and husky.

He closes the distance between us, and his lips meet mine, deliciously slow. Calculated. Lingering. As if he wants to sit in this moment for as long as possible.

The scruff of his beard rubs against my skin, like striking a match, igniting a heated thrill that spreads through me. I want more of him. I *need* more of him.

Despite my attempts to get closer, I'm held back by the seat belt I'm still wearing. He senses my struggle and pulls away from me, breaking our kiss. Our eyes meet, goofy smiles spread across our faces.

"Here, let me." Ethan presses the release button, the sound equivalent to that of a starting horn.

The moment I'm free, I leap across the middle console, Ethan simultaneously yanking me to him. This time, our lips crash against each other, demanding, carnal. I settle my body against his, straddling his lap. Every part of my body connects to him. Mouth to mouth. Chest to chest. My arms snake around his neck, eliminating any remaining distance, and we melt into each other. My hips involuntarily grind, seeking friction against his hardness. Ethan's fingers dig into my waist, sending a scatter of goosebumps up my spine, before releasing and sliding to cup my ass, forcing my core closer.

He moans into my mouth at the contact, and his hips flex, returning the friction. I'm a mindless pool of lust, surrendering my body to him. I can think of nothing but his touch and wishing our clothes would disintegrate off our bodies. I'm desperate for more, for his skin on mine, for relief from the throb pulsing between my legs. He releases my mouth and moves his lips down my neck, nipping and sucking until he reaches my collar bone, where his tongue darts out and licks a trail. He moves higher, licking up the column of my neck, kissing along my jaw until his hot breath is in my ear.

This is more than a simple kiss. This is possession.

I move my hand from his neck, dragging it down his torso, and cup his hardened length over his jeans. His cock twitches beneath my grip, giving me a pretty good idea of his size. Long and thick. *Massive*.

I give him a firm stroke over his jeans, and he grunts, the vibration from it making my skin tingle.

"We should stop," he says, as his teeth graze my ear and his hand slips under the waistband of my leggings.

"We should," I agree, matching his lack of conviction.

I tilt my head back, allowing him more access.

"It's a terrible idea." His lips press against my neck before giving me a pinching nip. The combination of pain and pleasure is enough to bring me to the edge of combusting.

"The worst," I moan.

Wandering fingers inch closer to the spot I need him, and

he groans. "Fuck, Marisa. Have you not been wearing panties this entire time?"

"I don't wear underwear when I wear leggings."

He releases a frustrated groan, and I giggle, giving him another stroke, but my giggle morphs into a gasp as he slips one finger inside of me and then slowly spreads my arousal around.

"Your pussy is dripping. Is this all for me?" he rasps.

I grind harder, letting him fill me more. "Every. Last. Drop."

He recaptures my mouth with his, roughly, frenzied, and I crumble, relishing in the loss of his control. While his fingers curl inside of me, teasing me, his other hand slides into my hair. He gives it a firm tug and starts twisting it around his hand. Parting our kiss, he firmly pulls on the strands wrapped around his knuckles, causing my head to angle back. "Fuck, this hair. I've been fantasizing about wrapping it around my fist for weeks."

I gasp, both from the dull ache at my scalp and from his confession.

Weeks.

My stomach flip-flops with anticipation. I don't care where we are. I don't care about repercussions. I can only think of what I need, and that's to be fucked right here and now.

The same thought is apparently running through Ethan's mind. He practically rips off my shirt, tossing it over his shoulder and exposing my bra. His eyes widen, taking in the sight, and I thank the universe I'm wearing one of my sexier lace ones. He drops the seat back, but rather than pull me against him, he forces me to stay upright, his eyes admiring me, drinking me in, before locking with mine.

"You're fucking incredible, you know that?"

I swallow, feeling like he's not just looking at me but that he truly sees me.

This doesn't feel like a heated moment between two friends. It feels like the precipice of something deeper. Something I'm not sure I can handle.

Ethan, sensing my shift, brings his hand up and caresses my cheek. It's such a gentle movement compared to what we were just doing. I search his eyes, looking for my fears reflected in them, but he's unwavering.

"Baby," he whispers, and I turn liquid. Sweet, warm liquid. "Tell me what's going through that beautiful mind of yours."

How do I explain that with every touch, every kiss, the less this feels like two people caught up in a fleeting act of passion, and more like the beginning of something real? Something that transcends attraction and hormones, something more profound. And it's overwhelming.

"I...I—"

My words are cut off by my buzzing phone.

I look away from him, already crawling off his lap. "I should get that."

As I'm digging through my bag for the phone, every sound feels like a door closing. His seat locking upright, the ruffling of adjustments being made to his clothing. The rattling of keys. I'm too distracted to read the caller ID before I answer.

"Hello?"

"Hello. Am I speaking with Marisa Castilla?"

"This is she." My eyes cut to Ethan as he hands me my discarded shirt, avoiding looking at me.

"This is Cherie with Skyline Solutions. Sorry to call at this hour, but I wanted to catch you before the day ended. We would like to extend an offer for you to join our team."

She proceeds to explain the particulars about the position

and that they will need an acceptance or rejection within two weeks. She then informs me an email is waiting in my inbox.

I feel Ethan's gaze as I end the call. When I look to face him, his brow is creased and he's nearly unreadable. Closed off once more.

"You got the job." It's not a question, it's a statement.

I nod, finally meeting his eyes.

"Congratulations." He smiles, but it doesn't reach his eyes. "When do you start?"

"I haven't accepted the job yet." The "yet" hangs in the air, bright and red, like a warning light.

"But you will. And you should. It's a great opportunity."

His eyes briefly land on my bra before he flicks them away. Quickly, I put my shirt back on.

The space between us is fraught with tension, made worse by my tangled hair and Ethan's twisted shirt, evidence of what almost happened.

"I should go inside." My hand is already on the handle.

I climb out and take a deep breath, letting the cool air fill my lungs. Ethan exits as well, fast at work, getting my suitcase out and taking it to my porch. We move in silence. I can practically feel the regret coming off him. Clearly, it's a good thing we got interrupted. It would've been a mistake, one I'm not sure I'd recover from easily.

"See you," I say, not looking at him, my chin remaining down, as I enter my cottage.

"Yep," he says, walking away toward his.

Once inside, I flop my head back on the door and slump down until I'm sitting, knees hugged against my chest. I close my eyes and press the tips of my fingers against my swollen lips, feeling where he branded me. If not for the evidence, I would think I imagined the entire thing.

CHAPTER 30

Marisa

FRIENDS MY ASS

"How many festivals does this town have?" I ask Suzy, hugging my arms against myself to keep warm.

"I'm not sure, I've never really counted." She considers it for a moment. "At least ten."

Mario was supposed to cover the Trunk or Treat Festival but came down with the flu that's been going around, so now I'm covering it, with the help of Suzy.

It's been windy for most of the day, a bone-chilling wind that cuts right through my flimsy peacoat. I purchased this coat more for looks than practicality, a choice I'm very much regretting.

Suzy looks at me, laughing at my shivering. "Once the parade is over, you'll have all the pictures you need."

Thank God.

Tonight's events are particularly bustling because, for a majority of the local wineries and farms, harvest has come to a close. A lot of people who would normally still be tied up are now out celebrating, causing downtown to feel overcrowded.

"What time does the parade start?"

"Six o'clock." She turns to me, arms crossed to keep warm, too. "You have forty-five minutes to kill. Go walk around, get your blood flowing. Or better yet, go mingle under one of the heated tents."

"And what are you going to do while I mingle?"

She shrugs. "Probably go check to see how my husband is handling the kids."

Suzy's husband Derek is taking their four kids around to the different cars parked along Main Street that are participating in Trunk or Treat, where local businesses and city services hand out candy to kids, rather than them going door to door to get it from strangers.

We split, Suzy going north while I head south. To be honest, the last thing I feel like doing is mingling. Ever since Ethan dropped me off yesterday, I haven't been able to stop thinking about what happened. In fact, it seems to be all I can think about. I woke up early this morning to go for a run, at least that's what I told myself, but really I think I was hoping to bump into him. But when I walked outside, his cottage was still dark. Either he already went in to work, or he was still sleeping. And I've spent the rest of the day searching for him, hoping to talk—or to avoid him, I haven't quite decided. As I walk, I make sure to snap pictures for the article. A pumpkin carving station, kids lined up for a costume contest, face painting, bobbing for apples, a mini corn maze for dogs. Several booths are set up with food and drinks, but I gravitate toward the one I know will warm me up. Hot cider.

I get in line and blow on my hands, rubbing them together to create warmth. Meanwhile, kids are running around in paper-thin costumes, perfectly content with the recent drop in temperature. Either I'm a weeny when it comes to cold weather, or kids are made out of some different shit these days. I take a picture of a group of kids in coordinating Minion costumes when I feel the presence of someone behind me. I turn to look at the source of the shadow, part of me hoping it's Ethan for some silly reason.

It's not Ethan. It's Cole.

"Heyyy, drunky," he says teasingly.

I wince at the nickname but give him a polite chuckle.

"Cole, right?" I don't want to further inflate his ego.

He places both hands over his chest. "You remembered. I'm touched."

"I wasn't that drunk," I defend.

He scoffs. "You definitely were. Lucky for you, though, my buddy Ethan was kind enough to carry you home."

My cheeks warm. "You heard about that, huh?"

His smile is mischievous. "Sweetheart, the whole town heard about that."

That's just great.

I'm saved from having to continue with the conversation since it's my turn to order. I order the cinnamon apple hot cider and wait off to the side for them to complete it. Unfortunately, Cole is close behind. He joins me in the waiting area, his face full of questions.

"So, what's the deal with you and Ethan? Are you guys together or fucking around?"

I suck in a sharp laugh. "Neither. We're friends."

At least I hope we're still friends. Things are a little murky right now after having mauled each other in his truck and not speaking since.

"Does *he* know that?" He smirks, his eyes trained on the crowded street.

My forehead scrunches. "What do you mean?"

Cole lifts his chin with raised brows, looking beyond my shoulder, and I whip my head around a little too fast to see what he's gesturing at. For a split second, I think Cole is messing with me, but in an instant, Ethan's eyes connect with mine from across the road. We stare for a moment, but a little girl—his niece, I'm assuming—asks him something, breaking the connection.

Cole snorts. "Friends my ass."

The booth attendant hands me and Cole our ciders. I ordered it for warmth, but my flushed skin seems to indicate I was warmed by something—someone—else entirely.

Cole is holding two ciders.

"Thirsty?" I ask.

He shakes his head. "One is for my date."

Date?

Relief sweeps over me, and I'm not sure why. Maybe because he's flirtatious but in a way that feels like an inside joke I'm not privy to. Or maybe it's that I don't want him to flirt with me at all.

He shoots me a sly smile. "Ethan and I have always been competitive."

"I don't understand."

He smiles again, this time more genuinely. "I had this theory, and you guys proved it."

With that, he turns to leave, and I'm even more confused than I was before.

As I'm walking out of the tent, Elyse flags me down with a wave. She's standing with some of her family—including Ethan.

"Hey! Are you here alone?" Her eyes dart around me while I will mine to not glance over at the tall, ruggedly handsome man to her left.

"I'm here for work. I'm covering the festival."

"Fun!" She does a spin, showing me her costume. "What do you think?"

I bite my lip, holding back a laugh. "What are you supposed to be?"

Her eyes roll playfully. "The sexy Wicked Witch of the East. Obviously." She gestures to her family. "We did a group

243

costume this year for my niece Lily. She's Dorothy, Gavin is the lion, Shane is the scarecrow, and Ethan is the tin man."

Gavin has his normally tied-back hair loose and free, with his face painted like a lion. It's a little comical to see a man like him going full out for Halloween, but it also warms my heart knowing it's for his daughter. Shane also has his face painted and is exposing his bare chest, revealing even more tattoos. And then there's Ethan, who, not surprisingly, is only wearing a gray henley under his open jacket.

"Where's your costume?" I ask Ethan, putting an end to our streak of silence.

Elyse nudges him. "Mr. Party Pooper agreed to wear the hat"—she rolls her eyes at me—"for pictures only."

"Because that hat makes me look like a conspiracy theorist," he argues.

She places her hands on her hips. "It's for your niece."

He looks at both of us through furrowed brows, internally debating, before he relents. "Fine."

Elyse does a little clap. "Yay!" She pulls the cone-shaped DIY foil hat out of her purse and places it on Ethan, snapping the chin strap for good measure.

His eyes flash to mine. "See? Ridiculous."

I bite my bottom lip to prevent my threatening smile. "You're supposed to look ridiculous. It's Halloween."

He crosses his arms, but his expression has a glint of humor. "And where's your costume?"

I shrug. "I'm on the job. I have to look professional."

Ethan shakes his head at me, the corners of his lips lifting. "Excuses, excuses."

"Speaking of which," I shout, so the group can hear me. "Let me take a picture of you guys for the *Herald*."

Lily runs out from behind Gavin to stand front and center. As she should.

I glance around for a spot to set my drink so I can take the picture, but before I can figure it out, Ethan quietly takes the cup from my hands. Our fingertips briefly brush, causing a subtle warmth to pass between us, and without a word, he slips it behind his back as he joins his family for the photo.

It takes me a moment to regain my composure, far more affected by him than I'd like to admit.

Shaking my head to focus on the task at hand, I step back to get the right frame. "Alright, everyone say 'cheese!'" I take a few quick shots. "Okay, I think I got some good ones."

Gavin approaches me. I thought Ethan was tall, but Gavin has him by a few inches. "Think you could send me a few copies of those?"

"Yeah, no problem."

He reaches out and gives me a brief handshake. "I'm Gavin, by the way. I don't think we've officially met."

"Marisa. Nice to meet you."

Lily stands at her dad's side, staring up at me, so I bend down to meet her at eye level.

"And you're a very pretty Dorothy."

She smiles brightly and does a twirl, mirroring Elyse's. "Thank you," she says, cheeks turning a light shade of rosy pink.

Lily spots a Disney princess and takes Gavin's hand to drag him away, leaving me with Ethan and Elyse.

"I'm going to go grab a hot chocolate. You guys want anything?" Elyse asks us.

We both shake our heads no, and she darts away for one of the various tents.

And then there were two.

Ethan takes a drink of my hot cider, and I can't help the blush that takes over my cheeks. I'm not sure why sharing a drink feels so familiar, but it does. Way too familiar when I remember that his mouth was on mine less than twenty-four hours ago. His lips linger on the rim of the cup a moment longer than necessary, and when he hands it back to me, his eyes lock with mine. There's a teasing glimmer in them, but something else, too—something that sends a spark of heat down my spine.

I swallow, trying to ignore the flutter in my chest.

The air between us inflates, and despite being steps away, he suddenly feels too close. Close enough for me to catch a hint of his scent, and it mingles with the faintest trace of cinnamon from the cider.

Ethan sticks his hands in his pockets, keeping his focus down while I bobble my head about as if I'm looking at the crowd, when really I can't focus on anything but the man next to me.

"The article turned out great. Thanks for focusing it more on the winery."

I tipped Marv, the man who delivers the paper, to deliver it to Ethan first thing in the morning. It should've been waiting for him at the winery when he got to work.

"Good." I smile tightly. "I'm glad you liked it."

Seconds tick by as we look at each other but don't speak. It's as if neither one of us is quite ready to address the metaphorical elephant standing between us.

"Well, this is awkward." I huff a laugh, hoping to dissolve this stupid tension.

"Yeah, about that," he starts, his head lifting to meet my eyes. "I was an ass yesterday. I should've been more excited for you. I am—I'm proud of you. And I'm happy you got the job."

He smiles, that soft, gentle smile I selfishly hope is only reserved for me.

"Thank you." My voice is a whisper as my throat tightens with emotion. It's one thing to congratulate me or say he's happy for me. It's an entirely different feeling to say he's proud of me. Growing up, it was the compliment I strived for the most and so rarely received. My dad was never easily impressed by my accomplishments. As soon as one was achieved, it was on to the next. The constant chasing of his praise led to burnout in my college years. Growing resentment combined with never feeling good enough made me believe that my achievements—or lack thereof—were tied to his love for me. I can feel my daddy issues surfacing, so I clear my throat and push them back down.

He nods, eyes boring into mine, before cutting away to look around us. When they meet mine again, they're laced with...worry? Embarrassment, maybe? I can't read him.

"We should probably talk about what happened," he says in a low, quiet voice.

My chest sinks down to my stomach. "Right," I breathe. "We should."

He rubs the back of his neck. A move I'm realizing he does when he's anxious. "I think it would be best—"

"You regret it, don't you?" I cut him off. "It's fine if you do. It was a heat of the moment thing, and I—"

"Marisa, stop," he says firmly, shaking his head, almost in disbelief. "I don't regret it." His eyes travel down the length of my body, leaving behind a heated trail. "I don't regret any of it."

"Oh." I swallow. I was fully prepared to brush it off to save face. Now I'm not sure what to say.

"Why? Do you?"

I hesitate only a moment and then give my head a shake. "No. I don't regret it either."

The corner of his mouth quirks as he looks down at me. "Good."

I press my lips together, fighting a grin. "Good," I echo.

"But," he starts.

I take a deep breath. "There's always a but."

His smile settles to one that is more even. More wistful. "But we probably shouldn't go down that road."

I know this. My brain knows this. But my heart? My heart disagrees. A pressure builds around it, heavy and insistent. I bring my hand to my chest and rub my sternum, trying to ease the pain. One kiss shouldn't have left me feeling this way. But here I am, fighting to keep my emotions in check.

"You're right. You're so right." I nod quickly, trying to sound casual, even keeled. Not at all dejected like I feel.

"It's just that you're leaving. And—"

"I get it." I didn't intend to say that with as much bite as I did, and I wince, mentally scolding myself. "Friends?" I ask, my voice way too cheerful. I even squeaked it went up so high.

God, I sound pathetic.

He blows out a breath, and it fogs between us. "Friends," he agrees.

CHAPTER 31

Marisa

PRACTICALLY OBSCENE

I t's been over a week since the Trunk or Treat Festival. It's also been over a week since I've seen Ethan. After we agreed to keep being friends, I thought we'd at least see each other, chat a bit, maybe even hang out. But nothing. I haven't even seen him in passing, almost like he's avoiding me.

It's not as if we were very close beforehand, but I thought after driving me over a snowy mountain pass and sticking his tongue down my throat, there would at least be a little texting. I could always reach out, but I don't want to come across as annoying or clingy. For all I know, he was only placating me to avoid the fallout of our kiss and intends to avoid me until I leave.

My fingers twitch across my phone screen, practically itching to text him. But I can't. I won't do it. I'm not going to beg for attention from someone who doesn't want to give it.

And what would be the point, anyway? Clearly, there's chemistry there and hanging out or talking would only make it that much more apparent after we both decided not to get involved with one another. Ethan's being the rational one, doing the right thing and avoiding—

My thoughts are cut off by the chime of my phone, alerting me of a text message.

ETHAN

Hey

I stare at the text as a line of heat works its way through me, lighting fire to all the feelings I've been pretending aren't that intense. It's a silly crush, that's all. It'll go away. It's not even a good text. I press the sleep button on my phone and toss it on the couch cushion next to me, purposefully choosing to distance myself from it and not respond to his shitty text. I mean, he didn't even use any punctuation.

Seconds tick by, the large, decorative clock on the wall echoing like a ticking time bomb. I stare at the phone and then, before I can second guess myself, reach for it and fire back a text to Ethan. What can I say? I have zero restraint.

Shane?

I can't help but giggle. He knows I have his number saved, but it's so fun riling him up.

ETHAN

Very funny. If Shane were texting you, he would've sent a dick pic and misspelled every other word.

So you're saying I'm not getting a dick pic? Darn.

A minute later a picture comes through and for a second, like a very, very split second, I worry he actually did send a dick pic. But then I remember I'm texting Ethan, and he would never.

A laugh bursts out of me as I open the picture, and it's of a banana. A banana being held in a very suggestive pose, much like a man would actually take a dick pic, down low, by his crotch, his hand fisting it. I'm momentarily distracted by the prominent veins in his forearms. The fact that he knows exactly how all guys take dick pics makes me think he's definitely taken one before. Maybe there's a side to Ethan I've never seen.

> Comparing yourself to a banana?
> Someone's cocky...get it 🍌

ETHAN

You have the humor of a ten year old boy.

> Thank you. It's one of my many positive attributes.

ETHAN

What are you up to tonight?

My heartbeat quickens. Where is this going?

> Just having a night in, watching trashy TV.
> What are you doing tonight?

ETHAN

Same as you, minus the trashy TV. I have the Discovery channel on for noise.

I smile into the phone. He's such a dork, and I love it.

> Ok old man.

> Want some company?

I hold my breath, waiting for his response. So much for not begging for attention. Thankfully, he's quick on the reply.

ETHAN

Sure. I'll come to you. Be there in about ten
minutes.

My heart practically leaps out of my chest with excitement, which evolves into pure panic. I have almost no time to
make myself look presentable and tidy up the place. Scrambling, I shove anything that's lying around out of sight,
jamming it into every nook and cranny I can find. The goal is
to look like I don't live here. There cannot be any evidence of
life. Thankfully, my dad was able to make room in his garage
for my boxes, so at least it's not as cluttered.

Racking my brain, I mentally cycle through my inventory
of clothing. I need to wear something that's cute and put
together while simultaneously looking casual and lounge-y.
My current outfit of decade-old flannel pajama pants—ripping
apart at the ass seam—and a stained band T-shirt aren't exactly
presentable. Strapped for time, I decide on a pair of flared
leggings with a cropped tank top and an oversize, relaxed cardi-
gan. Hopefully, it says *I was totally already wearing this and
definitely didn't change just for you.*

As I'm giving myself a quick once-over in the mirror, there's
a knock at the front door. A case of the jitters hits me. I wasn't
prepared to be this nervous. It's Ethan. We've shared a motel
room, we've kissed for crying out loud, but this feels like more.
Just us two, hanging out, alone, with really no reason other
than wanting each other's company. It feels like a date. But it's
not a date, right? Because we're friends. We're just friends.

"Hey, come on in."

My voice is too high. I need to calm down. *Calm down,
Marisa.*

He walks in and holds up a bottle of wine and a box of
Cheez-Its. "I brought sustenance."

He remembered. I'm positive there's a tinge of pink shading my cheeks right now.

"I thought you hated Cheez-Its?"

He sets the wine and box of crackers on the counter. "Oh, I do. They taste like vomit. But you like them, and I heard they pair well with Chardonnay, hence the bottle."

Why does this feel like the nicest thing a man has ever done for me? Jesus, I'm easy to please.

"What are you going to eat?"

He opens his jacket and pulls out a bag of popcorn from the inside pocket. "Popcorn for me and vomit crackers for you, win win."

I grab the popcorn bag from him and get it going in the microwave. I have no idea what to do, so I occupy myself in the kitchen, getting out bowls and glasses. I'm so nervous I could jump out of my skin. He walks in here with wine and Cheez-Its, and I'm ready to get down on my knees for the man. I need to get a handle on myself, and I need to do it now. We're friends. He's being friendly. Friends totally go out of their way to buy your favorite snack food, even if they themselves don't like it. Right?

"It smells good in here," Ethan comments.

My head gestures toward the vanilla candle I have burning on the coffee table. "It's the candle. I bought it the other day at the farmers market."

He shakes his head. "No, that's not it. It smells like you in here. It's nice."

"Oh." I giggle. If I wasn't blushing already, I am now. "Um, thank you." I turn away from him, opening a kitchen drawer. This is going to be a long night.

"Want to do the honors?" I ask, handing over the wine bottle opener.

He grabs the opener from me, and his hand lightly brushes

against mine, causing my stomach to dip. Very, very long night.

"This is our 2013 Chardonnay. It was one of our best Chardonnay years." He goes on to explain the tasting notes, but I can't seem to hear him over the distraction of watching his arms twist the opener. His forearm muscles are really working at it. Somewhere between when he walked through the door and now, he slipped off his jacket. He looks practically obscene in a simple black T-shirt. I've never noticed a man's arms so much in my life until I met Ethan. I think I'm developing a new obsession.

He hands me the glass, now filled with wine, pulling me out of my distracting thoughts. He's watching me like he's waiting to see my reaction to it, so I obey, because I'm completely weak for him, and take a sip of the wine. The cool liquid dances across my tongue, its buttery flavor lingering long after I've swallowed. It's delicious, but I would expect nothing less.

"Better than the fruit juice you're used to?" he teases, nudging his head to the crappy bottle of wine I have sitting on the counter.

"Slightly." I smile so he knows I'm teasing him, and he shakes his head at me, walking off toward the couch with our snacks.

"Don't make fun of me," I say as I take a seat next to him, careful to distance myself by keeping one cushion between us. "But I may have purchased the entire season of that telenovela we started watching at the motel."

He leans back and laughs. "Seriously?"

"See, I knew you were going to make fun of me."

He starts swiping through his phone. "I'm not making fun of you." He points his phone toward me, showing me the screen. "I did the same thing."

The screen shows his online purchase of the entire first season.

Color me shocked. I thought he was just pacifying me by letting me watch it when we were in the motel. Brandon would do that in the beginning of our relationship, act like he enjoyed watching one of my shows only to tell me he actually couldn't stand it once we were a few months in. It's silly really, because who cares? It's just a TV show. Except, I guess I did. He made my interests seem stupid simply because they weren't his. From the shows I liked to the books I read, even down to my taste in music, he thought they were all ridiculous. He wanted to make me feel small for liking things he deemed too feminine to take seriously.

"You actually liked it?"

He shrugs. "Well, yeah. I only stayed up all night watching it with you. I got invested. I have to know how it ends. Plus, I'm kind of fuzzy on some of the details, and I think it's because we missed the first couple episodes."

I must be staring at him with a weird expression because he says, "Why are you looking at me like that?"

"I'm surprised, that's all."

"Well, put it on. The popcorn is getting cold. And start on episode one."

I fiddle with the remote as Ethan gets settled. I try to ignore how aware I am of his weight pressing down on the couch, or how his scent is so much stronger when it's trapped inside this tiny cottage, or that I want nothing more than to crawl into his arms and let myself get completely lost in him.

As the beginning credits start, Ethan clears his throat. "So, did you accept the job?"

My pulse stills. I was going to tell him. I just didn't know how to bring it up. I turn to him, trying to look relaxed. "Yeah. I did."

He nods and his lips lift, looking content. "Good. Congratulations."

His genuine happiness for me shouldn't hurt my feelings, yet a corner of my heart cracks as I force a smile. "Thanks."

In the weeks that follow, Ethan and I fall into the rhythm of an unofficial routine. With harvest over, Ethan's schedule is much more relaxed and back to regular business hours. No more early mornings or late nights. His weekends aren't as chaotic either.

In a matter of days, we complete the entire novela we started with. From there, Ethan makes me watch *Top Gun*, which I only pretend to hate. And then I make him watch some of my favorite Nora Ephron movies, starting with *Sleepless in Seattle* and ending with *When Harry Met Sally*. I expected some protest, because most guys don't enjoy sitting through chick flicks, but he happily watched and even got a little antsy with how long it took Sam and Annie to finally come face-to-face in *Sleepless in Seattle*.

Sometimes we're at my cottage and sometimes we're at his. I prefer his, because Goose joins us and he's really good at keeping my feet warm. It started slowly, a night here, a night there, then two in a row, and so on and so on. Now it's nearly every day, and I'm not sure what that means.

Long gone is the grumpy man I met, though he does still have his moments, but never with me. No, with me, he's different. He pays attention to my likes and dislikes, learning that the only candy I'll eat is chocolate, that I can make one cup of coffee last an entire day, and that my feet are always cold, but I refuse to wear socks. I learn about him, too. I find out about his aversion to most vegetables and tease him about it constantly. He tells me about how he never planned to follow in his dad's footsteps. That he worries about disappointing his family if he makes a bad decision that hurts the business. He talks about living in Woodinville, and about the house he was supposed to build with his ex. That he's relieved they didn't get far in the process since he still hopes to build on the land someday. It reminds me of the conversation I had with Leanne about her dream of having all her children live nearby. I don't bring it up to Ethan, though. I sense that sharing the house plans with me was a big enough step, and I don't want to add any pressure.

We've grown a lot closer, but true to our agreement, we never cross the line. He stays on one side of the couch, and I stay on the other. We don't touch. Ever. One time we almost grazed arms in the kitchen, but he leaped out of the way like I was a hot stove.

In some ways, this friendship feels a lot like voluntary torture. Because as much as I enjoy hanging out with him—in fact, he's often the best part of my day—it's not enough. I thought I had feelings for him when we had only kissed, but now that I know him, my feelings have grown from hesitant to undeniable. Ethan doesn't seem to be suffering the way I am, though. Any feelings or interest he may have had are clearly dissolved.

"Do you have any plans for Thanksgiving?" Ethan asks.

I press pause on *Love Is Blind*. "Yes, I do." I can't contain my excitement. I meant to tell him earlier, but I got distracted after I dove into my next project for the second edition of *The Vine*.

His brows raise. "You seem awfully spirited over one of the more boring holidays we have."

I give a mock exasperated sigh. "I'm not excited about the actual holiday, silly. I'm excited because my mom is coming. She hasn't been home for the holidays in years."

His head cocks, and his eyes narrow slightly. "Your mom hasn't been home for the holidays in years? Who were you spending Thanksgiving and Christmas with? Because I know it wasn't with your dad."

The harshness in his voice catches me off guard. I decide to shrug it off to a stressful work day, because it feels like it's coming out of nowhere.

"With Hillary or my ex, Brandon." Saying Brandon's name out loud leaves a sour taste in my mouth. "Are you mad or something?"

Ethan's grip on his glass of water tightens. "What? No, I'm not mad. I'm just trying to understand how you've gone years without a family to spend the holidays with."

This time his voice is much gentler, but his words hit all the same. Pity. He feels sorry for me.

"Not everyone has a giant family like yours." My defenses are rising. "I've known Hillary's family my entire life, so it wasn't weird if I spent a holiday or two with them. And Brandon and I were together for four years. I don't get where you're going with this."

He sighs, running a hand through his hair. "You're right. I'm being a dick. I'm sorry, it was a stressful day, and I'm not myself."

Our eyes lock, an awkward dissonance settling in the air. His reaction has me feeling off kilter, and I don't like the small seed of doubt starting to take root in my gut. Rather than dwell on it, I try to dissolve the stilted atmosphere.

"Can you please be excited for me? It actually works out perfectly because my dad is going to spend it with Jenn's family in Spokane, and they were nice enough to lend me their house for my mom and I to celebrate in."

He smiles softly. "I am. I'm excited for you. I promise."

Some of the tension eases, but his initial reaction continues to linger in my mind.

"The reason I was asking," he continues. "Is because my mom wanted me to let you know you're more than welcome to join us. And now that your mom is coming, obviously, she's also welcome."

Thanksgiving with the Ledgers. If my mom wasn't coming, I would love to spend the holiday with them. Growing up, I always imagined what it would be like to spend the holidays in a big family. The chaos, the mess, the conversations. I used to be so envious of my friends who had lots of siblings. As I grew older, I became more appreciative of the quiet relaxation of my family's holidays, but a small part of me always wondered.

People assume I have a large family because my mom is Mexican, but that isn't the case. My mom left her family behind in Mexico when she was a teenager and never looked back. I used to ask questions about them when I was younger, wondering why all my friends had aunts and uncles and grandparents and I only had my dad's one living parent, my Grandpa Johnny, who passed away when I was eight. Eventually, I gave up, because the questions never got me anywhere, and I was still left wondering what became of that part of my family.

"Thank you for the invite, but I think we're going to keep it just us two. It's been so long since I've seen her. I'm really wanting that alone time."

He nods, understanding, and doesn't press any further. We resume the show, trying to get back to a comfortable place, but we never get there.

CHAPTER 32

Ethan

YOU TWO ARE SO DUMB

I can't keep doing this. The more time I spend with Marisa, the more intense my feelings get. I fooled myself into thinking her friendship was enough. It's not enough, it's so far from enough. Stopping at the kiss was supposed to protect me from getting hurt when she leaves, but this is an entirely different kind of pain. When I'm with her, all I want is to touch her, to feel her, and when we're apart, I'm plagued with thoughts of her. She consumes me. She has fully infiltrated me and I'm past the point of ignoring it any further. Something has to be done. Either we put a stop to the dangerous game of toeing the line we're playing, acting as if spending all of our free time together isn't a relationship, or we finally give in and act on it. There's also a major possibility that this is entirely one-sided on my part. Regardless, I'm at my breaking point.

"What's wrong with you?"

I look up to find Elyse walking into my office. "Nothing, why?"

Her eyes narrow. She doesn't believe me for a second. "Weird. Because I was standing here, staring at you for a good minute, and you were zoned out like a crazy person the entire time."

"Just tired." I try to lie, but even I can hear the lack of conviction behind my words.

"This wouldn't have anything to do with a certain someone, would it? Maybe someone named Marisa?"

My expression must give it all away, because Elyse's eyes light with excitement.

She walks closer and leans her hip against my desk. "Oh, you got it bad, huh?"

I look at her, trying to keep my face neutral, but Elyse sees everything. She's like our mom.

"You are so down bad for her, it's not even funny," she continues.

I give up. There's no use keeping this to myself. "And what if I am? It doesn't mean anything. She's leaving after the new year, anyway."

She smiles, apparently enjoying my torture. "You don't know that. Maybe she will, maybe she won't. But wouldn't it be nice if she had a reason, more than her dad, to stick around?"

"You have all the answers, don't you?" I grit. "I doubt she sees me as anything more than a friend. She's barely speaking to me."

Ever since she brought up her mom coming to visit, she's been noticeably distant. After that night, we haven't had our usual hangout. It's only been a few days, but enough for it to be obvious that I upset her.

"Interesting," she muses. "I had lunch with her the other day."

That catches my attention, and then I see it for what it was. She's baiting me, and it worked.

"I'm not lying. We did have lunch. And you know what's funny?"

I hate it when she's like this. "What, Elle? What's funny?"

She leans down, like she's about to reveal a secret. "She looked just as zoned out and distracted as you."

"I don't know what that means. Can you stop fucking with me and spit it out already?"

She rolls her eyes. "Fine. You're no fun." Laughing, she walks back toward the hall. "You two are so dumb. I mean, how much work does a girl have to do to get two people to realize they like each other? Those dates aligning with her interview and your meeting. It was kismet, like the universe plopped it in my lap and said, 'Elyse, work your magic.' The snow, well, that was Mother Nature, but I mean, come on. It's so obvious there are feelings there. It's like a game of ping-pong watching you two in a room, bouncing googly eyes back and forth."

My face heats, images of our kiss replaying in my head. I think about *that kiss* too often. I think about it when I wake up. I think about it when I'm at work. I think about it when I'm with her. I think about it when the ache for her becomes unbearable and I have to take matters into my own hands, literally. The amount of times I've come to thoughts of Marisa is embarrassingly high. If she knew she was the star of every single one of my fantasies, she would run back to Seattle a lot sooner than after the new year.

"What's that look on your face?" Elyse asks, her face twisting.

Shaking my head, I force away my indecent thoughts. "What look?" I say, feigning confusion.

Elyse's eyes crinkle, assessing me. "Did something happen between you two?"

She's like a damn bloodhound, unrelenting.

"I'm not talking about this with you. Boundaries, Elle."

She releases an exaggerated gasp. "Something totally happened!"

I rub the throbbing pain building between my brows. "Will you drop it already? Don't you have work to do?"

Elyse leans her head out of my doorway. "Tawn, get in here," she calls out.

Jesus Christ. I should work from home, if only to avoid shit like this. "Elle, seriously? Leave it alone. I will deal with things in my own way. I don't need you and Tawny and whoever else butting into my business."

She pouts just as Tawny walks in.

"What are we talking about?" Tawny asks, eyes brimming with curiosity.

Elyse turns to her. "Ethan and his big fat crush on Marisa."

Tawny giggles, leaning into Elyse. "Oh, I know. Aren't they adorable?"

Alright, now I'm pissed. "I didn't realize I pay you two to gossip like old women at the hair salon. Back to work."

Tawny shrugs, unaffected, but wanders out.

Elyse shakes her head at me. "Tsk, tsk. Careful, E, your misogyny is showing."

"Out. Get out and get back to work."

She huffs and starts to walk out but pauses and turns to look at me, her eyes devoid of their usual humor. "For what it's worth, I think you need to go for it. Forget about her leaving. Forget about the what ifs. Just try. Because you know what's worse than going after who you want and it not working out? Not trying at all and living with the regret."

Hell must be frozen over, because I'm taking advice from Shane. Willingly.

"Gray sweatpants." Shane throws the sweatpants at me.

263

"You gotta wear the gray sweatpants. The ladies go feral for them."

Somehow, one text in the group chat turned into Gavin and Shane showing up at my place with unwarranted advice. I invited myself over to Marisa's and after she took an hour to reply to my text, I started to panic and involved my brothers. I really wish I hadn't.

I look over at Gavin, needing his confirmation on this.

Gavin smiles and nods. "He's not wrong."

"So, what? I just walk in there shirtless with gray sweatpants and she's suddenly going to be interested in me?"

Shane laughs. "You're gonna wear a shirt. This isn't a porno. This is a seduction, young grasshopper."

Shane is loving this way too much, and my regret for getting him involved is growing by the minute.

"You know what?" I stand. "This was a mistake."

"E, I'm just joking around—"

Both Gavin and Shane stand, talking over each other.

"Ignore Shane, he's being a shithead," Gavin says.

I stop, fighting the instinct to kick both of them out. "This is ridiculous. It's probably all for nothing. I doubt she sees me the way I see her."

Gavin and Shane exchange a look and then bust up laughing.

"Bruh, you're blind as fuck," Shane says. "She may be treating you like a friend, but the eyes don't lie, and hers aren't looking at you like a friend. They're saying, 'Ethan, fuck me.'"

I throw a pillow at Shane to shut him the fuck up.

"Yeah, man," Gavin chimes in, ignoring Shane. "I've seen it, too. At the festival, she only had eyes for you."

"Well, besides when she was talking to Cole," Shane says under his breath.

Gavin punches his arm. "You don't know when to shut up, do you?"

I sit on the couch, slumping into the cushions, and let out a breath. "I don't know what I'm thinking. She's not planning to stay. It's pointless."

Gavin joins me on the couch. "Plans change."

"If this blows up in my face, I'm blaming you both."

Shane throws up his arms in defense. "I'll take all the blame. But it won't. Trust us."

My two brothers regard me with pleading, yet conniving eyes. Even Goose joins them, rubbing his head against Shane's thigh while shooting me puppy dog eyes.

I release a breath. "Fine, let's get this over with."

By the time Shane and Gavin are through with me, I'm wearing gray sweatpants, a black, long-sleeved compression shirt, and a backward hat.

"I never dress like this. She's going to think something is up."

Gavin shakes his head. "Don't acknowledge it. You're wearing regular clothes. You're overthinking things. Walk in and do what you normally do."

"I look like I'm going to the gym." I tug at the tight shirt, adjusting the fabric.

"Will you stop being a little bitch for one goddamn second? Be a man and go get your woman. The longer you go without making a move or trying to make something happen, the more of an opening you give to another dude. Cole Benton was already sniffing around her once. You think he won't try again? And he's just trying to get inside her pussy—"

"Hey," I snap. "One more mention of her pussy, and I'm going to punch the word right out of your mouth."

"Rawwr." Shane mimics a cat. "I see how it is. You really like this chick."

I grab Shane by the shoulders, forcing him to stand. "Alright, time to go before I lose my shit on you."

"Why is it always me you're losing your shit on and never Gavin?"

"Because Gavin knows when to keep his mouth shut."

Gavin laughs while Shane pouts.

"Bye, fuckers."

Shane turns to me at the front door. "Good luck getting that pus— I mean, um, you know what I mean."

Gavin smacks the back of Shane's head.

Tonight will tell if my brothers are geniuses or complete idiots.

My money's on idiots.

CHAPTER 33

Marisa

SACRED CALDO DE POLLO

I'm sick. It's the Friday before Thanksgiving, and I'm on my deathbed. The flu that's been spreading around town finally got me. I consider myself to be fairly tolerable in most uncomfortable situations, but when I'm sick, I may as well be a man, because I go full-on man cold.

I tried to deny it, but yesterday I woke up feeling off, and it only got worse as the day progressed. Today, there's no denying it. I attempted to go into work, but my dad took one look at me and sent me straight home. At the end of the day, I found myself in bed, eventually dozing off.

Hours must have passed since I fell asleep, because my bedroom is bathed in darkness, and a hand is resting on my forehead, smoothing down my hair.

"Hey," Ethan whispers. "How are you feeling?"

If I had any energy, I'd be shocked to see him here, but a small part of my memory recalls him inviting himself over. I'm not even sure if I responded. I'm positive my skin is gross and greasy, and there's probably snot on my face. I should be embarrassed about letting Ethan see me like this, but his face is showing nothing but concern for me.

"Like shit," I moan.

He chuckles, adjusting the surrounding blankets and tucking me in tighter. "You should've texted me that you weren't feeling well. I would've come over sooner."

"I didn't want to get you sick."

"Like I care about that." He shakes his head. "There's some medicine on the nightstand. Take it and you can go back to sleep."

He leaves, and I down the awful-tasting liquid, sleep coming fast.

When I wake up again, it's almost noon the next day, and the sun is shining brightly through my windows. Thankfully, I don't feel quite as shitty as I did yesterday. In fact, my stomach growls, reminding me it's been a while since I've eaten.

I get out of bed and walk to the kitchen, hoping there's magically going to be something in my fridge that's edible. Turning the corner, my steps falter as I stare at the man standing in my kitchen, cooking at the stove.

It's Ethan.

Did he stay the night?

"What are you doing here?"

He turns to me, still stirring something in a pot, and smiles casually, as if it's normal for him to be cooking in my kitchen. "Hey," he says cheerfully. "Hungry?"

On cue, my stomach growls ferociously.

"I guess so," I admit, still surprised to see him.

"Sit," he commands, and I do because I'm too sick to function.

He sets a bowl in front of me.

I don't know what to think. I look down at it and then back up at him.

What?

His grin is so big, you'd think the man never scowled a day in his life.

"How— Where— Explain yourself."

He sits across from me at the table, still smiling proudly. "Your mom called. And then she called again. And again. By the fourth time, I finally answered. I told her you weren't feeling well, and we got to chatting, and she gave me the recipe."

"You talked to my mom? And she was nice?"

"Yeah." He shrugs. "Well, at first she was a little scary and then she was nicer."

He talked to my mom.

I must be hallucinating.

"You're telling me that my man-hating mother gave you her sacred caldo de pollo recipe?"

"Yep. Try it." His eyes dart down to the bowl.

My senses are off, so I probably won't be able to taste much of it, but presentation-wise, it's spot on. I slurp a spoonful, Ethan watching me like a hawk the whole time.

"Well?"

"It's pretty good," I admit. "I wouldn't know the difference."

He continues chatting with me, and I hem and haw in all the right places, but my mind is somewhere else entirely.

My mom hasn't made this for me in years. I was probably in high school the last time. It's not a hard recipe, and I've made it a few times, but it's one of those things that tastes better when someone else makes it for you. The fact that she gave him the recipe is a whole other thing to unpack. What could he have said? I'll deal with that when my brain feels less like mush.

Maybe it's the fever, or maybe I'm seeing what I want to see, but I get the feeling Ethan wouldn't go out of his way like this for just anyone. What that means, I'm not entirely sure. But I can't keep pretending this is just a friendship. This is more. And I think it's more than I've ever experienced. But where does that leave us?

I finish my bowl, and even though my taste buds are a little off, it really did taste like my mom's. I don't know how he did it. I look at him, feeling more awake, and notice something is off. He looks...different.

"What are you wearing?"

"What?" he says, turning away to place my bowl in the sink, but I still notice the tips of his ears turning a shade of pink.

"Are those Shane's clothes?" I can't recall Ethan ever wearing something like this, but I know for a fact I've seen Shane wear something similar around town.

He shakes his head, keeping his back to me before turning around and looking everywhere but my eyes.

It's not that I'm complaining. He looks good. He looks more than good.

"Shane and his stupid ideas," Ethan says, more to himself than to me.

He looks younger somehow, with his face pinched, looking equal parts frustrated and annoyed. It's cute, and I feel the weirdest urge to squeeze his cheeks.

I think the fever is making me weird.

I stand, but it's too fast, and the vertigo makes me sway.

Ethan zips toward me, grabbing at my ribs to steady me. "Maybe I should take you to bed."

I still, letting my body go slack in his hold, and look up at him. I may be sick, but I'm not *that* sick.

He winces and shakes his head. "To lie down," he clarifies, but it's too late. My mind went there immediately.

He stays holding me as he guides me back to my bedroom. On the way there, I notice that either little fairies appeared while I was sleeping and cleaned the cottage, or it was Ethan.

"You cleaned?" I know it was him. Who else would it be?

"A bit," he says nonchalantly.

The heat in my chest rises a few degrees. He made me soup and he cleaned and he's taking care of me. It's too much. It feels too good. I don't know what to do with all the emotions flooding me at once.

I could easily get used to this. I can't recall ever being taken care of this way. Maybe as a child, but even then it's different because it's a parent. Brandon sure never did. In fact, he would quarantine himself whenever I would get sick, leaving me to basically take care of myself. I've been so deprived of care like this I don't know how to handle it. By the time we get in my bedroom and Ethan helps me climb into bed, my mind is a battlefield of emotions. I try to mask it, but I'm sure he can see the turmoil written all over my face.

Ethan's gaze meets mine, and he freezes. "What's wrong? Does something hurt?"

He's worried about me. Genuinely worried about me. And it's only a flu. My heart aches, the pressure of it cracking open my chest. That's how deprived I am, how desperate I feel. I'm so neglected, a couple of kind gestures are my undoing.

I look away, not wanting his concerned stare.

"My throat hurts," I lie. It's probably the one symptom I don't have.

His forehead wrinkles, but he doesn't question me. "I think I picked up some throat spray. Let me go check."

He leaves, and I let out a long breath. I'm not sure what's come over me. I think we've been spending too much time together, and it's confusing me. The lines are blurring, and the memory of our kiss is still sitting at the forefront of my mind. I can't let deep feelings develop. This feeling is fleeting, only a crush, an infatuation, nothing more. Our lives are going in two different directions. It would be pointless. It's why he put a stop to things. Because unlike me, he thinks with his head.

"Found it." Ethan returns, holding a bottle of throat spray.

"Thanks," I croak, twirling my thumbs. "You don't have to stay. You've been here since yesterday taking care of me. Go home, get some rest. Goose probably misses you."

"He's with my parents. And really I don't mind."

"I'm fine. Seriously. Go home." I offer a smile, hoping he'll buy it and leave.

He releases a long exhale. "I can't. There's something I need to tell you."

CHAPTER 34

Marisa

HIS HANDSHAKE WAS LIMP

"She's not coming," Ethan repeats.

I heard him the first time, but I didn't respond. My mom isn't coming.

"Oh," is all I manage to get out.

I should be feeling more.

More upset?

More emotional?

I feel none of those things. I feel nothing. A dark pit of nothingness.

"That's why she kept calling," he adds hesitantly.

"Well." A forced smile pulls at my lips as I sigh, my blinking eyes betraying what I can't hide with a smile. The sting of tears tickles my nose, so I take a deep breath and force them back. "Did she say why?"

He twists his watch nervously. When his eyes cut to mine, they're filled with sadness. He feels sorry for me. I look away, hating it.

"She didn't really say. She said she would call you to talk about it when you're feeling better."

I shrug, throwing the covers off myself, the bed suddenly feeling suffocating. "I'm sure she had her reasons."

A shower. That's what I need. I'm all goopy and snotty and clammy. I think a nice, hot shower would do wonders for me right now.

"Marisa," Ethan starts. "What are you doing?"

I grab a towel from my closet. "I'm going to shower."

"Do you want to talk about it?"

A bitter laugh jumps out of me. "No. I'm good."

He stands at the entry to the bathroom, blocking me from getting through. "Are you okay? You seem..."

His words die, but he holds his eyes to mine.

I offer him a brief, strained smirk. "I'm fine. I'd be even better if you moved."

His jaw tightens, lips drawing into a thin line as he stares at me for a few beats before stepping aside.

"You don't have to act tough around me. If you're upset about it, then be upset. Let it out."

My spine stiffens, annoyance working its way through me. "I really wish you'd drop it."

"I would if you weren't acting like a fucking mannequin."

"I don't know what you want from me," I bite. And then take a breath, trying to reel in my irritation. "Thank you for the soup and the medicine, but I'd like you to leave. I just want to be alone."

He nods, shoulders dropped and resigned, before quietly walking out. It's not until I hear the click of the door that my lip starts to tremble.

It's silly.

Stupid, honestly.

I don't even like Thanksgiving. The food is bland and boring.

I step into the shower, my skin rising with goosebumps even

as the hot water pours over me. My body is vibrating, shaking to the point that I feel like I'm swaying back and forth. It must be the flu, I'm probably still running a low grade fever. A loud choking noise blares over the sound of the water beating down on the tiles and I jump back slightly, trying to identify the source. It happens again, and I realize it's me. I'm the one choking.

Gasping.

My vision blurs under the fall of water. My chest heaves, shoulders dropping as the tension in my neck snaps like a rubber band. I break down, tears streaming heavily and mixing with the hot water.

My mom isn't coming.

Maybe I shampoo my hair, I'm not sure.

My mom isn't coming.

Maybe I wash my body, I'm not sure.

My mom isn't coming.

I let my skin turn wrinkled and pruny, standing under the water until it runs cold and forces me out.

As I'm wrapping the tie of my robe around my waist and knotting it, there's a knock on the front door.

It's probably Ethan coming to check on me.

I answer the door, ready to explain myself.

Except it's not Ethan.

"Dad?" I freeze for a second and then push the collar of my fluffy robe against my neck. "What are you doing here?"

"Can I come in?" he asks, already walking in.

I let the door fall open wider as he walks through and into the living room.

"What's going on?" Normally my dad would text or call before popping by. He's not really a random drop in kind of person.

"I ran into Ethan a few minutes ago." He takes a seat on the couch. "He told me about your mom."

Instead of answering, I stay quiet and close the door, keeping my head down.

"I'm sorry, sweets. I wish there was something I could do to change the situation."

I fuss with the tie on my robe. "Why are you apologizing? It's not like you're the one who promised you would come. The one who bought a plane ticket and even showed me a screenshot of the purchase. The one who hasn't been home to visit me in over three years."

He sighs, rubbing his face. "Your mom is—"

"Don't. If you're going to talk badly about her. Don't. I don't want to hear it."

He shifts his head, regarding me patiently. "Will you let me finish?"

I take a seat on the couch, curling my legs under me, and give him a nod.

"Your mom is a free spirit." He looks at me, asking for silent permission to proceed.

I give it to him with arched brows.

"I ever tell you how we met?"

I shake my head, biting down on my tongue. I'm not sure I want to know, but I do at the same time.

"She worked at this hole-in-the-wall ice cream shop right off campus. I would drop in there between my afternoon classes every Thursday. And every time, I would try to talk to her. Joke around, flirt. But she wasn't having it. Her accent was a lot thicker back then, and I thought it was the sexiest thing I'd ever heard."

I cringe, giggling. He chuckles, his eyes looking into the distance, as if he's remembering it. It's bittersweet hearing the origin of their story, knowing that the ending isn't a happy one.

"Anyway," he continues. "I kept going, and then one day she was like, 'Are you going to ask me out or what?' So I did.

And we fell in love. When we found out about you, we were excited, but we were also terrified because we weren't ready. I think we both projected a lot of our fears onto you. We wanted you to be everything we never could be. With me, that meant academics. I wanted you to have your pick of colleges, of career options. I wanted you to achieve all of your dreams. With your mom, she wanted you to be that free, young woman that she had to suppress while raising you. Her family...well, they weren't very kind. They were extremely religious, and she felt trapped in her upbringing. When she eventually found her way to the states, she was excited for some freedom. Neither one of us, but especially her, were quite ready to be parents. But she's been a good mom to you, and she loves you. You know she does."

"I know," I say quietly. "It just sucks."

"And I'm sorry for being so hard on you. For making you feel like you weren't good enough. I hated watching you settle for that job. Settle for that guy. You wanted to be a writer and when that dream changed for you, I guess I had a hard time letting it go."

My eyes look at his, glassy as they stare at me.

"You are more than enough. You're everything."

The dam breaks. I'm still unstable from crying in the shower, and now I'm crying again. My dad scoops me up in his arms and holds me while I cry.

Still cradling me, he clears his throat. "You know, I bought the *Herald* because of you."

My body stills, and I pull back, meeting his eyes. "What?"

"Sweets, I worked in publishing for twenty years. You think I don't know that newspapers are a dying media.

"I don't understand."

"I'd already ruined things with you and then an old buddy told me about a newspaper in a tourist down being for sale. He only mentioned it in passing, but it piqued my interest because I was ready to start slowing down. I don't know...I thought maybe you'd want to come along with me. Obviously, our relationship was too broken for that conversation, but I still held out hope that one day I'd get to see you become a journalist. I know it's not New York or some fancy magazine, but it's something."

A heavy knot weighs in my throat, only adding to the emotional overhaul today has been. "Why didn't you say anything?"

His shoulders lift with a sigh. "I was going to. You and I had plans to get dinner before I moved and I had it all prepared, but then you showed up with that piece of shit and stars in your eyes, and I knew I lost you. I also knew he was a twerp not good enough for my little girl."

I let out a watery snort. "You could tell in just one meeting?"

His lips contort. "Sweets, a man knows. His handshake was limp and he looked at you like a prize, like a pretty thing to have on his arm, not like a man in love. But you weren't a kid anymore and I couldn't tell you all of that. I could only hope that you'd figure it out, which you did."

As I wipe my damp cheeks, my mind is reeling. "I wish you had told me sooner about the *Herald*...and about Brandon, too."

He exhales a small smile. "I know you're heading back to Seattle and that job is an amazing opportunity, but just know you'll always have a place at the *Herald*, and you'll always have a place with me. I may not have been the greatest dad, but I love you very much and you're never going to stop being my little girl."

I'm not sure how long we sit, catching up on years' worth of conversations. An hour. Maybe more.

Eventually, we both pull it together. He tells me about

Caleb's football game. How Sadie showed up with a boyfriend she's been hiding from Jenn and they had a big blowup.

"Oh, I forgot to tell you. I met with my financial guy and we worked out a better deal for your loan. Payments are now a much more manageable $350 a month."

"Thank you for handling that," I tell him, still a embarrassed I got myself in that mess.

He waves it off. "If you don't make a bad money decision in your twenties, then you'll make one in your thirties, and that's worse."

The conversation shifts, and he invites me to Jenn's family's Thanksgiving, repeating several times they would welcome me with open arms, that they're really nice people. I tell him I'll think about it.

"Goodnight, sweets. Feel better and get some rest." He kisses my forehead and leaves.

Once my dad is gone, I continue to think about what he said about settling. Was I settling becoming a technical writer instead of continuing to pursue journalism? At the time, it felt like the more responsible decision. It's not as if dreams pay the bills, but now I'm questioning what I even want at this point. My job at the *Herald* is only supposed to be temporary. Everything about Red Mountain is supposed to be temporary.

Later on that night, I contemplate texting Ethan but decide against it. I think what I actually need is space. A day. Maybe two.

CHAPTER 35

Ethan

THAT'S WHAT SHE SAID

The day before Thanksgiving, the winery is a madhouse. It's an all-hands-on-deck kind of day. Even Ariana is hard at work, having shut down Novel early to help out. She and Layla are manning the tasting room so our regular attendants can have the day off. Between wine club members picking up their fall release cases, locals and out-of-towners doing tastings, and the restaurant overflowing, it feels like every corner of the estate is filled. To stay away from the commotion, I remain upstairs in my office.

"You mind if I cut out early?" Tawny asks. "I have a lot of prep work to do before my in-laws come over."

"Go ahead," I tell her absentmindedly.

She leans her body in through the doorway. "Oh, and by the way, you have a visitor." She winks and then disappears down the hall.

I get up and round the corner, about to ask who it is when I find Marisa, nearly running into her. She looks so fucking pretty.

But more than that, she looks healthy, too. The color has returned to her cheeks, and her eyes look much more alive than the last time I saw her. Apart from a text to ask how she was feeling, I haven't seen or spoken to her since she kicked me out after I told her about her mom not coming.

She looks at me, chin slightly down, lips rolled back and a hint of uncertainty in her eyes.

"Hey," I say, breathless.

"Hey." She smiles. It's her nervous one. "Busy?"

Extremely. "No, come on in."

I lean my hip against my desk, and she sits in one of the leather wingbacks. "I wanted to come by and apologize for the other night. I shouldn't have been so short with you, especially after you were nice enough to make me soup and take care of me. I feel really bad about the whole thing. I think it was the fever, you know? It was making me cranky and emotional, and really, I was a mess."

I love it when she rambles. "No need to apologize. I'm just glad you're feeling better. And that you don't look like a sickly Victorian child dying from scarlet fever anymore."

Her jaw drops, releasing a gasping laugh. "You're an ass."

"Go for Ethan," Gavin's static voice blares through my radio, causing us both to jump.

I grab the radio off my desk. "This is Ethan. Over."

"Do you have time to go down to the cellar? I think I left behind my stainless steel wine thief. Can you go check? I have to pick up Lily and don't have time."

"I'll handle it. Over."

Marisa rises, sliding her purse over her shoulder. "I'll head out. You seem busy."

That may be true, but I'm not ready for her to leave. "Have you seen the cellar yet?"

"No," she says hesitantly, but her eyes are curious. "It's not creepy down there, is it?"

"No." I laugh through my nose. "Come on. Come with me."

The stairs that lead down to the cellar are being renovated, so we take the elevator. When the doors open, there's a noticeable drop in temperature. Marisa instantly folds her arms. I take off my flannel, draping it over her shoulders before she can protest.

She shivers and blows on her palms. "I thought you said it wasn't creepy."

"It isn't," I counter.

She rolls her eyes at me, slipping her arms through the sleeves and clutching my flannel tighter around herself. The sleeves hang way past her hands and the fabric completely engulfs her. I don't think I'll ever not love the sight of her in my clothes.

"What are we looking for again?" Her eyes wander over the hundreds of barrels stacked to the ceiling. I've been down here more times than I can count and forget that it's something worth looking at. It's one of the most popular spots for first looks between couples getting married at the winery.

"A thief. It's a long, shiny, silver thing."

She snorts and says, "That's what she said," under her breath.

Gavin would've left it near the cluster of barrels, ready for racking. I glance around, and sure enough, it's sitting on a cart next to the barrels.

"Found it," I announce.

Marisa, who's wandered off, starts walking my way, the sounds of her shoes echoing closer and closer.

"Good, it's fucking freezing."

"Okay, let's go—"

A loud boom sounds, and the lights cut out. Marisa screams and grabs on to me, her nails digging into my skin.

"What was that?" Her voice is muffled from her mouth pressing into my arm.

The lighting is dim and terrible down here, but without it, it's pitch black.

"I'm not sure." I wrap an arm around her shoulders and pull her against me, telling myself it's for safety and has nothing to do with loving the feel of her in my arms. She grabs on to me tighter. "If we go this way, we can sit down and I'll make some calls."

I feel her nod as she walks with me to the edge of the wall. Together, we slide down onto our bottoms and sit on the concrete, pulling apart as we do.

Gavin beats me to the punch and calls through on the radio. "Did anybody else hear an explosion?"

"What happened? Marisa and I are trapped in the cellar."

"I think a transformer blew, but I'm not sure. I'll have Mom go get Lily. If you give me about twenty minutes, I'll come release the roll-up door and get you guys out. That is, assuming the power doesn't come back on before then."

"Sounds good. We'll wait."

Marisa tenses. "A whole twenty minutes in the dark? Thank God you're here with me. I think I'd be panicking if I were alone. At least with you, I know I'm safe."

Her words shouldn't affect me the way they do. She'd likely feel safe with anyone. It's not the person, it's the idea. It's not having to face the darkness alone. But in this instance, it is *me* who she feels safe with, and I'm going to let myself sit in that feeling longer than I should.

The darkness, the silence, it's like we've slipped outside of reality. Time is still.

Marisa shivers and, without thinking, I wrap my arm back around her and tuck her in close. She sighs, and it vibrates through my side.

"Thank you." Her teeth chatter. "I hope I don't get you sick, I'm probably still contagious."

"You're fine," I say in a low voice and pull her even closer.

We haven't been this close since we kissed. I missed her. Is that possible? To miss someone despite seeing her all the time? Her vanilla scent drifts between us. It's a drug. A drug I've quickly become addicted to.

She turns her head toward my neck, and her breath tickles my skin. "Ethan?" she whispers.

"Hmm?" I don't trust my voice.

"Do you ever think about it?"

My lungs squeeze. All breathing comes to a halt. I'm not sure if her mind is where mine is.

A silent beat passes.

"The kiss," she clarifies.

All the time. "Yes," I say hesitantly. I'm not sure where she's going with this.

"Me, too," she admits.

Silence.

It stretches between us, thick like dense fog. I don't know where to go from here. I feel like anything I could say would be wrong.

I want to kiss you again.

I think about kissing you all the time.

I wonder what would've happened had we not been interrupted.

So.

Many.

Thoughts.

Her fingers begin tiptoeing across my torso, as if they're dancing to a silent song. Is it intentional? Is she trying to kill me?

A pattern forms. Definitely intentional.

Her body shakes, and for a second, I think she's crying, but I quickly realize she's snickering.

"What are you doing?"

She snorts, laughing harder. "I don't know what you're talking about." Her voice is full of mock confusion.

I bark a laugh. "Are you sure you don't still have a fever?"

"I was feeling fidgety and didn't know what to do with my hands." She's giggling. That same awful giggle I heard that first night. I liked it then, but now I'm certain I love it.

She starts the dance again, but I quickly capture her hand in mine.

"Boo," she protests. "You're no fun."

She can't see my face. She can't see that I'm always up for a challenge. "That's it." I trap her so she can't move and tickle her under her ribs.

She squeals so loud it echoes. "Ethan," she screams.

Fuck, do I wish my name was being screamed like that for an entirely different reason.

She squirms, trying to escape, but I'm relentless.

Her shirt lifts.

My hands slip.

Her skin is so smooth right here. So warm.

"Ethan," she moans.

I still, my hands freezing.

She wiggles. Or maybe that's her hips grinding.

Her warm breath dusts along my earlobe. "Don't stop," she whispers.

My throat bobs. Am I hallucinating?

Moisture forms where her breath was a moment ago. I'm losing it. Imagining things that aren't real.

Then a pinch. A nip. Teeth pulling on the delicate skin.

I definitely didn't imagine that.

She wiggles again, moving her body. Now instead of

285

leaning on me on her side, she faces me, kneeling in the space between my widened legs.

"Ethan..." she says quietly. She's close enough that her whisper fans my face. She slides her hands up my torso, over my chest, snaking them around my neck. "I'm so tired of fighting this. Please tell me it's not one-sided."

Fuck...

My hand reaches for her, pulling her against me. Our foreheads press together as we share the same air.

"It's not one-sided." My hands dig into her hips, desperate to feel her closer. "Are you sure?" I ask. Three words that mean a hell of a lot more than what I'm asking.

Are you sure about this? Because we both know where this leads. We're about to cross the line.

Her forehead moves against mine. "Yes."

And it's all the permission I need. I grip her firmly, readjusting us so she's straddling me.

Her. Wrapped around me. There's no better feeling.

I tip her chin up and start trailing my mouth down her neck. Her breath hitches, and she angles her head back, arching into me.

"Oh," she breathes.

My hands glide up her neck and grab hold of her jaw as I finally let go of the last of my resolve.

Our mouths crash together. Lips parting, tongues plunging, moving together, completely in sync.

I thought my mind had warped the memory of our first kiss, making it better than reality. But I was wrong.

Nothing beats reality. Nothing beats her.

My hands slide under her shirt, around her lower back, wandering up and down in a feather-light exploration, before coming down and grabbing onto her perfect ass. I hold it firmly, my hands flexing over her rounded cheeks. I pull her closer, forcing her to press against my growing erection.

She moans into my mouth and voluntarily grinds down.

Two seconds of some light dry humping, and I'm ready to come in my pants. My body feels like a live wire. Everywhere she touches, everywhere she is, I spark.

"Fuck, it's so good," she breathes, pulling her lips off mine. "Why is it so good?"

I answer by kissing her again. Deeper. Harder.

She smiles against my mouth and starts tugging at my belt.

I work on her jeans, unbuttoning and unzipping faster than she can loosen my belt. I need to know how wet she is. I need to *feel* how wet she is.

My fingers slip into her pants, yanking aside her panties.

I sink in one finger.

So wet.

Two fingers.

So tight.

Her back arches.

Fuck, she's soaked.

My fingers curl. The sounds of her soaking pussy encourage me to go faster.

She squirms and wiggles and sighs and moans. I eat up every sound and stroke my thumb against her clit.

"Oh, God!" Marisa's hips jerk. A cry leaves her lips as I push in deeper, knuckles deep inside her perfect fucking pussy.

Her nails dig into my back, painfully, and I love it. I love being the reason she's unraveling, rolling her hips as I finger-fuck her into oblivion. She's writhing, moving uninhibited.

"That's it, baby," I murmur. Hooking my fingers further, I hit just the right spot. Her hips buck, and I hold her firmly around the waist, not letting her body jerk away from her building orgasm.

"Come for me. Come all over my fingers. Drench them, baby."

She tenses and her pussy spasms, gripping my fingers like a vise. Her moans and sighs are a sweet melody to my ears.

As she comes down, I remove my fingers, unable to resist the urge to taste her on them. I've regretted missing out on it when we were in the truck and promised myself not to make that mistake again. She tastes like sin. Like a sweet fruit I'd gladly let be my downfall. I knew she would smell good, and I knew she would taste good, but I wasn't quite expecting for my brain to be screaming *mine* the moment I got to actually do it. But fuck, does she taste like mine and smell like mine. She's fucking mine. Now that I've had her like this, I can't return to the man I was. I can't return to what *we* were before we burned every line we'd ever drawn.

She goes languid in my arms, and fuck, I can't decide which I like better. Giving her orgasms, or having the privilege to hold her afterward.

"How are you so good at that?" She moans lazily, her cheek pressed against my chest. "Actually, never mind. Don't answer that."

I rub up and down her back and toy with the ends of her hair. "A man knows how to work what's his."

She stiffens, and I worry I went too far. If only she could read my mind, she'd know my feelings for her are way past casual. She's given me this part of herself. Her body. But I want so much more than that, and I'm not sure we'll ever be on the same page. So I'll happily accept the physical in hopes that she'll get there. But I won't hold my breath.

The tension in her body releases and she relaxes against me again. I can barely make out her eyes, but I'm positive they roll.

"I'd have a witty retort, but you've rendered my brain useless."

I chuckle, giving her neck a nuzzle. "If my fingers did that, imagine what my co—"

Her hand grips me over my pants, giving my cock a firm stroke, and it twitches so hard I'm surprised my zipper doesn't bust. Quickly, I take her hand in mine and pull it away from my painfully hard dick.

"I want to touch you," she protests. "It only seems fair."

Snorting, I shake my head. "We're not keeping score. You don't owe me a hand job."

"It's not about keeping score. I want you to feel good, too." She pauses a beat and places a soft kiss on my neck. "And who said anything about a hand job? I want you in my mouth."

Jesus Christ.

I'm not strong enough.

"You're killing me," I grit.

She giggles and then sneaks her hand back to my belt, her dainty fingers working at it much rougher than I thought possible. My dick, with a mind of his own, stands at full attention for her.

I should stop her. I don't want this moment to be about me. But my resolve is gone.

Her hand edges my boxer briefs before sliding inside.

"Holy shit," she exclaims, causing my brain to short-circuit as she wraps her hand around my cock. "I knew you were decently sized, but I didn't know you were *this* big."

My ego inflates tenfold.

"I hate to break it to you," she says, as if I can concentrate on her words when she's pumping my cock. "But there's no way this thing is fitting inside of my mouth." She brushes her thumb over the tip, spreading around my bead of pre-cum.

"We could skip your mouth and go straight for your pussy," I joke. Which I immediately regret, because I shouldn't push my luck.

She laughs. "Definitely not fitting in there."

Oh, it'll fit.

This tease of a woman is going to be the death of me. I grab her, cupping her face, and kiss her roughly. She moans into my mouth, pumping my cock faster.

I'm so close to coming. I should be embarrassed that I'll blow my load faster than I think I ever have before, but I don't give a single fuck. I've wanted Marisa for so long, my body has been primed for her, just waiting to be touched by her and only her.

Metal panels rattle together at the far end of the cellar. Marisa throws herself off me, and I swiftly tuck my dick back in my pants. Slowly, the cellar fills with light as each panel of the roll-up door moves up the track.

In the darkness, it felt like we were in a haven, separated from the real world, but as the harsh light descends, reality sets in. Marisa is working on adjusting and smoothing her clothes, erasing all evidence of me. She finger-combs her hair and swipes her thumb along the edges of her lips. She won't even look at me.

Fuck.

"Gavin to the rescue!" Gavin shouts as he walks through the opening.

Marisa scrambles out of my shirt, tossing it at me as she steps away, putting a noticeable gap between us. She may as well be somewhere else entirely. When Gavin gets close enough to see us, there's no mistaking how we look. Marisa can try to hide the evidence, but it's obvious what we were doing.

He makes eye contact with me, wearing a shit-eating grin.

Definitely obvious.

"I guess it's time to put the man-door in that we've been discussing for years, huh?"

"Seems like it," I agree absentmindedly.

We walk out, and my eyes squint from the harsh daylight. It's a cloudy, dull day, but I still need some time for my vision to adjust. I look at Marisa, and she's using her hand to shield some of the light away from her eyes.

"What caused the power outage?" she asks Gavin.

He shrugs, shaking his head. "Probably a blown transformer like I said, but it's not just us. The whole mountain is without power."

It's a cool forty degrees with a northern breeze that chills right to the bone. And it's only going to get colder once the sun goes down.

"I should head back," Marisa states, already on the rounded path that leads back up to the winery.

I look at Gavin and nudge my head, indicating to give us some privacy. He bites his lip, holding back a laugh. Motherfucker. I'm never going to hear the end of this. But he does at least have the decency to turn around and walk the few hundred yards back to his truck.

"Marisa, wait," I call out.

She's already walked surprisingly far, so I do a half-jog to catch up to her.

She pauses, turning to me with a cheery smile. "What's up?"

She's going to try to pretend nothing happened.

Yeah, fuck that. Without hesitation, I pull her toward me and crash my lips to hers. She tenses for a split second before parting her mouth and letting me in. I try to tell her what I can't seem to vocalize.

I devour her, demanding her surrender. And she gives it, melting into me. I groan, gripping her harder, rougher.

Anyone could walk by and see us. And I don't care. Let them see. But I know if I don't stop now, I'm going to push her too far.

I pull away. Her eyes are dazed, lips puffy, cheeks pink. Fucking beautiful.

"We'll finish this later."

CHAPTER 36

Marisa

TASTE IT

I t's been three hours. Three hours of overthinking. Three hours of my mind reeling. And the power is still out. At first, it didn't bother me, but now the sun is going down and the cottage is getting colder.

And still no Ethan. Not a call, not a text, nothing.

A firm knock at the door has me practically jumping out of my skin.

I answer it and find Ethan standing on my porch steps. He changed. Earlier, he was wearing a flannel with a canvas vest and jeans, and now, he's wearing slim-fit jeans, nicer ones in a darker shade, and a forest-green henley that brings out the green in his hazel eyes.

"Hey," he says with his hands in his pockets. "Can I come in?"

I nod, stepping back from the door and opening it wider so he can pass through. A stupid mistake on my part. His smell invades my senses, and my knees start to wobble. My arms fold across my chest. Some form of self-protection, I guess. As he walks by me, I give him a once-over, my cheeks instantly heating as my eyes flash to his crotch. Earlier today, I had his rock-hard dick in my hands, and now, I don't know how to act like a normal person.

He's been inside for a second, and I'm overwhelmed. Not necessarily by him, but by the situation and where we go from here. It's enough to make me spiral.

I cough, swallow, and take a deep breath, trying to compose myself.

"The power is still out, huh?"

Obviously, Marisa.

"Yeah. I can't remember it ever being out this long. We had to shut down business for the day, but there were still a lot of orders that had to be picked up. It was kind of a shit show."

"Why's that? Just the chaos?"

His shoulders lift, and our eyes meet. "That and I had to talk to a bunch of people." He cringes, and some of the unease hanging in the air gradually lightens.

"Oh, no. Not people."

"Don't make fun of me. It was very exhausting."

I let out a bubbly laugh, daring to get closer. "You poor baby."

Ethan takes a steady step toward me, and one side of his mouth curves up in a lopsided grin.

But it drops before I get to enjoy it. "What the fuck is that?"

I look back over my shoulder at the kitchen, where I have several bottles of wine spread across the counter.

And they're not Ledger wine.

Oops.

Ethan brushes past me and picks up the first bottle, reading the label in disbelief. "Why is Cole's wine on my property?"

Oh, Jesus. Here we go. "It's not Cole's wine, it's Benton wine."

He releases a dry, humorless huff. "Like there's a difference."

I almost forgot how hot he looks when he's upset. He's been so nice lately.

"It's work related."

His eyes cut to mine. "How so?" he grits.

"Benton remodeled their tasting room, and they're doing a grand reopening next week. I was trying to educate myself, learn the tasting notes and what not."

Some of the annoyance softens around his eyes. But only slightly. "If you want to learn about wine, come to me."

I wasn't trying to learn about wine in general. I was trying to learn about Benton wine, but I don't correct him.

"Come on." He grabs my hand, dragging me toward the front door.

"Where are we going?" I ask, letting him pull me to keep feeling his hand over mine.

"Back to the winery."

"How is it warm in here?"

"Backup generators. We can't afford for the atmosphere in the temperature-controlled rooms to change."

Ethan leads me to the empty tasting room. I've never been inside after hours. A single row of dim recessed lights illuminates the space.

"Are we the only ones here?"

"Yeah, I sent everyone home." Ethan points to the barstool. "Sit," he commands.

"We don't have to do this right now. We can wait until after Thanksgiving when the winery is open."

The look he gives me tells me there won't be any changing his mind.

I take a seat, and he sets down two glasses for me and him.

"Too many people. I think a little privacy is needed for today's lesson."

Okay, well, that sounded dirty. Involuntarily, my thighs squeeze together, hidden by the imposing marble counter. Ethan's eyes drag from mine, down my neck, stopping at the cleavage poking out over my top, leaving a path of heat in their wake. He pulls his bottom lip in with his teeth, and a spark ignites in my core.

"What's the lesson?" I squeak, my voice revealing how much his eye-fuck affected me.

A haughty grin tugs at his lips. "Wine tasting, of course."

Of course. Because why would I be thinking about anything else?

He starts opening one of the bottles, a loud pop sounding as he pulls out the cork. He grabs my glass and pours the deep-burgundy liquid.

While pouring his own glass he says, "This bottle is this year's Ledger Estate Red Blend." His voice is a low murmur.

With both glasses holding a decent pour, our eyes meet and the room seems to shrink, the air growing heavier by the second.

"Taste it," he commands.

I think I'm going to melt into a puddle. I'm not mature enough for this. He says *taste it,* and it takes all of my willpower for my eyes to not stare directly at his dick.

I pick up the glass and bring it to my lips, but he stops me. "Wait."

My body freezes, waiting for his next command.

"Look at it first," he continues. "I know it's not very bright in here, but hold it up and let the light catch it."

I do as I'm told, holding it up for the dim light above to shine against the glass.

"You're looking for clarity, if there's any sediment."

I honestly cannot see anything, but I'm playing along because every other word out of his mouth sounds like an innuendo.

"Now, bring it down and swirl it gently before you smell it."

Following his directions, I do exactly that, inhaling the spicy aroma.

"Now you can taste it," he tells me, his voice a husky whisper.

I take a sip, closing my eyes as the liquid slides down my throat and spreads warmth through my chest.

When my eyes reopen, Ethan is no longer standing on the other side of the bar. Instead, he's next to me, spinning me in the swiveling bar stool. My legs fall open for him naturally, allowing him to step closer, my inner thighs brushing against his outer thighs.

My erratic heartbeat is so loud, I'm sure he can hear it. He leans in, and the world outside of this moment ceases to exist. It's only us and our warm breaths intermingling with one another. His heated, intense gaze sends thrums of anticipation through me, while an overwhelming desire blooms at my core, growing, building. I lean closer, on the cusp of begging.

"What did you taste?" he whispers against my lips.

"I...I..." My voice is a tremble. And just when I think he's going to kiss me, he pulls away.

"Let's try the next one, yeah?" He walks back around the bar and works at opening another bottle. Not particularly rushed, every move calm and steady. Meanwhile, I'm about to combust.

He fills another glass. This time, the liquid is a lighter red, almost hot pink. "With this one, after you take a sip, swirl it around in your mouth before you swallow. It'll release the aromas and let you evaluate the mouthfeel."

Swirl?

Swallow?

Mouthfeel?

Is wine tasting supposed to sound pornographic?

We lock eyes. The man is pure evil. He knows exactly what he's doing.

Well, two can play at that game.

I fix my eyes on him and tip my head back, taking a sip. And just as he instructed, I swirl it around, letting the liquid coat my mouth before swallowing it loudly. Just to fuck with him, I drop open my mouth and stick my tongue out. I may not be able to read his mind, but I'd bet good money he's picturing slapping his dick against it.

His eyes flare with heat, and a devilish grin spreads across my face.

"Brat," he mutters.

I've decided he's had too much control, and I think it's time he lost some of it. I slide out of the barstool and walk around, meeting him on his side of the bar as he watches me curiously.

"The lesson isn't over yet," he tells me as I inch closer.

"Let's take a break."

I reach for his belt, and he tenses but doesn't stop me. Once it's undone, I pull it off and let it fall to the floor. It lands with a clack as the buckle meets the tile. Keeping a steady stare, I slowly drop to my knees in front of him and tip my chin up to see his tense jaw and bewildered eyes. "I want something else in my mouth."

He sucks in a breath, and I lick my lips.

"Fuck," he breathes.

I was feeling overly confident, but now that I'm on my knees in front of him, some of that confidence is waning. This is a big step, a giant leap from some heavy kissing and a little hand action. If we do this, there really is no going back. But maybe I don't want to go back. Maybe I'm done trying to convince myself that I don't want this man with every fiber of my being.

"Marisa," he says softly. Gone is the commanding man, and back is *my* Ethan. The version of him reserved for me. "You don't have to—"

I don't second guess it. I undo his button and rip down his zipper. He sucks in a sharp breath as my hand wraps around his cock over his tented boxer briefs. In one swift motion, I pull down his jeans and boxers, and his cock springs free, fully erect, hardened, with a bead of pre-cum glistening at the tip. And fuck, is it massive, just inches from my face. Now I'm nervous for an entirely different reason.

"Eyes up here, baby."

My eyes shift from his cock up to those hooded hazels. He looks drugged, barely restraining himself. I keep my focus trained on him as I open up my mouth and take him, going as far as I can until his tip is down my throat. Ethan's head falls back, and he groans.

"Holy fuck." His voice is a moaning whisper, husky and shaky. And it's because of me. Because he's entirely bound by my will. Right now, I own him.

As my mouth bobs, I use one hand to pump him and the other to gently caress his balls. His hands tangle in my hair, gripping it roughly. He tugs on it and flexes his hips, fucking my face. Breathing through my nose, I try to take him deeper, and my nose gets flooded with his musky scent that forces a moan out of me. The sound vibrates up my throat.

"You like sucking my cock, don't you?" He sounds equally turned on and shocked, as if no one could ever enjoy this.

I drop my hand from his balls, unbutton my pants, and

start touching myself. I was already wet from the naughty wine tasting, but now I'm soaked.

Ethan's surprised eyes look down at me in complete amazement.

I jerk my head faster, pumping and twisting his base with my hand, all the while never breaking eye contact.

"Your mouth feels too good, baby," he grits. "I'm going to come embarrassingly fast."

His words only encourage me to move even faster.

"Fuuuuuck," he drags.

With a deep breath, I pass the point I thought I could take him and go deeper. My eyes water, and a lewd choking sound comes up my throat. "That's it, baby, choke on my cock like a good girl."

His filthy words cause my pussy to throb, and I start grinding my hips, chasing relief.

"I'm close. Pull away now if you don't want me to finish in your mouth."

I do the opposite and maintain my pace. Seconds later, his cock is twitching and jerking, his cum spilling into my mouth. The moaning that escapes him is feral and animalistic, and I fucking love it. When he's done, he slowly releases his cock from my mouth, but I remain on my knees, teary-eyed. When our eyes meet, I drop open my mouth to show him his cum sitting on my tongue.

He crouches down and drags his thumb along my jaw. "Holy shit," he says softly, drawing in a breath. "You look so good with a mouthful of cum. Now swirl it around in your mouth before you swallow."

I do as I'm told, just like I did with the wine, and make an exaggerated, audible swallow.

"Where did you come from?" he says in disbelief.

He crushes his mouth to mine, obviously not caring that he can taste himself. The kiss is blazing and intense. It's a thank you. He pulls me closer, and I wind my hands around his neck.

Slowly, he drags us to a standing position and pulls away from our kiss, leaning his forehead against mine. "That was the best blow job of my life." His breath fans my damp lips.

I giggle quietly and take a step back. So much just happened. My mind is reeling. With my head down and back turned, I hear Ethan zip up his pants.

A pit of insecurity forms in my stomach. Dread creeps in where I once felt powerful. Was that too much? Does he think less of me now that I've sucked his dick without so much as a date? I feel like that stupid archaic saying about buying the cow and free milk. I don't know where to go from here or what this means—

Soft lips meet the exposed skin on my shoulder and start littering light kisses. Instantly, the tension drops and my head flops to the side. His lips work their way up to my ear, and his warm breath tickles me.

"Now sit on the bar and spread those thighs. We're not leaving this room until I get to taste you."

CHAPTER 37

Ethan

CLEAN-SHAVEN CITY BOYS

Marisa looks up at me, biting her lip, her big brown eyes pinched in confusion. "Why?"

I laugh. She has no idea. Doesn't she get it? The question shouldn't be *why*, it should be *why not?* I've only been fantasizing about eating her pussy for far too long.

"Baby, I dream about getting to taste you."

I grab her hand that was playing with her pussy while she sucked me off and bring her fingers to my lips. Before I lick them clean, I take a big inhale, and my eyes roll back when I get a whiff of her intoxicating scent. Her rounded eyes watch me as I lick her fingers like a goddamn popsicle.

"Now take off your pants and sit that sweet ass on this bar. I'm starving."

Her cheeks turn bright pink, and she rolls her lips, trying to hide her smile.

Using my thumb, I free her bottom lip. "Don't hide this from me."

I press a soft kiss to her lips and tug at her pants. She helps me, and together, we slide them off her. I hook her lace thong with my index fingers and strip them down, helping her step out of them. Her stare holds mine as she hops up and sits on the edge of the counter. Just a few moments ago, she was looking a little shy, but the woman before me is all confidence, flashing me a sexy little smile as she spreads her perfect thighs, putting that glistening pussy on display for me.

"Is this what you wanted?" she asks coyly.

My mouth waters. And like the playful tease she is, she takes two fingers and uses them to spread her pussy lips.

So wet.

A growl crawls up my throat before I crouch down and run my nose along her seam, inhaling her addicting scent.

She leans back on her hands, watching me with lust-filled, sultry eyes. Those beautiful lashes of hers flutter slightly with each blink, drawing me in.

I flatten my tongue right at her center and lap up the pooled moisture. Arching her back, she drops her elbows, resting her back on the marble counter while her thighs fall open wider. She moans, squirming and flailing, but I keep a firm grip on her thighs to hold her in place while I devour her pussy like my life depends on it. Fucking her with my tongue and pumping two hooked fingers inside of her, I'm quickly drawing out her orgasm. Her hips start lifting, grinding against my face, while her strangled cries echo around me. She grips my fingers tightly, and I know she's close.

"I'm going to come," she breathes.

I keep pumping into her with my fingers curled, hitting against her inner wall, and press my thumb to her clit while licking and sucking the sweet liquid pouring out of her. She comes with a jolt, back lifting, a groaning sigh escaping her lips. Her body bends and twists as the orgasm releases, and it's the best fucking thing I've ever seen.

Seconds pass as her sprawled body heaves up and down from her deep breaths.

"Oh, my God," she sighs. "I've never come that way."

"If you've never had a real man between your legs, just say so."

She snorts, and it morphs into a fit of giggles. "The ego on you. I shouldn't have said anything. It was probably the beard."

"What?" I laugh. "Those clean-shaven city boys can't eat pussy? Can't say I'm surprised."

Still lying down, she gives my hip a playful nudge with her foot. "You're insufferable."

I pull her toward me and help her up to a sitting position. Her hair is a mess, and her skin is flushed. She looks like a dream.

"You like it." I place a soft kiss on her lips, unsure if it'll bother her to taste herself, but she opens her mouth to me and deepens the kiss. I'm getting hard again, knowing that not only can she taste herself, but she's enjoying it. Before we get swept up again, I step back and rest my forehead to hers, tucking a stray strand of her hair behind her ear.

"Go on a date with me."

Her head rears back, and she looks at me like I just asked her to go rob a bank. "What?"

My heart thunders in my chest. Fuck.

If she only wants to keep things physical, I think it would break a piece of my heart off. But I'll do it, if that's what she really wants. I'm in too deep to not accept crumbs.

"A date," I repeat. "With me."

A palpable quiet stretches between us, and I would give anything to go back in time to redo this.

Her expression is unreadable, and I'm starting to sweat, waiting for an answer.

"You know what? Never mind. It's fine. Forget I asked."

"What!" she shrieks. "No, I'm not saying no." She wraps her arms around my back and rests her chin on my chest, looking up at me. "I think we should talk about what it means."

"Okay," I say cautiously. "For me, it means that I like you. That I have feelings for you. And I want to see where this goes."

Her body melts a little more into mine. "I like you, too."

I don't think I realized how badly I needed to hear that. The pressure in my chest releases, and it feels like I can breathe a deep, full breath.

"But I'm still leaving," she continues.

My heart stutters. I know she's leaving. And I know I'm setting myself up for a world of hurt come January. But I also know I can't stay away from her anymore. She feels inevitable, as if no matter how hard I try, I'll still end up in this spot, hoping for a chance.

"How about this? We go on one date and then another date, and we keep going on dates, but only with each other. Do you see where I'm going with this?"

Her eyes regard me curiously. "So, like casual exclusivity?"

A dry laugh slips out, though I don't mean for it to. "Let me make myself clear. Nothing about *us* is casual."

She sucks in a breath, and her chest presses against me. "What happens in January?" Her voice is a low whisper, and I hear my own fears in the slight tremble of her words.

I don't have an answer for her. There isn't a solution to the warning sign in the room with us. What I do know is that I'm sure as shit not going to feel less for her.

"We can cross that bridge when we get to it."

Her lips press together as if she's mulling it over, her eyes darting back and forth, a faint crease forming between her brows, but she nods slowly. "Okay. Let's go on a date."

CHAPTER 38

Marisa

BUCKET OF COLD WATER

I think I'm going to puke. I can't remember the last time I was this nervous. Which is ridiculous, because it's Ethan.

The mascara wand shakes in my hand as I try to do a final coat. It's been three days since I agreed to go on a date with Ethan, and if I'm being honest, he's consumed ninety-nine percent of my thoughts. I remember being at Thanksgiving and meeting Jenn's family, but it feels like I wasn't really there. I was going through the motions. I've found myself drifting off into a dreamlike state, my thoughts wandering back to the wine cellar, kissing him, doing a lot more than kissing him. We went from zero to a hundred very quickly, but it also didn't feel fast because we've actually gotten to know each other.

A knock at the front door sounds and, by the grace of the universe, I don't stab myself in the eye.

"Coming!" I shout, my voice already vibrating with the anticipation of seeing him.

I open the door, and he walks in casually, like he's done countless times before. However, this time he is wearing the cheesiest smile, and I find myself mirroring it. I've never felt so giddy.

For a beat, we're standing, smiling at each other, the excitement unmistakable. Would it be silly to kiss him before the date even begins? Because I'm struggling to keep my thoughts on anything else.

Ethan laughs to himself, shaking his head. And then when our eyes meet, butterflies erupt in my stomach.

"Fuck it," Ethan says, backing me up against the wall. He wastes zero time, lifting me off the ground and capturing my mouth with his. I melt into him as his tongue works over mine. It's a dance of stroking and sucking and pulling and it feels practiced even though we've just begun. It's like we've been kissing each other for ages with the way he knows just how to curl his tongue to mine. My eyes are closed, but they still roll back in my head. He breaks the kiss and slides me down his body, back to solid ground.

Panting, he says, "I have no idea what happened. I got one look at you and had to kiss you."

Well, if I wasn't already dissolving into a puddle, I am now. My stomach flips and dips, and I feel like I'm going to soar out of my body. How am I going to survive dinner? We're a minute into this date, and I'm ready to rip off this dress and get naked with him. My hormones could use a bucket of cold water right about now.

"So, where are we going?" I try to change the subject, piercing through the fog of lust drifting around us.

"It's a surprise." He smiles boyishly, looking almost shy.

I'm not sure why I assumed we were going to dinner. Maybe because dinner is the standard first date, at least the standard first date I'm used to. His only instructions to me earlier today when I tried to pry information out of him about where we were going were to dress like we're going to a cocktail party and to pack an overnight bag. He made sure to clarify several times there wasn't going to be any pressure tonight, but that we would be leaving town.

"Calm down," he says, picking up on my panic. "You'll like it. Trust me."

I'm halfway shocked Ethan didn't blindfold me the moment we got inside his truck. He's being that secretive. As someone who equally hates and loves surprises, this is excruciating. I will commit sacrilegious acts to scratch the itch of instant gratification, such as reading the last page in a romance novel, even though I know the couple will end up together in the end. I have to spoil it for myself. Once, when we were in college, Hillary threw me a surprise party for my twenty-first birthday. I loved it, but I was also irritated I wasn't part of the planning process. Basically, there is no pleasing me, so whatever Ethan has up his sleeve has me both intrigued and frustrated.

"You're losing it, aren't you?" His lips twitch, the corners curling upward, betraying his attempt to suppress a smirk. He's clearly enjoying this a bit too much. I've already made up my mind to plan our next date.

Red Mountain disappears behind us as Ethan gets on the highway toward Badger Canyon.

"We're going to Badger Canyon?"

He nods. "It's our first stop."

First stop? How many stops are we doing?

The drive is silent, with the radio playing low in the background. My mind races, overthinking, worried that maybe agreeing to this date was a bad idea. My plans haven't changed; come January, I'll still be leaving. It's going to be so much harder with this added complication.

Rather than drive through town, Ethan turns on a

random road I don't recognize, and I couldn't be more confused. I assumed we were going to Badger Canyon because of their nicer restaurants, but we're nowhere near a restaurant —or town, for that matter.

When he turns again, my stomach drops as I read the *Badger Canyon Airport* sign.

My head whips to him. "Please tell me we're not jumping out of a plane."

He laughs, parking and turning off the truck. "Why would I tell you to wear a dress and then make you jump out of a plane?"

Opening the door for me, he grabs my hand to help me down.

"If this is our first stop? How many places are we going?"

"You'll see." He snakes his arm around my lower back. The heat of his large palm settling on my hip sends a thrill up my spine.

Obviously, we're doing something with planes, why else would we be here? I'm still convinced I'm going to be forced into jumping out of a plane.

I let him take the lead, and he guides us toward an open field, which I realize is more of a rustic landing strip.

"So, we're not jumping out of a plane and there isn't a plane nearby? I have to tell you, I don't think I've ever been more confused on a date than I am right now."

He laughs, pulling me closer to him, and places a light kiss on my forehead. The gesture makes me feel all warm and gooey inside.

A low whirr sounds in the distance, and it keeps getting closer and closer. Meanwhile, Ethan has his focus aimed at the sky, like he's looking for something.

After a while, the source of the whirring appears in the form of a helicopter.

What. The. Hell.

My head snaps to look at Ethan, where I find him holding back a smile.

"A helicopter!" I yell. "Are you kidding me?"

Now he's smiling so widely, it's nearly splitting his face.

Oh, he's good. I don't stand a chance at fighting this. Not that I ever intended to, but this is straight out of a reality dating show. This isn't real life. Everyday people don't fly in helicopters for a first date.

"You're kidding," I repeat. I keep waiting for the punch-line to hit.

He shoves his hands in his pockets and shrugs like it's nothing. "I'm quite serious."

"How much did this cost?"

"Nothing."

"So, you just happen to have access to a helicopter?"

"I'd tell you, but then I'd have to…" he says mischievously.

I give him a pointed stare. I'm not letting this go.

"Fine," he says, giving up. "I may have given one of our bigger clients, who's also a friend, a few pallets of wine in exchange for his helicopter."

A laugh bursts out of me. This is so ridiculous; it can't be real. There's no way.

I'm truly shocked. Not in my wildest dreams was I imagining something this extravagant.

"You mean to tell me you've had access to a helicopter this whole time and I'm just now finding out about it?"

"I almost asked for it when you needed to get to Seattle, but decided I'd rather be trapped in a car with you for hours instead."

"We were barely starting to get along. Even though things changed when we got home."

A knowing look passes between us, both of us recalling our life-altering kiss.

"Marisa. I liked you. Why else would I have agreed to drive

you? Why do you think I was always acting like a crazy person around you? I had all these feelings for you, and I had no idea how to handle it." He says it like it was painfully obvious. Maybe it was to everyone else, but certainly not to me.

"You liked me even before then?"

"I've liked you since the beginning. I didn't want to admit it to myself yet, but I definitely did."

"And now?" My gaze turns downward; I'm suddenly feeling shy.

He lifts my chin, forcing our eyes to lock. "And now, I really fucking like you."

The giddiness rising in my chest is effervescent. This must be what floating feels like.

"I think I liked you then too," I admit, biting back my smile.

The helicopter lands in the center of the field, and Ethan holds me close to protect me from the air whipping around us from the propellers. Thank goodness I thought to throw on my peacoat before we left, or I'd be flashing the pilot. It takes a few minutes, but the helicopter powers off and the propellers come to a stop.

"Come on." Ethan grabs my hand. "We have somewhere to be."

CHAPTER 39

Ethan

MR. AND MRS. LEDGER

L ake Coeur d'Alene shimmers below us under the night sky, reflecting in Marisa's sparkling eyes, and my chest squeezes at the excitement on her face. When ideas for our first date started floating around in my head, I knew this would be over the top. But for once in my life, I felt like being over the top, at least for Marisa.

In truth, most of life is mundane. We wake up and go to work and come home only to do it all over again, in endless cycles. We'll pepper in dinners out, weekends away, the occasional vacation, and all of those things are fine, because that's real life. But to truly wow her, to spoil her, to give her experiences beyond the norm, I want to be the one to give that to her. I want to give her the world. This vivacious, funny, caring, whirlwind of a woman crashed into my life in the best way possible, and now I can't imagine my world without her at the center.

She's deserving of so much more than the average first date dinner. We've already done the dinners and the movies and the car rides. Any man can do those things with her. Tonight is about proving how unlike any man from her past I am. I want

311

to ruin her for anyone who should try to follow. Because as far as I'm concerned, this will be the last first date she ever goes on. As soon as she agreed to this date, my mind skipped through all the hesitation and the fear regarding her move back to Seattle, and I decided that I'm not giving up without a fight. If that means making some changes of my own to be with her, then I'll gladly do it. I know we're not in the same spot. I know my feelings are more intense. This is my attempt to catch her up to speed.

The look on her face when she saw the helicopter eased any doubts I had that I was coming on too strong or pushing her beyond her comfort zone. At first she was nervous, watching our pilot like a hawk, but I would never risk her. He's a professional and very experienced. I would never put her in danger. But being Marisa, she's proceeded to remind me of the number of celebrities that have died in private plane and helicopter crashes.

"The Kennedys!" her loud voice bursts through my earpiece.

"What about them?"

"Dead. Mysterious plane crashes."

"They're cursed, so they don't count. Besides"—I point to the helipad on the rooftop of The Coeur d'Alene Resort—"we're here."

When the helicopter lands smoothly on the bullseye, I let out a steady breath of relief that we made it safely.

After the pilot powers down, I unbuckle myself and then turn to Marisa, grabbing her knees and spinning her to face me. I make slow, calculated movements as I unbuckle her, my fingers skimming along her waist. She lets out a faint gasp, her eyes turning hazy. Fuck, she's beautiful. I feel like the luckiest son of a bitch getting to share this with her.

I remove our headsets and hand them to the pilot, who's

already reaching for them. "You keep looking at me like that, and we're not going to make it to the rest of the date."

"Says the guy who was just feeling me up."

If not for the pilot and the resort staff waiting for us to de-board, I would be tempted to give in.

We give our thanks to the pilot and crouch down to exit the helicopter. Marisa clutches onto my hand, tightly gripping it until we're back on solid ground.

"Good evening, Mr. and Mrs. Ledger." The man shakes my hand firmly and Marisa straightens next to me. I'm getting dangerously ahead of myself, but I really liked the sound of that and do nothing to correct him. And neither does Marisa as he shakes her hand too. "I'm Joel, your concierge for the evening. I'll be escorting you to your dinner reservation." He grabs our bags and hands them to another staff member. "Your luggage will be placed in your suite."

We follow Joel as he guides us to the private dining room I reserved. It only took offering a couple hundred cases of our latest vintage to get it booked at the last minute. Thousands of dollars in lost profit, but completely worth it.

The private dining room is a 180-degree view of the lake. Despite the darkness, the water glows beneath the cloudless sky and full moon. Joel thanks us for coming and informs us our server will be with us shortly.

Once we're settled in our seats, Marisa regards me curiously. "Is this the Ethan Ledger special? Do all your first dates include helicopter rides and ritzy resorts and private dining?" She's smiling, but the smile doesn't reach her eyes, telling me she's genuinely worried I make a habit of this.

"Just you. I've never done anything like this for anyone. Ever. Only you."

Her forced smile falls, replaced with softening eyes. "I don't need anything fancy or extravagant."

"Need and deserve are two very different things, and you deserve the best."

"I don't know what to say." She looks around, taking in the room and the view before her gaze returns to mine.

"Don't say anything."

Footsteps approach, and a young blonde woman wearing a crisp white button down and black slacks greets us with a smile. "Good evening, folks. I'm Addie, and I'll be your server for the evening." She sets a stack of menus on the table. "Can I get you started with anything to drink?"

We both opt for water, Marisa wanting time to peruse the cocktail menu. When Addie returns with our waters, Marisa orders a fruity martini, and I order an old-fashioned.

"No wine tonight?" she teases.

"I drink more than wine," I defend.

Her lips tilt up as she runs a hand through her hair. "True. You had whiskey at the bar." She continues messing with her hair, twirling the ends of it absentmindedly.

And I'm struggling. I don't know what it is about her hair, but my hands always want to be in it. I could stare at her all day and never tire of the sight. Her hair, her eyes, her lips.

Her eyes flash to mine, lit with amusement. "Why are you looking at me like that?"

I swallow down the liquid pooling in my mouth roughly, salivating over her like a dog. "You look beautiful."

"Oh." She turns her head, looking away with a nervous giggle, and her cheeks take on a pink hue. "Thank you."

Every time I compliment her, she looks startled, like she's not used to it. I make a mental note to do it everyday, multiple times a day, until she believes it. And even then, I'm never going to stop.

She continues browsing the menu, occasionally taking in the view of the water.

"I can't believe I've never been here," she says. "It's not even very far."

While she admires the view, my mind is already imagining all the places I want to take her. All the experiences I want to have with her. I'm getting way too ahead of myself, but I can't seem to stop.

"Just so you know," I tell her. "The suite I booked us has two bedrooms. I don't want you to think this was all a ploy to get in your pants. I want you to feel comfortable."

She peers at me over the menu. "Good thing I'm not wearing any pants."

Fuck me.

Her smile is all innocence, but her foot running up and down my leg under the table is just the opposite. She puts the menu down and sets her elbows on the table, resting her chin in her palms, and regards me with a question in her eyes.

The waitress drops off our drinks and says she'll return shortly to take our orders. Marisa takes a sip of hers, releasing a little moan that hits me right in the dick. I take a sip of my own drink to calm down.

"So, you're like rich, rich?"

I nearly choke on my whiskey. "What?"

"It's just that I didn't realize..." she starts and then falters. "Which is silly, obviously you're well off, you're the CEO of a successful winery..."

Her face is etched with worry, brows furrowed, eyes downcast. We've never discussed money, so I'm only now noticing her discomfort with it.

"I wouldn't say I'm rich. There are plenty of people better off than me and my family. We have good years and bad years like any other business." Outwardly, I'm trying to remain calm, but internally, I'm scrambling. I'm not sure what the right thing to say is.

She looks away, breathing deeply, before her eyes look back

at me. "I don't want to be that person that brings up an ex on a first date. But my ex...Brandon"—her face twists saying the asshole's name—"he's wealthy. Very wealthy. And I got kind of lost in it all, and in the end ... Well, let's just say it pretty much screwed me."

My stomach sours at the thought of her with some other guy. One who clearly didn't treat her right. I'm reminded of that night at The Jackalope when she mentioned how she ended up in Red Mountain. Everything she's told me about him only makes me despise him more. He didn't realize what he had, but I sure as hell do. "This is the same guy who evicted you, right?"

She nods, avoiding my eyes. "Sure is."

"He sounds like an asshole."

A sharp laugh escapes her. "Yeah, and the worst part of it is we lived in a luxury waterfront condo. The mortgage payment was insane, and he made me pay half, and in return, he covered most of my expenses. So, here I am, making pennies compared to him and it's his name on the mortgage, but I'm paying half. By the time he kicked me out, I was broke. I couldn't build a savings, because I was paying so much of my income toward his place."

My fists ball at my sides, and my jaw tenses. I can't believe what I'm hearing right now. Who the fuck is this guy? Because I'd love to find him. Maybe get him alone for five minutes in a windowless room.

"What's his last name?" I grit.

Her brows shoot up. "I'm not telling you. Looking at you, I can tell you want to kick his ass. And as much as I would enjoy that, he's not worth it."

I shrug nonchalantly and take a gulp of whiskey. "Maybe I only want to Google him."

She shakes her head with a small smile. "Liar. But it's very sweet of you."

My head tilts. "Just what every guy wants to be...sweet."

Her smile broadens. "You're actually very sweet. You act like you're a big ol' grump, but you're really a softy."

I can't help but beam at her. "Only for you." And it's the truth. She makes me want to be better, to be the kind of man deserving of a woman like her.

The waitress returns and takes our food orders. Marisa orders the mussels, and I order a steak. I'm not entirely sure steak was on the menu. I was too distracted by the incredible woman across from me to read the words on the page.

After dinner, we take a walk along the boardwalk. It's cooler by the shoreline, so I pull Marisa in close to me with an arm around her. I can only imagine how cold she is in that thin peacoat.

We walk in silence as our breaths fog in front of us. I love having her curled around me, encased in my arms. I've never been the touchy feely type, and in the past I've had girlfriends complain they felt I didn't like them because I'm not overly affectionate. Maybe they were right, because if Marisa is around, I want to be touching her. I *need* to be touching her. And she fits against me like she was always meant to be there. I think I'm way past the like stage. I'm falling in love with her. Maybe I have been since she stepped out of her car on that very first day. Maybe that's why I tried to create distance.

She sighs deeply, hugging me close, as if she wants to dissolve into me. "I'm sorry for ruining dinner," she says quietly.

I let my hand play with the ends of her hair and look down at her. "What? You didn't ruin dinner. What are you talking about?"

Her head flops a little to the side, and she groans. "I brought up my ex. That's like the number one rule of dates. And now you're being all quiet. I shouldn't have said anything."

I stop walking and put both arms around her, fully caging her in. Her chin rests on my chest, and she peers up at me.

"Baby, the only reason I'm quiet right now is because I'm so fucking happy. Do you have any idea how much I like you? How lucky I feel to even get to touch you like this?"

Her breath trembles, vibrating against my chest. "You do?"

I tuck one of her silky strands behind her ear. "Like a lot. Like an amount that would probably make you want to file a restraining order."

She snorts and buries her face in my chest, giggling. When her laughter eases, she tilts her head up and our gazes lock. "I like you a lot, too. Maybe not restraining order levels, but it's up there."

I tip my head down and place a light peck on her lips. Well, it was supposed to be a light peck, but she grabs my face and keeps me there, deepening the kiss.

We make out, right there in the middle of the darkened boardwalk, and we don't pull apart until a couple walks by and whistles at us.

Marisa laughs against my mouth, and her kiss-drunken eyes meet mine. "Maybe we should go up to the room?"

I swallow before nodding slowly. I think part of me had been avoiding going up to the room because I meant what I said. I'm not going to pressure her into anything she isn't ready for. But it's going to be pure torment sleeping in one room, knowing she's in the next one. Close, but too far away. I need to think with my head up top, though. She's too important to fuck things up with. And I already pushed it, getting a taste of her the other day. I should've waited and taken her out on a proper date before burying my face in her pussy, and I definitely shouldn't have let her suck me off. With this, I need to remain strong. She calls the shots, she's in the lead.

"Okay, let's go up."

"Holy shit," Marisa exclaims when we get inside the suite. "This might be the nicest room I've ever stayed in."

Not if I have any say.

She grabs my hand and drags me through the room. "Come on, let's explore." She jostles her eyebrows, and I can't help but smile at her unadulterated excitement.

The suite is large, but it's only slightly bigger than one of the cottages, so it's not necessarily the longest exploration. The kitchen, living room, and dining room are one great room and then one bedroom is the primary, while the other is more standard sized. The primary is the last room we go into.

Marisa flops down on the bed and sighs. And of course, my dick decides to wake up.

She pats the spot next to hers. "Come on," she pats again. "Come lie down next to me."

I'm definitely not saying no to that. I loosen the collar of my shirt, undoing the top two buttons, and join her on the bed. She props herself on one elbow, resting on her side, and looks at me.

"I like this." Her fingertips come up to my neck and skid down to the uncovered part of my chest. "I remember the first time I saw you. I thought this open, exposed, little piece was so hot." Her cheeks blush, but her eyes stay on me while she licks her lips.

My own cheeks heat at her admission. I was such an

319

asshole that day, I can't believe she had one positive thought about me, let alone checked me out.

"Yeah?" I breathe, suddenly feeling overheated.

She dips her head and places a soft kiss where my neck meets my chest. She pulls back slightly, her lips hovering over the area. "So sexy," she whispers, and her breath sends a jolt down my sternum and straight to my hardening cock. And then her lips go back, pressing another kiss to me, but this one is wetter, and I just know her tongue is poking out.

"You're killing me," I sigh, sensing my restraint fading. "I am merely a weak man."

She laughs and moves off the bed to a standing position, and I sit up to watch her.

"Listen, Ethan, I get that you're trying to be a gentleman and wait." She pauses and slips a strap off that sexy little dress, letting it fall down her shoulder. "But could you maybe stop being so polite?"

The second strap falls, exposing more of her cleavage. She reaches around her back, and I hear the zipper being pulled down.

"I didn't wear this uncomfortable bra for nothing."

The dress falls, gathering at her feet before she kicks it away, standing in front of me in nothing but a black, lacy bra and thong, and strappy black high heels.

Fuuuuuck.

She walks up to me, closing the distance between us until she's nestled within my legs as I sit on the edge of the bed, very close to losing my goddamn mind. Her hands rest on the tops of my shoulders while mine stay tightly at my sides. With our height difference, her full tits hang heavy in my face, begging to be touched.

Her hands trail from my shoulders, down my arms, and the movement presses her tits even closer, close enough to take in my mouth.

"Ethan," she sighs. "I want you to touch me."

I can't deny her. I would never. As long as she knows she's in control. "Is this okay?" I ask, running a hand up the side of her torso, landing on the edge of her breast.

"More," she groans. "I need more."

God, that soft, sexy voice of hers, begging to be touched, is almost enough to make me come.

I slip my hand under the cup of her bra and grab a handful of her tit, lightly massaging it and then giving a firm tug to her nipple. Her back arches to me like she wants more of my touch.

Roughly, her hand grips at my chin, forcing my face up to meet hers. "Stop treating me like a delicate flower. I want you to be rougher. I want to be consumed."

Her words snap something inside of me, and my hesitancy flies out the window. I wanted her to take the lead tonight, and this is what she wants. If she wants to be consumed, I'll gladly devour her.

Standing, I encircle her waist with my arms, picking her up. I gently toss her on the bed. I'll be a little rougher, but I'm not going to treat her like she's not the most precious thing in the world to me. She lands with a relieved groan, and I crawl over her body, pressing my weight down on her.

"Yes, just like this."

Her hair splays out, wild and tangled, as her chest rises and falls rapidly. I pull down her bra, freeing her breasts. Her nipples are hard and pointing at me, her skin is flushed, and her eyes are glazed with desire. Starting at her neck, I work my way down, kissing and sucking at her soft skin until I reach her puckered nipples that are begging for my attention. I flick my tongue across one peak before pulling it between my teeth and giving it a gentle pull. She writhes, curving against my touch.

"Oh, God," she gasps.

I open my mouth wider, licking and sucking on her hardened nipple. The sweetest whimpers escape her parted lips.

"Such a needy girl," I tell her before swirling my tongue.

As I continue to shower her breasts in attention, my hand slides up her thigh and then cups her lace covered pussy.

"Touch me," she cries, letting her thighs fall open.

I pull her panties to the side and dip two fingers inside. She's fucking dripping.

"Baby, you're so wet."

"I know," she breathes. "Make it better. I need to come."

My fingers curl inside her, fucking her tight little pussy like my life depends on it, while I kiss and suck, nipping all over her perfect tits. She starts tugging at my shirt, trying to free me of my clothes. I pause just enough to take off my button down, likely ripping off a few buttons in the process.

"I love your chest," she says, digging her sharp nails down my torso, pinching some of the hair.

"Not too hairy?" I joke. My chest hair would probably be out of control if I didn't maintain it.

"Never." She sits up on her elbows and removes her bra, throwing it over my shoulder. "It's just right."

I pause, taking in the view. She's stunning, laid out before me topless with her legs spread. Every dream come true, and it's right in front of me.

"You're fucking gorgeous, a goddamn dream."

She swallows, and her eyes slightly ease out of their lustful glimmer. "Thank you," she says under her breath.

My hand reaches out to cup her jaw, and I lean over to kiss her. She meets my kiss and then some, snaking her arms around my neck and pulling me flush to her.

We've never been like this, skin to skin. Why the fuck have I not been doing this the whole time? How have I gone so long without feeling her nearly naked body against mine?

Apparently on the same train of thought as me, she starts

tugging on my pants while I tear off her panties. I don't give a fuck. I'll buy her hundreds more pairs.

Soon we're both free of any clothing, completely vulnerable and exposed to each other.

I kiss her, and her body grinds beneath mine.

"I need— I need.."

I press my forehead against hers, my breath ragged. "What do you need, baby?"

"I need you inside of me."

I don't have to be told twice.

I start to move, to grab a condom, but her hand grips my arm. "I have an IUD, and I'm clear. I got checked recently."

I would love nothing more than to not have any barriers between us, but I have to double check. "Are you sure? I'm clear, too, but I have condoms."

She laughs quietly. "So much for sleeping in separate rooms."

"Hey, a man can dream. I didn't come with expectations, just a hell of a lot of hope."

"I don't want anything between us." Her hand wraps around my hard cock, and she gives it a firm pump.

"Fuuuck," I moan.

She does it again and grabs the back of my neck, pulling me down to her lips. I hover there, holding her stare.

"Are you sure?" My voice comes out strained.

She nods, breathing into my mouth. "I'm sure."

Her lips capture mine, and I grip her waist tightly, changing our positions, so she's on top of me. "You're in control."

She adjusts herself, straddling me, her pussy just barely touching my cock. I take her hand in mine and place it over my cock.

"It's all you, baby. You take the lead."

She nods and, with our eyes held captive by one another,

she rubs the tip of my cock between her pussy lips, spreading around her arousal. "I have to go slow," she breathes. "I don't know if you'll fit."

I can't help it. My chest swells when she talks about how big my dick is. "It'll fit." I smirk.

She rolls her eyes while slowly sinking down over the tip. Her breath hitches, and she pauses, adjusting.

My hands are gripping her hips lightly, but I strengthen my hold and press her down to take more. "You can take it, baby. Your pussy was made for me. Now prove it."

She lets out a huff, and her eyes narrow in challenge as she continues to ease me inside her. My breathing quickens. The further she goes, the less I'm able to form a coherent thought.

So tight.

So wet.

Fucking perfect.

When she's fully seated, we both groan. Her head falls back as she sighs.

The room fades, the world ceases to exist, all I feel is her. My name falls from her lips, and my heart thunders loudly, only beating for her.

"You have to move, baby," I saw out between clenched teeth.

She nods, breathing deeply. "Just give me a sec."

A beat passes before she rises slightly and then sinks back down. The movement forces my eyes back, and my vision blurs.

Holy fuck.

"Do that again," I beg with my jaw tight.

She does it again, but this time she rises up higher and instead of slowly easing back, she slams down, and I watch my cock disappear between her legs.

"Just like that," I praise. "So fucking good."

As much as I enjoy watching her above me, seeing those

full tits of hers bounce as she takes my cock, I need to feel her. I want her on me. I've never felt such an intense desire to hold someone against me as I do now. My hands wrap around her lower back, pulling her down to me, and our bodies melt together. Her hair falls like a veil, cocooning us, and I'm enveloped by sweet vanilla.

Her forehead presses against mine. "Ethan," she whimpers.

I thrust my hips up, filling her deeper, and she shudders, her thighs trembling as they lift.

"Kiss me while you fuck my cock." I crush my lips to hers, and she moans into my mouth while bouncing her ass and riding me like her body was made to do it.

Heaven. This is pure heaven.

I place a hand between us, circling her clit. Her body jerks at the contact, but I keep my rhythm. "Come all over me, baby. I love your messy pussy. You take my cock like such a"—*thrust*— "good"—*thrust*— "fucking"—*thrust*— "girl."

She loves when I talk to her like this. I can tell by the way her pussy spasms around me every time I tell her something dirty. My filthy girl.

Soon she's crying out, quaking above me, unintelligible words escaping from her lips as her pussy squeezes around my cock. My own orgasm builds, and for a split second, I'm rational enough to think that I should pull out, birth control or not, it's probably smarter. But that idea is quickly squashed when she moans, "Fill my pussy up."

I guess my filthy girl has a mouth on her, too. I'm not one to disobey a direct order, so I do as I'm told and spill every last drop of cum inside of her.

I wake up with long, dark, silky hair brushing against my chest and the woman of my dreams nestled beside me. The warmth of her body is overheating the hell out of me, but I don't dare move. Not a fucking chance.

She's completely naked, with the most adorable little snore humming softly out of her. If I could bottle the feeling of this moment and drink it for the rest of my life, I'd be drunk every day. Drunk on Marisa and smiling like a lovesick fool.

Last night was the best sex of my life. After the first round, we showered. I meant to be sweet and wash her, take care of her, but soon her legs were wrapped around my waist and I was fucking her against the glass shower door. After that, Marisa wanted chocolate cake, and I aim to please, so we ordered room service. Somehow, that turned into eating the fudge frosting off her nipples and bending her over the kitchen counter. She told me if we went again, her pussy would be too sore, so I dragged her to bed and massaged her pussy with my tongue until she came, screaming my name.

I should still be fast asleep, but there's too much adrenaline pumping through me and my dick is as hard as a rock.

Her ass wiggles against me. "How are you hard right now?" she murmurs into the pillows. "That monster should be exhausted."

"Baby, it hurts my feelings when you call my dick names."

She giggles, and I pull her closer, nuzzling her neck.

"What time do we have to leave?"

I take a breath. The thought of leaving has me wary, knowing we'll break the bubble as soon as we do. But we can't stay here forever and pretend reality doesn't exist.

"I requested a late check out, so we don't have to be out of here until three o'clock."

She nods, peering up at me through her thick lashes. "What happens when we get home? What does this mean?"

I try not to let her use of the word *home* affect me, but it still does. The selfish, greedy man in me wants Red Mountain to be her home. I want to be her home.

"How about you're mine and I'm yours, and we take it one day at a time?"

"Okaayyy," she says, with a smile on her face. "I like the sound of that." Her eyes shift, looking away and then back to me. "Not to sound juvenile, but would that make you my boyfriend?"

Boyfriend. Fiancé. Husband. Baby daddy. I want every label in the damn book.

I tuck a piece of her hair behind her ear. "Yeah. As long as that means you're my girlfriend. Because in case it's not explicitly clear, I don't share."

Her smile widens, and her cheeks flush a light pink. "I'm all yours."

We stay in bed for the next few hours, exploring each other's bodies, a mess of tangled limbs. But this time, when I take her, I go slow, savoring her. I make gentle love to her body, worshiping her the way she deserves.

CHAPTER 40
Marisa
SAY SOMETHING IN SPANISH

"What now?"

We're parked between our two cottages, both of us unmoving, unsure of what to do.

"We could unpack?" Ethan suggests.

The last thing I feel like doing is unpacking. Normally, I would need some alone time after having spent the entire day and night with someone, but with Ethan, the need to recoup with some solitude doesn't hit me. Instead, I only want more of his company, but I know I'll come off as clingy, so I remain quiet.

Together, we get out, and Ethan helps me with my bags to my front door.

"I guess this is goodbye for now," I tell him, feeling shy despite having done very not-shy things the past twenty-four hours.

He bites his cheek, holding back a smile. "Goodbye for now," he agrees, and bends down to give me a light peck.

It doesn't stay light for long, though, because once his lips are on mine, I can't help but slip my tongue in and stroke it against his. He groans and backs me up against the door, deepening the kiss, and letting his hands roam my body.

I shamelessly rub myself against him, pleased to find his hardening length ready for me. I should be worn out and exhausted, but I can already feel dampness between my thighs.

He eases back from our kiss, and his ragged breath fogs between us. "What are you doing to me? I'm fucking addicted to you."

I toy with the collar of his flannel and sway a little, feeling ridiculously happy. "The feeling is mutual."

"New plan." He tucks a strand of my hair behind my ear. "Since we both have work tomorrow, let's each unpack and get ready for the work week. When we're done, we'll figure out whose place to stay at."

My head is already nodding in agreement before he's even finished. "I like the sound of that."

He kisses me again. "Good."

"Don't you usually have family dinner on Sundays?"

"Yeah, but it started an hour ago, and honestly, I'd rather be with you. My family can go without me for this one."

His admission makes something twinge in my chest. We've spent so much time together, and he's still not sick of me.

I fight my instinct to cling to him like a koala and let him go. Once I'm inside, the cottage feels dead and lifeless, like it's missing all the things that make it homey, even though everything is right where it should be.

I'm way too keyed up to unpack and opt for a shower instead. I lather on an extra amount of vanilla soap since Ethan seems to love it so much and I'm all for encouraging anything that keeps his hands and mouth all over me.

After the shower, I pack an overnight bag with enough toiletries and clothing for tomorrow. It's probably too soon, and moving too fast, but I have no interest in being apart from Ethan. What that means for the future is not something I'm ready to deal with right now. What I do know is this is the happiest I've ever felt, and I'm going to go with what feels right, and not let doubts start to creep in, and ruin this.

Ethan opens the door and looks a little taken aback to see me standing on his porch. Those doubts I was trying to suppress come rushing back, and my stomach sinks like a stone. *I'm too eager, too much, too everything.* But he quickly takes those intrusive thoughts and annihilates them as he pulls me inside.

A whoosh escapes my lips, and he captures it with his mouth, kissing me with abandon.

He moves from my lips and trails open-mouth kisses down my neck.

"Baby, I was going to come to you."

I let out a breathy laugh. "I figured Goose would be more comfortable in his own home."

On cue, Goose snores loudly, and Ethan shakes his head. "Shane made him gourmet dog food, and he ate himself into a food coma."

"Looks like I made the right choice then."

His lips press into a smirk. "I don't care where we sleep as long as you're in bed next to me."

Butterflies flutter in my chest, sending my heart into an erratic frenzy. "I can get on board with that."

He swoops down, wrapping his arms around me, right under my ass, and lifts me into the air. A string of squeals and giggles fly out of me as he carts me into his bedroom and tosses me on the bed. I land with a small thud and let my arms and legs fall freely, giving him space to settle over me. His heavy body moves over mine, sinking me into the mattress as his calloused fingers glide under my dress. Did I purposely put on a dress not at all appropriate for the weather? Absolutely.

"No panties, baby? Again?" he nearly growls as his hands

explore my inner thighs, teasing me by getting close but not quite close enough.

Squirming under him, my body searches for relief.

"Patience," he tuts. "I haven't fucked you in my bed yet, and you better believe I'm going to take my time."

I sigh, letting my head fall to the side. "I've slept in it, though." I offer him a mischievous smile and his heated eyes meet mine.

"Trust me." He pauses, slipping a single finger inside of me. "I remember. I even had a key to your place, but by that point, rational thinking was out the window."

I gasp both from surprise and from the way his finger is pumping in and out of me. "I knew it! I knew you knew about the keys."

A knowing grin lights his face as a second finger sinks in. "Of course I know about the keys. I selfishly wanted you in this bed because I never thought I'd get a real chance. Best fucking night of my life until I got to kiss you."

My back starts to arch off the bed as his fingers work in a delicious rhythm.

"Kissing me was the best night of your life?" I question, my words laced in obvious doubt.

His mouth runs down the length of my neck, scattering soft pinches. "Every moment with you is the best." He stops his attack on my neck and forces our gazes to meet. "Like right now? Best fucking night of my life. You in my bed, under me, soaking pussy, I could die a very happy man."

If I wasn't already falling for this man, he has to go and say the sweetest things I've ever heard. Before I can think to hold them back, tears begin to well in my eyes. I don't bother trying to blink them away, because even if Ethan wasn't looking directly at me, he would somehow still sense my sudden surge of emotion. It seems he reads me better than just about anyone.

"What's wrong?" The concern in his voice is so prevalent, it only makes my tears come on harder, blurring my vision. With the pad of his thumb, he swipes one away as it falls from the corner of my eye.

"It's nothing," I lie as I start to sit up.

He eases off me and moves to lie on his side, facing me.

He doesn't push me, instead he waits patiently while I gather my thoughts.

"Here I go again, ruining a perfectly good moment." I let out a quavering laugh, trying to make things feel less heavy.

Ethan cups the side of my face, gently using his thumb to rub at my temple. "Baby, tell me what's wrong."

"It's just that— It's—No one has ever said such nice things to me." Saying the words out loud feels like a whole different kind of embarrassment. He must think I'm pathetically sad. A sad, lonely girl. The thoughts are enough to force my eyes from his to look anywhere else.

Gently, his hold slides down to grip my chin, and he turns my head to face him. "Hey, I'm not feeding you a bunch of lines. I'm not sure if you've noticed, but I'm a pretty literal guy and I don't say things I don't mean. You're incredible, and I'm going to spend every day you let me reminding you of that."

My head tilts, resting on his hand, and I close my eyes, nodding and breathing deeply. "Okay." It comes out a muddled whisper.

He softly chuckles and shakes his head. "Well now that I've made you cry in the first five minutes of being here, should we watch something and relax?"

My lips roll together, biting my smile. "I would love to watch something."

We crawl under the covers, my body draping over his like he's my own personal body pillow. He doesn't seem to mind as he flicks through the channels and his hand that's wrapped around my shoulder draws lazy circles on my upper arm. We've done this countless times in the past few weeks— but not like *this*. All those times spent putting distance between us seem silly when I can't think of anything else feeling more right than being in his arms on a Sunday evening. Goose hops up on the bed and lies down at the foot, totally content.

"How about this?" Ethan asks. He's on one of the Spanish-speaking channels.

"Another novela?" I tease. "I'm starting to think you like them more than I do. It must be all the ridiculous drama."

He laughs, a low rumble. "Maybe I like watching you watch them."

I angle my head to meet his gaze. "Say something in Spanish."

"What?" A blush starts to bloom across his face.

"Please," I beg. "I only heard you speak it the one time, but it was really hot."

Still blushing, he adjusts me so I'm lying on top of him, resting on his stomach.

"What do you want me to say?"

My shoulders lift, my own cheeks flushing. "I don't know. Anything."

"¿Dónde está la biblioteca?" *(Where is the library?)*

I snort, falling into a fit of laughter. His deep voice speaking Spanish might be the most endearing thing I've ever heard. Of all the things he could've said, he chose to speak the one phrase everyone learns on day one.

"What's so funny?" His lips disappear as he bites them back to tamper down his amusement. "You said anything."

"Say something else. Something you don't learn in Spanish 101."

Sighing, he breathes a laugh. "Fine, how about this? Eres muy hermosa." *(You are very beautiful)*

"Better," I muse, unable to contain my cheek splitting smile.

He playfully rolls his eyes. "Okay, one more. And then it's your turn." Some of the playfulness in his expression eases, and his eyes regard me tenderly. "No puedo imaginar mi vida sin ti." *(I can't imagine my life without you.)*

I scoot up and place a soft kiss to his lips. "Like I said. You're a big ol' softy."

When I try to pull back, he keeps me in place, continuing to gently move his lips over mine while his fingers comb through my hair.

I take his bottom lip between my teeth and give him a little nibble. He responds by swatting my ass, forcing a yelp out of me while his brows quirk up.

"Your turn. Tell me something in Spanish and make it dirty."

I shoot him a narrowed, mock glare. "Oh, you're one of *those* guys. I see how it is. You have a Latina fetish."

"No." His face scrunches. "I am not one of *those* guys. I like hearing you talk, no matter the language. Ramble away, baby."

My heart skips, surging into my throat. I'm overwhelmed by the way his words heal a part of me I didn't realize was wounded.

"Just one sentence. Please," he begs. He even throws in a pout.

How can I say no to that?

"One sentence. And only because I'm nice."

His smile broadens, and it feels blinding with how bright it shines when it's directed at me. For a man who makes it his business to scowl, that grumpy scowl has nothing on his smile.

I open my mouth to speak but hesitate for a moment. "Just so you know, my Spanish isn't perfect. I'm only half-

Mexican. Everyone always expects my Spanish to be perfect, because I don't look half and then when it's not, I'm a disappointment."

His expression softens. "Baby, nothing you could ever say would be a disappointment to me. Fuck everyone else and their opinions."

Warmth settles in my chest. But the longer I watch him, as he patiently waits for me to speak, the more that warmth travels down toward my stomach and lands between my thighs. He requested something dirty, and I think I can deliver.

"Siempre estoy mojada por ti." *(I'm always wet for you.)*

He swallows, his Adam's apple bobbing in his throat. "I guess I am one of *those* guys."

I snicker, pressing my head in his chest as I laugh. "I was only fulfilling your request. Did you like it?"

He rolls us so he's on top of me, holding his weight with flexed arms on either side of my head. His veins branching across his forearm send my stomach into a somersault and force my thighs to involuntarily squeeze.

"Fuck yeah," he says and then brands me with a searing kiss.

I open my mouth, letting him sink deeper into the kiss. Our movements turn frantic, tangled limbs, pulling of clothes, sheets twisting around us. His hard cock nudges between my legs, and I roll my hips, aching for it.

"Let me go down on you first," Ethan says with a groan.

I roll my hips again, seeking friction.

"Please, baby."

I've never had a man beg to go down on me. Who am I to deny him?

I give a slight nod and smile. "If you must."

He tosses a smug smirk at me, and a rush of hot air flows over my body. As his lips travel their way down and his hands work at lifting my dress that's bunched at my waist, the building heat spreads across my skin, leaving me flushed. His rough palms pry my knees apart and his eyes stare directly between my legs.

"Such a pretty pussy." He uses his index finger to swipe at the seam, swirling my arousal around and causing my hips to buck. "I love how wet you get for me." His finger gently brushes over my clit, and I moan, tossing my head to the side.

My eyes shut as the overwhelming feeling of his touch courses through me. His hot breath blows over the sensitive skin, and the intense need for him almost feels unbearable.

"Ethan," I cry. "Please."

"Eyes on me, baby," he says with his head between my thighs.

I shift my head forward to meet his darkened hazel stare.

"Watch me make you come."

I watch him extend his tongue and bury it inside my pussy, swirling and lapping and sucking relentlessly. Two fingers slide in and out of me while his thumb circles my clit. Within seconds, I'm a mess of raspy exhales and desperate moans, only further encouraging every flick of his tongue and brush of his fingers.

Soon my thighs are shaking as my back bows off the bed. My vision goes hazy, the edges turning blinding white as an orgasm tears through me. Ethan continues using his tongue to draw it out as the ripples of pleasure pulse through me.

As I'm coming back to my senses, Ethan moves to hover over me, the last of his clothes now gone and his lips coated in a shiny sheen.

"Your mouth can't be real. I have no idea how you make me come so fast."

He shoots me a crooked grin, and I fight an eye roll, knowing the comment has gone straight to his head.

"Maybe my mouth was made for your pussy." He licks his lips and then presses them to mine.

I kiss him back, hungrily, sweeping my tongue around his.

"See how good you taste, baby? How sweet your pussy is."

Something about getting to experience this side of Ethan drives me absolutely wild. No one would ever suspect he has such a dirty mouth in bed. It's been the best, unexpected surprise, and it makes me completely desperate for him in a way I've never felt before. So desperate that I need him inside me more than I need my next breath. I reach for his cock and give it a firm pump as I rub my thumb over the bead of pre-cum at his tip before I guide him to my entrance.

Ethan rocks his hips forward and is inside of me, filling me to the hilt. We still for a moment, relishing in the feeling of being completely connected.

"Like I said, best fucking night of my life."

Ethan smashes his lips against mine, feverishly kissing me as he fucks me rough and deep and fast. The familiar build of heat starts to unfurl in my core, and my hips move up to meet his thrusts.

"Give me another one. I want to feel your pussy choke my cock as you come."

He drops his hand between us, as his fingers draw quick circles over my clit, and it's just what I need to fall over the edge, coming again. Except this time my cries of ecstasy mingle with Ethan's grunts as he comes along with me, filling me with thick, warm liquid.

"Holy shit," Ethan pants.

We stay a mess, wrapped in each other's bodies. He stays inside of me even though he's no longer hard, and I revel in the comfort of his weight blanketing me.

It's been my experience that most men don't want to touch after sex, but not Ethan. If anything, it's like he wants to touch me more afterward.

Eventually, we untangle and Ethan pads off to the bathroom. The moment he's gone, I feel the mattress dip. Confused, I look over my shoulder to see Goose on the bed, settling into Ethan's spot. His puppy dog eyes dissolve any part of me that would think to shoo him away, and instead I scratch his head and cuddle up to him.

I hear Ethan's footsteps returning and listen as they pause in the doorway. When I turn to meet his eyes, there's a small smile on his lips. He walks in, shaking his head in faux annoyance.

"Goose, are you trying to steal my girl?"

My heart skips a beat and then skitters erratically, a whirlwind of emotion rushing through me as I catch his eyes. *My girl.* Two words I never knew could make me feel so much happiness.

He scoots Goose to move back to his spot on the edge and crawls on the bed, resting on his knees.

"Spread your thighs."

My eyes nearly bug out. "Again? I need at least an hour."

Chuckling, he shakes his head. "No, not again." He lifts his right hand to show me he's holding a washcloth. "Figured I'd be a gentleman and clean you up."

"Oh." My skin flushes. "Um...okay." I do as he says, opening my legs for him. After everything we've done, I shouldn't feel self-conscious, yet this feels like the most intimate thing we've ever done.

The washcloth is warm against my over-sensitized skin as he gently cleans our shared release. It's not sexual; it's so much more than sexual. It's caring.

When he's done, he leaves to discard the washcloth before coming back to bed and settling in beside me. He pulls me close, my back to his chest.

"I love sleeping with you in my arms." He nuzzles into my hair.

"I love it, too."

I love it so much, I don't think I ever want to go without it. I didn't know it was possible to feel so blissfully happy yet so incredibly screwed at the same time.

CHAPTER 41

Ethan

SO GODDAMN MATURE

"Someone got laid," Tawny chirps as I pass her desk on the way to my office.

Rather than indulge her with an answer, I keep walking, ignoring her.

I barely have my coat off, and she's already taking a seat in the brown leather wingback across from my desk. Apparently, she can't take a hint.

"How was it? Tell me everything," she says with way too much enthusiasm for this hour before taking a sip from the steaming mug of coffee in her hands.

"Fine." A sigh slips out of me as I get my computer started up.

She grumbles something incoherent under her breath. "Come on, you have to give me more than that. Did she like it? What did she say? Was it a total disaster? Was it amazing? Tell me something!"

I pinch the bridge of my nose, already feeling a headache coming on. I knew I was going to regret asking Tawny to help me plan the date. Now she's going to be even more annoying.

"It was fine," I repeat.

She rolls her eyes. "Don't make me track down Marisa so I can get the dirt."

"It was good."

"Why are you like this? Does this mean you guys are together now, or what?"

I know she's going to continue to pester me if I don't give in a little. "Sure, yeah, we're together."

She squeals so loudly it hurts my ears.

"Will you calm down? People are trying to work, which is what you should be doing."

I'm being a dick on purpose. I don't want Tawny or the rest of my family putting their noses in my business, and spooking Marisa.

She hops up from her chair and some of the coffee in her mug sloshes over the rim and splatters on the floor. "Does everyone know? Have you told your family?"

I glance at my watch, hoping time has miraculously moved an hour so I can leave and get to my meeting at the warehouse.

It hasn't.

"I didn't realize I needed to make an announcement on matters pertaining to my personal life."

Instead of answering me, she sets her mug on the edge of my desk and starts vigorously texting. No doubt informing everyone in our entire family.

"Stop being so moody. We're happy for you, that's all."

"Go be happy for me at your desk."

She tosses her head back, likely frustrated that I'm not divulging every single detail of shit that doesn't concern her.

"You know, I thought you'd be a little more pleasant, maybe nicer, after an amazing date with your dream girl. Guess I was wrong."

I may not be acting like it, but I don't think I've ever felt so happy. Waking up this morning with Marisa wrapped around me, getting ready alongside each other for a boring workday, it gave me a glimpse into what life could be like with her. Squeezing together in the small bathroom of the cottage as we brushed our teeth, hearing her hum as she did her makeup, giving her a kiss goodbye before we went our separate ways, I couldn't have asked for a better morning. A random Monday morning made all the better because of the amazing woman I got to share it with. I could get used to it—I want to get used to it.

Just as Tawny's about to walk out I say, "I am nicer...to her. The rest of you I tolerate."

She squeals again, but this time she's smart enough not to linger.

By two o'clock, I'm considering leaving early. After Marisa sent me a text at noon asking if it was okay if she worked the remainder of her day at my cottage to keep Goose company, I haven't been able to focus on anything besides getting home to her.

As I'm gathering my things to head out, Tawny emerges with a weird look on her face.

"Whatever it is, it can wait." There's no way anything is so important it can't be handled by someone else, or wait until tomorrow.

She winces. "It actually can't. More like *he* can't wait."

I still, my forehead creasing as I look at her with complete confusion. "What?"

Her eyes close like it pains her to tell me whatever it is that's going on.

"Travis...he's downstairs."

My stomach sinks at the sound of his name. Why the hell would Travis come here? What could be so important? He wouldn't show up without a good reason. I don't owe him anything, and I should refuse, but my curiosity gets the best of me.

"Uh...okay. Send him up."

Tawny's eyes go wide. "Are you sure?"

"Just send him up," I bite.

She starts to slink away. "I'm not going to have to call the cops, am I?"

I shoot her a deadpan look. "Jesus Christ. No. It's the middle of the day. Send him up."

Besides the fact that we're grown ass men, I'm not about to fight him over a woman I don't give a shit about.

Forcing myself to keep my expression neutral and stay composed, I wait with clenched fists and a pounding heart for Travis to get here.

I don't have to wait long because less than five minutes later he's walking in, looking as nervous as I feel. Travis has always been the kind of guy that wears every emotion on his face.

He drops his head low and holds my stare for a beat, his jaw twitching. His throat clears loudly. "Thanks for agreeing to see me."

I'm silent for a stretch, watching him sweat bullets as he awkwardly stands in the middle of my office with his hands tucked in his pockets.

"You didn't give me much of a choice, showing up here unannounced."

He approaches slowly, like a timid animal. "Mind if I sit?"

My head nods slightly. "Sure."

He breathes a strained sigh and sinks down in the seat across from me. "You're probably wondering why I'm here."

I regard him with a flat expression. "I'm sure you're going to tell me."

"Laura and I called it quits."

Some of the rigidness in my spine dissolves, either from shock or maybe it's...empathy.

"Oh." My head nods in slow motion. "Sorry to hear that."

He scoffs with the shake of his head, a dull smile resting on his face. "I bet you are."

"I'm serious."

His jaw tightens, face twisting in disbelief. "Why do you always have to be so goddamn mature, taking the high road? Fucking hit me, man. Scream at me. I deserve it."

"I'm not going to do that. Maybe if this shit happened in high school, but we're not stupid teenagers."

He groans and then leans forward to rest his elbows on his thighs while his head hangs heavy. "Everything is so fucked up right now. I don't know why I came here. I guess I thought it'd feel better to add some physical pain to this nightmare, but you won't even do me a solid and punch me." He looks up at me, and the corner of his lip quirks.

I smile back, and for a brief moment, it feels like we're friends again, just like we used to be. But the moment is fleeting. Too much has changed for us to go back. I don't hate him, and I don't wish him any ill will, but I can't trust him either. There's no place in my life for that kind of relationship anymore, even if I once thought of him as family.

"You'll be fine. My fist in your face isn't going to dull that pain. You have to deal with it and move on."

He nods and stands to leave. "For what it's worth, I'm sorry for what we did—what I did. There's no excuse. She was just the first person, besides you and your family, that looked at me like I was worth something, and I let it get to me, let it turn me into someone I hardly recognize. If I could take it back, I would."

With that, he steps out, and a pressure that's been weighing on me eases. I wait for Tawny to come barging in and badger me about why he came by, but for once in her life, she minds her business.

"How goes it, son?" my dad calls to me as I'm walking to the parking lot.

"You do realize it's almost freezing, right?" I ask, barely containing my laughter at his ridiculous outfit consisting of a Hawaiian shirt and cargo shorts.

As he walks closer, his arms open wide, gesturing at his clothes. "I overdid it with buying Hawaiian shirts when we were on vacation and told your mother I wouldn't let them go to waste." His shoulders lift in a shrug. "Besides, I think she kind of likes them." He waggles his brows, and I scrunch my face at what he's implying.

Trying to change the subject, I let out a sigh. "Did you need something?"

Ever since he retired, he's been pretty checked out in terms of the business. There wasn't a transition of any kind, and when I do ask questions, his answers are vague. He's always happy to talk about the business side of things, but never in any way that's helpful.

"I was coming by to see you, but it's clear you're heading out. I can come by another day."

I'm dying to get home to Marisa, but this is the first time my dad has randomly dropped by, and I have to know the reason.

"I have time now."

We head back in, settling in the tasting room since it's closed and vacant.

"What did you want to talk about?"

He cocks his head with a knowing smirk, and for a second,

I'm a kid, feeling like I'm not going to like what's on the other side of that look.

"I peeked at the reports from this year's harvest and compared them to previous years."

My stomach drops. A collision of my fears and anxiety surges through me, coiling tightly. He's going to tell me I'm not fit for the job. Why else would he be here?

"I can explain—"

His hand lifts, stopping me. "There's nothing to explain. The numbers are phenomenal. You kept equipment costs down by keeping up on the maintenance of the harvester, gross tons harvested was more than last year, overall, it's looking like it's going to be a good rest of the year for production. I'm impressed."

After several seconds I say, "Oh...Thank you."

He shakes his head and looks up at me over the rim of his glasses. "You need to stop convincing yourself you can't do this. You can do this. It's in your blood, you grew up in this world. Trust yourself. You're the best person for the job."

"I don't know about that." I smile faintly. "Gavin is probably better suited."

His head turns, looking in either direction before speaking. "Don't tell your brother I said this, but thank goodness he turned it down. He's too calm and understanding. He'd let too much slide because of his good heart. Not that you don't have a good heart, but you don't take any shit. Not even from me, and I respect that about you." He pauses and leans back, resting his ankle on the opposite knee. "There's a reason I didn't hold your hand during transition. I did exactly what my dad did for me, absolutely nothing. He fed me to the wolves when I took over and then never checked to see if I was okay. Because that's how you learn, you figure it out yourself. I didn't want you to do things my way, I wanted you to do them your way."

"Would've been nice if you gave me some warning and told me that beforehand."

He chuckles. "Now what's the fun in that?"

When I get home, I find Marisa reading in bed with Goose cuddled up to her. My girl and my dog; it's the best sight to come home to. Within minutes I'm changed out of my work clothes and have her in my arms, my nose buried in her hair, inhaling her.

"How was your day?" she asks, closing her book, and giving me her full attention.

"Weird," I say hesitantly while twisting the ends of her hair between my fingers, the silky strands slipping easily through my hands.

Her eyes narrow, willing me to elaborate.

"Well, first Travis came by."

Her jaw drops while she stares at me with creased brows. "What? Why?"

I tell her about our conversation, and she's quiet for a beat, biting her bottom lip.

"How do you feel about it?

I have to think for a moment, because ultimately, what I really feel is surprising. "As strange as it sounds, I feel bad for him. I've been there, but I had my family to lean on. Travis doesn't have a family like mine, and he hardly has any friends. He's probably going to have a hard time getting over her."

Marisa caresses my cheek with her thumb and then runs it along my shave line. Her soft, smooth hands on me could calm even the worst of my storms.

"You're a good guy, you know that? Someone else in your shoes would probably scream 'I told you so' in his face."

I grunt a laugh. "I wanted to, but I held it in."

Her lips brush against mine, the faintest of kisses. I feel her smile against me as she pulls away.

"I should probably tell you I got added to a group chat today with your sisters and Tawny. Is that weird for you? I know things between us are still new, and I don't want to over-step a boundary you're not comfortable with."

"Baby, there is no boundary. I want you everywhere, in my house, in my bed, in my life. I pre-apologize for my crazy family, but they're kind of part of the package."

Her cheeks lift as a dazzling smile spreads across her face. "So, we're really doing this, huh? Full-on public, out in the open?"

"Definitely."

Marisa

MARK YOUR TERRITORY

L ife is bliss, or maybe it's all the orgasms.

"Come back to bed," Ethan whines.

"Can't." I spritz some perfume on my wrist and then dab it on my neck. "I'm interviewing Cole, and we agreed to meet at Sagebrush Diner at eight."

"Fuck that guy."

I have to stifle a laugh. Cole has been nothing but a gentleman since he found out about Ethan and me. In fact, he looks at us like he's brimming with satisfaction, as if he orchestrated the whole thing. But Ethan still hasn't moved on from watching him flirt with me at The Jackalope, and it doesn't seem like he'll be letting it go anytime soon.

I walk over to Ethan's side of the bed. The sheets are resting low around his waist, his bare chest on full display. The temptation to stay in bed all day is strong. Like really, really strong.

After we got back from Coeur d'Alene, we didn't come up for air for a while. I'm pretty sure our week of sex changed my entire gait. I'm still paranoid about it.

"My girlfriend is leaving me for another man."

My heart still pinches when he calls me his girlfriend. It's silly how happy one word can make me.

"You're being very dramatic."

I bend down to give him a kiss, but he surprises me by grabbing me around the waist and pulling me on top of him. I can't even catch my breath, because in one swift move, the room tilts and he has me pinned against the bed, my dress gathered up at the waist.

"Ethan!"

He settles between my legs, making it very evident how hard he is under his boxer briefs. "I promise not to make you late," he mumbles into my neck, sending confetti-like tingles down my back.

Goose, who was lying at the foot of the bed, lets out a groan and gets up to leave. He's had it with our antics.

Whipping my attention back to Ethan, I meet his stare. "I'm cutting it close." My words hold no conviction, since I'm already shamelessly rubbing against him.

He pushes my dress up even more and yanks my underwear to the side, hooking two fingers in my already drenched pussy.

"Always so ready for me." His fingers work in a fast rhythm, going in and out at just the right angle that disconnects every synapse in my brain, leaving me completely thoughtless. "Hear that, baby? Your pussy just loves drenching my fingers in a slippery mess."

The sounds of my arousal fill the room, tangling with my ragged breaths and guttural moans.

"You want my cock?"

"Y-yes," I stammer.

He keeps bringing me to the brink of orgasm and then pulling out his fingers, leaving me writhing with need.

"Yes what?"

"Yes, please, give me your cock."

That's all it takes for him to ram into me, filling me to the hilt. We both groan in relief at the connection.

"Every. Fucking. Time," Ethan groans. "Your pussy is my sweetest vice."

He pounds into me roughly, and I'm lost in the euphoria of being utterly possessed by Ethan. He's so gentle with me in every other way, but when it comes to sex, he treats me the way I've always fantasized about but could never vocalize for fear of being looked at like I was something less. Ethan manages to fuck me like the slut I want to be in the bedroom, while still making me feel like a precious stone, something to be cared for outside of the bedroom. Right now, he's filling me completely, almost painfully so. My wrists are pushing into the mattress as he holds them firmly down. I'm at his mercy, and the thought alone could give me an orgasm. He pulls nearly all the way out before slamming all the way in, my brain rattling inside my head.

"You like being fucked hard and rough, don't you?"

My back begins arching off the bed, chasing the build as I moan incoherent sounds, words escaping me.

"That's right, baby, squeeze my cock. Such a good girl with a needy pussy."

A familiar tightening blooms inside of me, spreading a welcomed heat. I'm steps from the free fall.

"I'm close," he says hoarsely, giving my pussy a light slap and then rubbing my clit. He continues this pattern while simultaneously fucking me relentlessly, and soon I'm right there with him, falling over the edge. My head whips back, my vision edging out into a bright light, and my body convulsing as the orgasm rings out of me, twisting and turning until the wave evens out.

We stay intertwined, our chests rising and falling together.

When I start to wiggle out from under him, he puts his arm out to stop me.

"I really do have to go." I giggle, trying to move past him.

"No cleaning up."

"What?" I'm confused by his devious grin.

He moves his hand to cup me, using his fingers to shove back in his cum that's now leaking out of me. "If you're going to have breakfast with Cole fucking Benton, then you're going to do it with my cum dripping down your thighs, covered in my smell."

I'm sorry, what in the fuck did he just say? "How *very mark your territory* of you. Want to pee on me, too, while you're at it?"

I like his domineering side, in the right moment, but this? Absolutely not. It's a little too caveman for me. A trickle of doubt starts to manifest like a red flag waving at me for attention.

"Peeing isn't one of my kinks. Not judging anyone who's into it, though." He shrugs, a smile still playing on his lips as if he's not acting like a territorial asshole.

"This isn't funny."

My tone must be enough to clue him in, because that smile falls real quick.

"You know, at some point, you're going to have to trust me. Do you not trust me to go have a work breakfast? Because Cole knows we're together."

"Of course I trust you." His voice is pitched, high, defensive.

I get up, shoving his arm out of my way. "Yeah, sure feels like it."

"Marisa—"

"Don't. I'm already late. We'll talk about this when I get back."

Cum is pooling in my panties, so wet it feels like I'm sitting in my own pee, making it extremely difficult to keep a straight face while Cole goes on and on about his organic practices. In all my anger at Ethan's ridiculous demand, I did, in fact, not clean up, just like he wanted.

"Wouldn't you agree?" Cole asks.

I missed whatever he was talking about. "I'm sorry. My coffee still hasn't kicked in. What was it you were saying?"

He smiles easily, completely unaffected. "I was saying that it's our responsibility as the next generation to move forward with more sustainable methods."

"Yep, I agree. That's very commendable of you."

He takes a bite of toast, assessing me with curiosity.

"What?" I ask, feeling self-conscious.

"You seem distracted. Is everything okay? We can do this another time."

"I really am so sorry. This is very unprofessional of me. I'm tired, long night," I lie.

"Want to talk about it?" He leans forward, looking at me expectantly.

"There's nothing to talk about." I give him my best customer service smile, hoping he'll drop it. "Everything is fine."

"Ahh, I get it." He takes another bite of toast, nodding to himself.

"What do you get?" My skin prickles with unease. He's too observant and I don't like it. He's the one being interviewed, not me. Not to mention he refused to meet me at Benton Winery or the *Herald*. I love a good diner, but it blurs the lines of professionalism to conduct an interview over a meal.

He sets down the toast and smacks his hands together, dusting off the crumbs. "Trouble in paradise already. What did he do?"

My breath stills. Something I won't be doing is talking about my relationship with Cole. What's between me and Ethan, stays between me and Ethan. "I'm interviewing you, not the other way around."

"Let me guess." He pauses, looking up at the old-fashioned diner lamp dangling above our table like he's deep in thought. "He's probably pissed you're here with me. Isn't he?"

"Cole, come on. Let's get back to the interview."

He blows out a whistle. "I know I'm right." Settling deeper into the booth bench, he crosses his arms. "There's always been some rivalry between me and Ethan. How could there not be? Same age, same year in school, played the same sports, same pool of girls. And now as adults, we compete with our businesses. We get each other, and he'd probably disagree, but we think alike, too."

"What's your point?" I ask despite myself.

He shrugs. "At the end of the day, I still consider him a friend, even if he's been looking at me lately like he wants to kick my ass. He'll get over it. You're nothing like Laura, and if he hasn't figured that out yet, he will. He's just scared."

"Thank you for your unwarranted advice. Ethan and I are fine."

He stands, gathering his coat. "I'm going to head out. Email me the questions and we can finish that way."

"But—"

"No, really, let's do it that way. Besides, I'm trying to get over to Novel before Ariana runs out of chocolate croissants."

He leaves me stewing in my thoughts, making me question if I was too quick to snap at Ethan. Honestly, I think my feelings are warranted. Still, I probably should've stayed to talk about it, not run off at the first sign of a fight. I can't help it. I hate fighting, but more than that, I hate dealing with it. I'm a sweep things under the rug kind of girl, and that has to change. Things with Ethan feel different than my past relationships. He feels like more. It's terrifying and exhilarating, and I don't want to mess us up, especially when a dark cloud the size of Seattle is hanging over us.

CHAPTER 43
Ethan

SAD PUPPY DOG FACE

I'm such an idiot. I had to open my dumb fucking mouth and vomit my insecurities all over Marisa. She has every right to be mad. It took all of five seconds after she stormed off for me to realize how in the wrong I was. I thought I had moved past this, but it's pretty evident I'm transferring my fears from my past relationship onto this one, and it's not fair to Marisa. The problem is, I'm not sure I can stop it on my own.

When her footsteps sound at the front door, my heart plummets to my stomach, my body tensing with each step closer. I'm already mentally preparing myself for a fight, truly our first one, excluding the bickering from before we really knew each other. When she walks into the living room, I'm thoroughly primed for her face to be tight in anger, but instead, she looks sullen, her shoulders sagging in sadness. Somehow, this is worse than anger.

"Hey," she says, her voice withdrawn.

I stand, feeling like a kid being called into the principal's office. "Hey."

She sets her bag on the coffee table and slips out of her

boots, plopping down on the couch. "You can drop the sad puppy dog face. I don't want to fight."

"We don't have to fight, but we should talk about it." I step closer. "Starting with me apologizing for being a massive, insecure dick."

She breathes out a laugh. "Okay, then."

Approaching her like she's a feral cat, I carefully take the seat next to her and push the boundary further by setting her curled up legs on my lap. I begin massaging her calves. She tenses at the contact, but quickly relaxes as I start kneading under her knee.

"I'm not her." Her voice is barely above a whisper, almost like she's talking to herself.

"I know."

"If you know, then why treat me like someone you think would cheat on you? I've been cheated on. I know how badly it hurts. That's not the kind of person I am."

"I know. I'm sorry. I panicked a little. My feelings for you have come on so fast and so strong it's honestly terrifying thinking of losing you. Especially losing you to someone else."

"The only way you're going to lose me is if you keep acting like a Neanderthal, trying to mark your territory."

"I'll never do it again—well, with that intention. No promises on not shoving my cum back in your pussy, because that was fucking hot."

"Always a perv," she teases.

Some of the unease slips away when I see a small smile play on her lips. "You liked it."

She smirks. "Maybe."

We sit in silence for a beat, her body slowly unraveling from the tension.

"You know," she continues. "I could easily compare you to Brandon, but I actively choose not to."

My hands pause. "I'm nothing like that piece of shit."

"In reality, of course not, but on paper, you two tick almost all the same boxes."

The back of my neck heats. I don't enjoy thinking about Marisa with that asshole, and I especially don't like the comparison game we're playing right now.

"I'm not him," I say, parroting her words back to her.

Her eyes catch mine, holding me in place. "I know." She reaches for my hand and laces our fingers together. "I accept your apology, and I'm sorry for storming off. That was a bad move on my part."

My pulse begins to settle. I fucked up, but we talked it out and survived. The guilt will continue to grate at me, though. I need to do something to show I trust her. It's easy to sit here and say I'm not going to be a jealous asshole again. It's a lot harder to prove it.

Unable to resist being this close to her and not kissing her, I lean in for a kiss, my chest swelling as she closes the distance between us. Quickly, the kiss intensifies. My tongue sweeping against hers, her mouth opening up for me, hands skimming down her waist to pull her in.

"Mmm mmm," she moans, shaking her head. Breaking the kiss, she breathes deeply. "I need to shower. You made a mess of me earlier."

"I don't mind."

She laughs, trying to squirm out of my hold. "I mind."

"Okay." I grip her waist tightly, standing and tossing her over my shoulder.

A gasping *ooph* sound escapes her lips. "Where are you taking me?"

I give her ass a light smack. "To the shower. So I can clean you up and make you dirty all over again."

CHAPTER 44

Marisa

MY SAFE PLACE

T he steam from the shower fills the air. Ethan strips off his shirt, his taut stomach drawing my eyes to him like a magnet.

"My eyes are up here." His cocky smirk only amplifies my growing need for him.

I meet his heated gaze. "I like ogling you."

"Lose the clothes, Marisa." His stare drags down my entire body, as if he can already see what's underneath. "And do it slowly." His voice is a low growl, starting a frenzy of butterflies swirling in my stomach.

My hands shake as I start to pull my dress up over my head, but I pause, letting it fall back into place. I don't know why I'm so nervous. We've barely come up for air, but never with the bright sun shining directly on me. The steady stream of water, the fogged mirrors, daylight pouring through the windows. He'll see all of me, every flaw, with nothing to mask it, no sheets or shadows to hide behind.

He must sense the nerves that have started flooding my veins. Lifting my chin, he says, "Hey, it's just me and you. Don't ever be afraid or self-conscious about your body around me, because I'm fucking obsessed with it, every curve, every freckle. I could spend an entire day worshiping every inch of you and still be in awe of how fucking sexy you are. My dick has been in a constant state of hardness since you crashed into my life with that smart mouth and perfect ass." He takes my hand and holds it so his cock is in my palm. "Feel that? That is what you do to me."

He's hard in my grasp, so I tighten my hold and run my hand up and down his length over his jeans, eliciting a moan. His eyes become hooded, gazing down at me and blazing with lust. I try to dig into his jeans and feel all of him, but he grabs my hand to stop me.

"Bad girl. Not yet." He backs me up against the vanity, and slowly eases me out of my dress. His eyes flare as they catch sight of my lace bra. "Your tits are amazing. One day, I'm going to fuck these."

He yanks the cups down, causing my breasts to spill over. Grabbing both, he uses his thumbs to draw circles around my nipples. I curve into his touch, goosebumps spreading across my chest as he bends to capture a nipple in his mouth, his tongue swirling over it. His hot mouth over the sensitive skin causes heat to build in my lower abdomen. My thighs squeeze together, trying to find relief.

In a quick, rough second, he has my bra off. My hips grind, trying to rub against him.

"Ethan," I whine. The feminist in me has left the room because I'm on the brink of pleading for his cock until he gives it to me.

I can't take it any longer. I need him now. I'm getting squirmy. I spin out of his grasp and remove the last bit of fabric covering me. I ball up my panties and toss them at him with a smirk before I get inside the hot shower.

The sound of denim slapping the tile floor echoes behind me, right before I step under the waterfall shower head. Ethan joins me seconds later, his hands sliding down my waist, tracing the curves. He captures my mouth. The hot water splashes down on our faces before he moves me against the shower wall. Shampoo bottles scatter around us in loud thuds.

Drawing back from our kiss, I giggle against his mouth. "Get it together. You're destroying the shower," I tease.

"I'm only concerned with destroying your pussy."

My body shakes against his, laughter bubbling out of me before it's replaced with a squeal as he lifts me, my legs winding around his waist and back scraping against the tiles.

"Are you laughing at me?"

I nod. "Always."

He smiles into my neck. "Such a brat."

His tongue flattens, licking down my neck and over my clavicle, causing the smile to drop. I moan, throwing my head back as he thrusts into me, filling me completely. He's so deep this way, it takes my body a second to adjust. His hands grip my ass, sliding me up and down his cock. I gasp, feeling completely out of control and loving being at his mercy.

"Fuck, you take my cock so good. Who does this pussy belong to?"

"You," I say, breathless. "Only you."

My words seem to be his undoing, because he picks up speed, pushing his cock in and out of me at a tantalizing rhythm. The familiar build of heat coils between my thighs, and my body goes slack, falling apart in his arms. His groans tickle my ears as his release follows mine.

Slowly, after we've caught our breaths, Ethan sets me back down, holding onto me for a second as I gather my footing. "You're going to be the death of me, woman. I'm going to run out of cum if we keep going multiple times a day."

His smile is so cocky. I know he's basically bragging that he can go several times a day.

"You'll live," I say, shaking my head, a smile playing on my lips.

I pick up the dropped bottles and start to actually shower. Ethan does the same. Our faces split into lopsided smiles while we stare at each other. I've never felt so comfortable and cared for in my entire life. He makes me feel cherished and special, looking at me like I hung the moon. My heart beats, infused with warmth, and I realize I've fallen in love with him. Is it even considered falling when he feels like the softest landing I've ever experienced? He's my safe place; he would never let me fall. He's always there to catch me.

CHAPTER 45

Marisa

CAN'T AVOID HER FOREVER

I t's almost Christmas, and I still haven't spoken to my mom. It's not from a lack of her trying. She's called me more over the last few weeks than she ever has before. And I know she's desperate to talk to me, because she even called my dad. After some of the shock on his part wore off, he told her I was fine and needed some space.

Despite the hurt I still feel, I also miss her. So much. And the holiday is exasperating that feeling, remembering all of our traditions. She used to make large batches of champurrado, so we always had it ready to heat up and enjoy. I made a small pitcher, and while it tasted fine, it was nowhere near as good as hers. When I was a kid, instead of your standard gingerbread man cookies, we would make Mexican wedding cookies that she renamed snowballs to make them seem Christmasy. And I'll never forget our several attempts to master tamales. She could never remember her family's exact recipe, and it's not as if she was ever going to call them to get it, so we were always guessing and failing before eventually giving up and ordering them from someone who knew what they were doing. Though a handful of Christmases have passed since we've spent the holiday together, this one feels particularly tough. It's also the longest we've gone without speaking.

"Hi, baby," Ethan says, placing a kiss on my forehead.

I still get a little flutter of butterflies when he does that, and I wonder if that feeling will ever go away. He slides his jacket off and hangs it in the coat closet.

We've unofficially moved in together. A lot of my things are still at my cottage, but I spend a majority of my time at Ethan's. We thought we were being sly about it, but one day my dad came looking for me and when he couldn't find me, he banged on Ethan's door, only for him to open it with me right behind him, wearing one of his T-shirts. It was very obvious we'd had sex shortly before he arrived. I've never seen my dad so embarrassed and uncomfortable. It took him a few days to look me in the eye again. It was mortifying. But after we got past that, he's been fully onboard with me and Ethan. Not that he was ever against it. I think he's hoping I'll stay because of Ethan, even though he's never brought it up.

"How was your day?" Ethan asks, embracing me from behind and drawing me close.

I can't help but melt into him, a soft wave of relief easing through me as his arms offer a sense of calmness.

"It was fine, nothing exciting."

He tenses slightly. "What's wrong?"

I forget how well he knows me. There's no sense in hiding anything. He'll just drag it out of me. "I miss my mom."

He smooths my hair and angles my head to place a soft kiss at my neck. "Call her. You can't avoid her forever."

"And say what?"

"You could start with hi and go from there."

On Christmas Eve, I finally cave and decide to call my mom. Ethan is right. I can't avoid her forever. The phone rings three times, long enough to make me think she won't answer, but then she does.

"Marisa." She sounds surprised. "Is that you?"

"Hi, Mom."

"How are you? Are you okay? I've missed you so much, mijita."

I can hear the emotion in her voice, the sound of a knot sitting in her throat. Guilt engulfs me. "I'm fine... I've missed you, too. And I'm sorry it's taken me this long to call."

She sighs, her breath shaky. "I'm the one that should be apologizing. I wish I had some grand excuse that sounded good enough to not come see you, but the truth is, I don't."

My stomach sinks, and I wait for her to elaborate.

"The truth is, I panicked," she continues. "All these years later, and it's still difficult for me to accept that your dad has moved on from me and is happily married."

"It's not like he was going to be here," I say with more bite than I intended.

"I know. But I would've had to come into his town, go inside the home he shares with her, and I wasn't ready."

I understand where she's coming from. I wish she would've discussed it with me before bailing. "Why didn't you say anything?"

She laughs, a sad chuckle. "Because you always think I'm so strong. I hate for you to see me weak."

"You're allowed to be human. I think I would prefer it, honestly."

"I'll keep that in mind," she says in a quiet tone.

We're silent for a few beats before I break it, practically shouting, "I have a boyfriend."

She laughs again, this time without the underlying sadness. "I know."

I wait for her tangent, but it never comes. "How do you know? Did Dad tell you?"

There's a pause before she takes a breath. "No, I knew when I talked to him. Ethan, right?"

"Yes." I hesitate, holding my breath, waiting for her to say something I don't want to hear.

"He seems like a special man."

I stiffen, my spine snapping straight. I think she's rendered me speechless.

"Marisa, are you still there?"

Coughing, I try to recover. "Who are you and what have you done with my mom?"

She laughs, a big, loud laugh, and it rumbles through the phone. Her laughter dies, but I feel like I can hear her smile. "He asked me how to make you feel better. He asked me how to take care of you."

"So, what...now you like him?"

"Mija, a man who wants to take care of you when you're at your worst? That's a rare find. He sounds like one of the good ones."

"Seriously, who are you right now?"

"Believe it or not, before I became a bitter old woman, I was a lot more like you than you realize. Sometimes when love sours, it can make you better or it can make you bitter. I'm sure you can tell which way I leaned." She pauses, sighing. "I don't want you to become like me. I thought I was protecting you, but now I see I was doing more harm than good."

When I don't respond, she continues.

"Do you love him?"

My breath catches. There isn't a doubt in my mind that I love Ethan, but we haven't said it yet, so the word weighs heavy in my chest.

"I— We— We haven't..."

"It's okay. You can tell me when you're ready."

We continue talking for hours, making up for lost time. She tells me stories from all of her adventures, and I tell her how much I enjoy working on *The Vine* and that I'm on the fence about moving back to Seattle. She tells me that the right man will stick around if I do decide to follow through with my plan. I'm not surprised she's encouraging of me still moving back, regardless of my relationship with Ethan. It's not as if I expected her to completely change. And maybe she's right. The right guy isn't going to let a couple hundred miles get between us, right?

Later that night, as I'm cuddled up in Ethan's arms, I think back to my mom asking me if I love Ethan. I want so badly to tell him, but something is preventing me from getting the words out. Maybe it's because I'm afraid to say it first, or maybe it's because I'm worried I'll make a fool of myself when reality sets in, and he breaks up with me the moment I'm back on the other side of the state.

CHAPTER 46

Marisa

CARHARTT TO CUSTOM SUIT

"What's this thing called again?"

Ethan and I are getting ready for some festival gala thing happening at the winery. With the amount of things this town turns into an event, I'm starting to think Hallmark is a lot more accurate than I believed it was.

"The Winter Wine Fest," he says, looking at me through the reflection in the mirror as he ties his tie. "It's another way to generate interest in the slow season, fill the lull between Christmas and New Years. Except this year, it's a little different, because Elyse is hosting a corporate holiday retreat, so she's playing double-duty tonight, with the other event happening in the downstairs ballroom. I'm assuming it's going to be hectic."

I'm not exactly dying to wear this tight dress and mingle, but any excuse to see Ethan dressed up is a-oh-kay with me. The man goes from Carhartt to custom suit very smoothly. The night hasn't even begun, but I already can't wait to come home and peel him out of that—actually scratch that. The suit stays on.

Before we leave, he takes a beta blocker and slips more medication in my purse, just in case. We're now at a place where he doesn't hide that side of himself. His anxiety is part of who he is and I would never shame him for it. I feel privileged to be one of the few he trusts. The fact that he feels safe enough with me to be vulnerable, knowing how hard it is for him to let anyone in that way, has made me fall even more in love with him.

We spent Christmas at Ethan's parents' house, surrounded by his siblings and extended family. Even my dad, Jenn, and the kids joined in, because a bout of freezing rain derailed their plans to spend it with Jenn's family. It was just as I predicted it would be, total chaos, loud conversations, and an absolute dream.

It didn't take me long to realize, though, that even in the presence of his family, Ethan was having a hard time. He was tense and quiet, keeping his fists balled at his sides. And all I wanted to do was fix it. It was such a helpless feeling, but I tried my best to be the calm and steady against his anxious mind. Staying by his side, distracting him with rambling stories, giving him a break by suggesting a walk, it was all I could think of, and it didn't feel like it was enough.

We agreed not to do presents—well I suggested it and tried to make him uphold his end of the deal. I didn't want to make the holiday about gifts, not with us. He hasn't admitted it, but I suspect the tires on my car are new and I miraculously found a brand new supply of all the expensive makeup and toiletries I use on a regular basis. He knew I wanted to be low key and still managed to find a way to make me feel special. I'm not sure how I got so lucky. He didn't just raise the bar, he made an entirely new one, one no one else could ever reach.

We get to the winery early to help Elyse with any last-minute things she may need, though, upon arrival, she clearly has it all under control. When she sees me, she rushes over to us and wraps me in a hug, shoulder bumping Ethan in the process.

"I'm so glad you made it. I was worried my shithead brother would bail and keep you two locked inside his lair."

"I'm the boss, I kind of have to be here," he says to her back.

"Well, you never know." Her voice is defensively high. "I mean, I've barely seen Marisa since you two became official."

In a shocking, not so shocking, turn of events, Elyse both loves and is very annoyed that I'm officially dating her brother.

Before we can continue dwelling on it, she gets pulled away to the kitchen, and Ethan guides us to the bar, where his parents are. The event doesn't start for another thirty minutes, so the bar is wide open.

"Don't you look beautiful, sweetie." Leanne hugs me tightly and fusses with my hair, like I've seen her do for her own daughters. The movement makes my breath hitch, and I clear my throat to mask the emotion I let get a little too close to the surface.

"Me? You're the one who looks beautiful." As usual, Leanne is absolutely stunning. She has such a graceful presence. I imagine even a paper bag would look glamorous on her.

"Oh, stop." She waves her hand. "It's the Spanx," she says with a wink.

Jack gives me a hug before taking the stool next to Ethan and talking shop, going on about numbers and distribution and projected sales, none of which holds any of my interest.

"Jack, honey, you're boring me to tears. These young people don't want to talk business at a party."

Jack smacks his head jokingly. "Apologies, Marisa, old habits are hard to break. You kids have anything fun planned during slow season? My son better be whisking you off somewhere." He turns to Ethan with his brows raised. "Leanne and I used to go somewhere warm and tropical during winter, get away from this bone-chilling cold weather."

"Actually," I say. "Ethan tried to convince me to get away, but my best friend Hillary is due with her first baby in a couple weeks and I want to make sure I'm around for that."

Leanne places both of her hands over her chest. "How wonderful. A new baby." She looks at Jack with a smile. "We were just talking about how great it would be to have a new grandbaby. Lily is already in first grade. If only our kids would ever settle down." She pouts, looking at Ethan.

"Mom," he warns.

She puts up her hands. "What? I didn't say anything."

"Of course you didn't. Because you're a mastermind. But you implied it."

She shrugs and smiles innocently. "All I'm saying is a new baby in the family would be happy news. Wouldn't you agree, Marisa?"

"And we're leaving." Ethan stands, pulling my hand while I try to hold in a laugh. He guides me until we're clear across the room.

"We didn't have to leave. I wasn't uncomfortable. It's a mom thing."

He shakes his head. "We've been together for like five minutes, and my mom is already trying to get a grandkid out of you. You don't need that kind of pressure. Besides, you're—"

He doesn't finish the sentence, but I know what he was going to say. I'm leaving, so there's no sense in planning for the future. Forcing away the negativity, I pivot the conversation to something lighter, something to distract us from thoughts of the future.

"You know," I singsong, playing with his tie. "I was

thinking it would be fun if we checked out the wine cellar. For old times' sake."

"Yeah?" Ethan's hand grabs at my hip, pulling me closer to him. "I think that's the best idea I've heard all night," he mumbles against my lips before giving my bottom lip a little tug with his teeth, forcing my mouth to drop open for him. His tongue slides in, lapping against mine, and I feel my feet hover off the ground as Ethan's arms wrap around my waist and he turns the corner into a secluded hallway. He carries me over to the elevators, and takes us to the cellar, holding me the whole way down.

Once the door pings open, he carries me over to a barrel and sets me on it. I'm already so overheated from his touch, I hardly notice the chill in the air.

"What if someone catches us down here?"

The space is wide open. Anyone coming off the elevator would spot us.

He nips at my neck as his hands grip under my thighs. My legs wind around his waist.

"Let them. But trust me, no one is coming down here."

"Ethan," I squeal-whisper as his tongue begins licking the sensitive spot where my neck meets the top of my shoulder.

"Do you like the idea of being caught? If I touched your pussy right this second, would I find you soaked for me? Excited that someone could walk in on us at any moment, maybe even while you're coming on my cock?"

His words unravel the last of my control, making me want him that much more.

"Answer me," he says. "Is your pussy soaked?"

"Yes," I moan. "I'm always wet for you."

Two fingers push my panties to the side and plunge inside of me. "Baby, I love how ready and wet you always are."

He angles his fingers, hooking them forward and pushing them in and out of me, the build in my lower belly already growing fast. When I feel close, like I'm just about to reach the edge, he pulls his fingers all the way out.

I whine, slumping against him. "Why did you stop?" I should be embarrassed by my ragged breathing, but my brain is too jumbled to care.

His smile is wicked. "I have a better idea."

In my fog of confusion, I barely notice that he's lifted and spun me around, bending me over the barrel.

"What are you doing?"

"Shhh," he says. Then his hands are under my dress, pulling down my panties. I step out of them without thinking.

He crouches down behind me, and cool air hits me as the hem of my dress is lifted and gathered around my waist. I start to squirm when his breath dusts across my ass.

"I know we're supposed to be getting dinner right now," he says quietly against my thigh, his head between my legs. "But I'm in the mood for dessert."

His hands grip my ass cheeks, spreading them.

"Fuck, I love your ass. You look so pretty like this, bent over my barrel, at my mercy."

I gasp when his finger trails a line from my pussy all the way to that sensitive spot where he applies a slight pressure. The feeling is foreign and curious.

"You should've seen my ass after Goose trampled me. I had such a big bruise."

"Was it here?" *Kiss.* "Or here?" *Kiss.* "Maybe it was here." *Kiss.*

He peppers kisses all over my ass cheeks.

"Are you kissing my ass, literally?"

The vibration of his chuckle sends a shiver down my spine. "It's an honor to kiss your ass."

I snort, but it quickly morphs into a moan as his tongue draws a languid lick from my pussy all the way to my back entrance.

He does it again, going deeper with his tongue, and it causes my thighs to shake of their own volition. "Do you like it?" Ethan asks, in a low murmur.

"I don't know," I breathe. It feels both good and wrong at the same time. No one's ever touched me there.

He repeats the movement. When he gets to the overly sensitive spot he sucks hard, forcing a cry out of me as my vision fades.

"I think you like it," he muses. He buries his face between my ass cheeks and loudly, relentlessly, slurps and licks, eating me from front to back like I'm his last meal. In a matter of minutes, I'm coming, riding out the wave of my orgasm.

While I'm still recovering, I hear the sound of his zipper, and he gives my ass a light smack. "This is going to be quick," he grits.

And then he's inside of me, fucking me rough and fast, another orgasm building with each thrust. Soon we're both coming, and I feel exhausted, completely spent, my limbs like jello.

He slumps his weight over me, his ragged breath fanning the back of my neck. "We're going to look so obvious when we go back up," he mumbles.

A giggle escapes me. "It's your fault."

"Worth it," he groans, standing and giving my ass another smack before he works at fixing my dress.

My dress is barely put back into place when the elevator pings. Our heads whip to see who has arrived. Footsteps sound and then stop, staying out of sight.

"Who's there?" Ethan says in a deep, commanding voice, already standing in front of me, concealing me from whoever exited the elevator.

"It's Shane. Chill with the Batman voice."

Ethan's shoulders instantly relax. "What the fuck do you want?"

"Mom wanted me to let you know dinner is being served, and I saw you and Marisa sucking face before you two snuck off down here. Didn't know you had it in you. I feel like a proud father."

"Get fucked."

"You know, I lost my virginity down here." He snickers.

"Why do you fucking talk?" Ethan groans.

"Hi, Marisa."

I clutch onto Ethan's back, shaking from silent laughter. "Hi, Shane."

"We'll be up in a second. And I'll kick your ass if you breathe one word of this to anyone. Got it?"

"Sheesh, so sensitive."

"Shane!"

"Alright, alright. Might want to remove that stick up your ass."

His footsteps fade into the distance and the elevator sounds, but Ethan doesn't move until he's absolutely sure we're alone.

"That little shit is going to tell everyone."

When we get back up to the party, the ballroom is packed.

We join Ethan's siblings, parents, and my dad and Jenn for dinner, which is several courses, each with a wine pairing from this season's release. Shane keeps shooting looks our way, and I try my best to avoid his stare. If he and Ethan didn't look so alike, I truly would not believe they're brothers.

"I'm going to go freshen up," I tell Ethan, rising from my seat.

He nods, mid-conversation with his dad, and gives my hand a light squeeze before I leave. I love that he does that;

small little touches to make me feel seen even when his attention is elsewhere.

As I weave through the ballroom, I spot my coworkers, Raquel and Suzy, and give them a wave as I pass. I round the corner toward the ladies' restroom. The line is so long it's filtering out the door. Lucky for me, I've become quite familiar with the winery and know there's another set of restrooms downstairs.

The staircase is vacant, and the click of my heels echoes with each step I take. On the first floor, the corporate holiday retreat is in full swing, with loud conversations and laughter mixing with a strange techno sounding jazz song playing in the background. Pieces of conversation come at me, mentions of "AI framework" and "infrastructure strategy." It's enough to make my skin crawl. A reminder of my life before coming to Red Mountain.

I notice Elyse standing against the wall, ferociously typing into her phone. She looks up at me, and her eyes shift from stressed to relieved.

"Oh, thank God. A normal person." She pulls me in for a tight hug. "This crowd is full of pretentious weirdos," she whispers in my ear, snickering.

"What are you doing down here?"

Her shoulders rise, and she rolls her eyes. "The douchebag president or manager or whatever he is made Bella, my intern, cry, so I came down to smooth things over."

"Sounds like a sweet guy." I laugh. "I came down to use the restroom. The one upstairs had a really long line."

She nods. "Good call. This thing is a sausage fest. The ladies' room should be wide open."

"Marisa? Marisa Castilla?"

My body freezes.

"It is you," the man's voice says. The very familiar man's voice.

I turn slowly, my chest already sinking, and come face to face with Aaron.

"I thought that was you," he says with the audacity to smile at me as if we're old friends.

"Aaron." My voice rises. "What are you doing here?"

"Oh, you know how Brandon is. He loves a fancy shindig. We've had a bunch of turnaround recently, so this is kind of like a get to know each other event."

My head whips to Elyse. "What's the name of the company this retreat is for?"

Her eyes stare at me, bulging. "Beaker Innovations."

This has got to be a joke.

"Is the guy you've been dealing with named Brandon Beaker?"

She nods, putting the pieces together.

"I should go," I tell her, already sprinting away. It's not that I'm worried about seeing Brandon again, it's that I don't *want* to see him again. How dare he show up in Red Mountain and encroach on my life here. Did he know? There's no way he could've known. But he knew my dad lived here. I punch the button for the elevator repeatedly, as if that will make it come faster. I'm too frazzled to walk back up the stairs without falling on my ass, and embarrassing myself.

Come on, come on, come on!

It dings loudly, and relief immediately floods through me.

That relief is short-lived though, because when the doors open, there's Brandon. He recognizes me immediately, as if he were expecting me to be there.

"Risy, what a nice surprise."

CHAPTER 47

Ethan

TALL WHITE GUYS WITH MONEY

Marisa left to go freshen up a while ago. Normally, I wouldn't care, but I haven't seen her in the ballroom and my gut is telling me something is off.

I walk the perimeter and don't see any signs of her. Her coworkers, Suzy and Raquel claim they haven't seen her in at least twenty minutes, if not more.

Now, I actually am worried. Leaving the ballroom, I walk into the lobby, and run right into Elyse.

"Oh, good!" she shouts. "Just the person I was looking for." She looks panicked, but I really don't have time to deal with her.

"Not now, Elle. I'm looking for Marisa."

"That's why I came to find you."

I still and look at her. My gut feeling souring even more. "What's wrong? Is she okay?"

Elyse takes a long breath. "You know that corporate retreat thing downstairs?"

"Yes," I hesitate.

"It's her ex's," she squeaks with her eyes squeezed shut.

My spine goes rigid. "You're fucking kidding me," I shout, catching the attention of the few people hanging out in the lobby.

I race down the stairs, Elle following right behind me.

"You're not going to do anything stupid, right? Because we could get sued."

I wheeze a laugh. "Let him sue me. If he so much as touches her, he'll be lucky to walk out of here with all of his limbs."

"Fuck. Fuck. Fuck," Elyse mutters.

As soon as I reach the first floor, I instantly spot Marisa by the elevators. Arms crossed, shoulders hunched, and that son of a bitch is smiling at her.

Elyse grabs my shoulder from behind, her nails digging in like claws. "Think rationally. She doesn't need you to kick his ass, she just needs *you*. It's not about him. Be the better man." She lets go, giving my shoulder a push.

I take a breath to calm down. Elle is right. As much as I want to go up and punch him square on the jaw, it's not what Marisa needs from me.

"Baby," I say loudly, cheerfully.

Marisa's head snaps to me, and her face immediately releases all of its turmoil.

There's my girl.

I pull her close, draping my arm around her, and give her a kiss on the forehead, all the while ignoring the piece of shit next to us. My palm cups her face, and my lips are on hers, a possessive, crushing kiss. And despite the situation, she molds herself to me.

Am I acting like a caveman, staking a claim to my girl? Yes, I fucking am. Do I give a shit? Nope.

"I was looking for you," I murmur against her temple, still holding her close.

Her eyes meet mine and the relief she expresses knowing I'm by her side makes my chest swell.

An obnoxious throat clears, forcing me to acknowledge him.

Having been on the job a few months now, I actually have picked up some useful customer service skills. I extend my hand to him. "Ethan Ledger. Welcome to my winery."

We shake hands, and he is very obviously trying to grip my hand with all of his strength, but it still feels limp and weak, like the bitch he is.

"Brandon Beaker." He looks between Marisa and me, his eyes lingering on her too long for my liking. "I see you have a type, Risy. Tall white guys with money." He chuckles, as if his joke is really fucking funny.

"Do you two know each other?" I ask, my voice overly bright. Maybe I have a little more of my dad's charm than I thought.

His jaw ticks, his eyes narrowing at Marisa before he plasters on a smarmy smile. "We used to date. Even lived together. Not sure if she mentioned it, but it was only a few months ago."

I shrug, shaking my head. "I can't say I recall hearing anything like that. She mentioned a piece of shit ex who cheated on her and fucked with her career, but never even bothered to tell me his name."

Marisa's lips roll, holding back a smile.

"Nice little winery you got here, by the way. Reminds me of a similar winery in Sonoma, but they're larger scaled, international. You know the kind."

He thinks what he said is a dig, but all that did was reveal how stupid he is. Like I give a shit about some winery in another state.

When I don't indulge him with an answer, he sets his sight on Marisa. "So, this is where you ran off to? The discount version of Napa." He laughs again, the sound like nails on a chalkboard. This guy is a fucking tool, and I can't imagine a world in which he was able to land a woman like Marisa.

"You're drunk, Brandon," Marisa says with a dull voice. "Go back to your party."

It didn't occur to me that he's drunk, but that's when I notice his glassy eyes and the way he's slightly swaying. I was too blinded by my simmering rage. I didn't see the signs.

"You moved on quick, huh? But I know the truth. You miss me, don't you, Risy. I bet it takes everything in you to not scream my name while he's fucking—"

"That's enough," I bark. Stepping away from Marisa, I grab him by the collar and pin him against the wall. A man can only be so tolerable, and I won't have him speaking to her that way. "I think it's time for you to leave."

"You think she's yours, but she's not," he says through his strangled breath. "She's always going to think of me. You should've seen her face when we broke up. Fucking devastated, it was pathetic."

I yank him forward and slam him back against the wall. "She can't even remember her own name after I've had her, let alone yours. Now, unless you want me to rough up that pretty boy face of yours, I suggest you leave. And if you're not off the estate property within the next five minutes, I'll have you arrested."

"Yeah," he huffs. "For what?"

I laugh a humorless laugh, shoving my face to his. "It doesn't matter. It's a small town, and I know every single person on the force. I'm sure they'll think of something to charge you with."

"Whoa, whoa, whoa. The fuck is going on?" Shane asks, with a devilish grin, Gavin behind him looking like Jack Reacher. Elyse must've grabbed them.

Gavin's gaze meets mine, and I slowly let up on Brandon.

"Why don't you go be with your girl and Shane and I will take care of our special guest?" Gavin nudges his head, and I look to see Marisa, watching everything with her face twisted in concern.

My hands release Brandon completely, and he slumps against the wall. Before I hand him off to Shane and Gavin, I can't help but get in one more dig.

"Might want to look into getting some plugs for that bald spot, looks like shit."

I leave him, letting my brothers handle the rest. An audience has gathered, guests from both events watching the drama unfold. But for once in my life, I don't give a damn. Because all I see is Marisa. She's all that matters.

CHAPTER 48

Marisa

A CAUTIONARY TALE

"It was pretty hot," I tell Ethan, as we're lying in bed, staring at each other, our cheeks pressed into the pillows.

He mutters a laugh and takes a strand of my hair, twirling it between his fingers before tucking it behind my ear. "I should've punched him. At least once."

"Nahh," I sigh. "He's not worth it."

"What did you ever see in that guy?" He asks it with a slight laugh, but his eyes regard me tensely.

"He wasn't always like that. He was...smooth, I guess is the right word. Smooth and I was lonely. I have a habit of trying to see the best in people and it leads to building them up in my head."

A husky snort escapes him. "Bullshit. You saw the worst in me from day one."

My hand reaches out and rubs over his cheek, brushing against his beard. "You're the exception. Obviously."

I start to pull my hand away, but he's quicker and grabs it, yanking me to him.

"Hmmm," he breathes into my neck. "You're my exception, too."

My throat tightens, a lump rising, and I bite my cheek to keep from crying.

It's almost New Year's Eve, and we haven't discussed what we're going to do. If we're going to try long distance or...not try long distance. I'm not ready to let him go, but I don't know if I'm ready to move here permanently when we've only been together for a short while. I was with Brandon for a whole year before we moved in together. I was cautious, making sure the timing was right, and it didn't work out. I don't know if my heart can survive the hurt of Ethan doing something to me like Brandon did. Not that I think he would cheat on me, but distance makes people act in ways they normally wouldn't. How am I supposed to expect him to wait for me to figure out where I fit?

It's like I'm being torn in two directions, my heart wants to stay but my brain wants to follow through with the plan, because I can't possibly stay here for a guy, right? I can't change everything, literally choosing to give up a great job and my old life for a guy I've been dating less than two months. That's crazy, it's the start of a cautionary tale.

He draws back gently and takes my face in his hand, peering at me intensely. The air feels thick, and I worry he's going to tell me something bad. Something terrible. He's never looked at me like this.

"Is everything okay?" I whisper.

"No," he breathes. "It's not okay."

I suck in a sharp lungful of air. "What is it?" My voice is barely audible, almost as if I don't want him to hear it.

His thumb glides slowly across my jaw, delicately, and it leaves me with a tingle running down my spine. "I'm in love with you."

My heart soars, the words eager to tumble out. "I—"

"Don't." He cuts me off before I can say it back. "I don't want you to feel like you have to say it back. I'm not saying it to pressure you or to make you stay. I'm saying it because I can't let you leave without you knowing that I love you. That I've been in love with you for a while, maybe since you bent that cute little ass over and huffed at me, trying to find your insurance."

I laugh, but it mixes with the moisture pooling in my eyes. A tear wells over and rolls down my cheek, and his thumb brushes it gently. We stay watching each other for minutes, maybe an hour.

"What are we going to do?" I ask, my voice low.

He smiles softly at me, but it's a sad smile. "You're going to leave and I'm going to stay, but it's not the end."

I roll my lips, not liking but not hating his answer. "What do you mean?"

"I'm not going to beg you to stay, as much as I want to. I think you need to go back and figure out if Seattle is where you want to be, if that job is the job you want to have. And if it's not, you come back home."

"And if it is?" My heart stills, waiting for his answer—worried for his answer.

"Then I'll recommend Elle for CEO and I'll go back to working in the finance department at the Woodinville location."

My head is shaking before he can finish the sentence. "You can't leave just for me. Your family is here, your whole life is here. And you didn't even like working in Woodinville."

"You're my whole life. I can be apart from my family, but I can't be apart from you. So whatever you decide, I'm there. If it's here, great. If it's Seattle, that's great, too."

I groan, pressing my head back into my pillow. "Why can't you tell me what I want?"

He chuckles, and it cracks some of the tension in my chest. "Baby, I can only do that in bed."

The new year comes and goes, but it's hard to feel like celebrating when every day that passes brings me closer to leaving. We spent New Year's Eve in bed, memorizing each other's bodies, even though neither one of us would admit it. Ethan's always been affectionate with me, but lately he's even more so. Almost as if he thinks I'm going to disappear on him if his hands aren't on me. It's getting to feel suffocating, if I'm being honest.

I've already made arrangements with Zoe to stay in her apartment. Apparently, she has a boyfriend now—who she met on a dating app—and spends most of her time at his place. She told me I was welcome to crash there for a couple of weeks before I find my own place. It's like I'm back right where I started, still trying to figure things out while staying in someone's guest room.

It's Friday, my second to last day in Red Mountain, and I'm a wreck. I've been snappy all day, forcing Ethan to give me space, even when the last thing I want is space.

"You okay?" Ethan asks as I'm cutting up some lettuce for a salad.

"Yeah," I say cheerily, faking it. "Why?"

His eyes look down at the lettuce on my cutting board then back up to my face. "It's just that you've murdered that lettuce. It's practically mush."

I look down, and he's right. *Fuck.* I set down the knife and walk out of the kitchen. I'm not hungry, anyway.

"What are you in the mood for? I can make you something else."

"Will you stop!" I yell.

Ethan halts, watching me like I'm losing it. Maybe I am losing it. "Stop what?" he asks, quietly.

"Stop being so nice. Stop being helpful. Break up with me already. You know you're going to. Maybe not at first, but you'll work late or I'll work late and then we won't get to talk and then we'll start fighting and resent each other. I'll go out with coworkers, and you'll wonder if I'm cheating on you. I'll hear about some pretty blonde in town for a wine tasting flirting with you, and then I'll think you're cheating on me. We'll have a big blowup fight, and it'll be over. Might as well do it now and save us the pain from dragging it out."

My chest heaves from the word vomit. Ethan is frozen, his eyes wide, and then before I know it, he's wrapping his arms around me. He rocks us gently back and forth, rubbing my back soothingly.

"Where is this coming from?" He says it soft and gentle, like he's worried I might break. He's been incredibly patient, and I don't deserve it—I don't deserve him. "Why are you freaking out? It's only a four-hour drive, and I'm already set to visit you two weeks after you get there."

"I'm scared," I choke out. "What if you forget about me?"

"I'm not going to forget about you. Stop freaking out. I'm this close to slipping you a beta blocker," he jokes.

I burry my face against his chest, inhaling him deeply. "Promise me."

"What's that?" he says, still soothing my back.

"Promise me it's going to work."

He pulls away and cups my face, staring straight into my eyes. "I promise."

CHAPTER 49

Ethan

PEOPLE ARE LIKE GRAPES

"So, you let her go, huh?" Gavin asks while he looks down at me from the metal staircase that reaches the top of one of the tanks.

"How did you know I was in here?" I snuck off to the lab because I was tired of Tawny looking at me with her depressing stare, asking if I had spoken to Marisa. She's been gone a week, and it's been the worst week of my life. Worse than catching Laura cheating, worse than breaking off the engagement, worse than Travis's betrayal, worse than saying goodbye to Marisa the morning she left. Everything feels fucking terrible. If a doctor told me I was dying, I wouldn't be surprised, because that's what this feels like. Death.

"Your footsteps. You always walk like you can't get somewhere fast enough. Like the pitter patter of an elf."

"Pitter patter of an elf? I see Lily is still deep in the Christmas movies."

He lets out a tired sigh. "All year round."

Walking down the staircase, he rips off the hairnet covering his man bun. The man bun we all give him shit for, relentlessly.

"Why did you do it? Why'd you let her leave?"

Because I'm an idiot, that's why. "Because I'm not going to force her to stay. She needs to make the decision for herself."

It was the right thing to do. Deep down, I know it was, but doing the right thing feels like shit. I should've been selfish and told her to stay. Then maybe I wouldn't feel like my heart is cracking in half inside my chest.

"Well, what the fuck are you doing here? Go get her. She left, she's there. Now go get her."

"It's not that simple."

He barks a laugh. "Yeah, it is."

Gavin doesn't get it. To him, everything is black and white, right and wrong. While I know some part of him will always carry love for Lily's mom, to honor her memory, he's never been in love. Not like this.

"People are like grapes," he says.

I fight an eye roll. Here we go with his philosophical advice. "Please don't keep going," I groan, annoyed.

He raises his brows and smiles. "Each grape variety is different."

"Jesus Christ. Why did I come here? At least Tawny doesn't speak to me like she's reading off a fortune cookie."

Gavin laughs, walking toward one of the tanks. "Take this cab franc. It's earthy, a little herbaceous. It can be a lot to handle." He walks with his hands clasped behind his back like he's in front of a lecture hall, enlightening his students. I couldn't stop him now if I tried. He's full-on philosophical chemist. He points to another tank. "But then there's this cab sauv. It's bold, complex, a little spicy, a real fan favorite."

"Am I the cab franc and Marisa is the cab sauv in this scenario?" I ask, my voice deadpan.

"Exactly," he yells, entirely too excited about this weird-ass conversation. "You see, when you mix them together, it makes for the perfect, well-balanced wine. Sometimes the most unexpected combinations create the best results." He walks over to me and pats me on the back. "On their own, they're great, but together, create something unique, something rare."

"That was deep, Gav. I'm moved."

He shakes his head with a perfected disappointed dad look. "You laugh now, but my words will haunt you when you lie awake tonight, alone."

Heading for the door, I give him a dismissive wave. "Thanks for the advice. I'll come back next time I need my palm read."

Back in the cottage, I feel worse. So much of Marisa is still present. Some of her clothes hang in the closet, a couple pairs of her shoes are scattered by the door, her ridiculous coffeemaker is sitting on the counter, and the most unbearable of all is the sweet smell of vanilla she left behind. She left her car here, too, because there was no way that death trap would survive driving over the pass. Her dad bought her a plane ticket, and the plan is for me to bring more of her stuff when I go visit. The downside of that is now I'm surrounded by her things and her scent, but she's long gone.

We were supposed to FaceTime tonight, like we do every night, so I've been sitting on the couch with my phone clutched in my hand for thirty minutes, but still no call. Just as I'm about to give up and call her, a text comes through.

MARISA

Sorry. Can't talk tonight. I'm at the hospital.

I shoot out of my seat, panicked.

MARISA

Hillary had the baby.

My breath eases. Jesus Christ. The woman nearly gave me a heart attack.

Ok. We'll talk tomorrow. Tell Hillary and
Archie I say congratulations.

I stare at my phone a bit longer, waiting for a reply, but it never comes. I hate this. I hate being apart. I hate not seeing her.

I wasted so much time trying to avoid her, to stay away, and now I'd give anything to have that time back. Goose paws at the door, looking at me, and then back to the door. He's waiting for her.

I rise and go to scratch his head. "Sorry, buddy, she's not coming."

He whines, making a circle around me.

"I know. We're two whiny little bitches without her."

Goose and I get in bed, but instead of reclaiming his spot that's been occupied by Marisa, he remains at the foot and stares at the empty pillow. He doesn't understand that she's not coming, and I think it breaks me even more.

I turn on the TV, playing it loudly because it's so goddamn quiet without her. Meanwhile, my mind keeps repeating Gavin's stupid wine analogy. Damn him for predicting it would haunt me. Of course, she's perfect for me and we fit together like I never imagined I could with someone else. I stare at the ceiling. I stare at Goose. I toss and turn for several minutes. I try to focus on the TV, but that doesn't work either. I'm a mess.

By ten o'clock, I'm still wide awake and anxious. My phone chimes, and Marisa's name lights up the screen. It's a text.

MARISA

You're probably sleeping but here's a pic of me and baby Josephine.

A few seconds later, a picture pops up of Marisa smiling brightly, holding the smallest baby girl. I stare at the image for far too long.

I've never seen her hold a baby before, and she looks so right doing it. The baby in her arms, an equal mix of Hillary's round eyes and Archie's red hair, soon distorts, and I'm imagining a baby with Marisa's dark hair and her olive skin and my hazel eyes. The perfect mix of both of us.

What the fuck am I doing and why did I let her go?! I jump out of bed, so abruptly it makes Goose jump too.

"Come on." I whistle. "Get your leash. You're going to go stay at Grandpa and Grandma's."

In less than thirty minutes, I have Goose loaded in my truck with his overnight bag in my passenger seat. I should've sent a text to my parents before showing up this late, but I'm not exactly thinking beyond getting to Seattle as quickly as possible. I knock harshly and press their camera doorbell.

"I'm coming, I'm coming," my dad barks through the speaker.

A few minutes later, the front door opens and both of my parents stand at the entrance, very clearly having been woken up.

My dad groans and grabs on to Goose's leash. "Drive safe. The pass is still shit."

"How did you know I was going to Seattle?"

He looks me up and down, regarding me, somehow both proud and annoyed. "Wild guess."

CHAPTER 50

Marisa

A FREAK OF NATURE

I 'm breaking the law...well, sort of. The laws of the hospital. It is well past visiting hours, but Hillary refused to let me go back to the apartment.

I don't know how she's not passed out. She's honestly a freak of nature. Not only did she work a full eight-hour day— because she refused to start maternity leave before the baby arrived—she gave birth without any drugs, and baby Josephine was almost a ten-pounder. If I'm fortunate enough to have kids, I'll be begging for pain meds.

Archie is snoring loudly on the pullout couch, looking totally exhausted.

"I think I broke his hand," Hillary says to me with a giggle. "Poor guy wasn't ready."

"Seems only fair, considering the state of your vagina."

She groans. "Don't remind me. She's never going to look the same again."

I laugh quietly, trying not to wake Archie or the baby. "It'll be good as new in a few months."

Her eyes roll. "I doubt it. Tonight, do yourself a favor and take some good vagina pics. You can send them to Ethan for safe keeping. That way you'll always remember how pretty she was before a baby, with a head in the ninety-eighth percentile, squeezed out of it."

"I'll keep that in mind," I murmur, distracted by thoughts of Ethan.

Hillary stays quiet for a beat, watching me. "You're going to marry him, you know. He's the one."

My eyes meet hers, and I breathe out, giving her a small smile, nodding. "I hope so."

She squeals and then realizes where she is and claps a hand over her mouth. Once she's calmed down, she gestures for me to come closer. "Why did you come back? And don't tell me it was for that stupid job. You don't even like being a technical writer."

"I know," I say, flashing my eyes downcast. "He was adamant that I needed to move back so I would know what I really wanted. But I knew, Hill. I knew I should've stayed. I just let myself think it was too soon. I've regretted moving back every second I've been here. The only reason I would consider staying is because I do love having you close by, and it's hard being away from you."

She snorts. "Sweetie, I can move. I got Archie to cross an ocean for me. If I wake up tomorrow and tell him, 'Babe, let's move to Red Mountain,' he would have the moving truck scheduled that week."

I cock my head at her. "You're not moving, Hillary."

She sighs. "Well, obviously not right now. I just had a baby. But I could, one day. What I'm getting at is don't stay for me. This isn't your home. You have nothing tying you to Seattle anymore, except that dumb job, of course."

"I quit."

Her head rears back. "Like you quit the new job?"

I nod. "Yeah. Technically, it wasn't a real quit, since I'm still within the ninety-day window, but yeah, I quit."

Her smile is soft. "Good for you." She grabs my hand and gives it a squeeze. "I'm proud of you."

At some point, I fell asleep in the rocking chair in Hillary's hospital room. My eyes squint from the bright fluorescents the nurse turned on. Apparently, staying in a hospital means getting woken up at three in the morning. I look around and let my eyes adjust. Archie is still hard asleep. Hillary is awake, but it looks like she was recently woken up based on her tired eyes. A nurse holds baby Josephine in front of Hillary.

I get up and walk over to Hillary and the nurse. "What's going on?"

"They want me to try to breastfeed. I guess she was fussing."

The nurse passes a bundled Josephine into Hillary's arms. I watch for a moment as she coos and shushes, rocking her gently back and forth, like a total natural.

"You're a mommy," I tell her, feeling emotional.

Her eyes meet mine, shiny. "Yeah, I guess I am."

I blow her a silent kiss goodbye and wave. After being awkwardly curled up in the rocking chair, I'm ready for a real bed.

The only nice thing about this hour is that it takes almost no time at all to get an Uber to pick me up from the hospital. With the lack of traffic and the driver slightly speeding, the normal twenty minute drive is only ten. When we're almost to Zoe's apartment, I slip the driver a tip to stop at the convenience store so I can run in and grab something to munch on. Between quitting my job and then racing to the hospital, I've barely eaten today. It's been a whirlwind.

As soon as we pull into the parking lot of Zoe's apartment,

the driver is quick to leave. A pang of unease hits me as I wander through the dark parking lot during the witching hour. Zoe lives in a decent area, but Seattle still has plenty of crime, enough to have me looking over my shoulders all the way to the complex. Just when I think I can breathe a sigh of relief because I'm almost to Zoe's door, I instantly freeze, seeing a man slumped over, passed out, and sitting in front of the door.

My large pop and hotdog drop to the ground, and I yelp. The man stirs, turning his face, and I'm immediately relieved. It's Ethan.

Wait! It's Ethan!?

I rush to him and squat down. "Ethan! What are you doing here? Are you insane?!"

He shakes his head, coming out of his sleepy state.

"It's fucking January. You could've frozen to death."

"Keep it down!" someone yells from up above.

"Come on," I whisper. "Let's get you inside."

I practically drag him in and close and lock the door behind us. When I turn back to face him, he's rubbing at his face, looking more awake.

"Why are you here?" I don't mean to sound upset, but had I known he was coming, I would've been here hours ago. He didn't call or text or anything. I'm feeling panicked. People don't show up out of the blue for no reason. The only thing I can think of is that he finally came to his senses and is here to break up with me, and because he's such a good man, he's doing it in person.

"Let's sit down," he says.

I stand my ground and cross my arms, popping a hip to feel a little more confident. "No, I'm not sitting until you tell me why you're here."

His eyes narrow at me, confused. "Are you mad at me right now?"

I throw up my hands. "I don't know Ethan? You show up here out of nowhere, and it's got me freaking out." I meet his gaze and then look down, feeling less and less confident with each passing second. Breathing deeply, I lock eyes with him. "Are you here to break up with me?"

He laughs harshly, tossing his head back. "Break up with you? Why would you think that?" He approaches me slowly, cautiously. Reaching his hand out, his fingers brush against my jaw, holding it gently. "Baby, I'm not here to break up with you. I'm here to take you home."

CHAPTER 51

Ethan

I HAVE RULES

"I'm sorry, what?"

I wrap my arms around her lower back and pull her against me, dipping my head to nuzzle her neck. "You heard me. We're going home."

She giggles, letting her head fall back. Fuck, I love that sound.

"You know, for someone who basically pushed me out the door, you sure are pretty demanding about me coming back home with you."

I place a soft kiss on her collarbone while inhaling the vanilla coming off her skin. "I'm a stupid man." I hold her tightly, probably suffocating her, but I need to hold her like I need my next breath. "The biggest mistake I've ever made in my life was letting you leave, thinking I could ever go without you, no matter how temporary."

She wiggles out of my grasp and goes to sit on the couch. I join her, but give her some space, even though it's the last thing I want.

"And you decided this in the middle of the night? It couldn't have waited until morning?"

I shake my head. "It couldn't wait. I can't go another day without you, baby."

"And if I refuse to go?" Her voice is stern, but her smile is pure sunshine.

"Then you better get used to me, because I'm done being apart. I can't do it anymore."

She crosses her arms, eyes trained on me. "How do I know you're not going to push me away again?"

"I wasn't pushing you away. I wanted you to be sure, I didn't want you to end up resenting me because you passed up a good opportunity."

She looks down, twisting the ends of her hair. "I know that's what you said, but it didn't feel that way," she says quietly.

"Come home." My voice is a plea. If I have to beg, I will.

She peers over at me with her head tilted. Her eyes have a little challenge behind them. "Give me one good reason why."

I reach for her, taking her hands in mine and hold her stare. "You're my first thought when I wake up, and before my eyes even open, they're looking for you. When I think about what I'm going to eat, I'm not thinking about what I want, I'm thinking about what you'll want, because food is tasteless unless I'm sharing it with you. When I see something funny, you're the first person I want to share it with, because your laugh is my favorite sound. When I pass a nice house, I don't think about whether I like it, instead, I wonder if it's your dream house and how can I build it for you. And when I walk by a jewelry store I'm thinking how long should I wait to go in there and buy the one thing that will make you mine forever. I'm more than in love with you, I'm in life with you. I want to do life with you, every day. I'm a greedy man, Marisa, I want all of your days, the good, the bad, the mundane. And after that, I want all your nights, buried between your legs, making you scream my name for the rest of our fucking lives. I want you forever, baby. It's as simple as that."

By the time I'm done laying it all out on the line, Marisa's eyes are tear-filled. She leaps across the couch cushion between us and throws her arms around my neck, pulling me in close.

"That was some speech," her garbled voice says into my neck.

"Thanks, I've been watching Nora Ephron movies all week, because I know how much you like them."

Her giggle trembles, and when she pulls away to face me, I wipe a tear off her cheek.

"I have something to tell you." Her tone is serious, and it makes my lungs squeeze. "I quit my job."

My eyes widen. "What?"

She nods, smiling. "While I appreciate the groveling grand gesture, since you're still only seventy-five percent forgiven, I was already planning to come back. As it turns out, I'm just as weak for you as you are for me and I couldn't stand being apart."

"So, you're coming home with me?"

Readjusting, she moves to straddle me, pressing her chest to mine. "Yeah, but—"

"There's always a but."

She smiles mischievously, cocking her head. "But I have rules."

"Really?" I play with the ends of her hair. "What are these so-called rules?"

Her lips roll, biting her smile. "Rule number one, no visitors."

I bark a laugh. She's such a brat.

"I'm serious Ethan, we can't have people dropping by our little love cottage. We have a whole week to make up for."

Still laughing, I ask, "And rule number two?"

Her head lowers, and her lips hover over mine. "Me and you, we're not friends."

"Oh, yeah?" I breathe as my hands roam her body.

"Nope," she sighs. "In fact, my feelings for you are way past friendly." She stills, and cups my cheeks, brushing her thumbs over my beard. "I'm way too in love with you to ever be just friends."

I close the distance between us and kiss her softly. "Say it again," I whisper.

She smiles and brushes her nose against mine. "I love you. I'm so, so, so in love with you."

CHAPTER 52

Marisa

BETTER THAN ANYONE

There better be a damn good reason why my boyfriend is waking me up this early.

"Stop," I groan. "Let me sleep." I turn away, curling into my pillow, but Ethan rolls me back to face him. It's only been a few weeks since I came back, but we've already fallen back into our rhythm. Except this time, there isn't a ticking time bomb. It's just us, and I've never been happier.

His beard scratches against my neck as he trails kisses along my jaw. "Time to wake up, baby," he singsongs.

"Too early," I protest.

I keep my eyes closed, even though I'm awake now. How could I stay asleep as his hands wander my body? His touch is electrifying, jolting me awake.

"I hate you," I moan. My lips press together, hiding my smile, and I keep my eyes squeezed shut.

"Liar." He continues to nip and suck and kneed and massage.

My body becomes more and more loose and malleable. And I don't mind it one bit. I love waking up with his lips on me and his weight pressing me down onto the mattress. It's like being cocooned in the most comforting way.

But I also love teasing him. "You're being too gentle. What happened to the grumpy asshole? Bring him back. I like him better."

"That's it," he declares, getting up and yanking the bedding off me.

My body screams in protest, instantly freezing from the loss of blankets. Before I get a chance to yell at him, he's picked me up and thrown me over his shoulder, fireman style.

"Ethan," I screech while giving his ass a hard smack. "Put me down!"

The bastard chuckles. "You said you wanted me to be a grumpy asshole. You got him now, too late to take it back."

I squirm. "Where are you taking me?"

Instead of answering me, he keeps walking, but I quickly realize he's taking me to the bathroom. Keeping me locked in his hold, he starts the shower. After a few beats, once the temperature has warmed, he finally lets me go, sliding me down his body, where I feel he's already hard for me.

"You woke me up this early for shower sex?"

He smirks, shaking his head. "We actually have somewhere to be, but now that you mention it." He pauses and strips out of his shirt. "Might as well fuck you awake."

He kisses along my collarbone, his lips never leaving my skin as he takes off my silky pajama shorts and tank top.

He picks me up, this time more gently, and just enough so that my feet are grazing the floor. Together, we stand under the stream of water. Wasting zero time, he crashes his lips to mine while hitching me higher and forcing my legs to wind around his waist. And then he's nudging at my entrance, tracing his cock along my seam to test my wetness.

"Fucking soaked," he whispers in my ear.

In one thrust, he's fully seated. Our gazes meet, lashes

dripping with water, and he smiles at me softly. "Good morning."

The corner of my mouth tilts up. "Good morning." Using the leverage of my hands around his neck, I lift my body, moving up his cock and sliding back down on it. We both sigh in relief.

"Fuck, baby. I'm never going to get enough of you." He pulls my bottom lip between his teeth, giving me a soft bite before invading my mouth and kissing me roughly. Slamming me against the tile wall, he fucks me at a relentless pace. I lose myself in him. He consumes me. He devours me. With each moment, the more we dissolve into each other.

Thirty minutes and two rounds of shower sex later, we're in the truck on our way. To where? I'm not sure, because Ethan won't tell me.

Strangely, the drive is very, very familiar. "Can you please tell me where we're going? You know I don't like surprises."

"You love my surprises."

I stay quiet, racking my brain, trying to think of what we could possibly be doing.

"Are we going to your parents' house?" He tried to take a roundabout way, but there's no mistaking the direction we're going.

He shakes his head. "No, not right now. We have other plans."

The anticipation is driving me crazy as he pulls alongside the empty lot next to Gavin's. He puts the truck in park, turns it off, and gets out, still not answering me.

Undoing my seat belt, I grumble while he holds open my door and follow after him.

"Well then, can you tell me what we're doing out here?"

The crunching of gravel draws my eyes to the hill where I see a Jeep rolling down, heading in our direction.

"Perfect timing," Ethan mutters.

"Who's that?"

"You'll see."

The Jeep parks next to the truck, and a professionally dressed, middle-aged blonde woman exits, walking toward us with a friendly smile.

"Ethan, so good to see you," the woman says, shaking Ethan's hand.

"Linda, this is Marisa, my girlfriend."

A blush scatters across my cheeks. I don't think I'll ever tire of hearing him call me that. Linda and I shake hands.

"Alright folks, let's design a house."

What?

My eyes fly to Ethan's. "What is she talking about?"

Ethan looks to Linda. "Can you give us a minute?"

She nods, smiling. "Sure, I'll go get the prints from my back seat. Be back in a jiff."

Ethan points to his parcel with a giant dirt pile at the center. I can tell it's been recently dug up, because the dirt looks fresh.

"Remember when I told you about still wanting to build a house on this land?"

"Yeah." I hesitate, wondering why it's dug up.

"I had a company come out and remove the foundation that was poured."

"Why?"

"Because I don't want to build that house. I want to build our house."

Our house.

My heart squeezes, and my throat tightens. *Our house.*

"What are you saying?" I need him to say it. To voice it out loud and bring it into existence. I need to know it's real.

His hand cups my jaw, and our gazes hold. With those gentle eyes and that soft smile, it's hard to believe he's the same man I met only months ago. "Let's build a house together, build a life."

"Really? Because that's kind of a big deal. What if you get sick of me a few months from now?"

He chuckles. "I'm never going to get sick of you. All I need is you. All I'm ever going to want is you."

He reaches into his pocket and hands me an envelope. "Here."

I grab the envelope and open it. Inside is a legal document. It only takes me a second to figure out what I'm looking at, and when I do, my eyes meet Ethan's. "How did you— Why did you—"

His hands grab my wrists, with the letter still in my hand, and I realize it's because they're shaking. "The deed is in your name. The land is yours."

When I don't answer because I'm too stunned to form a coherent word, he continues. "I don't want you to ever feel like at a moment's notice, you could lose everything. I thought, what better way to make you feel safe than to put it all in your name. You own it. And once the house is built, you'll own that, too."

"But what about you?"

"Baby, if you haven't figured out that you own every part of me, then clearly I haven't been doing a very good job of showing you that I'm yours. Completely."

"I don't know what to say."

"Say yes." He gives me a brief kiss and then pulls away. His lips quirk up as he hands me another envelope.

"Another envelope? What's happening right now?" I tear into it quickly, my curiosity getting the best of me.

It's a check. It's a check for a very significant amount of money.

"Why are you giving me money?"

Ethan laughs, only adding to my confusion. "When you told me that dick was making you pay half of his mortgage, I did some digging and found out he already owned the condo and was basically taking all of your money. I got my lawyer involved, and after some very non-threatening discussions, he was happy to hand over all the money he took from you."

I should be livid, finding out Brandon had been taking advantage of me, but all I feel is gratitude. Gratitude for the man in front of me who took on a battle he didn't need to. I'm not going to waste another second thinking about that time in my life when the present is so much better.

Linda returns with blueprints and pamphlets. Honestly, it's overwhelming. I'm still reeling from Ethan putting the property in my name and the unexpected check. I can't believe he did that. Maybe to him it seemed like a simple solution, but to me it's everything. He managed to make me feel safe and secure with more than words. I can't undo the years of my mom's warnings of never relying on a man and never putting myself in a situation that makes me vulnerable. I can't undo the damage and mistrust Brandon caused. Ethan took all of that and threw it out the window. Because he knows me. He knows me better than anyone.

There's a lot I don't know or understand about life. If all of our choices aren't our own and our futures are already determined, or if it's a series of decisions, each with their own path and the possibilities are endless. I'd like to think I ended up on the path I was always meant to be on. That getting fired and having to move to Red Mountain and crashing into the vineyard was all meant to be. Because not only did it lead me to Ethan, it led me back to my dad, and to this wonderful town, and to a job that makes me happy, and to new friends that feel like family. There's a cheesy saying I often see floating around that goes something like, *Sometimes things have to fall apart so that better things can fall together.* Now, having lived it, maybe it's not so cheesy anymore.

Later in the evening, over a bottle of wine and a box of Cheez-Its, Ethan and I start discussing all the things we want to include in the house—our house. We're cuddled up, making a Pinterest board, and it's so incredibly domestic. I love us. I love who we are together. We're a strange mix, a rare blend. Two people who shouldn't be compatible, yet somehow our jagged edges seamlessly align, fitting together in a way that feels both effortless and extraordinary.

ETHAN

THREE MONTHS LATER

"We're going to be late," Marisa calls from the other side of the door.

"Be right out." I've been ready for a few minutes, but I'm giving the beta blocker some time to work its magic so I can tolerate the large crowd that will be gathered at the winery. In typical Ledger fashion, everything must be celebrated and turned into an elaborate event, including my parents' wedding anniversary.

"You look very handsome."

I turn at the sound of Marisa's voice and watch as she saunters into our bedroom, wearing one of her sinful little dresses. The weather is still fairly cool for early spring, but you'd never know it wasn't blazing summer by the strappy, hot pink dress she's wearing. I can't wait to strip her out of it later.

"Behave," she warns with a sexy smile.

We're definitely leaving the party at least an hour early. I don't think I can last late into the night with her dressed like that and not being able to do anything about it.

When our gazes latch, I find the heat in her eyes mirrors mine and raise a brow at her. "Now who's the one giving the eye-fuck."

Her arms cross, only drawing more attention to her full, round tits. "What can I say, I'm weak for a rugged man in a custom suit. Something about calloused hands and cufflinks really does it for me."

"Baby, if that's your kink, I'll wear this monkey suit daily."

She laughs heartily and the huskiness of it warms my chest. Her laugh is the best damn sound I've ever heard—apart from her moans.

Sometimes I still wake up worried I dreamed the whole thing and she never came back. It's a nightmare that takes me a few seconds to shake until I realize it's her warm body next to mine. Right where she belongs. Forever.

I have no intentions of pushing Marisa before she's ready, but the ring I have hiding in my desk drawer is burning a hole in my thoughts. Every day I try to pretend it's not there and every day I fail. It's getting harder to wait, especially now that construction has started on our house. We had to wait for the harsh winter to pass, but once it did, it's been full speed ahead. We both know marriage is in our future, but I'm not going to ask until I'm absolutely certain she's ready. Until then, I'll continue to feel like the luckiest guy alive, because I get to share my life with this amazing woman.

"Come on, lover boy. We can't be late because we had a quickie beforehand. Your siblings will totally be able to tell. Especially Shane."

The party is in full swing when we arrive. I swallow the dryness in my throat, watching as large crowds filter in, and the sounds of a million conversations blur into one chaotic hum.

Marisa clutches onto my hand and gives it a squeeze.

"You give me the word, and we're out of here. We can tell people I have food poisoning or something."

God, I love her. I love that she gets it, and I don't have to explain it. I've never had to explain it.

"Thanks, baby." I bring up our joined hands and give her knuckles a kiss. "Let's go inside before I lose the nerve."

Inside, I immediately scan the overflowing ballroom for one of my siblings. Elyse spots us first and waves us over. She's the coordinator of the event, and looking very much the part, holding a tablet against her chest.

"I thought your mom said this was going to be a small, intimate event," Marisa says as we weave through to get to Elyse.

"This is her version of intimate."

She huffs, looking around. "I think she needs to look up the definition again."

"I sat you guys with the rest of the crew." Elyse points to a table near the stage and pushes us off, looking stressed.

I lead the way while we maneuver the round banquet tables decoratively covered in linen tablecloths and an array of centerpieces. This party looks a lot more like a wedding than it does a thirty-fifth anniversary celebration.

We spot Robert and Jenn as we get closer to our table, and they toss us a wave. Marisa also runs into a few of her coworkers, promising to meet up with them later.

The room is full of people I know, and it's both comforting and tortuous all at once. I give Marisa's hand a squeeze, telling her I found our table.

When we get there, Gavin and Shane are chatting while Layla and Ariana entertain Lily by coloring with her.

Shane's eyes give Marisa a once-over before cutting to me

and giving me a wink. He's always trying to get a rise out of me, especially when it comes to Marisa.

"Looking good, Marisa," Shane tells her.

Marisa smiles like she's holding in a laugh. "Thanks, Shane."

Gavin drums on the table. "Are we betting or what?"

I grumble at the same time Marisa asks, "What are we betting on?"

Gavin and Shane lean closer to her, as if they're divulging top-secret information.

"We always take bets on what ridiculous things will come out of our dad's mouth. Give the man a mic, and he's bound to say something embarrassing as shit," Gavin tells her.

Shane points between himself and Gavin. "We think he's going to go with the Stallone impression."

"My money is on the McConaughey one," Layla says.

Ariana nods. "Agreed. He's going to do McConaughey."

Marisa looks at me, amusement dancing in her eyes. "And you?" she asks. "What's your bet."

I shake my head. "No bet. I don't participate in their shenanigans. Last time they made a bet, Elyse lost, and she and Shane didn't speak for a week. They get too competitive."

"Just admit you're a pussy," Shane says, his tone full of challenge.

Before I can reply with a comeback, Marisa yells out, "Hey! Don't fucking talk to him like that."

The table falls completely silent, and all heads turn to Marisa. Her eyes flare, as if she's surprised by her own outburst. Layla and Ariana exchange a look with raised brows and rolled lips, like they want to smile. Seconds tick by, and then Gavin is the first to break.

He brings his closed fist to his mouth and his shoulders bounce in quick succession as a wheezing chuckle escapes him. Shane is fast to join him and together the two bust up laughing. Marisa looks at me confused and leans close to whisper in my ear.

"I was trying to defend you, but they seem to think it's hilarious."

Gavin clears his throat. "Damn, E, she's a keeper."

I wrap my arm around her and tuck her in at my side. "I know," I say and then kiss Marisa's forehead.

She melts into me and rubs her hand over my thigh. The movement short-circuits my thoughts, causing my dick to twitch. I place my hand over hers to stop her from doing any exploring under the cloak of the tablecloth. I'm not about to sport a boner surrounded by my siblings.

"Jesus Christ, get a room," Shane says with a snicker before making a gagging noise.

Marisa's eyes shoot daggers at him, but he ignores her, or he doesn't give a shit.

The tables around us start to fill, and Marisa tries to engage me in random conversations to distract me. I love her for trying, even if it's not really working. I don't think events like this will ever get easier for me, but they're definitely more tolerable with her by my side. She makes everything better by simply being there and noticing when I need a break. I didn't think it was possible to find someone who understands all the parts of me I try to keep hidden. My own family—while they're supportive—doesn't quite get it.

"Want to get some air?" Marisa whispers in my ear, already scooting to the edge of her seat to stand.

I nod. "A short one. Before the speeches start."

Instead of fighting the crowd, we take a side door that leads to a covered patio. The area is restricted, leaving just us two.

Black, wrought iron bistro tables line the railing. I take a seat in one of the chairs and Marisa curls up in my lap, winding her hands around my neck and resting her head on my chest.

"Your heart is beating so fast," she whispers, but it comes out muffled because of the way her cheek is pressed against me.

"I know. I'm kind of used to it."

We stay like that, cuddled together, for several minutes in comfortable silence. My hand rubs up and down her back, trying to keep her warm in this chilled spring air, while she stays wrapped around me. Now *this* I could do all night. The last thing I want to do is go back in and fake a smile, and act like I'm not a nervous wreck inside. But we can't stay out here forever.

Without saying anything, we simultaneously untangle and start walking toward the patio door. Just as we reach it, the sound of tires ripping across gravel has us both turning our heads at the erratic sound.

A deputy sheriff cruiser whizzes by, kicking up a cloud of sand in its wake.

"What the hell?" I say under my breath.

"Did someone call the cops?" Marisa asks as her eyes fix on me, filled with panic.

"I have no fucking idea, but we better go find Elle."

Marisa clutches my hand as I practically drag us to the entrance, where I suspect Elyse is.

When we get there, Elyse is on the phone. As soon as she spots me, she holds up her finger, indicating she needs a minute. The problem is, I don't think we have a minute.

"Clore County Sheriff's Department. Open up," a booming voice yells on the other side of the door with two loud, banging knocks.

Elyse's eyes nearly bug out of her head as she drops her phone and scurries to the door. She gestures her arm, waving it wildly for me to come with her.

I'm not sure if she's waving me over because I'm the CEO

or because I'm her older brother. Either way, I'm right next to her when she swings it open.

Standing at the entry, we're met with a deputy sheriff staring back at us.

"We got calls of a noise complaint. Is there a manager I can speak to?"

Elyse crosses her arms and squares her shoulders, not one to shrink under the stare of someone trying to be intimidating. Cop or not.

"Bull fucking shit."

My entire body freezes. I didn't expect her to be so abrasive. He's still a cop. Before I can cut in, she continues.

"Just exactly what are you trying to pull Dominic?"

Dominic?

I look at the deputy again. Really look at him. *Shit.* I can't believe I didn't recognize him. I think the uniform threw me off.

"Dom?" Our eyes meet, and he gives me a smirk. "Holy shit, man. I didn't know you moved back."

He moves toward me and clasps my hand in a brief shake as he claps me on the back.

"I've only been back a few weeks." His eyes break from mine and go straight to Elyse, who's still holding her rigid stance. "Hey, Ellie girl."

Her shoulders tense even more, and her face pinches into a painful expression. "What are you doing here, Dominic? There isn't really a noise complaint, is there?"

His chin dips, keeping his eyes on Elyse. "No, you got me. I heard it was your parents' wedding anniversary and wanted to stop by and see everyone."

"And you thought this stupid charade was the way to go?"

He rubs the back of his neck and tosses Elle a sheepish grin.

I can practically feel the irritation rolling off her, sharp and palpable, as if it could spark the air around us.

Marisa clears her throat, and I glance back at her, catching her eyes swinging like a pendulum between Elyse and Dom, trying to piece it all together.

Nodding my head, I gesture for her to come closer. "Baby, come meet Dom."

Marisa steps forward and comes around to my side, tucking herself under my arm.

Dom reaches out to shake her hand. "Dominic Alvarez. I grew up here."

"Marisa, Ethan's girlfriend."

Despite the icy air between Elyse and Dom, my chest still warms when I hear her call herself my girlfriend. I can't wait until the title is wife, but girlfriend still makes my heart thunder.

As they shake hands, Dom says, "I've known the Ledgers a long time."

Elyse scoffs. "Knew," she corrects. "You knew us. You don't anymore."

Marisa's stare is equally confused and amused.

"Should we go sit down?" I ask Marisa. Clearly, Elyse and Dom have some issues to work out and I want no part of it.

"Yes, let's go sit before things get started," Marisa says and then turns her focus to Dom. "It was nice meeting you."

"Nice meeting you," he tells Marisa, and then he nudges my chest. "Let's catch up soon man, it's been a long time."

"Yeah," I tell him. "You know where to find me."

As soon as we're out of earshot, Marisa ushers me into a quiet hallway outside the ballroom.

"Okay, spill. Who was that and why did Elyse look like she wanted to murder him?"

"Like he said, we've known him for a long time. He grew up with us. His family used to own a farm that bordered our property until they eventually sold it to us a few years ago, and we turned it into more vineyards."

Marisa rolls her eyes at me. "Like I care about any of that. I want the juicy shit."

I take a breath, not sure if Elyse would appreciate me talking about her personal life behind her back. But I also don't keep things from Marisa.

"They dated in high school and a little into their first year of college. Elyse is the one who broke up with him, but for whatever reason, she's harbored an anger toward him ever since, even though she insists he didn't do anything wrong. None of us know exactly what went down, but he was friends with all of us before they dated, and the few times I've run into him, we've been friendly. They probably broke up because they were going to different colleges and the distance was too hard. Elle is being dramatic about the whole thing, because she's dramatic about everything."

Marisa's lips purse, and her head cocks, taking in all the information.

"I don't think I've ever seen her look so affected by a guy. She looked pissed. I'm going to bet there's a hell of a lot more to the story than some simple breakup. People get over stuff like that. It's been, what, ten years?"

I shrug. I don't like to speculate, and frankly, it's none of my business. Unlike my siblings, I know when to not stick my nose somewhere it doesn't belong.

"Enough about my sister and her love life, let's go inside. The sooner we get this over with, the sooner I can get you home and naked."

As I'm about to turn, Marisa grabs my tie and pulls me back.

"Just a few more minutes." She stands on her tippy toes even though she's already in high heels and wraps her arms around my neck, bringing my head down to hers. "Have I told you how good you look tonight?" she whispers against my mouth.

My senses are flooded with the smell of her signature vanilla as it mingles with the sip of wine she had earlier. She crashes her lips to mine with an unexpected eagerness. It takes me a second, but I'm quick to catch on and pull her close. My hands wander down to her luscious ass, and I grab each cheek roughly as I hoist her against me. She moans into my mouth, sending a tingle down my spine. If we were in the privacy of our bedroom, I'd be seconds away from being inside of her, but that's not an option in this exposed hallway.

I draw away from her lips and nuzzle her neck. "What has gotten into you? You know I can't fuck you out in the open, no matter how badly I want to be inside of you right now."

She giggles and presses her body even closer, rolling it forward like she's desperate to ride my cock.

Fucking hell. Maybe I will fuck her here after all.

"It's just that I realized something," she says, but I'm almost too distracted to hear her, my mind drifting to thoughts of the empty upstairs and the lock on my office door.

She taps on my chest, bringing my focus to her face. "Are you listening to me?" she exhales.

"All ears, baby." I place a delicate kiss to the dip where her neck meets her shoulder. "What did you realize?"

"That I'm so lucky to have you. That *we're* so lucky to have each other."

The lust fog in my mind clears, and I pull back to meet her stare. Her eyes are slightly glassy, turning her chocolate browns into a black abyss, and there's a tightness in her voice that makes my heart lurch. Her crying can bring me to my knees. In fact, it has brought me to my knees.

"Why are you crying, baby?"

"I'm not crying, just a little misty." She sniffles. "Seeing Elyse get flustered over her ex reminded me that I have you to fight those battles for me and I never have to worry about stuff like that."

"No, you fucking don't," I say firmly. "If that asshole comes within a mile of this town, I actually will kick his ass."

She laughs a watery laugh. "No, what I mean is, I have you. I only want you. And that's never going to change."

"It better not." I tuck a piece of her hair behind her ear and try to ignore the way my heart is hammering in my chest. I'm nervous, and I'm not entirely sure why.

"Ethan," she says, meeting my eyes. "You're it for me. No one, no ex, no other guy, is ever going to come along to make me question if you're the one. You're it, it's only you, and I want you to know that. I know it's only been a few months, and I'm sure I drive you crazy with my messes and my rambling and my obsession with trashy TV, but just know that I love you so fucking much and I'm so happy you're mine and I'm yours."

A burst of emotion starts to work its way up my throat, and I clench my jaw to hold it back. My hands settle around her jaw and cup her face to hold her gaze.

"I ever tell you how lucky I feel that you even gave me a chance? That I get to wake up to you every day? I'm so in love with you that I can't remember the man I was before my heart belonged to you. And I don't want to remember him. You make me better. I'm a better man because I want to be a man deserving of you. You've been it for me since day one and you're going to be it for me until my heart stops beating. And even then, you bet your ass I'm finding you in the afterlife. It's a forever kind of love, baby. And I'm yours"— I take her lips in mine and give her a soft kiss—"always."

Eventually we leave the hallway and join the rest of the partygoers. My dad does his McConaughey impression, and my siblings exchange money across the table. The celebration passes in a whirl as speeches are conducted and my parents do a repeat of their first dance from thirty-five years ago. As I watch my parents, I can't help but wonder if one day it will be me and Marisa. If one day, we'll be the ones celebrating our thirty-fifth anniversary in a room full of friends and family. I highly doubt my anxiety will ease with age, but I wouldn't be opposed to celebrating the day with any kids we might have.

That's the amazing thing about our relationship, with Marisa by my side, the possibilities are endless. She's a rare find and the perfect match for me.

Bonus Epilogue

THE FOLLOWING OCTOBER

"**B**aby, I'm home," Ethan shouts from downstairs.

His voice sounds echoey, and I know he's in the formal dining room, because there isn't any furniture in there yet.

We've officially been in the new house—*our house*—for a little over a month. Just in time for harvest. I was excited for this new chapter of life with Ethan, but it was bittersweet leaving the cottages. We fell in love with each other within those tiny walls, and it felt like the end of an era. Though change is hard—even welcomed change—it's been an adventure filling our home with all the pieces of us.

I would've been happy with a smaller house, something simple, but Ethan convinced me to go bigger. I think sometimes he's more like his dad than he realizes, wanting to build me an ostentatious, oversize home, just like Jack built the chateau for Leanne. We compromised somewhere in the middle, and the house is still almost five thousand square feet.

I asked him, "What are we going to do with all this space?" Instead of answering me, he smiled shyly and shrugged. It made my stomach dip in that way it always does when I'm reminded we're intertwining our futures together.

He didn't say it and I didn't press, because we both knew the answer. A family. We're nowhere near ready to jump on that train but once I came back from Seattle, the space to discuss the future opened. As an only child, I've always dreamed of having a larger family, and Ethan, despite his siblings driving him crazy most of the time, also wants a large family.

"Coming," I shout, descending the stairs as quickly as one can in four-inch heels.

It's our anniversary. One whole year since I plowed through a vineyard and flipped my life upside down. I tried to argue that our anniversary should technically be from when we had our first date but, in all honesty, I feel like I've been his and he's been mine from the moment we met. It was like a shift in the planets, the falling of an asteroid. There would be no reverting, no going back. We may not have realized it at the time, but our lives were irrevocably changed from that point forward.

His back is to me as I approach, and from the looks of it, he changed at the office. Gone is his uniform of Wranglers and a flannel. They've been replaced by a pair of camel slacks and a checkered button down. Still ruggedly handsome, just a little dressier.

He turns at the sound of my heels clacking against the hardwood floors. His eyes trace my body, leaving flares of heat in the places they linger for a second too long.

"You look so fucking beautiful."

Before I can get a word out, his hands are on me, gripping my waist and pulling me against him. His lips capture mine, and my body melts into him. The kiss starts out slow and languid, but quickly transforms into a desperate mess. My wrists cross behind his neck, dragging him down to my slightly taller level thanks to my sky-high stilettos. Meanwhile, his hands explore my hips before traveling further to my ass, where he grabs a handful of it, and I feel it all the way to my core. A moan floats out of me as his lips pull from mine and he starts trailing kisses down my neck. You'd think we hadn't seen each other in months, but really, it's because it's harvest season.

The past few weeks have felt like we're passing ships in the night. He's awake and out the door before I've even woken up, leaving Goose to keep me warm. And then he comes home just in time to eat dinner before passing out from exhaustion. I can understand now why he was such a cranky ass when we first met.

Somehow, he still manages to find the energy to mold his body to mine in the middle of the night, and show me all the ways he's missing me. I have no complaints there, but it doesn't stop me from missing him throughout the day.

"Ready for dinner?"

Truthfully, I'd rather have a night in. Ethan is having Gavin cover winery operations for the remainder of the day so we can have a quiet evening together. I know how much he wants to take me out and spoil me, but cuddled up with him on the couch, watching a silly TV show is really all I need. I didn't have the heart to try and change his mind, especially when he's been so determined to do something special for today.

"Let's do it."

I already know we have reservations at an Italian bistro in Badger Canyon, so I relax into my seat and let my gaze fall to the rolling hills of vineyards that flank both sides of the highway as we leave Red Mountain.

Not ten minutes into our drive, Ethan's radio blares

loudly between us. He grabs it from the middle console, and I try my hardest not to look irritated. One night. That's all I wanted.

"Go for Ethan," David's static voice says.

Ethan sighs and then pulls over to the shoulder of the road, shooting me an apologetic expression. I smile tightly at him, because it's all I can muster without looking fake.

"This is Ethan."

"Something weird is going on at the Syrahs in sixteen. Might want to check it out."

Now I'm not just irritated. I'm pissed. Why is David calling Ethan when he should be calling Gavin?

Ethan breathes a groan, and I can feel his stare on me. "We're close by. It'll only be a few minutes. I promise."

I nod, not trusting my mouth to not say something snarky that will ruin the evening. This is what I signed up for. This is his job, and I need to respect that. No matter how much it upsets me that I can't get him to myself for one night.

"Ten-four," Ethan says into the radio, before putting the truck in drive and flipping around to go back to Red Mountain.

The drive is quiet and tense. He can clearly tell I'm upset. Why didn't he call Gavin? Why is he letting one radio call derail our plans? I can feel myself getting madder and madder. By the time Ethan pulls over to check out whatever this weird emergency is, my skin is flushed with anger. I take a few big inhales, trying to calm down.

Ethan hops out and then pauses, looking at me.

"I know you're wearing heels, but would you mind getting out with me? I don't feel comfortable leaving you in the truck by yourself."

He has to be joking.

"I'll sink into the sand if I have to walk out there." I wiggle my feet, showing him my heels.

His shoulders lift to a shrug. "I'll carry you."

The thing about Ethan is that he's stubborn. More stubborn than me.

My eyes close, and my shoulders sag, resigned. I think I'm going to have to chalk this night up as being a fail.

"Fine," I tell him. "Let's get this over with."

He comes around to my side, and I reach out for him, wrapping my arms around his neck as his calloused hand slides under my bare thighs, the other holding me at the small of my back.

"Reminds me of carrying you out of the bar," his voice rumbles in my ear as he walks us into the vineyard, and despite my irritation, it makes my spine tingle with awareness.

"That night was embarrassing." I'm being a bitch, but I can't seem to help myself.

He chuckles, and his breath dusts over my ear. "It was the first time I got to feel your tight little ass."

My head whips, meeting his eyes. "You felt me up that night? And here I thought you were a perfect gentleman."

He laughs again, and it reverberates through me. "Just a small graze. But enough for me to jerk my cock to it while you were sleeping in my bed."

My jaw drops, and a laugh escapes me. "Ethan Ledger! I can't believe what I'm hearing right now."

I hold his stare and his hazel eyes light up, the corners crinkling from his smile.

"Baby, I had it bad."

My head falls back, and I giggle. "Well, it's a good thing your feelings weren't one sided. Who knows what would've become of your poor cock," I tease.

We continue walking further in, my irritation subsided and replaced with curiosity. We've been walking for a while, and I have yet to see anything that warrants an emergency.

"Do you know exactly where David was talking about?"

Ethan nods and looks around.

"Should be right about here," he tells me. "Mind if I set you down so I can check it out?"

I nod, confused because I don't see anything.

He sets me back to solid ground easily, making sure a firm patch of grass is beneath me, so I don't sink into the ground.

I expect Ethan to run off and figure out what's going on, but he remains at my side.

"Look familiar?"

My eyes take in the expansive vineyard. "Looks like a vineyard." I laugh.

"Look harder." There's a mischievous smile playing on his lips. He's up to something.

A surge of excitement courses through me. My eyes dart around trying to latch onto something recognizable. Eventually they land ahead, on the opposite side from where we came, toward a different part of the highway. I look back at him and the question that was building in my head is all but confirmed by his expression.

"Is this *the* vineyard. The one I crashed into?"

He nods slowly. "Sure is. We came a different direction, so you'd be thrown off."

Now I'm even more confused. My forehead creases as I stare at him. "Why would you want to throw me off?"

He takes a step back, and I watch as his trembling hand reaches inside of his pocket. It suddenly hits me, and I realize what's happening. My vision starts to blur, and I don't know if it's from utter shock or tears welling in my eyes, but when the image before me clears, it's Ethan, down on one knee, presenting an open ring box.

"What are you doing?" My voice is garbled with tears. Both my hands are immediately cupped over my mouth.

"Marisa," he starts and then pauses, because I'm a total mess.

I knew he would be proposing at some point, yet I'm completely unprepared. I also thought I would have picked up on his plans, but it seems I was oblivious. How could I not have seen what was happening? And then I think back to Hillary constantly mentioning getting a manicure as if she was trying to bury it into my subconscious.

"Baby, you have to stop crying. I have a whole speech planned."

I take a big inhale, and it comes out embarrassingly snotty. We both laugh, easing some of the weight of this monumental situation.

"Marisa," Ethan starts again. "From the moment I met you, my life has never been the same. I took one look at those beautiful brown eyes of yours and knew I wanted to look into them forever. I love you, baby, and I love our life." With one hand still holding the box, his other reaches for me, shaking as he envelops my hand. When our eyes lock, I find his looking at me like they never have before, glassy and red and filled with so much love. "Will you please marry me?"

I'm a blubbering, crying mess as my head nods profusely. Just when I think he's going to slip the ring on my finger he stands and pulls me against him.

"I can't not touch you when you're crying, even if they're happy tears."

He cradles me in his arms, running soothing motions up and down my back and smoothing my hair. "They are happy tears, right?"

My eyes meet his. "Yes, very happy."

I crane my neck up to kiss him, and his lips collide with mine in a searing kiss. I coax out my tongue and he welcomes it, deepening the kiss.

My heart beats at an overwhelmingly fast tempo as Ethan consumes me, moving his lips over mine, grabbing at my hips and digging his fingers into my flesh like he's holding on to me for dear life. It's desperate, and tangled, and all encompassing. It's us.

Drawing away from our kiss, Ethan litters my face in kisses, kissing at the drying streaks of my tears, and then rests his forehead against mine, our breaths ragged against each other.

"Ready to marry me?"

I nod, unable to utter words over the clog of emotion sitting in my throat.

"Ready to be Marisa Ledger?"

"So ready," I manage to get out.

"I can't wait for you to be my wife." His voice is a hushed whisper.

My eyes close, letting the significance of the word wash over me. Wife. I'm going to be his wife.

"You better put that ring on my finger before I change my mind."

I toss him a teasing smirk, and he playfully rolls his eyes.

"Always such a brat," he says as he reaches back into his pocket and retrieves the velvet box.

I was so overcome when he was down on one knee, I never actually looked at the ring. This time when he opens the box, I make sure to inspect every detail.

Though we both knew marriage was the path we were on, we never discussed rings or what I would want. I've never been a big jewelry girl, usually keeping it simple with a dainty necklace or a modest pair of earrings. The ring Ethan chose is absolute perfection. A sleek, gold band with a single, oval-shaped diamond at the center.

"What do you think?"

His voice comes out husky and thick, like he's nervous about my reaction.

"I love it. I love it so much," I say and tilt my head up to kiss him softly. "I love you more, though."

He plucks the ring out of the box and takes my left hand in his.

"I had to sneak one of your rings out of your jewelry box to figure out your size, so hopefully it fits."

The cool metal slides around my finger, fitting like it was made for me.

I stare at it, once again flooded with a rush of emotion.

"I can't wait for you to be my husband."

Ethan brings my hand to his lips and kisses my palm, brushing his thumb over the diamond.

"You look good with a ring, baby." He kisses my palm again. "You look like mine."

Once we're back in the truck, I catch a glimpse of myself in the visor mirror.

"Why didn't you tell me I look like a scary racoon?" Frantically, I start wiping at the runny mascara under my eyes.

"A very sexy racoon," Ethan says with a chuckle.

"We're going to have to run by the house before dinner. There's no way I can go to the restaurant looking like this."

"About that..."

I still, as whirls of nerves and excitement dance in my stomach. "What? What is it?"

Ethan dips his chin, watching me with a mischievous glint in his eyes.

"The whole dinner thing was more of a distraction."

"What are we really doing?" I ask hesitantly.

This is the same man who whisked me away in a helicopter on our first date and hasn't stopped surprising me since. I don't think I could guess even if I tried.

"We're going back to our house," Ethan says casually.

"And?"

"And...there might be some people there waiting for us. They might have been hiding at Gavin's earlier, waiting until we left to sneak over."

I shake my head, biting my lips to suppress my smile.

"Always full of surprises."

When we get to our house, my dad, Jenn, Sadie and Caleb are there, along with Ethan's parents and siblings. Even Hillary, Archie, and baby Josephine made the trip over. Leanne connects with my mom over a video call, allowing her to join in on the celebration despite being thousands of miles away.

A year ago, I was broken. Stripped of all the hopes and dreams I had for myself. And thank goodness for that. I've never been more grateful for that lost girl, because she got me here, to a room surrounded by the people I love, with the man of my dreams. I thought I knew what I wanted. I thought I knew exactly how my life would go. Turns out it took a minor car accident, a grumpy neighbor, and a reset on life to realize sometimes you have to lose your way to find the journey you were always meant to take.

As my gaze meets Ethan's from across the room, everything else fades away, the chatter becoming a distant whirr, leaving just the two of us in our own world. He smiles gently, stirring a familiar rush of warmth through me as my chest swells, fuller than it's ever felt. I can't wait to see what the future holds for us, knowing no matter what life throws our way, our love is rare, rare enough to last a lifetime.

The End

Curious about Hillary and Archie's story? Read their novella, Last Call!

Thank you so much for reading Rare Blend. If you enjoyed this story, please consider leaving a review. Reviews are instrumental to the success of indie authors. Scan the QR code below to leave a review on Goodreads:

Also By Michelle Naomi Mosley

RED MOUNTAIN SERIES
Rare Blend (Ethan & Marisa)
Double Barrel (Elyse & Dominic)
Bottle Shock (Gavin & Scottie)
Blush Crush (Ariana & Cole)
Perfect Balance (2026)
Bright Finish (TBD)

RED MOUNTAIN SERIES NOVELLAS
Last Call (Hillary and Archie)

Find signed books and merch at
www.authormichellenaomimosley.com/

Xo, Michelle

Newsletter Sign-Up

Do you want to stay up to date with Marisa, Ethan, and the rest of the Red Mountain crew? Scan the QR code below to sign up for my newsletter, where I'll be sharing exclusive updates on the Red Mountain Series and future projects.

Stay Connected

Want to chat all things Rare Blend and the Red Mountain Series? Consider joining my Facebook Reader Group. Scan the QR code below for unhinged commentary, bonus content, and exclusive sneak peeks.

Content Warnings

Please review the following content notes before continuing and proceed at your own discretion:

- Cheating that occurs off page (not between MCs)
- Divorced parents
- Strained parental relationship
- Anxiety disorder
- Debt/money problems
- Career struggles
- Strong language
- Sexually explicit content
- Alcohol consumption
- Pregnancy (not MC)
- Financial abuse from a partner (not between MCs)
- Brief mention of a gun
- Brief mention of drug use
- Brief mention of domestic violence
- Brief mention of racism

Acknowledgments

First and foremost, thank you, reader, for picking up this book and taking a chance on a new author. I've dreamed of writing a book for as long as I can remember and finally decided to be brave enough to try. I can't even begin to express my appreciation that you not only picked up my book, but read it far enough to make it to this point.

A big thank you to friends and family for supporting me on this journey and offering the encouragement I needed to make this dream a reality. To my mother-in-law, Marie, for being even more excited about me writing a book than I was. To my sister, Kari, for making sure this book was perfect. To my bestie, Litzuli—our friendship inspired the friendship between Marisa and Hillary. I couldn't do life without you. You were my everything throughout this process: my alpha, my beta, my therapist, and my biggest cheerleader. I love you like a sister.

A huge thank you to my editor Andrea. Thank you for being flexible around my chaotic brain and allowing me to turn in multiple drafts because I couldn't stop making changes. You have the patience of a saint and I'm so thankful for your meticulous eye and attention to detail. Rare Blend would be a disaster without you.

Lauren, thank you for helping me make the story richer. Red

Mountain came to life because of your suggestions and it really set the tone for the rest of the series.

To my beta babes Rose, Sydney, Corrine, Madeline, Shelby, Rachel, Luna and Izabela—your opinions mattered so much to me, and your comments (mostly unhinged) and feedback were incredibly helpful. I'm so lucky to have had such an amazing group of beta readers. Rare Blend would not be the book it is today without all of you.

Jess at Truly Yours PR, thank you for handling ARCs and blowing my mind with how many sign-ups we got. I look forward to future projects together. Thank you to Sarah for schooling me in all things wine and owning a winery. A big thank you to Sandy for all of your journalism knowledge. Thank you to my Aunt Darla, for answering all of my mental health questions and providing professional feedback.

To my fellow indie authors, for graciously answering my annoying DMs and guiding me through the publishing process. I'm so thankful to have met you all.

To my parents, I know what love is because of the love I was lucky enough to witness for almost thirty years. I'll miss you forever, Mom, but Dad and I continue to talk about you and remember you, keeping you alive in our memories.

To all the amazing women I'm lucky enough to have in my life (sisters, cousins, aunts, friends). Writing strong female characters comes easily because I'm surrounded by wonderful examples. My favorite female characters all have little pieces of you.

Thank you to my husband. From late nights to stressful days, you were always encouraging and supportive. And thank you for looking so cute in Carhartt vests and backward hats—I just had to write a male character who wore the exact same thing.

To my ARC readers. I'm writing this before you even get the book, but I'm so thankful for your support. Your impact is huge and I can't truly express the gratitude I feel toward you for taking a risk on a new author. Thank you for the reviews and the posts, and above all thank you for taking the time to read Rare Blend.

And lastly, thank you to me (insert Kanye voice). Writing a book is HARD and finishing a book is even harder. I didn't anticipate making one of my biggest dreams come true while battling a huge health hurdle at the same time. I wanted to quit A LOT, but I'm glad I didn't. I poured my soul into this book and yet as I sit here and type this, there are four open WIPs on my laptop. It seems I have a lot more of my soul to give and I can't wait.

About the Author

Michelle Naomi Mosley is a biracial Mexican American contemporary romance author. She writes stories about men who fall pathetically in love and women who refuse to settle for anything less.

Michelle lives in Washington State's wine country with her husband. When she's not bringing her characters to life, she works a corporate job by day to justify the debt she accrued earning her BA and MBA. In her free time, she enjoys reading, cooking for the people she loves, and tackling DIY home projects.

You can follow her on Instagram and most socials @authormichellenaomimosley. For more information on books, merchandise, and newsletter sign-ups, visit authormichellenaomimosley.com.

www.ingramcontent.com/pod-product-compliance
Lightning Source LLC
Chambersburg PA
CBHW020003120726
47903CB00004B/1116